QUANTUM GIRL
RESURRECTION

BEING THE FOURTH BOOK IN
THE QUANTUM GIRL SAGA

BY

DONALD KIERAN AUSTEN

AND

PEYTON ELISE HERRON

INNER SPACE MEDIA
2023

Quantum Girl Resurrection / Donald Kieran Austen, Peyton Elise Herron
     p.   cm.

ISBN 978-1-7377812-4-0 (pbk. : acid-free paper)

Library of Congress Control Number: 2023914305

1. Science *Fiction*[1].   2. Superheroes   3. Alien Civilizations
4. Time Travel   5. Parallel Dimensions   6. LGBTQ
7. Bullying   8. Teen Suicide   9. Self-Harm

122024

Cover images designed by Donald Kieran Austen

Printed in the United States of America

---

[1] So stated as science *fiction* for the sake of Library of Congress Card Catalog classification and search engine visibility, though, most assuredly it is not.

to

Anya

Always

Quantum Girl Resurrection

FORWARD

There is a difference between reality and fiction. When seemingly remarkable things happen, often there is an assumption on the part of the reader that they did not occur at all or were drawn far out of proportion. Should there be even a modicum of science involved, the work might be labeled science fiction, but I assure you that what you are about to read is not, remarkable as the facts may seem. My name is Peyton Herron. I am the reincarnation of a long-dead alien (meaning extraterrestrial or in this case extra-universal) woman whose name was Khattaaara. Of course, I am now asking that you take two leaps of faith. The first is that what pages that follow are all based on true events. The second is that you concede the existence of the soul, for in its absence reincarnation could not occur.

Several years had passed since my last entry in *Quantum Girl Nexus*. I had taken up residence on the East Coast with my young daughter and for the majority of the time I had abandoned using my powers and left my costume to quantum mothballs, so to speak. But then something happened that I couldn't ignore and that is where this story begins.

With hope for a continued future for all,

PEYTON ELISE HERRON

CHAPTER I

Peyton

Earth Year: 2035

It had been six years since I took it upon myself to reshape reality. There were no more parallel dimensions—no more Quantum Girls other than me. And how strange it was to have learned that I was the beginning and end of everything without any real explanation of how that could be. The seven god-stones in my head were proof of that, though. I had power over time and space. I could create universes if I chose. I could create life and I could fend off death. I could rule over everything that existed if I so chose and no one could ever stop me. In Shropshire, England, on the 5th of April, 1887, John Emerich Edward Dalberg, aka Lord Acton, wrote in a letter to Archbishop Mandell Creighton, "Power tends to corrupt and absolute power corrupts absolutely." But Lord Acton was wrong, at least about the last part. Power does tend to corrupt but there is no absolute. Power is a tool, not a weapon and how it is used or misused depends on the person who wields it and their morality. My parents taught me right from wrong and they raised me to be Christian which in my vocabulary means something other than believing in Christ but, rather, someone who's selfless and caring and kind. Like Lazarus, I was resurrected. I had taken my own life but then had it thrust back into me along with powers beyond the scope of my imagination. I was fourteen years old at the time—a child, yet to even discover her womanhood, who in one fell swoop became someone whose life was threaded through eternity, and who was destined to try and save her universe from obliteration. My name is Peyton Elise Herron and I am

1

Quantum Girl.

Five years ago, my father had a massive heart attack. Whether it was congenital or from tension, the doctors couldn't say, but he died as a result. I did all that I could to try and save him. I went back in time to the moment that it happened and phased him to the hospital but he died anyway. I went six months back in time and convinced him to see a cardiologist. He did. He went. They ran tests, but in the end, nothing changed. His right hand grasped his left arm at the exact same moment as it had before and he collapsed and died for a second time and then a third and again and again. No matter how many times I went back in time to try and save him, each time he died in the end.

I knelt down beside him that last time—the time when I finally gave up, defeated by what for him was an unalterable fate. I wept out words he couldn't hear, climbed to my feet, looked toward the sky, and cursed any gods who would have let my father die. It was then and there that I gave up believing in the Bible, but not in believing in what is righteous and good.

My mother was a believer. She would presage the coming of light in a world filled with darkness. She believed in Heaven and the Ultimate Reward. I believed that God, were he to have existed, had abandoned us. I loved my father greatly. I loved him as much as he loved me, and I wished that I could have changed things, but at least I was beside him in the end.

The funeral that followed was met with solemnity and tears. In the church, as I held her by the hand walking in, Jordan, my now six-year-old daughter, broke free from me and raced up to the casket, perching on her toes to see her grandfather in his Sunday suit, looking as though he were asleep.

"Wake up, Grandpa!" she said. "Wake up!"

I walked up to her and gently placed my hands on her shoulders and she looked up at me.

"Why won't he wake up?" she asked.

"I told you, Lovebug, he can't," I replied. "Grandpa's gone to

2

Heaven."

"But he's still here!" she insisted.

"But his soul is gone," I said.

"I don't want him to go!" Jordan wept. "Make him come back!" she wept. "You're Quantum Girl! Make him come back!"

"I can't," I said. "I tried. I can't."

"You can do all kinds of things!" she insisted. "You have superpowers!" She glared at me, and then she ran off to my mother, her Grandma, and buried her tears in her lap. Such was the reaction of a six-year-old to death.

On Rendenaaar, Jordan had never met her grandparents. She grew up on an alien world and, but for her aunt and mother, she was totally alone. She'd never missed her Grandpa or Grandma because she'd never met them. In this life, it was different. Familiarity breeds sadness once it's taken away.

Distance hadn't been an issue, my having built a life in New York, more than twenty-seven hundred miles from where I used to call home. I had phased us back there every week to spend time with Mom and Dad and visit with my now happily married twin sister—except for December when we stayed from Christmas Eve through New Year's Day. I missed Dad, though, now that he was gone. Sometimes, I'd phase back in time to spend moments with him. During a few of my trips, I'd brought Jordan with me, back to when I was Jordan's age. How strange it was for Jordan to be playing with me and with Ophelia, barely kindergarten age. But then when we left, I would have to erase all their memories—all except Jordan's—so as not to interfere with the timeline again.

Jor and I lived in Lennox Hill on the Upper East Side of Manhattan, overlooking Central Park, in the six-story brownstone that I owned. I had carved out the entire top two floors for my apartment. The lower level serving partly as office space and partly as a dance studio. Jor's ever-present playmate was Niska, a blue merle collie, who came with me unscathed from the previous reality and to

3

whom I've added decades of life. How unfair is it of Nature that dogs should die at only twelve or fifteen years old?

Ever since creating the new reality, I'd taken a step back. I'd taken up the role of mother, rather than Quantum Girl. It seemed there was nothing major that absolutely needed my intervention. The world had turned on its axis without me since long before I was born. I had to recognize the fact that I was not God and that people could survive on their own. I wound up spending a lot of time with Phee and Claire. While Mom, as I have mentioned in the past, is a devout Christian, she accepted the marriage of the two, *unholy* as it was in her eyes. She recognized all that both of them had been put through, though it took a whole lot of explaining to her how Phee and Liam were in reality one and the same with their *souls* temporarily split apart by what had been a quantum divergence. Meanwhile, I had used my abilities to fertilize an egg in each of them by pulling Liam temporarily from Phee to impregnate them both. In Phee's case, it gave literal meaning to the expression, *Go fuck yourself!* But nine months later, Phee and Claire each gave birth to a beautiful girl, Zhana and Samira respectively, so named to pay homage to the twins I was carrying and lost when the reset took place. Phee pretended to not realize that Jordan was the same little girl she had given birth to in the old reality. She knew in her heart that she was the exact same child she had raised to young womanhood on Rendenaaar but she held her tongue, recognizing how important it was to me to have someone in my life to love. Regardless, she remained the very best of aunts and the very best of sisters as well; and with the other two births, Jor had inseparable cousins for playmates. In this life, she didn't need a god-stone to create other versions of herself to serve as playmates. In this life, she had two cousins to take their place.

It was just two weeks after Jor's sixth birthday had come and gone that something happened to change the world forever and cause me to resurrect my quantum self—the realization of the disaster that was about to unfold. The universe—this universe—was about to end.

Astronomers around the globe had all noticed a rapid acceleration in the redshift between galaxies. The night sky in every direction was growing darker with every passing day. Speculations arose that some form of dark energy was rapidly expanding space, but I knew better. I recognized the truth that Krotaaarak of Rendenaaar had predicted trillions of eons ago if there could be such a yardstick of time.

Years ago, when I was fifteen, I had tried to explain to my physics teacher, the rather obtuse Mr. Chatterjee, that it was not spacetime that was expanding, but rather that matter was contracting. Simply explained, there are five dimensions, not four. The first three are length, breadth, and height, which form the basis of matter. There are also the dimensions of time and magnitude. It was the last, though, that was most significant to what was happening to the universe. Each universe is created from the stuff of the one before it through what is called a Big Bang. Most astronomers incorrectly believe that our universe began from a singularity—a single point that exploded and stretched out spacetime in a cosmic instant to nearly 4.6 parsecs—roughly 14 billion light years—in each direction and then began expanding, tripling in size due to some undiscovered force they named dark energy. That, however, was not the case. Rather, the size of all matter had diminished by nearly one-third.

Present physics has maintained that there are four fundamental forces of nature: the electromagnetic force that creates electricity and magnetism, the strong nuclear that binds atoms together, the weak nuclear force that allows interactions between subatomic particles and which can influence quarks and neutrinos and gravity, the latter of which in legend caused Sir Isaac Newton to be whacked in the head by an apple falling from a tree. And while no one is certain as to whether he afterward ate it or hurled it away in anger while rubbing his injured skull, it supposedly inspired him to hypothesize a nonquantum view of gravity. He didn't know what gravity was—only what it did, which was to keep his two feet planted firmly on the ground. Physicists today have posited an imaginary (and nonexistent) subatomic particle they have named the graviton, which, per its name, is responsible for gravity. Unfortunately, their speculation about it is, as some might say, a lot of hooey.

Magnitude is the physical size of subatomic particles at any point in time relative to any other point. To be clear, there is no such thing as matter, per se. When you hold a book in your hands, no part of your hands is actually in contact with it. Rather, the subatomic force fields that surround the atoms of your hand are in contact with those that surround the atoms of the book. You can feel a similar force on a larger scale by trying to push two like polar ends of magnets together; the point being that what we perceive as matter is in reality an illusion created by subatomic fields moving so fast they appear to be solid. In other words, everything is made up of energy. A Big Bang is created when those energy fields collapse into a critical mass wherever they are and then—kaboom!—they explode, not just a little bit, but on a massive scale, though when that happens, the seedling galaxies are so far apart that they do not interfere with each other or things would be a mess. In our case, our universe had been spread out to what we calculated was 28 billion light years. But at that stage, the *matter* began to contract again as its magnitude began to diminish. As matter shrinks in size, spacetime appears to grow with the end result that there is the illusion of distant objects moving away from each other. Meanwhile, as that occurs, spacetime is deformed on a fourth-dimensional scale, causing objects to fall into the deformation; the result of that phenomenon is what we refer to as gravity.

The reason that I have brought any of this up is because at that time, critical mass was about to be reached, and the moment that it did, our universe would be erased in favor of another one. Everything we knew would suddenly cease to exist. As Quantum Girl, I was determined to not let that happen. I had so recently saved my world and everyone I loved, and I refused to let it all be destroyed by some random act of Nature.

I phased into a pocket dimension near the front door to Phee and

Claire's beach house in Malibu. The place had been my gift to both of them—a wedding gift as it were. Glancing around to make certain that no one would witness my sudden appearance, I phased into the real world and rang the doorbell. Upon seeing me, Claire answered with a brimming smile.

"Hello, Love," she announced in her Aussie accent and then looked around and past me. "Where are Jor and Niska?" she asked.

"They're with me back home," I replied. "Or did you forget I can be in more than one place at once?"

"I just thought," she began, "Sami and Zhan so love playing with them both."

"Maybe next time," I said. "But I need some advice—input, I suppose, would be a better word."

Claire took note of my serious tone. "What's wrong?" she asked. "Come on inside. Pheeli's in the kitchen. We were about to sit down to lunch. There's more than enough. We can talk after." She looked at me with concern. "Unless you need to talk right now."

"It can wait," I said with irony in my thoughts. "Twenty minutes more or less won't be the end of the world."

As I walked into the living room with its open kitchen, as Phee turned and saw me and was about to say hello, Zhana and Samira, who had been on the floor playing with their holosphere, ripped off their Vision goggles and jumped up.

"Auntie Peyton!" they both called out at once, as much an announcement as a greeting. Then they both rushed over and wrapped their arms around me.

"Mommy," Zhana cried out to Phee, "Auntie Peyton's here!"

"I know!" Phee said smiling, as she came up to me to give me a hug. "Now, the two of you go wash up. We're going to have lunch."

"What are we having?" Samira asked.

"Well, we adults," Phee replied, "are having Caesar salad. But there are chocolate waffles for the two of you."

"Yay!" the two cried out in unison. They looked at each other and then raced to the bathroom.

"Sit," Phee said in a more than friendly tone, indicating a seat at the table with a glance. I went there and sat down. Claire sat facing me. "Tea or hot chocolate?" Phee asked, her back turned away as she faced the stove.

"Hot chocolate, I think," I answered, apparently rhetorically as Phee had already set the cup down in front of me after my barely having spoken the words.

"I don't know why I bother to ask," Phee said with a smile. "The answer's always the same."

"Force of habit from when you were a server, I suppose," I replied.

"That was Liam," Claire interjected. "It's still so confusing, all that went on. I'm still bothered that Clairey doesn't exist anymore. She was such a sweet girl. It was as though she was made to not exist."

"I keep telling her," Phee said to me. "Clairey was *her*."

"You say that," Claire objected. "But when the two of the adult versions of me merged, we both had a choice. Clairey didn't and I feel as though I took away her ability to live her own life, become a teenager, and experience growing up. It just seems as though she were... erased."

I turned to her with sympathetic eyes. "Can we go somewhere?" I asked. "Away from the children."

Claire looked to Phee for approval.

"You two go disappear for a few," Phee said and smiled at both of us. "I'll keep the kids corralled."

Claire and I rose from the table and led me to the bedroom. I shut the door behind me.

"I want you to think about Clairey," I said. "Picture her in your mind." As she did, I caused Clairey to emerge from Claire. She quite literally stepped out of her and then looked at the two of us, from one to the other.

"How is it that I can see things in color?" she asked. "I don't have

8

a god-stone anymore. I can feel that I don't."

"That was my doing," I said. "I repaired your optic nerve when I separated you from Claire."

"This is all so strange," Clairey confessed. "I remember being me, but I also remember being you." She stared at Claire. "I remember going to middle school and high school and going to Australia and not going, though that doesn't make any sense. And I remember falling in love with Liam and then with Pheeli." Suddenly, she began to tremble. "What's happening to me?"

I squatted down in front of her and took her hands in mine. "Clairey," I said. "I want you to come with me."

Clairey nodded and I phased from the room with her. I returned alone a moment later.

"What happened?" Claire asked. "Where did you go? Where's Clairey?"

"It was wrong of me to merge her with you," I said.

"So, what did you do?" Claire asked. "Surely you didn't uncreate her?"

I scowled at the remark. "Of course not," I replied. "I simply took her back in time and merged her with the ten-year-old version of *you*. I'm going to have to do the same with young Liam and Li. I'll merge Liam into Li and then merge Li into the ten-year-old version of Phee. That way adulthood won't have been thrust upon them either."

Claire thought hard for a moment. "I suddenly remember," she said. "I was playing with Niska and you were there but I didn't know you and there was a girl with you who looked just like me and then suddenly she was gone and so were you." She looked up at me. "Thank you for that, Peyton. Now, I don't have to be concerned."

After we went back to the table and sat down, I looked at her with the most serious expression on my face I could muster. "I just have one question," I said.

Claire looked at me as though to ask "What?" without vocalizing the word.

"Are you going to eat your croutons?" I asked.

"Take as many as you want!" Claire replied with a laugh.

Lunch came and went without incident. True to form, Phee held her tongue in not asking what had gone on in the other room, though I knew from having grown up with her that the question was burning madly in her brain. Claire, of course, would clue her in later on. Phee, I must tell you, had become a great culinary artist by this time, self-taught, but with a natural flair for it. As for myself, despite being Quantum Girl, left to my own means in a kitchen, I would probably wind up burning water over a stove.

After we had all had our fill of lunch, followed by the tiramisu Phee had made—totally from scratch I might add—having left Zhana and Samira to frolic on the beach under our watchful eyes, we all sat down at the round, glass-topped table on the wooden deck.

"So, what's up?" Phee said, breaking the lull of the splashing waves and the laughter of the children in the distance.

"The universe is coming to an end," I said. My tone was unwavering. My expression was marked, perhaps, with a bit of sadness. I glanced briefly westward, thinking how those two precious little girls might never have the chance to grow up in this world.

"Why do you say that?" Claire's voice trembled with her words. Both she and my sister, now her wife, knew that I would never make light of such things. But it was Phee, so fair-complected, blue-eyed blonde that she was, who turned even more pale.

"The energy fields that form the basis of all matter are contracting toward a critical mass. I have seven god-stones. That's enough to save all of us—the two of you, the children, and Chloë, but that's all."

"What about the rest of the world?" Phee asked. "What about Mom?"

"And my parents?" Claire chimed in.

I shook my head. "And it's not just our world," I said. "There are billions of planets in the universe with life and millions with intelligent civilizations."

10

Claire appeared perplexed. "I don't understand," she said. "Nearly every scientist I've ever listened to says that the universe is expanding. How can they all be so wrong?"

"Because they are," I said at which point Phee laid her hand on top of mine, as it rested on the table.

"She's Quantum Girl," Phee said to Claire, never taking her eyes away from mine. "If she says she knows, she knows."

Claire rose from her seat. "I'm going to play with the children for a while. I need to be with them right now." And so she went.

Phee watched her as she walked barefoot down the sand and then called Samira and Zhana to come sit with her, placing an arm around each of them as they all faced the waves that came crashing to the shore. But all the oceans in all the world couldn't dilute all the tears that bled from her eyes.

"What are you going to do?" Phee asked.

"I don't know," I admitted. "I don't know how all of this works."

"Maybe there's someone on some other world who can help," Phee suggested.

"And how do you propose I find him or her? There are literally hundreds of billions of galaxies in the universe, each with hundreds of billions of stars. Multiply that by ten for the number of planets. It would take a trillion lifetimes to find anyone who might have the knowledge as to how to prevent the collapse."

"What about Krotaaarak?" Phee asked. "Why not go back to Rendenaaar and ask him? You speak Gaaalthaaaran. Surely, he'd be willing to help."

"Krotaaarak," I said, "lived nearly a thousand of their years before Khattaaara was born. And there's a problem. The god-stones had just been discovered around that time. I have no idea where they were, but they had yet to be placed in the sphere under the throne. They could be absorbed from my head and I'd wind up stranded there with no way to get back to help. Beyond that, I'm afraid to interfere with the timeline again."

11

"Just be careful," Phee said. "I have faith in you."

"Thanks, Sis," I replied. "I just hope it's justified."

"It is," she said back with assurance.

I smiled. "I need to talk to Dad first," I said.

Phee looked at me with a puzzled expression on her face.

"I've been visiting him back when we were small," I told her. "But we have a pact. Every time I leave, I bury the memories of his having seen me and reawaken them the next time I come. I've told him about you and Claire and what a wonderful mother you've become. He's very proud of you, you know."

"I was never Daddy's little girl like you were," she said.

"Come on," I assured her. "He would have jumped off a cliff to keep you safe. Besides, you have Mom and you always were her little darling."

Phee smiled. "Just tell him I miss him so much," she said.

"I will," I replied. "Wish me luck." Then I became Quantum Girl and phased into the past.

Most people wish they could talk with a dead parent one last time. There are always words that were left unsaid—sometimes good, sometimes not—but I am not like most. It was a bright spring day when I appeared. Dad was in his office on the thirty-fourth floor of the Constellation Tower in Century City where he worked as an accountant at Tenley, Delano, and Umbridge, which, growing up I always thought serendipitous, as taking the first two letters of each of the names sounded out *tedium*. To me, his job would have been boring beyond belief, but Dad had a mathematical mind and an innate imperative to take care of his family whom he dearly loved. The door to his office was closed when I phased into the hall as myself just outside it. No one else was around when I did, though one of the interns walked past me with a stack of files a moment later. Having knocked and been greeted with a cordial, "Come in," I entered. It was May 8th, 2014, twenty-nine years into the past. Dad was thirty-eight years old and quite handsome with a loving wife and two four-year-old daughters back home who were his life and his reason to exist.

He stared at me like one would a stranger. It was no wonder, as, like I had said, each time I left I had suppressed his memory of our visits together.

"May I help you?" he asked as he had a hundred times before.

I smiled at him. "I hope so," I said as I restored his memory of me. I remember the first time I went back in time to see him. It was all so strange in that he was so much younger than when he passed away. His hair was still sandy brown without the suffusion of gray that later came with age.

"Peyton!" he proclaimed, rising from his tufted leather chair.

"Hi, Dad!" I replied and we met and embraced at the corner of his desk.

"How are you and Jordan doing?" he asked, "and how's Ophelia and her *wife*? I still can't wrap my head around that."

"Claire," I said. "And she's about as close to being her best friend as she could ever hope for—other than me, of course."

"I guess I'm just from a different generation," he replied.

"You'll meet her someday," I said. "You'll see. The world has changed—hopefully for the best. And their kids are both so adorable!" I paused and then became almost dour. "But I'm here for a reason," I said. "I need your advice and your strength."

He smiled. "Quantum Girl needs *my* strength," he replied.

"How about we talk over dinner?" I said.

"It's barely noon," he replied, glancing at his wristwatch.

"Not in Paris," I said. "Give me your hand."

In another instant, I had phased us both to an alley behind *La Rôtisserie d'Argent* on *Quai de la Tournelle* in the heart of gay Paris. Still holding onto his hand, I led him around to the front and we entered. Dad glanced around.

"It looks expensive," he said.

"Dad," I replied, "I'm rich,"

It was at that moment that the *maître d'* approached us.

"*Bonsoir*," he said to me, slightly nodding his head. "*Bonsoir*," he said again, this time to Dad, assuming that he could speak French, "*Le monsieur,*" he went on, "*préférerait-il une table devant ou derrière?*"[2]

Dad who had no command of any language other than English, just stood there staring back, bewildered. The moment, though, revealed an edge of humor. I smiled at the waiter. It was my turn to speak.

"*Pourrions-nous, peut-être, avoir une table près de la fenêtre?*" I asked. "*Mon cher père est nouveau à Paris et je voudrais qu'il en profite pleinement..*"[3]

"*Mais bien sûr,*" he replied. "*Suis-moi s'il te plait.*"[4]

And with that, he led us to a table for two near the window, pulling out my chair for me.

"*Merci,*"[5] I said with a smile.

Then he placed menus down in front of us, nodded once more, and went back to his station near the door.

"I didn't know you spoke French," Dad said.

"I'm fluent in over seven thousand earth languages," I replied with a smile, "and a few from," and I paused, "other places."

Dad picked up the menu and stared at it. "Sorry," he said, "it's all Greek to me."

"I'm sure Napoleon would have found that comment amusing," I said, which elicited a look of curiosity from Dad. "Napoleon fought for Greek independence," I added, taking his menu from him. "Let me order," I insisted.

A few minutes later, our server arrived, a thirty-ish man wearing a black suit, white shirt, and black bow tie.

---

[2] "Good evening. Good Evening. Would the gentleman prefer a table in front or in back?"

[3] "May we have a table near the window? My dear father is new to Paris, and I would like him to take in its full ambiance."

[4] "But, of course. Please follow me."

[5] "Thank you."

"*Bonsoir, Monsieur, Mademoiselle,*" he said in a cordial voice. "*Puis-je prendre votre commande?*"[6]

I smiled and set down my menu.

"*Oui, s'il te plait,*" I replied. "*Nous voudrions deux verres de Morey-Saint-Denis 1er Cru 'Clos de la Bussière' Domaine Georges Roumieret Côte de Bœuf, sauce béarnaise & chimichurri, et pommes allumettes, por deux personnes. Et pour le dessert, mousse chocolat argent noir.*" [7]

"*Un excellent choix, Mademoiselle,*"[8] came his response.

After the man left, Dad stared out the window just as a red Switchblade was taking off. "Just when are we?" he asked. "There aren't any flying cars in my time." He looked back at me.

"2035," I replied. "My time. I couldn't risk us interfering with the timeline. I have to tread with caution whenever I go back into the past. Once, when I returned, Jordan's eye color had changed from dark to medium blue." It was at that moment that the waiter reappeared with a bottle of wine. He poured some into a glass for Dad's approval. Dad tasted it and then nodded to the man, who then poured out two glasses, bowed his head to each of us, and then departed.

"How are Mom and the twins?" I asked.

"Better now," he replied.

"Did something happen?" I asked.

"You came down with the flu," he said, "and gave it to the rest of us."

"I've always been a very giving person," I replied. "What about between you and Mom? I remember there was a lot of tension over something."

"She lost the baby," he replied.

---

[6] "Good evening, Sir, Miss. May I take your order?"

[7] "Yes, thank you," I replied. "We would like two glasses of *Morey-Saint-Denis 1er Cru 'Clos de la Bussière' Domaine Georges Roumier* and rib of beef, béarnaise sauce & *chimichurri,* and *matchstick potatoes.* for two. And for dessert, dark chocolate mousse."

[8] "An excellent choice, Miss,"

"I'm so sorry," I said, "I forgot she was pregnant back then. How far along *was* she?"

"Six months," he replied. "We were driving home from a movie and wound up being rear-ended."

"I remember now," I said, "Phee and I were in the hospital room afterward. Mom was all in tears. You did your best to comfort her. Then the nurse came in and gave her a shot and she fell asleep. You took Phee and me out into the waiting room and told us that the baby she was carrying had been taken to Heaven by angels. Thomas. You said you and Mom had named him Thomas."

"Thomas," he repeated wistfully.

"Odd," I said.

"What is?" he asked.

"Thomas was the name Dhraaal had taken when I found him. On Rendenaaar he was my half-brother."

Just then, the waiter returned with our meal.

"Enough of this talk of old times," he insisted. "You said you needed my strength. That's a tall order coming from a young woman who has the entire universe at her command."

"That's just it, Dad," I replied. "I don't. The universe is about to end. Hubble and Einstein were wrong. Space isn't expanding. Matter is contracting and according to my calculations, there are only days remaining before all matter reaches a critical mass and explodes as another Big Bang."

A curious look took over Dad's face as he asked me a question. "But didn't you tell me you had met a version of yourself from many years in the future?"

"I don't know," I replied. "I met two of them. But Liam and Li were from a parallel universe where time moved slower. The Quantum Women I came in contact with might have been from a dimensional plane where the reverse was true or maybe parts are or were elastic but now they're one and the same. All I know is I've phased into the future and witnessed the explosion. It will rewrite

16

everything and I don't know how to stop it. Dad, I'm scared. Everything will be gone."

"What about getting help from the other Quantum Girls?" Dad asked.

"I can't," I said. "I mean, I could recreate Demi or Pay, but the reality is they were both just projections of *me*. I might as well just duplicate myself, but it would be like me talking to my reflection in a mirror."

"How can I help you, Peanut?" he asked.

I smiled. "It's been a while since I heard you call me that," I replied. "You called Phee, Sunflower."

"Because of her light blonde hair," he explained.

"And I was Peanut because of the color of *my* hair?" I asked.

"No," he replied. "You were Peanut because you're twins and peanuts come two to a shell, and I couldn't call you both peanut, could I?"

"I suppose not," I laughed and then turned serious. "Honestly, I don't know what to do. My plan is to go back in time and ask Krotaaarak. He was the greatest physicist Rendenaaar had ever known. The problem is that he lived thousands of years before Khattaaara was born and I'm concerned about altering the timeline again."

Dad sat staring for a moment, immersed in thought. Then he spoke. "You once told me that you could reverse time," he said, "like when you brought the other dimensional me and your mother back to life. What if, after you discuss things with him, you reverse time to the very moment you arrived? No harm, no foul that way."

"That's why you're my Dad," I said, smiling. Then my face took on a serious mien. "I'm sorry I couldn't save you."

He laid his hand on mine. "Peanut," he replied, "we all have our time and place on this earth. We try to spend it the best way we can and, hopefully, make a difference. I hope I've accomplished that with you."

After dinner, I phased us back to his office the moment after we had left.

"You won't remember any of this until next time," I told him. "If there is a next time."

"I have faith in you," he said.

"Like father, like daughter," I replied. "Phee said the exact same thing."

We hugged and then I vanished, leaving him back at his desk to sort out the deficits and surpluses of whatever account he had been working on before I came. And, despite all that he had eaten, his stomach was empty once again and the thought of the ham and cheese sandwich that Mom had packed for him earlier that day made him yearn for his lunch break that was still half an hour away. He had that to look forward to and a loving wife and two children, all of which made his life complete. As for myself, I phased into the quantum fabric to return to Rendenaaar.

CHAPTER II

Peyton
(The One Who Stayed Behind)

Earth Year: 2035

Jordan had fallen asleep on my bed next to me. Sometimes she did that—climb into my bed when awakened by nightmares in her sleep. Most children have bad dreams now and then; they come in the form of boogiemen or goblins, but Jordan's were of her past life on Rendenaaar and, despite that it had filled me with endless concern, I didn't know what to do. My own childhood sleep was plagued much the same with visions of demons—some of them with pointed ears—all of them with tails. I would sit up screaming in the middle of the night, waking my sister and my parents. Eventually, it was decided that I should see someone to try and get to the root of it.

The psychiatrist I went to was Dr. Yulia Petrovna. She was my mother's age, so I guess in her early thirties at the time. I remember seeing a picture on her desk of a young girl who resembled her. I wondered if it were her daughter, but I didn't think it proper to ask. Young children are hardly ever schooled in how to make small talk. The conversations we did have were all about *me*, not *her*. At first, there were a lot of simple questions. *What was my favorite color? What was my favorite food? Did I get along with my sister? Were there jealousies between the two of us?* Then came others that were more uncomfortable like, *Was there anyone I was afraid of?* or *Did anyone ever touch me in the wrong place?* Finally, came one I answered yes to—*Was I afraid to go to sleep at night?*

Dr. Petrovna offered various suggestions, like going to bed cuddled up to a teddy bear or leaving a light on at night or sleeping in the same bed as Phee. We tried all of them. None of them worked. Eventually, I was put on a drug called prazosin. It helped to suppress the nightmares most of the time. Later, though, after I had the god-stone put in my head, I realized that the demons of my youth were just memories of my former life. No doubt, Jordan was having the same issue. I would have made an appointment for her to see someone as well, and perhaps get a similar prescription, but there just wasn't enough time—not with the world and everything else coming to an end.

Jordan stirred as I switched off the lamp on my nightstand.

"Don't worry, Mommy," she mumbled, half awake.

I turned to her and gently stroked her hair. "Why do you say that, Lovebug?"

"Because the lady told me to tell you," Jordan replied. "She said, 'Everything's going to be all right.'"

"And where did you see her?" I asked.

"When I was asleep," she replied. "She said not to be afraid."

"Did she say anything else?" I asked.

"She said there's a part of the answer in each of us," Jordan replied.

"What did she look like?" I asked.

Jordan closed her eyes. "She looked a lot like Auntie Phee. She said her name was Jordan, just like mine."

I stared at her as she fell back to sleep. *How was it possible?* I wondered to myself. *Could it be that part of the adult version was still alive in her? And what did that riddle of an answer mean?* Dreams clouded my focus as I followed her path toward sleep.

As morning woke, it appeared that Jordan had completely forgotten the vision she had had of her adult self, but it still concerned me. Was the consciousness of my former niece, now daughter, trapped within the quantum fabric, or had it been somehow ingrained in her subconscious mind, corridored in her brain like a split personality?

After a short breakfast and a shower with her, Jordan and I phased to *Grandma's* house in Santa Monica. I had just appeared when my mother walked in and saw us, stopping short, and grabbing her chest.

"Dear Lord!" she exclaimed. "Haven't you heard of a doorbell? You nearly scared the life right out of me."

"Sorry," I said, "but it's safer than appearing out of thin air in front of any neighbors who happen to be looking in our direction."

"I understand, Sweet Pea," she replied, "but you're dealing with an aging woman with an unpredictable heart." She glanced down at Jordan. "Well, hello there, Sugar Pie!"

Jordan, who had been totally engrossed in the reborn infant doll that my mom had sent her for her birthday, suddenly looked up. "Gramma!" she shouted and then ran up and hugged her legs. My mom responded by trying to lift her up in her arms but failed.

"My goodness!" she said. "What have you been feeding this child? Lead pellets?" She squatted down and looked Jordan in the eye. "You certainly have grown since Christmas!"

"I'm six years old now!" Jordan bragged.

"By the way," I said, "She loves the doll. I can't separate her from it. Say 'Thank you, Grandma.'"

Jordan looked back at me. "I said thank you on the phone!"

"This isn't the phone," I replied. "Now, say, 'Thank you.'"

"Thank you, Gramma," Jordan said to her.

"You're very welcome, Sugar Pie," she replied with a smile. Then she stood again and looked at me. "I wish you would visit more often," she said.

"Sorry, but I've got a lot on my plate," I replied. "I went to see Dad yesterday."

"It's often comforting to talk to someone you love," she replied, "even after they've passed on."

"No, Mom," I explained. "I went back in time to when Phee and I were the same age as Jor is now."

"Lord have mercy!" she exclaimed. "I thought you'd sworn off all the Quantum Girl time travel superhero shenanigans."

"I did for the most part," I replied, "but what's about to happen is too serious to ignore. Everything—the entire universe—is coming to an end."

"As the Bible predicted. 'For the Lord himself shall descend from heaven with a shout, with the voice of the archangel, and with the trumpet of God: and the dead in Christ shall rise...'"

"Mom!" I insisted, interrupting her. "This is not about the Bible. The universe is collapsing in on itself and then it will explode. Everything will be erased. You may be convinced that everyone who believes will ascend to some Heaven, but I don't! I witnessed the end of the last universe and I saw the creation of this one. The same thing is going to happen all over again in a matter of days! I don't know how many, but it *will* happen and soon! All the galaxies and stars are moving away from us at an accelerated speed. The night sky will grow dark. The moon will move farther and farther from us. No one will witness the explosion, though. Everyone will be dead by then. As the sun grows more and more distant from the Earth, the temperature will drop to nearly four hundred degrees below zero. Nothing will survive. One of me has gone back to Rendenaaar. There's someone back there I hope can help."

I paused and then stared hard into her eyes. "I know that you and Phee have been on the outs since she married Claire. I know that the two of you had words. But this is a time for forgiveness and understanding and love. Whatever you may think you know about her, know that she's a moral person—maybe not your definition of morality, but she's never harmed anyone. All she's ever given is love, and what she has been through in her life I wouldn't wish on anyone, and neither would she. As for Claire, she's given Phee the love she'd lacked throughout a lifetime of pain."

I turned into Quantum Girl and took Jordan by the hand. "I know she meant everything to you once and you everything to her. Go to her. If Jesus could find forgiveness and acceptance in *his* heart, so can you."

Those words spoken, I phased us back to our apartment and in half an instant we were there. I turned to Jordan.

"Hey," I said to her. "I'm sure you're hungry. There are cookies on the kitchen table and I'll get you some milk from the fridge."

I followed her to the kitchen, got the milk, poured some into a glass, and then walked toward the table where she had sat down. The glass, however, dropped from my hand as I looked to where Jordan should have been. Instead, there was a young girl who looked like her only older—perhaps fourteen years old. She was dressed in a white blouse and a jumper. There were schoolbooks beside her on the floor and there was breakfast in front of her, half-eaten on a plate.

"Mom?" she said. "What's wrong?"

"Jordan?" I gasped.

"You're not upset, are you?" she asked.

"Upset about what?" I asked in return.

"My revealing myself to the world that I'm Quantum Girl," she replied.

This was insane. "Jordan," I said with hesitance in my voice, "what year is this?"

"Again?" came the reply. She looked at me, at first with amusement and then with concern. "Mom, are you all right?"

"I need to know the year," I said. My voice must have carried a bit of insistence, for she seemed to turn quite pale.

"It's 2044," she replied and then stared at me with great concern. "You're serious," she said.

"It was just 2035," I replied. "I don't understand. Everything was going to end."

"Mom," Jordan said. Her voice was insistent. "You fixed all that. Don't you remember? You and Chloë. You're not still blaming yourself for her death, are you? She helped you save everything. None of us would still be here if it weren't for the two of you." She stood up, her eyes fixed on me. "Can I get you anything? Do you want me to call Dad?" She touched her left temple with her index finger. A moment passed. Then she spoke into the air. "Dad," she said as she stared at me with concern "something's wrong with Mom. Call me a.s.a.p. In the meantime, I'll try your office. End message."

She touched her temple a second time. "Hi, this is Jordan Galathar. Would you please try and locate my dad?" She stared at me again. "Yes. I'm Thom Galalthar's daughter. It's important. Thank you. He has the number. End comm."

She shook her head to herself and then suddenly perked as she touched her temple once again. "Dad," she said. "Thank Taaarak you called!" She stared at me, again with concern. "I think it might be the transfer. She thinks it's 2035. Yes. Please. I'll phase you here right now."

Instantly, a man identically to the young Thomas Drall I had met in the past appeared in the room next to Jordan, dressed in suit and tie—not the Thomas Drall I had left in 1990. This *version* was older by a good fifteen years.

"Hey, Kiddo," he said to Jor.

"*Hey*, Dad," she said back. Then took his hand in hers, as both of them began to stare at me. "She's drifting again," she went on. "Her mind is back nine years."

"Her brain is reacting as though the god-stones were still in her head," he replied.

"Excuse me," I said. "You don't need to talk to each other like I'm not six feet away."

"Sorry, Mom," Jor replied, "but this isn't the first time your consciousness has been phased through time. We think a temporal anomaly was created when you gave your one remaining god-stone to *me*."

"In English, please," I replied. "Gaaalthaaaran if you prefer."

"The fact that you had a god-stone in your head for so many billions of years," Jor explained, "affected your atoms on a quantum level. It's caused you to shift back and forth through time like a pendulum."

I stared hard at her. "You talk as though this isn't the first time,"

24

I said.

"It isn't," she replied. "It began just after you came back from Rendenaaar."

"And who is…?" I began to ask.

Jordan glanced at the man who looked exactly like Thom—like Dhraaal.

"He's Dad's reincarnation," she said, "fourteen thousand years from now. You brought him back through time and caused him to remember."

"You *do* remember Ruby's?" Thom asked. "Don't you, *Elise*?"

He looked hard at me and then cast a faint smile. Then, suddenly, Jordan became Quantum Girl, but not the Quantum Girl I was. She glowed red and her outfit was different. I had worn a tunic and a cape. Hers was… less. There were bands around her chest and her hips and each of her thighs, but the rest of her was bare, including her feet. And, instead of a cowl, was another band with cutouts that went around her head like a mask, all of which iridesced with her skin.

As I looked at her, she stared out and away and, where she did, a three-dimensional scene appeared. It was of me at Ruby's back in 1990 singing,

Fish gotta swim, birds gotta fly,
I gotta love one man till I die,
Can't help lovin' dat man of mine.
Tell me he's crazy, tell me he's slow,
Tell me I'm crazy, maybe I know,
Can't help lovin' dat man of mine.
When he goes away,
That's a rainy day,
But when he comes back,
The day is fine,
The sun will shine!
He can stay out as late as can be.

Home without him ain't no home for me.
Can't help lovin' dat man of mine.

The scene then shifted to Thom's bedroom back then. The two of us were naked in bed making love.

"That was the night I was conceived," Jordan said. The image faded. I looked at Thom and then at her.

"Surely what you're wearing—that's not your Quantum Girl costume?"

"Mom," she protested, "although you may not remember, it's 2044. Half of the girls wear revs[9] to school! This is considered conservative!"

I shook my head to myself. "I'm not sure what a rev is," I replied, "or how you got a quantum seed, but I still don't understand. The last thing I remember was that the universe was about to end. How did that *not* occur?"

Jordan took a deep breath and then sighed as though she had told me so many times before. "Try and think back," she said. "After you came back from Rendenaaar, you and Chloë…" she began to say, and that was when everything around me changed again.

·

---

[9] Originally called reverse bikinis, they were skintight outfits girls wore that, other than the head, covered up everything but what bikinis would.

CHAPTER III

Chloë

Earth Year: 2033
Alternate Reality I

I was sitting in the bleachers with Erin Masters. We were both cheerleaders at Braxton, both still in our uniforms from practice half an hour earlier. *"Gimme a B! Gimme an R! Gimme an A X T! Gimme an O! Gimme an N! Go-o-o-o-o Braxton!"* The air was chilly, heightened by the fact that the skirts we wore only just barely hid our butts and a gathering wind blew them even higher, forcing at least one arm down on top of them for reasons of both modesty and warmth. Of course, there were matching high-cut shorts underneath, but still... This wasn't a usual place for us to sit and talk, but that day was different. Erin was upset to the point of tears, a condition I'd tried to console her from, for most of the time we were there.

"It's not the end of the world," I insisted in a grim foreshadowing of what would soon turn out to be the inevitable truth. "We'll figure something out."

The back of her left hand wiped away tears that had escaped from her deep blue eyes. Erin was probably the prettiest girl at school, but she'd been raised a devout Catholic and that meant strict abstinence from sex until marriage—not very conducive to holding onto a boyfriend, especially when you're a sophomore dating a senior, unless you choose to disregard it. Erin was a year younger than me. Regardless, we were best friends.

"He blocked me," she wept. "He texted, 'There's no going back,' and then he blocked me. He didn't even let me explain."

"There's nothing *to* explain," I told her. "If it weren't for the fact that I'm straight, I'd marry you myself."

"Oh, my parents would just *love* that!" she said, laughing through her tears.

"Hey," I said, "what do lesbians need to get married."

"I don't know," she replied.

"A liquor license," I said.

"Ewww!" came her reply along with half a laugh.

I wiped away her tears with my fingers and stared into her eyes. She smiled and it seemed as though she was about to say something when she vanished—right in front of me. I froze for a split second and then stood up and stared around. She was nowhere to be seen. I called out her name again and again to no avail. My sweater protected me from the chill but my legs were cold. Befuddled by the disappearance, I headed back to the lockers to change back into my street clothes. The locker room was coed. I was okay with that, other than that, probs a hundred-ten percent of the guys, seeing the unclothed girls, walked around with flagpoles, as we called them, their immoral compasses always pointing toward this or that naked chick. There weren't any rapes—at least not at this school—but there were more than occasional incursions meaning vag penetrants and more often than not girls piping off some guy. The woke gym structs didn't appear to care one way or the other. Sex had gotten to be regarded as more or less passé, especially since the contra implants prevented unwanted pregnancies. As for me, I was no angel, but I limited my promiscuity to my steadies and no one else.

"Nice bongos," one of the football dufuses called out at me.

"Yeah," I replied without the slightest hint of invitation, "they came with the package."

"Well, *my* package would like to come visit *yours*," he laughed in moronic tones.

That'll be a cold day in July, I thought to myself without the slightest consideration of me being back in Australia! I shivered at the very thought. "Hey," I called out, "any of you guys seen Erin?"

There was a bout of twisted expressions from those who were listening, and a general, "Who?" or "Who's Erin?" that was uttered by every one of them.

"Erin Masters!" I said.

"Never heard of her," came the sound of a female voice next to me.

I turned and saw a pretty redhead standing with a towel to her hair, still dripping from the shower. I stood up and faced her.

"Who are *you*?" I asked, staring mostly at her face. Huge boobs, though. Natural. I was jealous, but my thoughts were focused on Erin.

"Come on," she said. "Always joking. Hey, you going to spend the night at my digs or with Brad?"

She glanced behind me. I wheeled around to see him—Brad Warren, all-star quarterback on the school team with great prospects for a full ticket to half a dozen universities and the reason Erin had been in tears.

"*Hey*, Cups," he said. He was dressed in his gear, probably just having come in from practice, helmet under his left arm, wreaking of mud and sweat. He set the helmet down on the wooden bench I'd just risen from and then pulled my naked body up against him.

"Hey!" I said.

"What?" he laughed. Then he tilted his head and kissed me as he grabbed my ass with one hand. I could feel his fingers move around me as he tried to maneuver them into my vag.

I pulled away from him. "Hey!" I said again, this time with more vehemence. "What the fuck! First, you break up with Erin, leaving her nearly suicidal, and now you try and rape me with your filthy hand!"

"Babe," he said, staring at me as though I was gonzo. "What's going on? Seriously, I washed my hands when I took a leak just now. You always said you love it when I finger you from behind! I don't get it! You're not on the rag till next week—at least that's what you said. And who's Erin?"

"Your girlfriend?" I replied. "At least she was until just before practice when she said you broke things off with her!"

"What are you talking about?" he said. "The three of *us*," and he motioned toward Red, "have been together two years!"

I turned and looked at Red. She looked back at me and nodded.

"I don't know what's going on," I said as I began to get dressed. "And I'm not fucking either of you!"

Brad and Red exchanged what appeared to be confused looks with each other, shrugging their shoulders as I slammed my locker door shut and then stormed off.

Once in my car, I tried to ring Erin on my cell. A man answered. I didn't say anything. I just hung up. This was all beyond creepy.

"*Car*rington," I said.

"Yes, Miss Salinger?" the car replied in Michael Caine's voice.

"Take me to Erin's house," I said.

"I'm afraid you don't have an Erin listed in your contacts," came the response.

"Well, then," I sighed, "just take me home."

"Yes, Miss," it replied.

The car moved into the street and began its journey, the whole of which time I sat immersed in thought. "People don't just vanish," I said to myself.

"What's that, Miss?" Carrington asked.

"Nothing," I replied.

No further words were uttered or exchanged until the car pulled into the driveway.

"Here we are, Miss," Carrington announced. "Home sweet home."

"Thank you, Carrington," I said, getting out.

"You're very welcome," it replied. "Would you like me to lock up for the night?"

"Yes, please," I said as I got out. I took the flagstone path to the front door. I had a bit of trouble with the grip recognition on the doorknob but, after a couple of tries, it did open. Mom and Dad were away for the weekend with Mona and Jack, meaning I had the house all to myself. But the sense of freedom didn't even flit through my mind at that moment. I rushed to my bedroom, pulled a yearbook from the shelf over my desk, and began flipping through pages till I came to the *ems—Manners, Magellan, Mellman. No Masters!* Her photo wasn't there! I closed the covers and sat there wondering what I was supposed to do next. Erin was my best friend. We'd known each other since first grade. Now, it was as though she'd been written out of existence. A sudden thought occurred to me. I got out my cell and called Peyton. She'd still be up. It was only nine o'clock in New York. The phone rang a couple of times then I heard, "The number you reached is not in service at this time. Please check the number and try your call again."

"Fuck!" I muttered to myself. I decided to try Claire. Maybe Ophelia knew how to get in touch with her. Claire picked up. "Hey, it's me," I said. "Would you please ask Ophelia if she knows how to get a hold of Peyton?"

"Ask who?" came the reply.

"Ophelia," I repeated. "Pheeli!"

I could hear as Claire spoke to someone else in the room. "Liam," she said, "do you know anyone named Ophelia?"

"No, Babe," came the reply.

"Sweetheart, neither of us know of any Ophelia," she said, "but Peyton should be at home with her mom." There was a short pause, then, "Is everything all right?"

"I'll have to get back to you on that one," I replied and then ended the conversation with, "I'll call you tomorrow."

I had a restless sleep. It seemed that Erin's existence had been erased. The photo of the two of us on my dresser was now of me and Red; the same with those on my phone. Even the texts and VIMs[10] were from her. "Hey, Cups. Just thought I'd check in to see how you were. You seemed kinda misted in the locks. The Bradster's upset, too. He spent the night here. Fucked his brains out. That calmed him

---

[10] Video Instant Messages.

down a bit. Miss you in bed, girl. Both of us do. Miss you all around. Kinda worried. You didn't answer our calls. Probs you're asleep. Hope you've calmed a bit. VIM me back when you wake up. Love you much."

Twilight Zone shit! That's what kept running through my mind. *Who on earth was she? How did any of this happen?* I needed to get a hold of Peyton. That was all I could think, and that she had to know what was going on.

I must have checked the time on my phone a hundred times until exhaustion got the better of me and I fell asleep. I was rudely awakened by the doorbell being rung again and again interspersed with banging on the door. The app on my phone showed Red and Brad as the culprits. Throwing on my robe and slippers, I went to let them in.

"Oh, my God!" Red exclaimed as she rushed up to me and hugged me. "We thought you might have cided yourself or something!" There were tears in her eyes. "Don't ever do that again!" she said, pulling back a bit and staring at me. She kissed me on the lips and then hugged me again even harder this time. Not only could I feel her breasts pushing up against mine, but her nipples as well, which seemed to grow erect as she hugged. It was uncomfortable and a bit unnerving. Despite that Claire and Ophelia are a couple, I myself have never had even the slightest proclivity in that direction, and so when the hug had finally ended, I took a small step back.

"We were so worried!" Red went on. She glanced over at Brad. "Weren't we?"

"Cameron wanted to call the cops," he replied, "but I said we should come here first."

Cameron, I thought to myself. *So that was her name.*

"I'm fine," I said to both of them. "I'm just concerned about Erin."

"Who *are* they?" Cameron asked.

"She," I said.

"Well," she replied, " I didn't know if it was Erin with an E or Aaron with an A! But in either case…"

"In either case," I snapped back, "she's gone and I'm concerned. Everything's suddenly changed and I need to talk to Peyton."

"Peyton Herron?" Brad asked. "You *do* know she's off her nut."

"What are you talking about?" I said. "She's the most together person I've ever met."

"Well, then, you apparently haven't met a lot of people," he replied.

"Peyton Herron tried to kill herself her frosh year at Brax like what… a decade ago?" Cameron said. "I was like six or seven when it happened. Her brother woke up in the middle of the night, read the note she'd left on the bed, and then broke down the door to the closet where she'd hanged herself. Her Dad managed to revive her, but it was really too late. Brain damage and all. She's been a virtual zombie ever since. Her Dad died in a car crash a year later. DUI. Her poor mom. She's had to take care of Peyton ever since. My heart goes out."

"Where did you come up with all this?" I asked.

"From you," Cameron said. "You get hit on the head or something? Seriously, like, Claire's married to Peyton's brother." She looked hard at me. "You know, *Liam*?"

I just shook my head. "I need to go talk to her," I said.

"Who?" Cameron asked.

"Peyton," I replied. "Sorry, but I need to see for myself, because either you're crazy or I am or the world just flipped on its head!"

I took a deep breath and then glanced down to notice Cameron take Brad's hand. Both of them seemed—I don't know—anxious.

Carrington drove me to see Peyton. It was late morning. Cameron asked me if it was all right if she and Brad stayed behind and had sex in Claire's old room. Actually, they'd asked me to join in. I declined on five counts: One, Brad had been the love of Erin's life, even after the breakup. Two, I didn't know Cameron from Cara Delevingne. Three, I was *not* bisexual. Four, Erin was still MIA. And five, I needed to figure out what the fuck was going on!

"Here we are, Miss," Carrington announced. "The Herron house."

"Thank you, Carrington," I replied.

"Have a nice visit, Miss," Carrington said. "I'll be parked right outside."

It was Mrs. Herron who answered the door after I rang the bell. She looked much older than I'd remembered; perhaps *worn out* was a better word.

"Hello, Chloë," she said with a smile. "You look prettier every time I see you. Please come in."

I followed her inside. The dining room table was set for two. "I came to see Peyton," I said.

She stopped at the table and turned to me. "We were just about to have lunch," she replied. "Please join us."

"I, um," I stammered out. "I had a micro about an hour ago."

"No excuses!" she proclaimed. "I've made a German pancake and there's more than enough. Sit down. I'll set another place." She exited into the kitchen. "Have you ever had one?" she asked from the other room. I could hear the rattle of plates and flatware.

"No, Ma'am," I replied.

She returned a moment later with the place setting.

"It's filled with baked apples and cinnamon and topped with powdered sugar."

"It sounds wonderful," I replied.

"And what's with this Ma'am?" she asked as she set the plate and fork and knife and tumbler down. "It's been Aunt Katherine ever since you and Claire were little. Clairey and Chloë! The two of you were always such beautiful children. Of course, now that Claire and Liam are married, I'm Mom to her! And the twins! They're like you and Clairey all over again!" She turned and stared down the hall. "Peyton!" she called out. "Lunch is ready! And we have a surprise! Chloë's come to visit with you!" She turned back to me. "She's so alone, poor thing. Ever since the incident. Well, God will make all

34

things right when it's finally her time. Be gentle with her, dear. She tries so very hard to fit in."

I don't know if it was sympathy or shock, though perhaps a bit of both when I saw Peyton come to sit down. Mrs. Herron helped her with her chair. This was not the Peyton that I had come to know. She was thinner by at least ten pounds. She looked anorexic. Her cheeks were caved in. There were circles under her eyes. Her hair appeared thinner. And despite that she and Claire were the same age, regardless that she wore no makeup, she looked older than her twenty-two years.

Mrs. Herron turned to Peyton. "Sweet Pea," she said, "isn't it nice that Chloë came to visit?"

"Hi, Peyton," I said to her.

Peyton stared at her mother with glassy eyes. "Mama," she said. "Phee wasn't there when I woke up. Is she at school?"

"Yes, dear," Mrs. Herron said. "I'm sure she'll be back this afternoon." She turned to me and said in a quiet voice, "She has delusions about a twin sister named Ophelia. Her father and I had tried to tell her that she only has a brother, but she refused to listen. I'll go get the food."

After she left to go back to the kitchen, I turned to Peyton. "I know all about Ophelia," I said.

"You do?" she replied and began to cry. "I haven't seen her in so long. Mama and Papa said she didn't exist but I knew better. She got kidnapped by aliens. They replaced her with one of them named Liam. They tried to convince me that he was my brother and that Phee never existed, but I know better. I miss her. I miss her so much! We were best friends, you know." She then began to call out in a loud voice, "Phee! Phee!" until Mrs. Herron came rushing in and took hold of her hands.

"She gets like this sometimes," she said in an apologetic voice. "I'm so sorry."

As I rose from my seat, Peyton's expression suddenly changed from one of tears to rage. "*Sdraaalknaaad!*" she spat out.

"*Ghaghavag naaarderaaan Khattaaara graaaj Rendenaaar!*"

"Peyton!" her mother wept. "Not again!" She glanced over at me. "Perhaps you should leave," she said. "I think your presence here is upsetting her."

And so, without a word, I left. Once back in the car, I called Claire.

"Hey, Sis," I said. "We need to talk."

"What's up?" she asked.

"No," I replied. "I meant in person. Can we meet up at Starbucks in the Promenade in like half an hour?"

"What's Starbucks?" she said.

"Over on Santa Monica and Third," I replied.

"You mean Stubbs?" she asked. "Make it forty-five. The twins aren't dressed."

"Twins?" I muttered to myself and then to Claire, "Okay, I'll see you then." I clicked off and then repeated, "Twins again? What the heck is going on?"

So, Starbucks was now Stubbs. The mermaid in the green circle had been replaced by a similarly crude portrait of Neptune or Poseidon or whatever one wants to call him. Hell, it might just as well have been Aquaman! I had already secured a table outside when Claire arrived with her twins in a double stroller.

"Hey," she said upon seeing me.

"Hey," I said back. "I took the liberty of ordering you a Strawberry Crème Frap," indicating the one already on the table. "It's still your favorite, isn't it?" to which Claire looked at me and smiled. "And some Madeleines for the kids."

I got out of my chair and squatted down in front of them. "How are my little Samira and Zhana?" I said to them.

"Who's Samira and Zhana?" Claire asked. "Did you forget the names of your own nieces?"

"Their names being?" I replied.

"Dargra and Katara," Claire announced resolutely.

36

"You named your daughters after two aliens?" I asked, incredulous.

"You *are* joking?" Claire said with growing concern.

"Actually not," I replied. "It's why I asked to meet you here." I stared at her hard. "Don't you remember *anything*?"

"Remember what?" she asked.

"Ophelia for one," I replied.

"That's the second time you've mentioned her," she said.

"I'd think you'd remember your wife," I told her.

"What on earth are you talking about?" she replied. "In the first place, I'm not a lesbian. I realize that you're heavily involved with your thruple thing and if that's what butters your biscuit that's fine, but I'm straight. And in the second place, I'm married to Liam—quite happily I might add."

"The only problem," I said, "is that Liam isn't real. He was just an abstract of Ophelia. Peyton merged all the versions of her together, just like she did with you."

Claire stared at me wide-eyed.

"Like the never-went-to-Australia version of you," I said, "who got swarmed by killer bees, and Clairey, the ten-year-year-old version who was struck blind when she saved Niska from being hit by a car. You remember Niska, don't you? Collie? Blue merle? Peyton took her when you and Ophelia hooked up. The Khattaaara from Earth III turned you into a Rend. Then Jordan turned you back."

"I don't know anyone named Jordan," she insisted, "and I haven't the slightest idea what you're talking about!"

I tried to calm down. I took a deep breath and then said in a steady voice, "Ophelia Herron, Peyton Herron's sister. Light blonde hair, pale blue eyes. Gorgeous. The two of you moved in together as roommates and then fell in love. I know because you went on and on ad nauseam about her. Then you two got married. Mr. Herron walked her down the aisle. Dad walked you. You were both wearing wedding gowns that were made of sheer cloth with butterflies sewn all over them. Yours had monarchs and hers was covered in blue morphos. It was the most beautiful thing I had ever seen. Peyton had them designed for the two of you. I remember when you kissed her after the I-dos, my heart literally stopped in my chest. Only suddenly yesterday things changed. My best friend, Erin, vanished in front of my eyes. Brad wasn't her boyfriend anymore. He was mine, and there was a girl named Cameron, and I was supposedly sexually involved with both of them. Hell, the two of them are probably still at the house fucking each other's brains out. I went to visit Peyton, but she's now a total mental case, literally. With all that's gone on, I had hoped to talk to Quantum Girl, not someone who's fifty-one cards short of a full deck." I looked at her teary-eyed. "Look, I know this all sounds insane and if I were you I'd have a hard time believing me, too, but you're my big sister and I need you to at least try."

"The only sibling of Peyton's I know about is Liam," she said resolutely. Ever since she was a teenager, my now sister-in-law has had severe mental problems, but she did it to herself—sadly—we never found out why. It's funny, though. that you should mention Quantum Girl, as Liam said she used to mumble the name in her sleep when they were growing up—well after she tried to end her own life." She scooched her chair closer to me and took both of my hands in hers. "Glowworm," she went on, "I know you have a vivid imagination that gets a hold of you sometimes. Your description of the wedding sounded beautiful, but I'm married to Liam, not some imaginary Ophelia, and even though I may not believe what you've said, it doesn't mean that I love you any less. You're the best sister I could have ever wished for. I hope you know that."

"I know," I said, weeping out the words. "I just need you to believe me."

Claire stood up and faced me. "Come here," she said. I rose from my chair and she pulled me close and wrapped her arms around me. "Hey, Glowworm," she whispered in my ear. " I want you to spend the night at the house with Liam and the girls and me." Then she pulled back just a bit to look at me. She cradled my face with her fingers and wiped away my tears with her thumbs. She loved me and I loved her back and in that moment I began to wonder who was crazier, Peyton or me. "Come on," she said. "You follow us home."

I nodded, picked up my purse, got in my car, and followed her there.

CHAPTER IV

Quantum Girl

The Quantum Fabric
Quantum Date: Incalculable

The quantum fabric was different when I phased into it to go back to ancient Rendenaaar. Before, it had been a dark place with glowing paths from those versions, mostly of me, who had traveled within it. To move through it, though, was more a journey of thought, focusing on a destination, whether through time or space, other universes, or alternate dimensions. In this instance, however, it was white in all directions with glowing spheres of different sizes floating through it. Some were immense; others microscopic. They were like globs of oil, each black and pulsating. Some of the larger ones, the size of small planets, collapsed into what appeared to be nothingness, only to burst out again as their previously massive dimensions. With others, the effect was less dramatic but still followed the same rhythmic pattern. It was both beautiful and frightening in its own way.

Thou art correct, a young female voice said to me, but the sound was in my head.

"Who are you?" I asked looking this way and that.

I have many names, she said. *Khii on Rendenaaar, Gaia on Earth, or perhaps thou knowest me best as God.*

Your voice sounds familiar, I thought back at her.

That is because we have met before, she said. *I was the silver being in the castle when thou as Khattaaara stole the gaaarlefflah.*

It was then that she appeared before me just as she had countless ages ago, the personification of both beauty and power to their ultimate extent.

Behold thy vision from the past, my daughter, she said into my brain.

Daughter? I thought back. *What do you mean?*

Ages ago, she said, *so long past that even I cannot clearly remember, I came into being in a place where there was nothing else but me, and all there was of me was thought. Long was I lonely; so long that even I as God begged for the mercy of death until at last, and I do not know how, a single wave of energy shot from me weaving back and forth through time so that in one instant it appeared as though there were uncountable numbers of them that formed the very first universe of many more to come. From them, I created that which became matter and from the matter came stars and from the stars spewed the dust that became planets and ambient things.*

I looked at her, but that one word still echoed in my brain, begging for a reply—*Daughter.*

At long last, I thought to myself, I shall have others as companions, and so I went from universe to universe, from world to world until I found thy mother. Here, I knew, was a good, kind woman who believed in me. I decided it was she who should bear my progeny, but, alas, she was already with child, albeit but an embryo. Thus did I make her pregnant with a second in her womb, and that, dearest Peyton was thee, the most beautiful daughter any mother could imagine.

But, I begged the question, *how could I be the reincarnation of Khattaaara or Cleopatra or any others when I came to be born so long after them?*

Who is to say, she replied, *in which direction time must flow?*

If you are God, I asked, *then who is Jesus to you? Is He your son, my brother?*

The being smiled. *I shall not destroy the faith of more than two billion souls for the sake of a yes or no.*

My universe, I went on, *is on the verge of collapse. Surely, you will help me stop that from happening.*

It is not my place to meddle, she answered, *Only to observe.*

But if you are all-powerful, I replied, *you can save us from extinction. I'm begging you!*

When thou wast Cleopatra, she said, *thou didst dissolve a priceless pearl in a goblet of win, just to witness its destruction. Regardless that thou was Pharoah with legions at thy command, thou couldst not undo what thou had done to that gem. Yet now in thy head are seven other gems that can work miracles shouldst thou command the power they hold. Go now and learn what thou can, my child. Make thy mother proud, for in thee lies the sum of my strength and the breadth of my wisdom, thy beauty notwithstanding.*

She vanished with those words.

Wait! I called out to her from my mind. *How do I find Rendenenaaar? All I see are black globules everywhere I look!*

Thou must look deeper, she said. *That is always the answer in life!*

There was only silence after that. I had no whistle such as I had given to Payton or to Phee with which to call her. I was totally on my own.

CHAPTER V

Peyton

Earth Year: 2033
Alternate Reality I

They keep taking me to doctors trying to figure out what's wrong with me when everything wrong is with them I can see it as clearly as I can see the invisible map that's been drawn on my bedroom ceiling by I don't know who but whoever it is they'd better not show themselves or I'll claw their eyes out not that I'm violent or anything I'm as calm as anyone else but sometimes I hear their thoughts thinking Peyton this and Peyton that and they look at me all of them like I'm the one who's crazy when it's them they who can't see past their noses sniffing the air waiting for any foul smell to waft in up their nostrils and then probably blame it on me like Peyton probably didn't take a bath or a shower never stopping to think that maybe just maybe I was killed in the shower by Thara-Klo dear daughter such a disgusting bitch with her four breasts and pointed ears and that tail or yaaargh or whatever the fuck it's called speaking of which fucking I mean I miss the times that I fucked Theresa but Theresa got killed by Khattaaara or was it by me but it served her right for bullying me because she shouldn't ought to have done it and it doesn't matter if she was upset by the fact that she thought that I would have rejected her and she may have been right except I didn't at least not the part of me that was reflected in the other world the other dimension only there aren't other dimensions now because I put them all together including one set of Moms and one set of Dads with maybe a couple of dead ones thrown in for good measure except they never cared for me, no, no, no, only they would pretend as if they did only Phee did but she's gone now and forgotten and supposedly Liam is her but Liam is a guy and Phee was Phee unless somehow Phee decided that

43

she was transgender and had an operation and became Liam so that she as he could fuck Claire whom she used to be married to only now Claire is married to Liam who may in fact be Phee but presumably now with a dick that she or is it he can fuck Claire with living in their house by the ocean that I bought them but no one remembers and Liam who is probably Phee probably takes credit for I wonder if Phee and Liam are one and the same if I call her or him or whatever LiPhee as in Leafy if she or he would take notice and turn and say Hello, Peyton, yes, you're right we are us and them and our preferred pronouns are shut the fuck up and me I would look at them in the eye and say I don't care if you are a he or a she because I know you're my twin and when you were two people you committed incest and you're not even from Kentucky which is a bad joke I suppose though really nothing's funny anymore not really though what is in fact funny is that sometimes especially at night I have phantom sensation imagining that I have two sets of breasts one set over the other and that I have a tail that I pull between my legs and plunge it into my vag like Liam must do with Claire not that he has a tail but rather with his non-phantom limb that he uses which he couldn't do if he were Phee but it's funny how I sometimes remember growing up with both of them and the fact of the matter is that I miss Phee and I can't understand why she can't come visit I would like that only I seem to remember throwing her up against a wall and trying to kill her so maybe just maybe that's what happened and Phee was resurrected as Liam maybe by Theresa before she died because I'm pretty certain she was able to do that sort of thing bringing dead things back to life but none of that matters because I'm hungry and I want to know when Mama is going to bring me supper though I hope it's not roast beef because I'm a vegetarian or was it Phee who was I forget but anyway I'm more tired than hungry so I think I'll just take a short nap and dream of Rendenaaar and how I was a princess there.

CHAPTER VI

Ophelia

The Next Universe
Planet Vesta: Year 1
Alternate Reality II

Peyton had rescued the five of us from the destruction of the universe and phased us to a planet she had named Vesta. In that all six of us were female, there appeared little hope of repopulating that world. We had been there eight months. Claire, now my partner, still mourned the loss of her sister. I couldn't say that I blamed her. I had come to love Chloë more as though she were *my* sister, rather than just Claire's. But Chloë was not the only one lost. The collapse of spacetime that exploded into a new creation caused the end of everything and everyone we had ever known as well as the end all life, even that beyond human reach. Nothing about existence it seemed was fair. I had gone through grief and mourning ever since my father died but now my mother was gone as well—my mother who fervidly believed in a Heaven where her soul would go to after her death. Peyton as the reincarnation of Khattaaara from a world, trillions of universes in the past proved that consciousness could in fact transcend death. I can only pray that our parents will have found their place together whether in Heaven or in some other universe at some future time.

Vesta was similar to the Earth in terms of its gravity and atmosphere, though its star was blue and thus considerably hotter than Earth's sun. That caused the temperatures to be sweltering, especially during the summer months. The children ran around naked. Claire and I wore as little as we could and sweated profusely. Peyton appeared unaffected by the heat. The hothouse effect, however, encouraged the proliferation of flora across the planet on a massive

45

scale, including gargantuan trees, some of which rose nearly two hundred feet into the air. Everywhere, in each direction, was a jungle yet to be tamed. Hardly any part of the ground lay untenanted by one sort of foliage or another. Beyond that, it was different from anything we had ever seen in that all of the leaves were shades of red, perhaps due to a different type of chlorophyll or some other pigment that served the same function. As for the fauna, much of it looked reptilian, of virtually every shape and size with either feathers or fur or scales for covering. The creatures roamed the ground, swam the oceans, or flew across the skies. There were ones like dinosaurs that were fearsome beasts. Others were harmless to the point of being tame. Claire took on the role of Adam, deciding to name them all, an insurmountable task but, beyond motherhood and wifery, what else did she have to do? I thought that we should try to domesticate some of them and suggested as much. Both Claire and Peyton agreed, though it would be an arduous task. The process on Earth had taken thousands of years. The time needed here, no doubt, would well exceed our lifetimes, but, again, it gave us something with which to fill our days.

Setting up camp was somewhat of a challenge in that all we had come with were the clothes on our backs. Whatever tools we needed, we had to fashion from wood or stone. Oddly, there was a preponderance of gold nuggets virtually everywhere, but in its pure state, it was useless for anything other than ornament. The children made mounds of it simply because it glittered and there were no toys or dolls for them to play with. Peyton promised to "scour the new universe" for any civilizations from which to purloin whatever amenities she could in order to make our lives more comfortable.

According to her, she had phased us more than eight billion years forward from this universe's inception. But it was just the six of us to survive as best we could. She went out exploring the far reaches of outer space *en mass*, dividing herself a thousandfold, though she left one of her behind to care for Jordan and to protect us all if need be.

As for the future, Peyton drew Liam out of me once more in order to impregnate Claire, hopefully with a boy and she drew up a male version of Claire whom we named Clark to plant his seed in me to the exact same end. The creation of the two males was, unfortunately, only temporary, such as had been the case on Rendenaaar when Khattaaara pulled out a version of me from herself. I will admit, albeit sadly as it was just for several hours, that having sex with a man again, feeling his strength, his arms around me, his manhood inside me, brought back memories I had almost forgotten—memories that would have brought me to tears had my love for Claire not been so great. How strange it was that in all my growing up I had never considered myself lesbian—not even bi. But here I was, allured by her beauty and aroused by the scent and taste of her sex when she, too, became aroused by *me*. How my dear mother would chide me whenever I broached the subject of our love. "Jesus this and Jesus that," she would say. "Jesus was all about love," I would say back and she had no answer for that. But as much as she frowned at the love that I'd found, I still loved her, and I missed her very much.

It on was day two hundred, forty-six that I opened my eyes to see Peyton standing near my side of the bed. We had built an adobe hut with four separate rooms: one for Claire and me, one for Peyton, a third for the girls, and a fourth that was sort of a living room. It was tolerable, though challenging when it rained.

"What's up?" I asked, squinting from what was blinding light coming through the window. As my vision cleared I saw another Peyton appear just behind her and merge into her.

"I found a planet with technology," she said. "It's uninhabited and looks to have been that way for quite some time. There are buildings and tools—even electronics. There's a lot of work to be done but it's better than here and there's a brutal storm headed this way." She paused and then looked at Claire who was still fast asleep. "How's she doing?"

"The morning sickness seems to have passed," I told her. "Just one question. How do we know if it's a boy?"

"Because," she said, "I saw to it that the sperm that fertilized her egg was male. When she was a Rend, Jordan had promised to give her back the little boy she'd miscarried. Watch."

Peyton stared at Claire once again. As she did, Peyton's eyes began to glow. Part of the sheet covering her became invisible. Then the flesh around her abdomen did as well, revealing first the amniotic sack and then the fetus which proved undoubtedly male, even at just five months.

"So, what are you two going to name him?" she asked.

"Liam," I said. "I really wished I could have gotten pregnant myself."

Peyton looked at me and smiled. "There's plenty of time," she said.

"Do you think there's any chance you can go back in time and save Mom and Dad and Claire's parents and Chloë?" I asked. I rose from the bed and led her off to one side. "I don't want to wake Claire. I've done my best to keep her relaxed. I don't want her pregnancy to take a turn for the worse. She had a hard time with Sami. We thought she was going to lose her a couple of times."

"You're asking a lot," she replied. "Maybe Chloë, but as for the rest, they're too old. Their brains are too wired. The god-stones wouldn't work on them and they can't cross universes without them."

"So, Mom and Dad," I said, "they're really dead forever?"

"They have their Heaven," she replied. "Let's hope for their sake it's real."

It was at that point that Claire stirred. "What's going on?" she asked. She sat up a bit and saw Peyton through squinting eyes. "Morning," she said, yawning. "Is everything all right?"

"We're moving on to another planet," Peyton replied. "It'll be better for us there. No more gigantic monsters. Just a lot of ancient electronics gathering dust."

CHAPTER VII

Chloë

Earth Year: 2033
Alternate Reality I

I found it unnerving when, after arriving at Claire's house, there was Liam in the flesh. The two of them acted as though that was how it always was. Neither had any recollection of the multiple dimensions that had existed or that Liam had been absorbed into Ophelia, who in this version of reality didn't exist. Here, as on what had been Earth II, it was Liam and not Ophelia who was Peyton's twin. Dargra and Katara, no longer half-sisters, born from separate wombs, were now fraternal twins.

As for me, the word was that I had been very open about my supposed bisexuality by frequently offering public displays of affection with Cameron and/or Brad in instances of which I had absolutely no recollection. All I knew was that I had a lot of different memories about a lot of things. Liam insisted that while he had heard Peyton's ramblings in her sleep when they were both children, he always thought it was from some comic book she had read or from some television show or cartoon she had watched.

"Poor Peyton!" Claire proclaimed when Peyton's name came up. "Liam still blames himself for what happened," she said, taking his hand in hers "I keep assuring him that it wasn't his fault. None of us noticed how despondent she'd become, she hid it so well. Besides, no one can change what was meant to be."

Beyond the obvious, there were other differences on a broader scope—significant ones. The Covid-19 pandemic had never happened. Instead, Sars-24 had been *accidentally* leaked from the same Chinese lab in Wuhan, but this time it was far more deadly and affected only Caucasian males, wiping out nearly seventy-five percent of that population. Vaccines were produced by China. It was touted that the serum caused white blood cells to produce antibodies, though conspiracy theorists believed that it also contained proteins able to breach the blood-brain barrier where they attached to brain cells in order to create a more docile and obedient population. While Claire rode the fence on that, Liam was one of the anti-vax adherents and quite outspoken about it. Meanwhile, the now decidedly socialist government had seized ownership of all buildings and land under the guise that such would eliminate the need for property tax. That meant that Claire and Liam no longer owned their home. At first, that seemed all right, not having to make payments every year, but then the government began charging rent—a little at first, but that soon began to increase. Food was in short supply unless one had enough money or else knew someone high up. The worst, according to Claire, was that everyone was now required to have electronic chips subcutaneously implanted at their temples. These were promoted as being able to allow anyone to watch movies and even be in them without the need for a display.[11] Gen Zs and Gen Alphs jumped on it, but then it became the law, maintaining that the implants were also there to monitor health conditions and would call 911 in the case of an emergency. The problem was that it also allowed the government to track anyone anywhere. It all seemed both a sad and frightening time in history. That was what Liam insisted, and I couldn't help but agree.

"Don't worry, Husband," Claire said to him. "The chips aren't allowed to listen in on private conversations."

"Not yet," came the reply. According to him, rumor had it that the next hardware upgrade would allow the chips to actually read minds.

I had sincerely hoped that morning would awaken me from the nightmare I had just lived through, but, as they say, good fortune only favors the few. Liam was still Claire's husband, the twins were still

---

[11] The technology had been developed by Apple through a government contract and was the fifth generation of its Vision Pro goggles.

called Dargra and Katara, and Peyton was still batshit crazy. After some hug-filled goodbyes, Carrington drove me back home. Amazingly, Brad and Cameron were still going at it, naked in bed. It was Cameron who first noticed me standing jaw-dropped in the doorway. She was on her knees, Brad riding her from behind. She pulled away from him and rolled onto her back in such a position that nothing was left to the imagination, not even to the most nearsighted of gynecologists. Meanwhile, Brad turned toward me, revealing, at attention, more than I cared to see.

"You're back," Cameron exhaled, her ample breasts sagged toward her sides.

"Have you two been fucking ever since I left?" I asked.

"It's a new upgrade in the chip," she replied. "Here," she said, getting out of bed. She grabbed her cell phone from off of one of the nightstands and walked over to me.

"Wait!" I said, but before I could move away, she reached out toward my left temple with her phone in one hand and pressed a button on the screen with the other.

"You need to be within six inches for this to work," she said. I could feel her still erect nipples rubbing me through my blouse. It made me feel uncomfortable. "There," she went on. "Done."

"Done?" I asked. "What's done?"

"You'll see," she said. "Just give it a second or two."

Suddenly, I felt strange. I remember shaking my head to try and ward off the effects.

"Don't fight it," she went on. "Just enjoy the experience. The app just came out yesterday. I set the duration to six hours. Come on, you. Let's get you undressed."

I could feel her unbuttoning my blouse. I caught words from Brad saying something about "grabbing something to eat from the kitchen," and then I was naked in bed with Cameron—doing things.

"I'm not a lesbian," I muttered.

"Of course, you're not," Cameron said back. "You're bi." She

51

paused. "You seem a bit muggled. I hope I didn't mess up the dose." She grabbed her phone again. "Shit," she spat out. "Well, you'll be a bit out of it, but I take it from where your hand is that you're feeling severely aroused."

My hand *was* there, my fingers moving rhythmically, my brain reeling from the intense pleasure of it all. Mostly, it was all a blur. Digits and tongues—that's what she called it—me and her, each enacting ecstasy upon the other, furthered by deep penetration when Brad returned. There was the smell of sweat and the musty odor and sourdough taste that came, literally, from Cameron—well, from one *part* of her at any rate. I was in a daze through all of it with orgasm after orgasm that refused to relent. And then I woke up. I was alone in the room and in bed. I didn't want to get up but I desperately needed to pee. Standing took an effort and, walking to the bathroom, I could feel the muscles around my vag aching. Some small relief came as a thick stream of urine splashed down from me into the toilet. I just sat there for a moment, my forearms on my thighs, trying to clear my head.

Oh, God! I thought to myself. *I hope I'm not pregnant!* I calmed myself a bit by theorizing that by the time Brad got to me, after a night of sex with Cam, his semen was too diluted to do its work. Finally, deep breath taken, I toilet-papered, rose, flushed, and then jumped into the shower. It was one of those ungirlish moments when I sniffed at my right armpit and threw back my head in disgust, and that didn't account for all the other scents I had acquired during what I can only describe as an at-home orgy.

The water felt refreshing as it rained down on me. The strawberry body gel helped wash away the images of the long sensual night. I had always looked at Claire and Ophelia with curiosity as to how two women could have and enjoy sex with each other. *Well,* I remember thinking, *that all was now in the past.* Snatching a towel off its hook, I dried myself as best I could, then, wrapping it around me—why, I didn't know, as I appeared to be alone in the house—I set down a path of wet footprints to the kitchen where I drowned my throat in peach yogurt.

It was after I finished off the tub that the front door opened and my mom and dad walked in. *Thank God Brad and Cameron had already left!* Mom came into the kitchen with a bag of groceries and began putting them away. I wasn't sure where Dad went, though generally, he sacked out after coming home from a vacation.

"How was your trip?" I asked.

"It was all right," she replied. "Your father and Jack went off fishing, so Mona and I wound up having sex by ourselves while they were gone."

"Ex*cuse* me?" I said, totally shocked to say the least.

"We were planning a swap," she replied, "but you know how the men are when it comes to trying to reel in trout."

"You and Mona," I said. "I had no idea the two of you…" I paused as the thought of what she said suddenly struck me. "Swap? As in you and Jack and Mona and Dad?"

"Glowworm," she said glancing back at me. "You act as though this is all new to you. I've never said anything to *you* about Brad and Cameron and your ever-more-frequent sexploits with them, although I do wish you would ask Brad to please remember to put the toilet seat down when he's through. You cannot imagine how cold the porcelain feels, especially when it comes unexpectedly."

"Twilight Zone," I muttered to myself.

"What, Dear?" Mom asked.

"Nothing," I replied, and then said, "Mom?"

"Yes, Dear?" she answered.

"Do you remember Erin?" I asked

"Who?" she asked.

"Erin," I said emphatically.

Mom turned toward me, "Is she one of your schoolmates?"

"She's my best friend," I said.

"Is she the skinny young thing with pink and blue hair you were having sex with last week?" she asked.

"No, Mom!" I replied. "Erin's blonde, very, very pretty with blue eyes and I would hardly describe her as skinny."

"Sorry," she apologized, "but maybe you could introduce me to her sometime." Her head perked. "I thought you and *Cameron* were best friends."

"So, I'm told," I replied. "The thing is, Erin just vanished and no one seems to remember her. And then there's the fact that everything seems to have changed."

"Changed?" Mom asked. "What on Terra do you mean?"

"Like *that*!" I insisted. "This isn't Terra! It's Earth! And those *things* in our heads apparently cause everyone to go full throttle, sexually. Oh, and then there's Kamala Harris! President? Really? The woman has the brains of a jellyfish! Claire is now married to Liam! Again—instead of Ophelia."

"Instead of *whom*, Dear?" came Mom's response.

"Ophelia! Ophelia Herron!" I shouted back. "But *she's* now disappeared along with Erin! And I can't ask Peyton to use her Quantum Girl shit because she's now totally bonkers! Jesus!"

"Dear," she replied, "it's pronounced *Heysoos*, and what does our gardener have to do with any of this? It's obviously a malfunction with one of your implants."

I looked down at my chest and felt my breasts.

"In your head," Sweetheart. "The others are real. My side of the family has always been blessed when it comes to our cup size."

"My new nickname, It seems," I replied.

"We'll have Carrington take you to the clinic," she said. "They can check out the electronics." Her attention suddenly turned. "Where is your father? He was derelict in his duty all weekend. If he's gone to sleep without giving me my morning orgasm, I swear to the gods..." And with that, she left the room.

I ran my fingers through my hair and groaned. It seemed that this was all a nightmare I couldn't wake up from.

Half an hour later, Carrington was driving me to the local (apparently there were a lot of them) S.O.M.A. clinic. S.O.M.A., it turned out, was an acronym for Subdural Optimal Mind Assistant, which is someone's fancy name for the chip implants. How or when I got mine put in I had no idea.

"Carrington?" I said.

"Yes, Miss?" came the Brit-inflected response.

"Are you aware of any changes to the timeline?" I asked.

"No, Miss," came Carrington's response. "Is there something wrong, Miss?"

"Oh, Brother, you can say that again!" I replied.

"Is there something wrong, Miss?" Carrington repeated.

"I didn't mean," I started to say and then finished with, "Just forget it."

"As you wish, Miss," the car system replied.

The rest of my *journey* went without conversation.

The S.O.M.A. building, or rather, complex, was a breathtaking gasp of modern architecture—colored glass windows, waterfall fountains, as well as holographic guides positioned at this obelisk or that. My immediate take on it was that whoever owned the place had money to burn. As it turned out, my assumption was correct. S.O.M.A. Corp., it turned out, had the exclusive contract for the implants and there was nothing like it anywhere else in the world.

Tall glass doors led into an atrium that revealed at least ten floors with a columnar hologram perhaps fifteen feet in diameter that reached up to the multi-colored glass ceiling and consisted of hundreds of naked figures of Cameron and Brad and me making love. I surmised that the images were specific to whichever person viewed them, generated in one's mind by the temporal implants. After just a moment, a rather beautiful woman appeared out of nowhere beside me and addressed me by name.

"Hello, Chloë," she said. "We've been expecting you."

Her sudden appearance startled me. Turning toward her, my arm accidentally went through her, disorienting me for a moment or more.

"What are you," I asked her or it.

"My name is V.E.R.A.," came the response, "a virtual electronic remote assistant, projected into your mind through your S.O.M.A. implants. Please follow me."

My guide led me to a transparent elevator that took me to the sixtieth floor and then walked me to a room at the end of the corridor that it opened out into. Once inside, I found myself alone once again. Seconds later, I heard a female voice in my head: *Chloë Salinger, born November 4th, 2016, sex: female. Sexuality: bisexual; presently involved with Brad Warren, age 18, and Cameron Barkley, age: 17. Bioscan reveals no physical abnormalities. Cerebral scan indicates the possibility of dissociative identity disorder. No malfunction in either S.O.M.A. Corp. biometric implant. Convergence indicated.*

"Please remove your shoes and socks," my holographic guide ordered, and so I did; I saw no harm in complying at least that much.

Once I was barefoot, I stood waiting. *What did they want with me?* I wondered. Then, all at once, I felt excruciating pain in both of my temples. My hands went up and pressed against them as I dropped to my knees. The torturous effect lasted for what seemed to be an eternity but was in reality probably no more than a minute or so. When it stopped it was as though an entire other lifetime had been impressed into my brain. While I still remembered everything about the world as it had been with multiple versions of everyone but me, I also remembered another reality where neither Erin nor Ophelia nor Quantum Girl existed. Strange, too, was my newfound incongruity with my sexual orientation, in love and lust with both Cameron and Brad. I shook my head, briefly pressed my eyelids together, and then climbed to my feet. But if what had just been done to me was effective, I wondered, how was it that I still remembered what used to have been? *Unless*, I thought to myself, *there was still some connection in my head to the god-stone that Liam and Li had given to me.* Suddenly, I heard an alarm, but it wasn't in my head. It was pulsing loudly, echoing within the room.

"Attention!" the same voice said. "Failure to correct biometrics! Subject: Chloë Salinger. Disposal personnel report to ground floor clean-up at once!"

Disposal personnel? I remembered hearing rumors in the other existence of individuals being murdered when the chips could no longer control them. Memories of the existence of the person killed were then erased from everyone else's minds. I needed to get out of there if I wanted to survive! It was as I turned toward the door that the floor I was standing on fell out from under me.

I was on the sixtieth floor and falling. I screamed without a stop. The air rushed past me as I accelerated, face down, toward impending death! Below me was an empty steel trash container, painted red if that made any difference—red, like the god-stone that had been in my head. I laughed in my terror at the irony, my eyes now burning from the air. Then, just as I was about to hit, as I realized that my life would end in one split second, wondering what it would feel like as my head was crushed against the hard metal, I found myself face up, lying on soft sand!

Above me was the blazing sun; I lifted my arm to shield my eyes, and squinted against its brightness—and then I sat up. I was still alive, *but how?* I wondered. The heat was blistering. In the distance, I could see the Sphinx and three tall pyramids behind it. Off to my right was a caravan of several camels with riders. I was about to stand up, but then I paused. Something was wrong. The Sphinx looked different—not as time-worn as I had remembered when Claire and I were in Egypt, and each of the pyramids was faced in white limestone, all of which looked hundreds of years old, but not thousands. It was clear *where* I was. The question was *when?* And how was it that I was here and not lying dead at the bottom of a dumpster?

CHAPTER VIII

Quantum Girl

The Quantum Fabric
Quantum Date: Incalculable

Of all the nearly infinite bloblike universes, my quantum sense guided me to the one that contained Rendenaaar; or perhaps *it* was guided to *me*. As with most of the rest, within the universe I had chosen, there were hundreds of billions of galaxies, each one seemingly microscopic, each shaped as a rotating sphere or spinning disk, and, like snowflakes, no two were alike—no two are ever alike! As with all of the others, the Rendenaaar universe expanded and contracted, pulsating as though it were a living, breathing thing, for within each quantum bubble lay trillions upon trillions of instants of time, defining the existence of that particular one. But the one that I had chosen was my destination, and so I phased down into the undulating expanse that contained the planet where once in another life I had lived out a separate life, although that would have been much further back in time than where I first emerged.

The Rendenaaaran universe, though older and larger, was not much different than my own but I was a colossus among the myriad of galaxies. All of them passed through me as though I wasn't even there, the matter that comprised me being so diffuse I was incorporeal to even the hottest stars. This was the universe I had been born in as Khattaaara. On Rendenaaar they called it the *chaaagargafal*, which in the Gaaalthaaaran tongue meant *all that is*. Visually, it was beautiful beyond belief. Galaxies swirled like pinwheels of fiery gas. Nebulae shed out rainbows of color that peppered the vast expanses between those august suns. This, though, was not just a bucket of stars. There were more lights around me than all the grains of sand on the Earth. It would have taken a million lifetimes to count them all.

Such was the majesty of this universe—of mine as well. I might have been lost in it all, but for my ancient daughter, Thara-Klo, for it was her words and thoughts that guided me once again to that same bright cluster where Rendenaaar spun its path around its star and from there to the planet itself, to set my feet down on its soil once again, having diminished myself in size as I did.

I found my way back to that desolate time when I and Payton stood before the remains of Khattaaara. I watched the scene replay as I slipped on the bracelet and observed from a pocket dimension how the avatar of Khattaaara had spoken to me, while my other-dimensional self stood frozen in time. All of that vanished, however, as I phased farther into the past with one eye on the skeleton that lay on the ground. Eventually, the flesh and blood returned to it. More than five thousand times did Rendenaaar circle its sun for this to happen but eventually the corpse that was Khattaaara rose backward from the grass that then surrounded it and turned to face a version of Dargra-Tol that had not ventured forth into the future—Dargra-Tol, who it seemed, from her perch in the air, had shot forth a fatal surge of quantum force to murder my incarnation. Going forward just a bit I watched as the *Thaaagran* phased down to the surface, stooped down, ripped the heart from Khattaaara's chest then crushed it in her hand so that the azure blood that had filled it dripped down into the Rendenaaaran soil.

How tempted I was to destroy the syth there and then, but I dared not for fear of upsetting Earth's timeline once more. I knew from all that had happened in the past that my footfall on this world needed to be gentle. And so I watched with neither action nor words as that artificial lifeform vanished, perhaps to join with itself in the universe whence I came. None of that mattered, though, for unlike the Tralfamadorians' perception of time in Slaughterhouse-Five, I knew that all that had or would happen was subject to irreversible change.

My journey soon led me farther back in time. I looked on as Jordan left this universe and traveled back to mine where she had been born. I wept as I watched Phee as she was electrocuted by Dargra-Tol, her body then taken by the synth as though it were some carrion it had found. I wanted to wrap her *yaaargh* around her throat and strangle her to death, but that would have altered the course of what was to be and so I just stood there, helpless, with tears raining down upon my cheeks. After that, I could bear no more. I phased to one of the libraries to learn where and when Krotaaarak had lived and then journeyed back in time to find him.

CHAPTER IX

Claire

The Next Universe
Planet Erebus: Year 1
Alternate Reality II

We named our new home Erebus. Erebus was the god of darkness, but also, through his sister and wife, Nix, the goddess of night, he was the father of Aether, the god of brightness, and Hemera, the goddess of day. It was our future, however, that remained dark to us so, ultimately, the name seemed appropriate. Still, we hoped that this forsaken planet would allow us to bring new life to its timeworn ruins.

According to Peyton, who had briefly traveled back to the civilization's past, the last inhabitants were metallic cyborgs, creations of carbon-based beings that had preceded them and who had died at the hands of their creations who, in turn, met with extinction when a computer virus spread throughout their kind. But that was hundreds of thousands of their years ago.

Most of the buildings were overrun with vegetation or else in utter ruin, but Peyton, through an effort that left her unconscious for nearly two weeks, placed a quantum field around one of the dwellings and reversed time within it so that we had shelter—a place to live that with a bit of effort proved both safe from the more aggressive wildlife and comfortable.

The girls spent their time being schooled either by Pheeli or myself or else played amongst themselves. There had been seven god-stones, but when the time came to leave—when our universe was about to go critical—Chloë's was nowhere to be found. Peyton had frozen time in an attempt to find her. She divided herself into millions of Quantum Girls but the forces of the collapse were so intense that she could only postpone the inevitable for a minute or two and, sadly, without success.

The explosion was cataclysmic as the old universe gave way to the new. It came in the form of a gravitational wave and felt as though the force of a thousand atom bombs was tearing through us, but the god-stones protected us from the devastation it created. Even photons were annihilated. Everything became dark. As Peyton moved us forward through time, particles were formed, gases comingled around the focal points of stars from the previous universe, and from those gases emerged the first light—faintly glimmering against a background of electrons and quarks that had yet to become anything. The process took more than three hundred thousand years for solid matter to begin to form. How small we seemed in the wake of it all. There were no stars—not yet. It would take millions more years for the first stars to be formed. But the nebulae that formed around us glowed with a spectrum of colors. It was fortunate that there was a quantum field around us so that we had air to breathe while we floated in this new outer space and so that we were all protected from the freezing cold and the deadly radiation. The twins cried, so frightened all that was going on. Jordan wept because there had been no way to take Niska with us. Pheeli and I were scared as well, but we tried our best to be brave for the sake of the children. Only Peyton remained calm in her Quantum Girl attire. I don't know if it was necessary for her to appear that way in order to use her powers or if it was just for a show of strength for us all.

"I'm going to take us all forward in time again," she said, and then she formed a platform beneath us so that we could sit or stand and watch as the universe quickly began to change.

She told us she had sent several divisions of herself on ahead to scout out a planet we could live on. I never bothered to ask her about it, but I saw at least half a dozen merge back into her before she announced that a suitable world had been found. Phasing was a strange experience, though one I was not a stranger to, as the part of me that had been a ten-year-old blind girl had experienced it more

62

than once. Still, it was like we were moving through Jell-O and then, suddenly, having it all disappear; you're in one place and time one second and then you're in another without physically having moved.

We wound up in a clearing in the pouring rain. It wasn't just a hard rain, it was a fucking monsoon! I wondered why Peyton didn't just phase us past it all a few days ahead, but she said she was exhausted. Not only did she take us billions of years through time, but had to match all of our energy fields to that of the rest of the universe in the time we were now in. Thankfully, she was able to throw up a quantum barrier that shielded us from being drenched anymore just before she collapsed into what I can only describe as a coma. We watched as the unrelenting downpour slid around the invisible barrier, pooling at its edge. We slept on bloodred, wet grass for four of this planet's days and were grateful when the storm finally broke. It took six more days for Peyton to regain her senses. In the meantime, it was up to Pheeli and me to search for food. The fact was we were hungry, only having had water to drink since we had arrived. In a short bout of consciousness, we got Peyton to remove the barrier so that we could look. I was the first to go. We had to take turns in order to watch the children and keep them from wandering off. I found some berries and small fruits, gathering them in the skirt of my dress. I volunteered to be the taster. The red berries caused me to throw up. The rest proved safe. Pheeli speared a couple of alien fish or whatever they were in a nearby stream, but we had no way to build a fire. We told the girls the raw fish was sushi. It kept us alive. Pheeli squeezed some of the fruit into Peyton's mouth, lifting up her head so that she wouldn't choke. We gathered leaves for beds and slept huddled for warmth as the nights were somewhat cold.

On the tenth day, sitting on a rock next to Pheeli, I broke into tears. "What's the good of it all?" I wept to her. "There's nothing here! There's no shelter and barely any food! Our clothes are becoming rags, not to mention that they stink which is not surprising considering that there's no soap to clean them with!"

63

"Peyton will wake up soon and things will get better," Pheeli said.

"You've been saying that for days!" I replied. I stood and turned toward Peyton who still lay unconscious. "Look at her!" I shouted through my tears. "She keeps phasing from herself to Quantum Girl! She may never wake up and what then? What are we supposed to do on this godforsaken planet in a universe we're not even from?"

"You need to have faith," Pheeli told me.

"Faith!" I repeated the word, shaking my head. "You were raised Christian. I was raised to believe what I can see and hear and feel. You still have your sister, but mine is gone. Everything we ever held dear has been obliterated. We're all that's left and even if we manage to survive, what sort of a life will we have? What sort of a life will there be for the children?"

Pheeli stood up and held me. "It's going to be all right," she said. "I know it will."

I knew that I shouldn't have, but I pulled away from her and went over to Sami, who was playing with Zhana and Jordan. I took her by the hand and led her away.

"Come on," I said to her.

"Where are we going?" she asked.

"Just for a walk," I replied.

"Is something wrong?" she asked.

"Everything's fine," I said.

"Then why are you crying?" she asked. "Doesn't Mommy Ophelia love you anymore?"

I turned to her and squatted down. A smile broke through my tears and I wiped my eyes with my fingers.

"*I* love you," she went on.

"I know you do," I replied and I hugged her.

"Mommy," she said when I pulled back just a bit. She stared into my eyes. "Is Auntie Peyton going to die?"

"No," I said. "She has god-stones in her head that will heal her. It just takes time. She's been through an awful lot."

"We had god-stones in our heads, too," she replied. "Why did Auntie Peyton take them out when we got here?"

"Because they can be dangerous," I replied, "if you don't know how to use them. She just didn't think she'd become unconscious when she did."

"What's unconshcus?" she asked.

"Unconscious," I repeated. "It's sort of like when you're asleep, only you don't dream."

"When will she wake up?" she asked.

"After she has time to heal," I replied. "She brought us from our universe to this one and that was a very hard thing to do."

"But why did we have to come here?" she asked. "I don't like it here and neither do Zhana or Jordie. Can we go back home?"

"I'm so sorry but we can't," I said.

"Why not?" she asked. We hadn't told any of the children the reason for our leaving.

"Because our universe and the Earth don't exist anymore," I told her.

"But what about Gramma and Grampa and Auntie Chloë?" she asked. "And all my friends at school?"

"I'm afraid they've all gone to Heaven?" I told her.

"You mean they died?" she said and began to cry. "I don't want them to die!" She broke away from me and ran over to where Peyton still lay unconscious, fell to her knees, and began to shake her. "Wake up, Auntie Peyton! Wake up!"

I walked over to her, squatted down, and held her from behind. Pheeli and Zhana and Jordan came over as well. Sami turned to look back toward me. "She's Quantum Girl!" she wept. "She can fix things!" She began to bawl. "I don't want Gramma and Grampa and Aunt Chloë to be dead! I want to go home! I want to go home!" Then she turned back to Peyton and began shaking her again. "Wake up!" she wept. "Wake up! You're Quantum Girl! Wake up!" Then she fell down upon her and continued to cry.

I was never one to believe in miracles or in the power of love, but as Sami clung to Peyton, suddenly Peyton lifted up her left arm and wrapped it around her. A moment later, she opened her eyes.

"Hey, Mira Dira," she said in a weak voice, "Everything's going to be all right."

Sami raised her head and stared at her. Then she threw her head back down on her chest and hugged her with all of her might. Peyton looked up at me. "Hey," she said in a weak voice, and then looked at Pheeli and smiled. Pheeli couldn't help but burst into tears. We didn't know what was going to happen from that point on, but at least Peyton was back among the living and that was a miracle in and of itself.

QUANTUM GIRL RESURRECTION

CHAPTER X

Chloë

Earth Year: 48 B.C.

Walking on desert sand is not an easy task. It gives way beneath your feet, beyond which it's extremely hot. It took me half an hour under the blazing sun to reach the Sphinx. It was different from what I had seen up close when Dad had business dealings in Egypt, and Claire and Mom and I all tagged along. The massive sculpture was worn, but not to the extent that I remembered. The nose was still intact, the features more crisp as was the headdress onto which there was a Uraeus with a reared-up cobra at the center. The Sphinx's head sat squarely on the body of a lion, much of the surface of which had been lost from sandstorms that had blasted away its limestone fur over the hundreds if not thousands of years since it had been carved from the living rock. Whenever I was, I was most certainly far off in the past. Meanwhile, the pyramids in the distance had yet to be stripped of their white limestone surface by the Romans in order to build their city and its temples to their ancient gods. But magnificent as the Sphinx was, it was just a lifeless block of stone that couldn't think or speak or feel.[12]

The heat had left me parched, so much so that it became difficult to swallow. The sun in a cloudless sky burned down on me and the sand reflected the heat and burned my bare feet. There was a small oasis nearby that a lone riderless camel drank from—a got-away, I thought, since it still wore its saddle. I trudged through the blistering sand, praying that it wasn't just a mirage.

When I finally made it there, I knelt down at the water's edge and

---

[12] Unlike the monstrous ancient Greek version that would devour travelers who could not answer her riddle, the Sphinx of the ancient Egyptians had been carved out of an outcropping of rock as a benevolent protector of its people.

drank my fill as the camel stared at me. After rising to my feet, I went up to it slowly so as not to frighten it away. Claire and I had ridden camels more than once on our trip. I got it to kneel down by first pressing gently on the top of its neck, then its back, and then its loin. Once it was down on all fours, I climbed up into the saddle. Reins in hand, I urged it up and toward the ancient city of Giza in the distance. It took ten minutes at a full run to reach its gates, the city itself located on the west bank of the Nile with its rushing waters giving off a cool, refreshing breeze.

While there were no walls surrounding the ancient city, there were sentries posted at intervals along those sides facing the desert as well as lookouts where it faced the Nile. Two shirtless bronze-skinned men saw and then approached me, each with armbands, ornamental skirts, and elaborate collars around their necks, all of which were either made of gold or turquoise or a combination of both. Each held a long crook, probably more ornamental than functional as they appeared to be carved from ivory. I halted my camel as I saw them, urged it to kneel down on the sand once again, and then dismounted. To be perfectly honest, I was frightened beyond words, being alone, not just in a foreign land but so far back in time. I spoke not a word of ancient Egyptian and I most certainly was not dressed for the occasion.

The sentries or guards, both Egyptian in feature, stared at me strangely. I thought perhaps that it was my pale skin and blue eyes. Few Romans or Greeks had advanced this far south other than those soldiers who had seen many years of sun. Then, after glancing at each other and mumbling something in their ancient tongue, they prostrated themselves in obeisance before me.

"*Consurge!*" I said in my first-year Latin, causing the men to rise to their feet, though they continued to cast their gaze down at the sand. "*Aperi ostium et me intus!*" I then commanded at which point they turned and began to lead me into the city. Taking up my camel's reigns and mounting the beast once more, I followed them.

This was Giza or, as the ancients called it, *Kher Neter* which meant *the Necropolis*. Here was where the Pharaohs lay buried and here, too, was where most of the great monuments had been built. The streets were lined with date and fig trees. Buildings were decorated in blue paint. Craftsmen, tradesmen, women, and children peopled the walkways. One of my escorts called out to an older man, who came up to me with eyes that refused to meet mine and indicated, first by words and then by gestures that they wished to lead me farther in; but when I began to walk, a thrust out palm and a bowed head begged that I wait, which I did. A moment later a rather ornate palanquin[13] was brought up by four bearers for me to ride in.

After fifteen minutes or so, the litter stopped before the entrance to a temple that stood in the middle of a massive isosceles trapezoid where on each side sat the same woman carved out from the same living rock that formed the temple's face. Each statue was at least sixty feet tall and wore a crown that depicted a vulture with its wings draped down, while their carefully sculpted dresses began just beneath their breasts. But it was the twelve-foot statue in a hollowed-out rectangle above the doorway that caused my heart to stop. Carved from the bedrock, timeworn for what must have been thousands of years, towered an Egyptian version of Quantum Girl!

How strange, I thought, that there were no guards at this entrance. As the palanquin was carried past it I felt an odd sensation against my skin as though I were passing through an invisible barrier. The corridor soon opened up and then it was as if I had gone from the ancient past to the distant future. Before us was a vast terrain filled with fruit-laden trees, brightly-colored flowers, and tropical birds of all kinds. Somewhere in the near distance stood a building that would have been an architectural wonder even in my time, but there it was, truly an anachronism, far beyond the technology of the day. It was a house that looked as though it had been designed by Tiffany with what must have been millions of pieces of colored glass of different shapes and thicknesses that were illuminated by some kind of

---

[13] A closed litter carried on the shoulders of four bearers.

artificial white light from within. The house and its gardens stood silently in a vale with green hills on each side and a river whose banks gently caressed the roots of a fig tree that stood silently off to one side. The air was scented and cool and crisp, welcoming the songbirds that chirped out their mating calls. *But how could this be,* I wondered, *in the middle of an ancient city that bore no resemblance to any of this? And where, between all of the buildings, would it have fit?* It was as though I had been miraculously transported—or phased—somewhere else! The mystery of it all churned unceasingly through my brain.

My small caravan stopped just before the door to the stained glass wonder. The vehicle—if one may call it such—was now set down for the first time, and so I took the opportunity to step out of it. As I stood once more on solid ground, the bearers picked up the litter and headed back the way they had come. I stared at the wonders all around me and before me. Then I made my way to the door which opened on its own.

Inside was as magnificent as out. Almost everything was made of colored glass, exotic wood, silver, or gold. As I tried to take it all in, I heard a voice from behind me.

"Hello, Chloë," it said in a fragile tone.

I wheeled around to see a woman—old beyond years—about ten feet away. She was a bit shorter than me with thin gray hair and with wrinkles that would have put a Shar Pe to shame.

"We've been expecting you," came a second but similar voice from behind me.

I wheeled around to see an identical old woman staring at me with a crooked smile. Both of them wore silk robes—floor-length and heavily embroidered with flowered designs.

"Who are you?" I asked, my head whipping back and forth like a spectator at a tennis match.

"Chloë," said one of them.

"Salinger," said the other as though my name was spoken by just

70

one.

"Yes," I said. " I know who *I* am, but who are *you*?"

"We are you," the pair said in unison.

"Have a seat," said one.

"Would you like a refreshment?" asked the other.

I looked at the two of them again, shrugged, and then found my way to a leather sofa. One of the women brought me a jeweled goblet filled with a dark liquid.

"What is it?" I asked, sniffing at it.

"I told you she would question it," said one. "It's grape juice mixed with apple and lime."

I brought the goblet to my lips and took a small sip. "It's good," I said.

"You see?" went on the one who had just spoken. "She likes it."

"Of course, she does," said the other. "I know her like the back of my hand."

"Your wrinkled *old* hand," came the snarky reply.

"I don't understand," I interrupted. "How can the two of you be me and why are there two of you?" I put the drink down on the table in front of me.

"It was," the first started, pausing as she thought a bit, "nigh on twenty-five hundred years ago."

"Chloë and I were Nuit," said the other. [14]

"Until we split apart," said the first. "Then we didn't know who we were."

"Nuit was not a twin," said the other.

"Nowhere was that written," said the first.

"Or quadruplets," the other went on. "We placed the capstone on the Great Pyramid. It was covered in electrum."[15]

---

[14] Nuit was the ancient Egyptian goddess of the sky, the daughter of Shu, the god of the air, and Tefnut, the goddess of water and fertility. With her brother and husband Geb, the god of the earth, she bore Osiris, Isis, Set, and Nephthys.

[15] An alloy of silver and gold.

"It was a bad choice," said the first. "It acted like a lightning rod. And when a bolt of lightning struck we lost most of our powers."

"We were never able to put ourselves back together," the other went on. "It either did something to our brains."

"Or to the god-stone," her mirror said.

I looked at them from one to the other. "How did you get a god-stone?" I asked.

"She doesn't know," the one on the left said staring at me.

"Of course, she doesn't know!" exclaimed the one on the right. "We didn't know when *we* were *her!*"

"Before the universe collapsed," Left said.

"Peyton willed it into your head," Right finished her phrase. "That's how you were able to travel back in time!"

"But now," Left said, "you're finally here like we knew you'd be."

"And we need you," Right insisted. "After all, we've waited a coon's age for you to come."

Left stared at her. "You are so politically incorrect," she exclaimed. "Coon's age indeed! What if one of the Nubians overheard you?"

"And what if one did?" Right scowled at her. "They don't speak English! English won't even exist for another fifteen hundred years!" She turned to me. "If it weren't for the company, I'd have left her ages ago!"

"Ahem!" I said, trying to calm things down a bit. "What do you need me for?"

"Why, to put us back together, of course!" said I don't know which one as they had paced back and forth during the argument.

The other one stared hard at me. "We really do need your help," she said. "We knew you were coming. We just had to wait."

"Two thousand, four hundred years give or take," came the other's aged voice.

"Will you help us?" the other, other one asked.

"If I can," I replied.

"Good," she went on. "Chloë and I will each take one of your hands, and then we must all concentrate on becoming one again."

And so we did, though their hands were so cold and frail it was like grabbing hold of a skeleton. Suddenly, I felt myself being pulled into them. I felt all of us merge into one and then, just as suddenly, everything around me blurred, the room vanished, and I was standing in the desert once again. This time, though, it was different. This, however, was not the Egypt that Claire and I had seen. It was not a desert, but lush and green with a branch of the Nile nearby and a canal that led up to the base of the pyramid. Sluices had been built to raise the level of the water to accommodate the levels that the blocks needed to be set on after they were lifted off of the barges that had brought them from the quarry site miles away. Meanwhile, what would later be arid sand was filled with trees and fields of wheat and barley stretched as far as the eye could see along with outcroppings of small houses, presumably occupied by the farmers. Scattered throughout in corrals or on fields were oxen or cattle or sheep with an occasional dog to herd them.[16]

As for the Sphinx, it looked almost new and was painted—the face to resemble flesh, the headdress blue and gold. As for the Great Pyramid, it was still under construction, unfinished, sand piled up almost to the top with the capstone in the distance being pushed and dragged on wooden rollers, yet to be set into place. I trembled at the realization that it was now nearly forty-five hundred years ago. Back then, there would be no other versions of me and my high school Latin would be of absolutely no help. Rome wouldn't even be founded for another seventeen hundred years. I felt more frightened than I had ever been in my life. The world began to spin around me. My thoughts began to blur and that was when I must have passed out.

---

[16] Contrary to popular belief, slaves were not used in the construction but, rather, paid workers.

CHAPTER XI

Ophelia

The Next Universe
Planet Erebus: Year 1
Alternate Reality II

Claire and I had warned the children to not wander off but, being children, they tended to not listen unless they knew they were being watched. Jordan was the one who generally took charge, especially in that she was a year older than Sami and Zhan. Peyton's recovery was slow, but she was on the mend, though not well enough to Quantum Girl this place into something more habitable. The trip through universes, her search for this planet, and then bringing us all here had taxed both her physical and mental states.

"The god-stone is still working," she would tell us, "but my head is still worn out. Just give me a little time and I'll l be totally back on track."

"Are there any other civilizations out there?" I asked her. That was on the afternoon of the third day since her awakening.

"None with anyone that you'd want to invite to dinner," she replied with a smile. "More likely they'd want to invite *you* to *be* dinner for *them*."

"*That* bad?" Claire asked.

"Oh, yeah," she said back. "Most that I saw were reptilian and others that were I don't know what. There was even one world with intelligent plant life that would definitely frown on vegetarians."

It was at that moment that the girls ran up to us, with Jordan in the lead.

"We found a habitant," she said.

"You mean an *in*habitant," Peyton corrected her.

"It's a robot!" she exclaimed.

Peyton wearily climbed to her feet. "A robot?" she repeated.

"Yes, Mama!" she replied and then engaged a frown. "But I think he needs batteries."

"Where *is* he?" Peyton asked. "Let's go have a look."

Sami and Zhana began to run off in what we assumed was the robot's direction. "This way! This way!" they both exclaimed, to which Jordan ran after them.

"Hey!" she called out. "Who's in charge here? I'm the one who found it!"

The three of us followed the children to a small room in one of the other buildings. The robot, as Jordan called it, was seated on the floor bent over, its head tilted to one side, looking like a life-size Raggedy Ann doll without the raggedy. The *robot*, it turned out, was one of the cyborgs Peyton had described that had inhabited the planet thousands of millennia ago. I stared at it and then glanced at her.

"I thought you said they were all gone?" I said.

"I thought they *were*," she replied and then went over to examine it. "There's a quantum fuel cell in it that's depleted." She looked up at me. "But why would they have left it behind? Surely, it could have been repowered."

"Can you fix it?" I asked.

"I suppose," she said. Then she moved her hand toward its back.

"Wait!" I shouted.

Peyton froze. "What?"

"How do we know it's not violent?" I asked her. "What if its kind killed its creators?"

She phased into Quantum Girl. "If it is, I can freeze time around it," she replied. "I can do that much." She focused on it, made it transparent to locate its power source, and then caused the power source to glow. "I would never let anything happen to any of you," she said, followed by, "There!" and "Voilà!"

It was as though she had flipped a switch in it. The robot or cyborg or whatever it was sat up a bit, turned its head this way and that, and then opened its eyes. I glanced at the kids whose gazes were all fixed on it with childlike fascination. The thing looked at Peyton but its head went back as though there were something amiss. As it turned out it was trying to read her mind but couldn't due to the god-stone in her head. Then it looked at me. I could feel it in my head. I raised my hands to my temples.

"Stop!" I shouted.

And so it did, turning to Claire whose gaze became fixed. Peyton was about to freeze it, but Claire held out her arm.

"Wait!" she cried out. "I think it's trying to communicate!"

But then something else happened. Its outer covering began to change. It was as though it were trying to become human, and not *just* human—*female*! There was the appearance of flesh covering what before looked like plastic and metal. Fingers and toes—even breasts—began to take shape. Dark brown hair grew rapidly from its scalp and then there was the face! Oh, my God! The face! The thing had morphed into an exact likeness of Chloë! Claire had been thinking of her, no doubt. She was always thinking of her and it used her thoughts to become her! Moments later, the Chloë clone stood up and faced me, naked and perfectly formed.

"Hello, Claire," it said in a mechanical version of her voice. "I've missed you. Long time, no see. I'm happy to be here with you and Ophelia and Peyton and the girls."

I turned to Peyton in shock. She shook her head but remained as Quantum Girl. The Chloë clone cocked its head as it stared at me.

"Is something wrong?" it asked and then glanced down at itself. "If it's the fact that I'm naked, I apologize. I don't know what happened to my clothes."

She turned to the girls, who were now staring at her with their mouths wide open. "Did you all undress me while I was asleep as a joke?" she asked them, her hands on her hips. "Very funny! Ha ha! Oh, well." It sighed. "What can I say? I mean, you've all seen naked girls before, so it's not like I need to be ashamed or anything. I guess

I need to go back home and put something on." It started to leave but then paused and added, "Wait! I seem to recall..." She turned to one wall, pressed on a panel, entered a hidden room, and a moment. later reemerged wearing a short, sleeveless dress made from some extremely thin gold metallic fabric. "No worries," it said. "I totally forgot about the fabricator." It spun around, still barefoot, the dress lifting up as it did. "How do I look?" it asked in its still slightly mechanical voice, with a smile painted on its perfect Chloë face.

"You're not my sister! You're not Chloë!" Claire shot back.

"What are you talking about?" the clone asked.

"Hang on!" Quantum Peyton said and her entire being appeared to blink for a second.

"Wait for what?" Claire asked.

"I went back in time," Payton said.

"When?" Claire asked. "You didn't even leave."

"She does that sometimes," I explained. "She can be gone for hours or even days but to us, it's like she hasn't even left."

"The Peytonization of time!" Claire sighed, "I'm still not used to any of this, no matter how much I see!"

"Anyway..." Peyton went on, turning back into herself. "It seems that this—it—she—is a companion model. At least that's the best I can describe it as—designed to be protoplasmic. It read your mind. That's how it was able to replicate Chloë—from your memories of her."

"Well, tell it to change back," Claire said. "It's really creeping me out, especially since Chloë's dead."

Peyton took a deep breath. "Unfortunately, the change is permanent. What's more, it now believes that it *is* Chloë."

"Great!" Claire said with exasperation. "So, now I have a robot for a sister!"

"Excuse me?" Chloë clone said in a now less mechanical voice. "Whatever you may think of me, Sis, I am *not* a robot! Do I call you a prom queen? No, I don't! *I've* always accepted you for however you

77

are, so kindly extend *me* the same courtesy. Robot! Ugh!" She shook her head to herself and then added, "I'm going for a walk!" and with that she headed off, calling out, "You know, Claire, Mom and Dad would not have been proud of what you just called me, and I miss them so much!"

Jordan started to go after her. Peyton instantly called out, "Jordan, come back here!"

Jordan stopped and turned and hung her head. "Yes, Mama," she said. Then she walked over to her. "Is that really Auntie Chloë?" she asked.

"No, Lovebug," Peyton replied, putting her arm around her as Jordan came up to her. "But she thinks she is."

CHAPTER XII

Quantum Girl

Rendenaaar
Trillions of Universes Ago

It was off-putting at the very least that when I finally found Krotaaarak the physicist, Krotaaarak, the philosopher, Krotaaarak the wise, I discovered that he was but a child, neither female nor male, for that time had not yet come for future her or future him to choose. Alas, it was destined that Krotaaarak would die before that choice ever came and he knew it. I say *he* just as a matter of convenience, for Krotaarak's gender or lack thereof was and is irrelevant to all of this. He said he was an omnipath. His mind absorbed the thoughts of everyone in the universe. He told me that, at first, it was like bombs going off in his head—endless noise and emotion—pleasure, pain, happiness, despair—until he lapsed into a coma. When he finally awakened, all of it had stopped, but what he was left with was the accumulated wisdom of the inhabitants of the more than eight trillion planets that had spawned civilizations. But despite that he was no longer a omnipath, his mind remained telepathic and savant, which was how by just reading my mind, he was able to speak perfect English, albeit with the accent of a Gaaalthaaaran with Gaaalthaaaran anatomy.[17]

"You actually lived through a genesis," he said with some amazement, genesis being what he called the Big Bang.

"It nearly killed me and drove me mad for hundreds of millions of years" I replied.

"To survive an ordeal," he said, "is to give meaning to what comes

---

[17] I was rather shocked when I first saw him. He was not very tall but his head was enormous, even for an adult, which, more than likely accounted for his unprecedented intellect.

after." He paused and looked at me, considering his words as they applied to my plight. "You want to save your universe," he went on. "The Silver Goddess has given you great power but you wonder if it is enough. Doubt can be a greater enemy than the prospect of failure."

"But the entire universe!" I said. "I've never even tried to change the course of a planet let alone all of spacetime."

"Consider the simple rubber band," he replied. "When it is stretched, does one think about the atoms of which it is comprised? Tug both ends and the rest of it follows."

"But I'm just one person," I said.

Krotaaarak looked hard at me. "You are Quantum Girl," he insisted. "You do not bend to time and space. It bends to your will."

I shook my head. "I tried and failed," I said.

"There is another," he replied. "Between the two of you, there is hope and from hope, you may find the resolution you seek."

"How can you know this?" I asked.

"The same way I know," he answered, "that within less than one hundred days I shall die."

"That will be a sad day for Rendenaaar," I mused aloud. Then another question raced through my mind. "What other person?" I asked, "Who?"

"Another Quantum Girl," he said, "emphasizing the word. But she is from a universe made up of antimatter."

"I wasn't aware that was possible," I replied.

"In your ancient Chinese philosophy," he went on, "there is what is called yin and yang that are opposite but interconnected forces. You are hers and she is yours. Hers is a realm that my mind has not reached. Her path may be different from yours but from the intersection of two lines is a singularity. You must return to your universe while there is still time and find her."

"And if I can't?" I said. "Hardly any time remained before I left."

"Then she will find you," he said. "Such is your destiny."

"And yours is to die?" I asked.

"Death is never an end," he replied. "It is like a ripple in the ocean of time. Perhaps we will meet again, Peyton Herron. One never knows what Fate has in store."

Taking my father's advice, I reversed time to just before we had met and then went back to my own time.

CHAPTER XIII

Chloë

Earth Year: 2489 B.C.

I awoke in a tent—not one of those put-it-up-in-five-minute pup tents one goes camping with, but a full-blow Lawrence of Arabia, Peter O'Toole, Omar Shariff, caravan sort of thing. It was the first thing I was aware of as my vision came into focus and my eyes stared upward at the inside of the vaulted linen top. As I turned my head this way and that, the realization of my surroundings became more and more evident. It was nighttime, and so it was rather dim where I was, but not cave-dark. What light there was filtered through the entrance from a large campfire outside some ten or more yards away. The entrance to my newfound shelter consisted of two flaps that were each drawn in opposite directions and held in place to the rest of the structure with ropes. The heat of the day had gone and had been welcomingly replaced by the chill of a desert night; chill is so much better than sweltering heat, even dry heat, as there is only so much you can take off but an entire Forever Seventeen's worth of clothes you can put on. Regardless, I still shivered a bit, bringing my arms across my chest to find that I was no longer in my clothes but in thin, if not immodest, garments. As I propped myself up on my elbows, I could see that I was wearing what was what I later learned was called a *kalasiris*, more or less a close-fitting thinly-woven linen tube over which was a net of long turquoise beads that had been diagonally threaded. My breasts—ample as they were/are—were noticeably bare—at least the sides of them were. Just below them was a *belt* just below the breasts,[18] with the belt comprised of long closely-woven

---

[18] Presumably to hold them up—my breasts, I mean (or is it bosom?). Anyway, in that I was just seventeen and possessed the right combination of mammillary genes, they were supportive without any help whatsoever from outside forces.

turquoise beads of the same sort but arranged vertically. The *kalasiri* ended mid-calf with that part having a loosely beaded fringe attached. The dress was held up by two wide straps, each with wide horizontal bands of beads in the same manner as the *belt*, only horizontal. Attached to the bands and over each breast was a woven beast cap of turquoise that had been carved to resemble an areola, complete with a nipple, Expensive though it might have been, truly, it was not the most comfortable of outfits, since the beading made it somewhat heavy and the close fit made it cumbersome. But this was the style of the day. Apparently, women were to only take small steps, reflective of their station in the universe. But it was when I threw my legs over the edge of the bed that I felt first the weight and confinement of my new attire.

It was the act of my having sat up, however, that caught the attention of two naked Egyptian girls, no more than ten years old, who each had been in a chair on opposite sides of the tent, each of whom immediately scurried up to me and placed leather sandals on my feet.

"Where am I?" I asked. "Where *is* this place?"

One of the girls looked at the other and then said something incomprehensible to me. Her words sounded Middle Eastern, but *different* from any language I had ever heard, similar to the banter spoken in the streets of ancient Giza, but decidedly *different*.

"I need to get into something," I said, half to them, half to myself. I looked around, but the clothes I had come in were nowhere to be seen. It was as I stood up that a hairless man entered wearing a wraparound white linen skirt, a broad, beaded turquoise collar, and sandals. He ordered the girls to leave, which they immediately did, scurrying out. Seeing them gone, he turned to me. He looked at me as though he were attempting to affirm something about me in his mind; then he bowed his head, so that his eyes did not meet mine, and spoke in a much kinder manner than he had to the girls. The only word I could make out was A*set* which he repeated several times. When he had finished whatever it was he was saying, he backed out of the tent with his head still bowed in obeisance, all the while gesturing with his hands for me to follow him. Outside, stood two strong black men, also with shaved heads and sandals but only wearing loincloths. Each held large sun shades made of ostrich plumes that had been widely striped with dyes—coloring them turquoise and wine—that were attached to long, carved ivory handles. These were held over me, one on each side, meeting over my head; this as I was led by the first man—whom I later learned was a priest—to a tent much larger than the one I had just left. It was at this point that the men with the feathers stopped and I was led inside where there were perhaps thirty men and women, dressed similarly to those who had brought me there, though with decorations added that made me think that the men were of a nobler class. The women wore sheer linen dresses, some adorned with gems, though none as elaborate as the one that *graced* me. Toward the back of the tent or, rather, yurt, was a more regal-looking man in his mid-thirties who wore a tall hat with a gold uraeus at the brim and gold striped adornments on the sides. The remainder of his crown— for that was what it was—stood covered in small feathers that had been dyed Egyptian blue. Meanwhile, around his neck was a collar similar to that worn by the man who had fetched me, but far more elaborate and decorated with gold. I was struck with horror, though, as before him, lying upon a stone dais on her back was a naked girl no more than ten years old who appeared very frightened, her flesh trembling, tears bleeding from her eyes. Such was quite understandable, as just to her right stood a powerful, muscled man, also hairless and with a shaved head as was the case with all of the men present. Meanwhile, high over the girl's neck, the man held a broad bronze axe. One did not need to feel it to know the sharpness of its blade.

The king or pharaoh—I did not know which at the time—spoke to me in words I did not understand, but the man I had come with urged me to the throne to the ruler's left and so I sat. The man then chanted what sounded like an incantation. Then came a command from his highness at which point the executioner—for that was what he was—raised his weapon even higher and was about to liberate the poor girl's head from the rest of her when I called out, "Stop!"

And stop everything did, from the wielded axe, to the sadistically delighted murmurs from the crowd that suddenly went silent, to the fly that had been buzzing around my head that became frozen mid-air.

I tried to rise from my seat but it was like attempting to run underwater, while trying to breathe was like inhaling sand. I began to panic. I wished that at least the air around me would be unaffected by whatever was causing this—and then it was so. With breath once more in my lungs, I began to think more clearly. Those ancient versions of me had said that Peyton had placed a god-stone in my head just before the universe had collapsed. I didn't understand how she could have done that, especially from a distance, but that explained how I had traveled through time and how I had caused it to stop.

For the moment, though, my thoughts focused on the child. I realized that once time resumed, the blade would descend and liberate the poor girl's head from her neck. I wasn't a stranger to the god-stone's power. I had one in my head when I was twelve years old. I had crossed dimensions with it and phased through time. But there was so much more to it that I had learned from all of the Peytons and from Jordan—the grown-up one. And so I willed the axe out of existence or, rather, I caused all of the quarks and gluons and electrons to revert to their quantum state of *infinite* existence. I spread them out through time rather than allowing them to remain in one instant. I wasn't quite certain how I knew to do that or how I could understand the basis for quantum reality, but I just did. It seemed to have exploded in my brain the same way it had caused me to phase back through time—twice now. Still, I needed to know more about where I was and so, one by one, I merged into each of those who were in the room—all except the girl. She was the one innocent in all of this. *How*, I thought, *could she be anything else?* She was just a kid.

The ancient Egyptian language came to me quickly. There were far fewer words back then than in English. Regardless, the tongue was colorful and expressive. They called their country Kumat. Their spoken language, Ranikumat, later evolved into modern-day Coptic, though I had no idea how I knew that fact.

Anyway, back to the beheading... What I gathered was that the girl appeared in the Pharoah's tent while he was having sex with one of his three wives.[19] Khufu, who as it turned out, was the one sitting next to me, had flown into a rage. To his mind, this was a demon in the shape of a Nubian child, no doubt to lay a curse upon his bedchamber. His thoughts were guided by the raiment in which the girl had been attired, the likes of which he had never seen. Had she been a slave, clothes of any sort were unbefitting her station, as the law ordered all slaves to be naked. Clothing represented position and slaves had none. Furthermore, when questioned by his guards as to how she had managed to enter, the girl refused to answer but only spoke in indecipherable tongues which only reinforced his belief that she was a demon from the *Duat*, the realm of the dead and, as such, needed to be sent back. As for myself, due to my fair skin and blue eyes, I was mistaken for the goddess, Isis·—Aset in their native tongue—and it was believed that my timely appearance was so that I might witness the return of the demon to its rightful realm. It was the belief of the Pharaoh and his priests that I had appeared from *Aaru*[20] and that the treacherous journey had rendered even me, an assumed goddess, unconscious. And so, by royal decree, I was anointed with oil by two female servants and then dressed as I have described. For whatever reason, when I had traveled back in time from the oasis or whatever it was, my clothes had remained behind. When morning

---

[19] It seems that all of the tents were temporary constructions while the Pharoah, Khufu—also known as Cheops by the Greeks—was there to observe the laying of the foundation for what would later be named the Great Pyramid of Giza.

[20] Aaru or the Field of Reeds was, in Egyptian mythology, the heavenly paradise that was ruled by the Egyptian god, Osiris. Isis was his wife.

dawned in that distant past, a water-bearing slave discovered me face down in the sand and immediately called his master. There were no camels. There were neither hoofprints nor footprints in the sand, nor had there been any storm to have erased them. To their minds there was no doubt but that I had fallen from *Duat* to watch as they sent the demon back to the underworld.

Ancient Egyptians firmly believed in an afterlife. That was why the Pharaohs built the pyramids and why they went to such great lengths to preserve their bodies and tell their life's tales in hieroglyphs on the walls inside. Those who were considered unimportant, such as workers and slaves, were left to rot and turn to dust with time to replenish the sand. The Pharaohs, conversely, were considered to be gods, and so when they died careful attention was taken to preserve their remains in order that their *ka* or soul would have a place to go in the afterlife. All organs other than the heart, which was left in place, were placed in canopic jars, while the body itself was packed with spices, wrapped in long strips of linen, and placed in a wooden coffin with the deceased's likeness painted on its lid. This, in turn, would be encased in a stone or gold sarcophagus. Little did any of them realize that most would find their final resting place in the basement of some museum, on display with the same dignity as a taxidermized lion or moose, for with the passage of time, greatness evaporates into dust like water into the air.

So, there I was, supposed omnipotent, brought beside Knufu, the self-proclaimed god of Kumat and all of its people. Undoubtedly, he wished for a fourth wife in me, the woman he believed to be the goddess of healing and magic, having come to earth to sit by his side and harden his cock in his bed. Would that he had known the truth that I came, not from his Heaven, but from some future that regarded him as a grandiose barbarian who spent his days building monuments to his fatuous existence. But there I was, a goddess in my own right or, rather, a Quantum Girl—perhaps inexperienced at her powers, but with powers nevertheless. And so, negating much of her weight, I lifted the girl into my arms, phased us back to the other tent, laid her down on the bed, and then allowed time to resume its natural course.

In only seconds, the girl opened her eyes, glanced at me, and then stared frightenedly around her new surroundings. She was a beautiful child, her features dark like the Nubian slaves but more chiseled—more refined, with hazel eyes.

"How did I get here?" she asked. There were tears in her eyes as she sat up. "I don't understand what's going on."

"You speak English!" I said with astonishment.

"Why shouldn't I?" she wept. "I'm from L.A. I don't know how I got here. I was walking home from school when a man attacked me. I think he wanted to kidnap me but then Quantum Girl, she saved me."

"Wait!" I interrupted her. "You know about Quantum Girl?"

The girl wiped her tears with the back of one hand. "Of course, I do," she said. "Everyone does."

"Really," I replied. "And how did you wind up here? I mean, *here* in ancient Egypt?"

"I'm not sure," she said. "It was as though the sky opened up and some sort of energy hit QG—that's what me and my friends call her—and then it was like she turned *negative* just as she reached out and touched me. Then I was in the desert. Some men on camels found me and brought me to this place. I tried to tell them what happened but they couldn't understand me. I got scared. I broke away from them and tried to hide in one of the tents but wound up in the tent of the guy that's in charge while he was having sex with two women. Then a couple of other men burst in and grabbed me. They took my clothes and brought me back to the same man, the one you were sitting next to and he started talking with the guy you were with before. Then they put chains on me. They would have killed me if you hadn't shown up. How did you save me?"

I ignored the question, asking instead, "How long have you been here?"

"Two days ago," she replied and then wept again. "I want to go home! I just want to go home!"

"What's your name," I asked her.

"Nefra," she said. "Nefra Meeks."

She looked around the tent, stood up, took a blanket, and wrapped it around herself.

"Here," I said, handing her a short decorative rope that lay nearby.

"Thanks," she said as she took it from me, using it as a belt.

"Tell me," I asked, "what year do you think this is?"

"2042," she answered. Then she stared at me. "Isn't it?"

I shook my head. "As best I can tell it's around 2500 B.C. give or take."

"How is that possible?" Nefra asked.

"I don't know," I admitted. "But I'm from 2033 and no one there knows about Quantum Girl but me and *her* sister and mine."

"And who are *you*?" she asked.

"Chloë Salinger," I told her, "and also a Quantum Girl," and with just a moment of reflection, I turned into an ancient Egyptian, Isis version of QG as Nefra called her. "Call me Isis," I said.

"Like the terrorist group?" she asked.

"No," I answered, "Like the Egyptian goddess they believe me to be."

CHAPTER XIV

Peyton

The Next Universe
Planet Erebus: Year 1
Alternate Reality II

Jordan woke up screaming in the middle of the night lying next to me in bed. Some kneejerk reaction caused me to triplicate myself with one of me being pushed off the mattress to fall on the floor, resulting in a bit of a groan from all of us. But as my attention quickly turned to Jordan, my selves merged back together.

"Hey, hey, hey!" I said to her gently as I bent over her. "It was just a bad dream."

"It wasn't a dream, Mommy!" Jordan cried with tears in her eyes. "It wasn't!"

"What do you mean?" I asked. I put my arms around her as I sat her up, and she wrapped hers around me. "What did you see?"

"There were a bunch of kids and all of them were naked," she wept, "and they were laughing at me because I had long hair and they didn't have any. Then one of them sneaked up behind me and tore off my dress and they pointed at my jay jay and started laughing and calling out, *'Zhardaaan, Zhardaaan, Zhardaaan! Praaagth! Praaagth! Praaagth!'* And then you and Auntie Ophelia rushed up and covered me up with my dress that got torn off, but both of you had pointy ears and tails and that's when I screamed and woke up!"

I laid my cheek against her head.

"It was just a nightmare, Lovebug," I told her. "Would you like it if we went to the kitchen and I got you something to drink?"

"'kay," she said, so we went into our ancient kitchen where I programmed the synthesizer to create a sweet nectar that the long-dead civilization had programmed in.

As she sat slowly drinking the teal liquid, I couldn't help but worry about what had just occurred. Of course, it was no nightmare, but, instead, a memory from when Jordan had grown up on Rendenaaar. Being human, she was different from all the other children there and they recognized that fact and teased her and bullied her without a stop. Perhaps if Dhraaal hadn't murdered Thara-Klo she would have had a big sister to look after her and protect her, but that was not the case. Jordan had to grow up in a universe where she was the only one of her kind and an outcast among those her own age. How it was that her past memories were coming back to haunt her troubled me to no end.

Moments later there came a gentle wrapping on the door jamb for there were no actual doors anywhere except to the outside. Whoever built these structures must have thought there was no need for them. Apparently, privacy had not been an issue for their kind. But then, this *was* the kitchen.

It was the Chloë clone robot android who stood looking in. "I heard sobbing," it said. "I thought there might be something I could do to help."

So odd, I thought to myself, for there stood Chloë—almost— probably not on the inside, but her figure and face—even her voice replete with the overtone of those of now extinct Australia—were the spitting image of her, not that images have ever been known to spit.

"We're fine," I said.

The Chloëbot, as I came to think of it, went over to Jordan and squatted down beside her. "Hey, Jordache," it said. "Did you have a bad dream?"

Jordan nodded.

"I have them, too, sometimes" it went on. "Did you see monsters?"

Again, Jordan nodded her head.

"I once dreamt that *I* was a monster," it said.

"What kind of monster?" Jordan shyly asked.

91

"A tickle monster!" it replied and then began tickling Jordan who started to laugh uncontrollably until it stopped.

It seemed odd that Jordan was able to accept it as Chloë when she clearly knew it was not. I supposed it was because it had seemed to have become her, and perhaps there was a bit of wish fulfillment there as well. Jordan had loved Chloë, her "very favorite auntie!" she always said. Chloë would always play with her—dolls, house, hide-and-seek—and tell her stories at night when Jordan lay in bed. She would often come to babysit and even though I was able to divide myself so that it wasn't necessary, I thought it important that Jordan, being an only child—again—with no other children around other than Zhana and Samira, who were both settled on the West Coast, to have at least someone other than me to broaden her scope. It saddened me, though, to no small extent, to realize that Chloë had perished with the rest of humanity when the universe came to an end. Would that my other self—the one I had left behind to try and fix things—could have prevented that from happening. *Had she died trying?* I wondered. So many months had gone by without any sense of her still being alive.

It was as the Chloëbot gently caressed Jordan's cheek with its right hand that, for just an instant, its hand and arm and then that half of its face flashed back to the android it had been But then all of that part of her returned to its Chloë form. It was in that instant, though, that Jordan saw it with me and it brought back the realization that the Chloëbot was not really her favorite aunt, and she began to scream.

The Chloëbot which believed she was, in fact, Chloë Salinger, became distressed at Jor's reaction, not realizing what had happened. She tried to console her—tried to touch her. She reached out to take her in her arms but Jordan pulled away and rushed into mine.

"I don't understand," the Chloëbot said to me with tears in its eyes as *I* held Jor and *she* held *me*. "Did I do something wrong?"

"No," I said. "But I think it best if you leave right now. We'll talk about it later."

"All right," the Chloëbot said and then, filled with genuine sadness, rose to her feet and left the room.

"Mommy," Jordan wept after the Chloëbot had left, "that wasn't Auntie Chloë, was it? I wanted it to be but it wasn't her. Auntie Chloë's dead, isn't she?"

"Yes, Lovebug," I replied. "Auntie Chloë's dead, but she's with God now."

"I thought you said you don't believe in God," she said.

"Do you remember I told you about the silver woman?" I asked her.

"The one who gave you the god-stones when you were Khattaaara?" she replied. "Is she God?"

"I don't know," I said, "but she just might be."

Jordan pushed out her lower lip. "I thought God was supposed to be an old man with a beard," she replied.

I lifted her chin and looked her in the eye. "That's just what people wanted everyone to think," I said, "because they're afraid to admit how strong and powerful we women are."

"Mommy?" she went on.

"Yes, Lovebug?" I replied.

"Why didn't any men come with us when we came here?" she asked.

"Because," I replied, "I only had seven god-stones and there were seven of us."

"One for you," she said and began to count on her fingers. "And one for me and one for Auntie Phelia and Auntie Claire and one for Zhana and one for Samira. That's just six. What did you do with the other one?"

She looked up at me wondering.

"I put it in Auntie Chloë," I replied.

"Then where *is* she?" she asked. "Why isn't she still alive?"

"That's a very good question," I said. "I guess it just didn't work for her."

"I miss her," Jor replied.

"I do, too," I told her. "I do, too."

CHAPTER XV

Quantum Girl

Rendenaaar
Trillions of Universes Ago

Aside from the lesson in Gaaalthaaaran philosophy, my trip back in time to see Krotaaarak had been useless. What was worse was that when I traveled back to my universe, I arrived only seconds before it was about to implode. Frantically, I went back two years to give myself more time. The end would still come but two years still remained for me to figure something out. The Earth beneath me, I phased into what I thought was my house in Manhattan—what *before* had been my house—only to find that my living room was part of an office suite filled with desks and people. Upon second glance, I realized that it was a newsroom. There were at least fifteen persons, male and female, sitting or standing. A woman at one desk looked up at me still in my Quantum Girl attire.

"You're here for the Comicon story?" she asked with little emotion. "Marsden's the one you're probably looking for. Down on the right near the window—sandy hair, wire-rimmed glasses." She looked at me then with an up-and-down stare. "Cool threads. Captain Marvel?"

I shook my head.

"Marsden!" she yelled across the room. "Your interview's here!"

She looked up at me and then raised her eyebrows as if to ask who I was.

"Quantum Girl," I replied.

"Quantum Girl!" she yelled out again at the reporter and then addressed me again. "He'll come in a second." She paused and then added, "Say, you wouldn't have any passes, would you? I've got a ten-year-old who goes gatflin over all that stuff."

95

I shook my head just as Marsden walked over.

"Mark Marsden," he said, introducing himself.

I turned to face him.

"I do the entertainment spread," he said. "I also cover Comicon, but I don't seem to recall any Quantum Girl." He shrugged. "Anyway, perhaps you can clue me in. We can talk in the conference room. Follow me," he went on.

He led me down the hall to a medium-sized room off to one side. He glanced at me with an eyebrow raised. "Those are some threads you've got on," he said as he opened the door and gestured for me to go in first.

The room was what you would expect for a small conference area. There was a rectangular table with eight chairs, a large window overlooking the pedestrian life below, and a small stand in one corner with a water cooler and a coffee maker that brewed the stay-awake kind. He went over to it and began to pour a cup from the half-filled pot into a Styrofoam cup. As he did, he glanced back at me.

"You want coffee or anything?"

"No, thank you," I said.

He walked over to the table, cup in hand. "I'd offer you a doughnut," he said, "but they're two days old and they've lost their palatability which I can personally attest to as I tried one this morning." He looked at me and then added, "Have a seat."

I sat down in one of the side chairs. The reporter pulled the one facing and followed suit. He took a sip from the cup and then set it down. He stared at me curiously.

"How exactly do they get you to glow?" he asked.

"Trade secret," I replied.

He continued to stare and then broke out of it. "I don't remember scheduling an interview," he said. "I didn't catch your name."

"Quantum Girl," came my reply.

Marsden offered a slight chuckle. "No," he said. "I meant your real name."

96

"Can I trust you?" I asked. "Secret identity and all."

He continued to stare at me as though trying to unravel a mystery. "Say, did Gloria in editorial put you up to this?" he asked. "I accidentally walked in on her last week while she was using the bathroom and…"

"No," I replied. "No Gloria."

"I just thought," he went on.

"No," I said. "But, off the record…"

"Not a word will leave this room," he replied.

"This used to be my bedroom," I said.

"I think you'd have to be pretty old for that to be true," he replied. "The paper's been here since, well, long before I was born."

"And yet," I said, "I purchased the building three years ago… just in a different timeline."

"Are you sure you have the right address?" he asked.

"Positive," I replied. "My name—my real name—is Peyton Herron." And with that said, I phased back to myself causing Marsden's jaw to drop as he stared at me with a *what-the-hell's-going-on?* expression on his face. He turned left and then right, looking around the room, and then focused back on me. "What in the Sam Hill?" he said. "Who or what *are* you?"

"I told you," I replied. "My name is Peyton Herron. And I'm not from Comicon. Eleven years ago, when I was fourteen…" I began, and then went on to tell him all that had happened and how I'd gone back to Rendenaaar to try and save the universe but when I got back, some things were different—how the room we were in had been my bedroom—that I had no idea what else had changed; but what I was certain of was that the universe had only a few short years left to exist.

"You *do* realize," he replied, "that I write an entertainment column. I cover movies and theatre and ballgames."

"And Comicon," I added.

"*And* Comicon," he repeated.

"But you do have a computer," I said, "and you *can* write."

97

"Yes," he replied, "I can write," then stared at me vacantly. "A computer? What does one of those monstrosities that can only spit out punch cards have to do with any of this?"

Thinking back, I suddenly realized that the room I'd materialized in had only been filled with reporters banging away at typewriters. It became obvious that my journey into the past had not been without consequences.

"So, if *you're* here," he said, "and things have changed, where's the other one of you that you supposedly left behind? I thought you said you could sense your duplicates or whatever you call them?"

"Good question," I replied. "but I don't know the answer... yet."

"So, how can I help?" he asked. "I'm assuming you don't want an article panicking everyone... about the end of the world, I mean."

"Universe," I corrected him.

"Say," he replied, "you're not one of those psychics I always see on the front page of the tabloids, are you?"

"Can I ask you something?" I said.

"Shoot," came the reply.

"Why are you still here," I said, "in the chair, in this room?"

"Because," he replied, "we supposedly had an appointment that I don't remember scheduling."

"No," I said. "I mean why didn't you run off screaming when I changed in front of your eyes?"

"Well," he replied, "perhaps if you'd turned into some sort of monster—Bride of Frankenstein, Hillary Clinton—I might have, but the truth of the matter is that I find the uncostumed you rather charming—and very attractive, I might add."

"Are you trying to hit on me?" I asked.

"Am I succeeding?" he asked.

"Maybe," I replied.

"If you can try and track down my sister and her wife," I said.

"Wife?" he replied.

I cleared my throat. "As I said," I reminded him, "things were different before I left. Anyway, my sister's name is Ophelia Jane Herron, born September 24, 2001. Her wife's name is Claire Wrenley Salinger, born April 6, 2001—and Wrenley is spelled W-r-e-n-l-e-y—both born in Los Angeles County, though Claire and her sister, Chloë Anne Salinger, born November 12, 2005, spent quite a bit of time in Perth, Australia."

He was writing all of this down in a notepad he'd taken from his pocket. When both he and I had finished, he looked up at me.

"Is that all?" he asked and then he paused. "Just one question," he went on. "How do you know they're all missing if, as you said, this was the first place you landed, so to speak?"

"Because," I replied from behind him as Quantum Girl, "while you two were talking, we were out locking."

Hearing my voice come from another direction than across the table from him, he turned and saw more than a dozen others of me and jumped in his seat.

"Jesus!" he exclaimed.

The other me shrugged and then all of them merged back into me. "Anyway," I said, reaching over for his pad and pen and beginning to write. "Here's my cell number. You can text me if you find anything."

"Text…" he said. I don't understand. "And what do you mean your cell? You didn't just escape from an institution or anything?"

I shook my head, produced my iPhone, and then stared down at the screen. "No signal," I said and then looked up at him. "I take it you don't have cellphones here."

"Just plain, ordinary telephones," he replied, "but nothing out of Buck Rogers or Dick Tracy."

"I guess then," I sighed, "I'll just have to touch base with you back here."

"I can give you *my* number," he said.

I shook my head. "It'll just be easier for me to phase here. Anyway, I appreciate your wanting to help." That said, I phased from the room, leaving him completely nonplussed; no doubt in my mind.

CHAPTER XVI

Chloë

Earth Year: 2489 B.C.

Despite that I had little experience mastering my powers, I wanted to take Nefra back to her time. I tried. I really did. At first, it was only some hours forward, then a day, then a week, and then a month at a time. Thus, did we witness the Great Pyramid of Giza as though it were being built, stone by stone, at miraculous speed.

As we made our way further in time, we beheld the giant capstone, that proved a challenge for even the Egyptian architects. We watched from afar as they struggled to remove it from the barge it was on like a team of Siberian huskies trying to drag their master's sledge through ten feet of snow. But then something happened. It began to topple into the canal, threatening to crush the twenty or so men who had fallen in with it. I could not let that happen. There were dark clouds overhead. Lightning ripped through the sky. Thunder cracked the air. I remembered with a bit of irony what my two old selves had told me; how they had split apart and then were stuck—all of them—by immeasurable amounts of electricity that left them with little control of the god-stone in their heads. Regardless of any consequences to me, I could not stand still when the capstone was about to crush at least twenty men. It was then that I materialized as Isis and tried to lift the giant marble block with quantum forces from my hands. And yet it was too much for me. It was so large and off-balance that I could not do it alone. But I feared that if I split into just two history would repeat, and so I divided into four and then lifted the capstone into the air and set it in place. *But wait!* I suddenly remember. *One of my ancient selves had used the word quadruplets! I wasn't about to change anything! I was just repeating what had already been done! Shit!* All of me thought at once. That was when the lightning struck two of me, causing them to fall, unconscious, five hundred feet to the ground. Bolts of lightning burst from the clouds, one after the other, melting the sand into glass. The third one of me, after being struck, vanished entirely. As the only one left, I rushed to protect Nefra to try and phase us both as far into the future as I could, which I did, just as another bolt of lightning bolt struck.

We materialized in the same spot, but how far we had traveled I had no idea. To our backs was the Sphinx, while there before us stood the Great Pyramid partially faced with white limestone but most of the blocks were missing with some dozens lying scattered or broken at the base. Those that remained glistening under the light of an almost full moon.

"How far ahead did you take us?" Nefra asked.

"I'm not sure," I replied, "but apparently not far enough. When my sister and I lived in Egypt there weren't any limestone blocks on the pyramid's face and none were left on the ground. I remember reading that there had been a massive earthquake here around the start of the Fourteenth Century B.C. that shook most of them off, so at least we've come that far."

"I thought I felt it," Nefra said, "as we were moving through time."

"So did I," I replied. "I think that's what caused us to stop."

"I'm scared," Nefra said.

"I am, too," I admitted. "These powers are fairly new to me. I can't control them all that well."

Suddenly, I felt weak. The world around me began to spin.

"What's wrong?" I heard Nefra ask, only her voice was like a distant echo. Then everything went black.

When I finally opened my eyes, I found myself in a comfortable bed of soft pillows in a room lit by an ornate ceramic oil lamp. Nefra was seated beside me in a small chair though she appeared to be asleep. Reaching out, I took hold of her wrist causing her to awaken. As I did, though, I could see that I still appeared as Isis with *radioactive* skin.

"Oh my God!" she said in half a whisper. "You're awake!"

"How long have I been unconscious?" I asked.

"Nearly six years," she replied. "It's a good thing that your powers kept you from needing to eat or drink. I tried to feed you but, no matter how I tried, I couldn't open your mouth. I thought you were going to die."

"You've been by my side all this time?" I asked.

Nefra smiled. "Not *all* the time," she replied. "Only sometimes I'd come and sit next to you hoping that one day you would wake up."

"How did I—we—get here?" I asked.

"After you passed out," she replied, "there was a caravan and they brought us here. I told them as best I could, mainly through gestures, that you were the goddess, Isis, and that you had gotten into a battle with another god and had become injured. I told them that you had come from the sky to protect them and that I was your daughter that you had made out of clay."

She shrugged at the explanation she had given them. I sat up and stared at her. She had grown into a beautiful young woman. The blanket had been replaced with clothes marked for royalty.

"So, what have you been doing all this time?" I asked.

"Well," she said, "being the daughter of a goddess, I've been treated very well. And I met a really cute guy. I call him *Ah*kee. He's next in line to become Pharaoh and he's asked me to marry him."

"Don't you want to go back home?" I asked.

"To what?" she replied. "I had nothing there but pain. And, beyond all else, I'm pregnant."

I had a sudden thought. "Wait a minute!" I said. "Ahkee. Akhenaten?"

Nefra smiled and nodded.

"The Greeks called him Amenhotep?" I said.

"The Fourth," she added.

"And if you're to be his wife," I went on, "that would make

you…"

"Nefertiti," she said with a smile. "I've tried to convert him to Christianity but it's been a bit difficult seeing as Jesus is not going to be born for at least a thousand years! However, I did convince one Bedouin named Abram that there was only one true God."

"How did you explain me as Isis?" I asked. "I mean, Isis is a god… was a god… goddess."

"I've described Isis as one of God's angels," she replied. "Besides," she added, "Ahkee would never let anything happen to you. You're his future mother-in-law. We're to be married next month on the first day of *Meshir*. I hope you'll attend, *Mother*," she said as a broad smile shone on her face.

"I wouldn't miss it," I replied and then added, "*Daughter*."

"Just one thing," she added. "Please don't change back to Chloë. It's best to keep up the pretense."

"Of course," I assured her. "Of course."

On the wedding day, thousands were present to witness the royal union between Akhenaten and Nefertiti. Flowers of all kinds decorated the palace and its pavilion. Akhenaten was dressed in a white robe, embroidered with gold thread. A crown of blue and gold striped cloth hung down widely on each side of his head, tapering to points at the shoulders as a golden uraeus, reared up over his forehead—a symbol of strength and power that the Egyptians called a *Jirt*. Meanwhile, Nefra was adorned in a similar robe, although hers was embroidered in blue. On *her* head was the tall, flat-topped cap she became known for, from the one bust of her that survived the centuries. Akhenaten promised to love her and, unlike his predecessors, never take a concubine. I, as Aset, blessed them both, promised to watch over them for the rest of their earthly lives, and then, wishing to add a touch of the dramatic, vanished in front of everyone, as I phased back within the palace walls.

"I need to leave," I told Nefra after the ceremony was done.

"Do you have to go so soon?" she asked.

"I have to find Peyton," I said. "The one not mentally ill. She once told me that she had been Cleopatra in a former life. If I find her *as* her, perhaps she will recognize me."

"And if she doesn't?" came Nefra's response.

"I have to try," I said.

"If you ever have the desire," she went on. "you know where to find me."

"Yes, my Queen," I said with a smile.

We both moved in toward each other, hugged as though we would never see each other again, and then I phased into the future, away from her embrace.

CHAPTER XVII

Chloë
(The One Who Vanished Alone)

Earth Year: 2033
Alternate Reality III

One moment I was in ancient Egypt in the middle of a lightning storm; the next I was back home in my bedroom. The room was dark, but I heard the moans of two females in the bed whom I could discern from the red glow of my Isis Quantum Girl presence. Both appeared to be about my same age. As it turned out, one was Cameron, the other Erin—the same Erin who had vanished in front of me—the same one that Cameron swore she never knew! The two of them were making love; well, having sex to be precise. *But the hell with what they were doing*, I thought to myself. Erin was alive! Both of them stopped as they saw me and then stared at me, wide-eyed!

"Holy crap!" Erin exclaimed. "It's Quantum Girl!"

"In the bedroom with us!" Cameron chimed in.

It was Erin who switched on the lamp on the nightstand nearest her.

"Cool threads!" Cameron said. "I like the new look."

"No," I said. "It's me. Chloë!" and I instantly changed back to my normal self.

"No way!" That was Erin's response. Cameron just sat there naked, gawking at me. Well, both of them were naked and unashamedly so.

"Wait!" Erin went on. "Do you mean to tell me that all this time we've been getting it on with Quantum Girl? Fuck me. Literally. Get into bed with us, like right now!"

"Okay," I said. "But the two of you need to chill. I have questions. God, do I have questions! First of all, Erin, where the fuck have you been you all this time? How are you two together? And where is Brad?"

"Brad Warren?" That was Cameron. She turned toward Erin and both of them stared at each other with a *What the fuck?* look and then they turned back to me.

"Where have *you* been?" Cameron asked. "Did someone hit you on the head or something? Brad Warren died with all the rest of the men four years ago."

"How?" I asked.

Erin stared hard at me. "You don't remember," she said, not in the form of a question. "Seriously." I shook my head. "Very well, Quantum Girl. In order to curb toxic masculinity, the New World Order passed a law requiring all males, regardless of age, to be inoculated with the Estron pathogen, only it turned out to be death-in-a-syringe, killing them all within thirty days. You know this. This is a joke, right?"

"This wasn't the way it was," I insisted, "before I went back in time."

"Why would you go back on your word?" Cameron said.

"What do you mean?" I asked.

"Your—Quantum Girl's—promise" she went on. "never to interfere with history?"

"I didn't go back willingly," I said in my defense. "I just found myself back there."

"Regardless," she went on, "apparently it caused a Turing effect to occur." She shook her head. "Just get undressed, get in bed with us and we'll talk about it in the morning."

What the hell! I thought to myself. *Why not?* So I did. To this day I attribute my decision to the implants. The thought of being drenched in orgasms had nothing to do with it—at least that was my moral justification for all that went on that night.

"By the way," Erin said as she gently ran her fingertips up from my thigh to the nape of my neck while Cameron gently kissed my lips, "What's with the Aussie accent?"

"Don't know," said Cameron, "but it's sexy as all hell!"

I had awakened alone in bed come morning, stretching out my arms luxuriously, though that brought a whiff from my pits which reminded me that in a coma and *quantumfied* all that time, I hadn't had a bath or shower in more than six years. But while being Quantum Isis had protected my skin from bacteria, the last night of *activity* caused me to require immediate attention to my hygiene. I could hear the water from the shower in the bathroom attached to my room. It was a Jack and Jill loo that Claire and I shared growing up after we moved back to the States. The shower was one of those walk-in kinds—a small tiled room that was open on one side. Two voices echoed from within. Barefoot and still naked, I walked over to the toilet and sat down to pee. Peeing is like sex of a lesser degree. There is the urge, the unabating need, and the almost orgasmic sense of relief as the urine streams out of you. Three sheets dropped down to the pool beneath me afterward and I flushed, only to hear an unexpected "Ow!" and "Hey!" echoing within the ceramic shower walls.

It was Cameron who poked her head out, gripping the thick tiled wall with both hands, her red hair now plastered against her freckled skin. "Hey, Cum Muffin. Don't you know the rule? *Don't rush. Never flush when someone's in the shower.*"

"Sorry," I said ever so apologetically.

"Come join us," she said.

"That's all right," I replied. "I'll just wait till you two are done doing whatever it is you're doing, not that I can't imagine."

"There's only so much hot water!" Erin called out from within. "Get it while you can!"

I shrugged and then reluctantly stepped in. This girl-girl or, in this case, girl-girl-girl thing was still somewhat new to me, despite that six years ago (to me) I had had that *menage a trois* that one night with Cameron and Brad. There'd been nothing in the Christian church growing up in Perth about any of this. It gave a whole new meaning to the term *down under*-pun definitely intended. But I guess there was no choice anymore. Men were a thing of the past, all as extinct as the *Brontosaurus*. My mind reeled as I saw the two naked Aphrodites there with me in the shower, the water beaded on their flesh, dripping from their nipples, cascading down to the seat of *their* passion—and *mine*. Bodies touching each other. Fingers reaching, probing. It was all so arousing, so sensual, the liquid soap acting as an emollient to my sexual desire. My head reeled from the pleasure that fled upward to my brain. And then a wave of coherence hit me. This wasn't who I was. Never in my life had I been hedonistic; but I felt powerless.

"Turn back into Quantum Girl," Cameron begged. "Only naked this time."

"Yes," agreed Erin. "Turn into her, please!"

Caught up in that moment of passion, I found no will to refuse. In an instant, I phased into Quantum Girl, the Quantum Girl who was me, my skin glowing red, the ends of my hair seeming to burst with red light, the irises of my eyes dilated wide with crimson lust, and at the same time naked. Beads of water on my skin glowed like scarlet fireflies, merging and dripping down between my legs like a ruby-red waterfall that Erin had squatted down to drink from. In that moment, I forgot who I had been. I left my soul behind. I only knew the want of my desire.

I was the last one out. Erin and Cameron had toweled off and were back in bed and I was me again. The water rained down on my face and then, turning around, on my back. It all felt so wonderful after having been in the desert for so long. At last, I shut off the faucet and whipped my head around, my hair splashing water in every direction. For some reason, I felt more alive than I had ever been. I had experienced passion with both of them but it was more than that. It touched upon love—love that rose from the seat of my passion to the heart that fluttered in my chest at the mere thought of either of them. But then I heard her voice—*my* voice—coming from just outside the bathroom door, only the Aussie accent was gone.

"Hey, guys," it said. "Did you miss me? My flight got delayed and I didn't have change for the phone."

"What are you talking about?" said Cameron.

"I thought you were still in the shower?" That was Erin, her voice expressing utter bewilderment.

"What are you talking about?" my American voice said. "I just got back. Traffick was murder."

It was then that I chose to make my entrance, wrapped in a towel, my hair still sopping wet. All three of them just stared at me. Erin and Cameron kept looking from me to her and then back and again as I stared at what appeared to be my doppelgänger and she stared hard at me until our eyes locked on each other's.

"Who are you?" we both said at once.

"Chloë Anne Salinger," we answered in chorus.

"What the fuck is going on?" Cameron said, climbing naked from the bed. I would have said that Erin was beside herself but I already had that one covered with me.

"I think all this is part of the rewrite," I said. "This happened before with Sarabeth."

"Who's Sarabeth?" Erin asked.

"Peyton Herron's alternate reality self," I said, "before Peyton merged back all the dimensions and put everything back together."

"Peyton Herron?" Cameron replied. "The one who works at the Pink Lady?"

"Isn't that a strip club?" I asked. "She's not all there in the head. Why would they even hire her?"

"Oh, she's totally all there," Cameron chimed in, "'nips to lips' as they say."

"Hey!" my dop said, pushing out her hands in a back-off gesture. "Who the hell is *she* and why does she look just *like* me?"

Erin shrugged, "We thought she was you," she replied.

"I *am* her," I protested, "but I'm her before reality changed. It must have had something to do with my having wound up in ancient Egypt."

"This is bullshit cray!" my dop exclaimed. There was anger in her voice. "And from the looks of it—of her," she went on, "I assume the three of you all had sex together!"

"We *thought* she was you!" Cameron said defensively. "And *she* didn't say anything. Well, unless moaning counts."

"Grrrr!" came my dop's response. "That's it! Everyone out. This is *my* house, *my* bedroom! Gather up what clothes you have that you haven't borrowed from me and head back home or wherever!" She *looked at me.* "On second thought, *you* stay! I need to get to the bottom of this!"

As Erin and Cameron dressed, Cameron glared at Dop and said, "You can drop the pretense. We know you're Quantum Girl."

Dop shook her head to herself. "Whatever!" she said back. "Right now I'm Angry Girl and *you two* who had sex with *her* need to leave as I seriously need to blow off some steam!"

When the two of them had gone—in silence I might add—Dop turned to me. "I assume you came here wearing more than a towel," she said, "which, by the way, is mine."

I just shrugged.

"Being an only child," she went on, "I've always wondered what it would have been like to have had a sister."

I paused for a moment as a thought came to me. *"Only child?"* The words echoed in my brain. *Where was Claire in all of this?* I wondered.

"Now, I'm wondering," she went on, "if my parents had lied to me all these years. What if when they divorced, they had each taken one of us, like in *Parent Trap*? That would make you my twin sister and not my *alternate self* as you put it. I mean, it would make a whole lot more sense."

"It would," I replied, "only that's not the case. And fuck the towel! This is what I came in with!" And I phased into Isis right in front of her.

"Holy shit!" came the somewhat expected response. "You're Quantum Girl!"

"No," I said as I phased into the illusion of a dressed version of me, "but I have a god-stone in my head the same as her."

"Wait!" she said. "You're not the bad one of her, are you?"

"What do you mean?" I asked.

"It's all over the news," she replied. "She went on a rampage. There were two of her, one black, one white—their costumes. I mean. They were hurling energy blasts at each other, and then both of them just disappeared."

"Two Quantum Girls," I repeated. "I wonder if one of them was Khattaaara."

"Who?" Dop replied.

"Long story," I said.

"I've got time," she said. "You can tell me over breakfast."

I followed her to the kitchen where she took some plates, glasses, and flatware, laid them on the table, and then went to the fridge.

"I hope you like heggsberry," she said as she took a few things out.

"What's that?" I asked.

"Scrambled eggs and ham, topped with acai berries," she replied, carrying the ingredients to the counter near the stove.

"Sounds fantastic," I replied.

"Not as much as the story you're about to tell, I'm guessing," she said as she placed a frying pan on one of the burners and greased it from a stick of butter.

And so I told her everything I knew about Peyton and Ophelia and Claire and about Quantum Girl and Rendenaaar and Khattaaara and all the parallel dimensions and how in the end Peyton put everything right—that is until I wound up back in time where, presumably, something I did changed what was to what had come to be. Toward the end of my story, I began to feel sick.

"I'm sorry," I said. "I'm not feeling well."

"Perhaps," she replied, "that's because you've been eating deadly nightshade berries not acai."

I stared up at her, grabbing my throat. "Why would you do that?" I asked.

That was when she phased into a Quantum Chloë, full-on Egyptian. "Did you honestly think you were the only Chloë Salinger with a god-stone in her head?" she yelled.

"I wasn't raised to be a killer!" I shouted back.

"Neither was I!" she scowled, "But all that's changed! Funny, I didn't expect the antimatter version of me to also have a god-stone!"

"What do you want?" I said, now collapsed on the floor. "Who are you really?"

"I'm Chloë Anne Salinger," she replied in scathing tones. "Quantum Queen in my plane of existence. But your Peyton Herron with her dimensional meddling destroyed the entire universe I was in and everyone I ever loved!"

"So when she merged all of the dimensions..." I said.

"She wound up destroying mine!" came the bitter response.

She shook her head, a deprecating expression on her face. "There *are* universes other than yours!" she raged on.

"But what," I asked, gasping for breath, "did *I* ever do to you?"

"I can't let you interfere," she snarled. "and I want her dead! Every version of her. I want her extinguished from existence!" Her eyes began to glow as she looked at me and then I was somewhere else.

Weak and doubled-up in pain, I found myself on my side in a hollow beneath the soil, dimly lit by patches of light that poked through from above. I could smell the rot in the dirt and the worms as they ate their way through it. I could feel the roots of plants brush against my face like cobwebs. In front of me was the decaying corpse of a man, lying in a rotted-away casket, wearing a dark suit that had itself been destroyed by water that had seeped through the soil and by time. I cringed at the sight. I screamed and tried to move away but that only dislodged the moist dirt above me that got into my mouth and eyes. I twisted and turned the other way and that's when I saw her—Peyton—dressed in a silver Quantum Girl outfit that still glowed. But half of her head was gone! One of her eyes, the one nearest me stared out vacantly from a skeletal socket, and above that was her shattered skull with part of her now naked brain. It was all too much for me—the poison, the horror—I screamed and screamed. I was in the grips of hysteria. I clawed at the soil above me, trying to escape, but the dirt got into my eyes and my mouth, blinding and choking me. *I don't want to die here like this*, I thought to myself. I lost consciousness after that.

CHAPTER XVIII

Chloë
(The One Who left with Nefertiti)

Earth Date: August 11, 30 B.C.

Nearly twenty-five hundred years after I had left Nefra, I was back in that same part of Egypt where I had first found myself. No longer Aset in the language of the Old or Middle Kingdoms, I was Isis, wife of Osiris and mother of Horus. Add another two thousand years to that and the name Isis would become synonymous with an Islamic terrorist group. Apparently, greatness has its limitations.

Forty-eight years before the birth of Christ, Gaius Julius Caesar stood as Dictator of the Roman Empire, while Cleopatra sat as Queen of Egypt—Cleopatra VII Thea Philopator, Cleopatra the Father-Loving Goddess—olive skin, dark hair, hazel eyes, considered the most beautiful woman in all her land, lover to both Caesar and Antony—she who once dissolved a gem in a goblet of wine—a priceless pearl earring to prove that she could drink away a fortune. After watching it dissolve in the aromatic liquid, she downed the liquid, not realizing that with that pearl was a god-stone that would endow her with powers beyond her imagination—she, who might have destroyed all of the Roman legions with but a single thought—she, who was a past incarnation of Peyton Herron, Quantum Girl.

I phased into Cleopatra's bedchamber late at night. I was Isis Quantum Girl. My body glowed in the darkness, but to awaken her, I increased the intensity to an almost solar glare. She awoke from her sleep shielding her eyes with her left forearm.

"What sort of witchery is this?" she asked in her ancient Greek that I could now understand.

"If it be witchery," I answered in that tongue and with a voice that echoed my words, "it is the witchery of the gods."

114

"Reveal thyself," she commanded, "Whatever the source of thy light, I demand that you cause it to cease!"

"I am Isis," I said as I dimmed the light from me, "Queen of the Throne and of the souls of all Egyptians. And thou art Cleopatra, Queen of the Nile and all its fertile lands."

"Forgive me, my Queen," she begged. "Thy godly presence blinded me from knowing. Hast thou come to end my life?" she asked. "To cut me into pieces as was thy husband's fate? If that be thy will, pray just let me look upon my children one last time."

"What idle talk!" I said. "Am I not the goddess of healing? Did not I gather the pieces of Osiris into a basket and then reassemble them so that he would again sit by my side? Nay, I have come to cure the memory in thee that was lost from the life which thou now owns."

I looked at her—past the heavy makeup that she wore, even to bed. It was the same face as Peyton's, regardless that she was by all accounts a decade older. *How?* I wondered until I sensed the god-stone in her head, though at the time I had yet to understand how it had come to her. Regardless, age had not touched her much, her years dispelled by the quantum gem. The question remained, did she know it was even there or of the incredible powers that lay at her fingertips?

"Tell me, my daughter," I said, "hast thou had dreams that thou couldst not explain?"

"Throughout my life," she said, "dreams that I was a monster—like the gorgons Antony would tell of. I had a tail and pointed ears and—oh, the horrors of it all! Again and again, I had such visions in my sleep—nightmares to be sure."

"Thou hast lived many lives," I told her, "yet the one of which thou speaks, then thy name wast…"

"Khattaaara," she said, finishing my words.

"But thou art more than that," I said. "In days to come, born Peyton Herron, thou shalt be known as Quantum Girl, with powers as great as mine."

"Canst thou truly see into the future?" she asked.

115

"As I can into the past," I replied. "I know that in this room in a cage breathes an asp with which, two days hence, thou seeks to end thy life."

"Better that than submit to Octavius," she said, "who already has bled to the sand my poor Caesarian, such son who not so long ago did suckle at my breast."

As I stared at her, I saw neither Peyton nor Khattaaara but rather a woman whose pride had brought her to the precipice of death. And yet her soul, scattered through time, had found its place in three of the most powerful women in all existence.

"Hast thou had any strange experiences?" I asked, curious to know if there had been any interaction between her and the stone.

"Aye," she said. "Just one night ago, I awoke to find the likeness of myself beside me on my bed. Thinking that this was my *ka* somehow fled from me, I ordered it back inside. To my great horror, it sat up and claimed to be me! 'I am Cleopatra!' it claimed. Thus vexed, convinced it was a demon of sorts, I grabbed its throat, pushed it down onto its back with my weight, and strangled it until it breathed no more." She stared hard into my eyes. "It is I who bears the right to my name and not some demon from the netherworld."

"And what became of the demon?" I asked.

"'Tis in the cedar chest across the room," she answered, "where I dragged it so that 'twould stay hid till I could think how best to dispose of it."

I walked over to the chest and opened it. Causing myself to glow brighter, I could see the body—her divided half, now dead—its knees pressed up against its chest. I quickly shut the lid, paused to take it all in, and then turned back to the one with breath still in her lungs.

"Afterward," she went on, "I was so weakened that I thought it must truly have been my *ka* that I had murdered with these hands. Thus, was I asleep until thy glorious presence awakened me."

It struck me that the death of her other half presented the perfect opportunity for me to prevent her suicide and take her somewhere to try and awaken the Peyton part of her.

"There is no need for thee to die," I assured her.

"Where then shall I go?" she asked.

"With me," I replied. "Bid thee farewell to thy children but say no more."

"Dost thou take me to the netherworld," she asked, "where sits Osiris on his throne?"

"I shall take thee to a land filled with wonder," I told her. "Fear not. Thy children shall be sent to Rome with Octavian's sister and shall prosper there, remembering their mother with great honor and love."

"To see them once and never again," she said, "is an unbearable thought."

I took her hands in mine. "Would death present better options?" I asked. "Or life with the hearts of thy children cut away to stab at thine? Trust thy goddess that in days to come thou shalt be able to visit with them again and witness the flowering of their lives."

Cleopatra nodded. "It is with reverence that I trust thee, Great Isis, for beneath my tainted flesh dwells the spirit thou breathed in me at my birth."

The next day Cleopatra spent with her children. Her twins, Cleopatra Selene II and Alexander Helios were ten years old while Ptolemy Philadelphos was only four. They were all quite lovely, though one could easily see that Ptolemy was the most spoiled, being the youngest.

"I shall disguise myself as a Macedonian girl visiting Her Majesty so as not to attract attention," I told her. "You may refer to me as Chloë."

"A young green shoot," she replied in a pondering tone. "I should have thought thou wouldst give thyself a name such as Hathor might have chosen. Nevertheless, I shall accede to thy choice, most cherished goddess. Thou shalt be called Chloë to all who wish to know."

Thus, did I phase into myself, though in Grecian attire. Cleopatra looked at me and smiled. "Thou still art beautiful," she said, "even in mortal form."

It was strange and somewhat exciting to engage with the children of Egypt's pharaoh. We all played tug of war with victories on each side and then I taught Cleopatra Selene— Seelee, as Cleopatra affectionately called her—how to jump rope, which I was quite proficient at growing up. The young girl took to it quite well. By the time evening came, the children were quite worn out. After a meal of squab dipped in honey, along with figs, dates, and beer—honeyed milk for the children—Cleopatra, with the aid of her maidservants, tucked them into bed and kissed them all goodnight.

Moments later, she and I were back in her chamber. Going over to the chest in which the body lay, I lifted the lid once more, only to find that, from it, now came an overwhelming stench like rotting meat with a fruity overtone. The cadaver, already having gone through rigor mortis, its abdomen had begun to swell from the bacteria within. I held my breath, briefly turning my head away, but then used my quantum abilities to create a time field around it, as Peyton had once done, in order to bring it back to its state just after death. I suppose that I could have brought it back to life, but that wouldn't have served my purpose of having a dead corpse to substitute for Cleopatra when I took her away from there. I found it curiously strange that when Cleopatra bent over the chest to view her other self, the part of the god-stone that was within it went *from* it and into her, pushing her back just a bit as it did.

"What spirit is it," she asked in terror, "that flies from the demon and strikes me in the head? Doth it seek to possess me?"

"Nay, Daughter," I assured her. "'tis but the dying breath of it, begging for forgiveness with a kiss." Then I phased it onto her bed.

Cleopatra walked over to it, staring at it by the torchlight on the walls. "One would think 'twas myself," she said, "laid out upon the bed, not dead but in dreams."

"We do not wish her to be asleep," I said. I walked to the cage where the asp slithered like the serpent in the Garden of Eden, only this one could not speak. I picked it up, holding it by its neck, and stared at it as it stared back at me. The venomous serpent opened its mouth and hissed at me, its eyes fixed upon mine as though there was some invisible thread between us.

I turned to Cleopatra. "Bare her breast," I told her.

Reluctantly, she went to the body of her other self and pulled back the cloth of its robe. I caused it to be warm, went over to it, and held the snake up close to the dead Cleopatra's skin. The creature reared its head, sensed the body heat with its tongue, and then struck the left breast just above the areola. The job done, I phased the asp out into the desert.

"No need to have anyone else bitten," I told her.

"Thy magic is truly great," Cleopatra replied.

"Once gone from here," I said, "I shall make thee a goddess as well." I paused and then sighed, "Anyway…" in English.

"What means 'annhiweighe?" she asked.

I smiled. "It is a word in a language that has yet to be invented," I said. "It means, 'despite all else.'" I looked at her make-up and the clothes she was wearing, and then said. "We need to change how you look for where we are going."

Per my request, she brought me some cleansing oil and softened papyrus in order for me to remove the heavy eyeshadow and mascara. After I was done, I took a step back and viewed the result. It was like looking, not at Cleopatra, but at Peyton Herron.

"Art thou ready?" I asked her.

"Thou doth promise that I can see my dear children again?" she asked.

"If thou chooseth," I replied.

"How could I not?" she proclaimed. "How could any mother not wish to see her children? Would that I might have bid farewell to Caesarin, but I sent him off to Berenice." Cleopatra stared at me with

119

sadness in her eyes. "Will I see *him* again as well?" I asked.

"Thou asketh many questions," I replied knowing that in only a few short days, the seventeen-year-old son of Rome's last dictator would be strangled to death upon orders of Octavian, later to be known as Augustus Caesar. "Give me thy hands," I said to her. I took hers in mine and then phased us both to 2033.

CHAPTER XIX

Claire

The Next Universe
Planet Erebus: Year 1
Alternate Reality II

It was hard enough for me to accept the death of my kid sister—the one who always tried to act like a *big* sister to *me*—but now there was a robot or android or whatever it was that had taken not only her shape but her identity as well. She looked like Chloë. She sounded like Chloë. She even appeared to think like her. And while she appeared harmless enough, I was still concerned for the children's safety around her. I even questioned my calling it a her. Beyond all else, she was a distraction that tended to constantly tug at my heart. Life on the planet was difficult enough without having to cart around the constant reminder that my sister was irrevocably dead.

The air on this planet was cooler than it had been on Vesta which was a good thing. There were billowing clouds that blocked half the sky most of the time, shielding the blue star that Erebus revolved around. There were also windstorms, but they were few and far between and we were able to take shelter from them in the buildings of the long-dead civilization that had once lived there. Pheeli and I often wondered what had caused their demise. I silently questioned whether or not Peyton knew, but if she did, she didn't share that information—at least not for a long while and neither I nor Pheeli pressed that issue or any other as she appeared strangely distracted for reasons unknown to either of us. I remember thinking how strange it was that not only were we on a different planet, but in a different universe—the sole survivors of our entire species; not a very earth-shattering realization. I laughed at the thought—so strange an expression—earth-shattering—considering that the Earth did not exist anymore. Pheeli was much stronger in her makeup than I was. I could never have endured what she had—she who had spent a lifetime in the form of an alien, on a long-forgotten planet in a universe that had been extinguished so long before our own. She didn't talk much about it, though. I remember what it was like to have only briefly been turned into a Gaaalthaaaran. I couldn't even begin to imagine how it must have been for her to have lived for so long with her humanity having been stripped away from her.

One thing that constantly weighed upon my mind was our future. *How*, I wondered, *were we to perpetuate the human race without men?* The fact that there was a chance that either or both Pheeli and I might be able to become pregnant was only due to Peyton having temporarily pulled out Liam from Pheeli—Liam who was but an alternate possibility of her—and, all too strange—an alternate male possibility of me we called Clark. We both had sex with each of them. Having sex with Liam brought back painful memories. Having sex with Clark felt kind of strange, knowing that he was kind of sort of me. It was sort of like being able to pull another one of you out of yourself in order to masturbate with the other one doing most of the work, only the one you pulled out was a guy who looked like he could have been your twin brother. I always wondered how Pheeli got around that fact. Regardless, I was in a committed relationship, and, even when I was having sex with Liam, I just kept telling myself, *It's really Pheeli. It's really Pheeli.* I loved her so much!

And while it was genetically unwise for siblings to perpetuate a line, our girls would need to man up as it were to at least be artificially inseminated by their brothers if the human race was to survive. My initial thoughts were *Why not just say fuck it all and go back a hundred years or more into our past so that we all could live out our lives before the universe ground to a stop*? It was Peyton (party killer!) who said that were we to do that we would interfere with the timeline and could potentially prevent any of us from ever being born as had been the case with the twins she had been carrying prior to her merging together all of the parallel dimensions.

"What if," Pheeli suggested to Peyton, "you go back in time with the god-stones and bring back three boys?"

"The problem with that is," she said, "if I do that, it would change things. This universe wouldn't be the same. Regardless that I would have left you safe and sound, this planet might cease to exist and all of you would die in empty space. The absolute best I could do," she went on, "would be to bring us back after Samira and Zhana were conceived but that would mean having to live in those few years over and over again, eventually resulting in hundreds of each of us existing at one time. Worse, theoretically, if any of us encountered our original selves, changing the timeline, we ourselves might cease to exist—the children as well."

As it stood, without any pregnancies, the human race would end in less than a century. It was the Chloëbot that came to me shortly after that conversation.

"What?" I said with some irritation in my voice.

"Did I do something wrong?" it asked.

"No," I sighed.

"You know that I love you," it said. "I love being with you, but I want to go home."

"If only we could," I replied.

Tears came to its eyes. "What do you mean?" it said. "Why can't Peyton just phase us back? I miss Mom and Dad and my friends." A frightened look came over its face. "Why can't I remember any of my friends' faces or names? All of my memories of them are shadows. What's wrong with me?"

"Oh, my God!" I exclaimed. "There's nothing *wrong* with you. You're just not my Chloë!"

Tears flooded from the Chloëbot eyes and down its cheeks. "Why are you being so mean?" it said. "I've always been there for you! I always looked *up* to you! Why can't you just accept me for who I am?"

It was all so strange. The automaton from this world's ancient past appeared to believe that it actually was my sister. I assumed that all the memories it possessed came from my memories of Chloë down to her mannerisms. It seemed that I was the one who by whatever mechanism had breathed life into this artificial creature. It was as if it were Galatea somehow come alive from a lifeless block of stone. It had no recollection of it ever being anything *but* Chloë Anne Salinger. Apparently, such creations had been devised to replace lost loved ones by those long dead in some forgotten past. Chloë was gone, the very fabric of her existence torn apart by the creation of this new universe. There before me was more than a portrait or a photograph. This was her recreated; and while I deeply mourned my sister's loss, I could not help feeling love for this Geppetto-like creation who believed it was real. But the only memories it had were those that I'd shared with Chloë. I'd never met any of her friends. That was why it couldn't remember them.

"I'm sorry," I told her—I thought it best to think of it that way. "I didn't mean to snap at you."

"It's all right," she said. Wiping away her tears.

Suddenly, the ground began to rumble. I could hear Samira scream from outside. The Chloëbot became a blur and then vanished entirely followed by a sonic boom. I quickly rose from where I had been sitting and raced outside. The Chloëbot, who had been holding onto Pheeli, let go as Pheeli vomited. Zhana was nearby. Jordan and Sami were running up from a short distance, while on the ground lay a large gargoyle that had been dislodged by the ground quake. I rushed over to Pheeli.

"Are you all right?" I asked with great concern. "What happened?"

Pheeli stared back at the fragments of the gargoyle on the ground. "I would've been killed if she hadn't saved me." She threw up again and then went on, wiping her mouth with the back of her hand. "She pushed me out of the way at incredible speed."

It was at that moment that Peyton phased up to us. "I was taking a nap," she said. "What happened?"

"Our Chloë saved Pheeli's life," I said. "I don't care where she came from. She's earned her place with us."

Pheeli, with Zhana now by her side, walked over to us. As she did, the ground rumbled again. "What's going on?" she asked Peyton.

Peyton stared out into space for a moment, her eyes glowing brightly as she did. "The fabric of this universe is being altered," she said.

"What do you mean?" I asked.

Her brow furled as she spoke. "It's as though something changed in our universe that's causing a ripple effect."

"How could that happen?" Pheeli asked.

Peyton shook her head. "I don't know," she replied, "but I hope this one ripple is all there is."

CHAPTER XX

Peyton

Earth Year: 2033
Alternate Reality I

I had more time to figure things out, but what had been my home was now the headquarters for a newspaper—the New York Herald which I had never heard of before—and the self I had left behind along with Jordan were nowhere to be found. Time had been rewritten. Everything was gone, including my dog.

With nowhere else to go, I phased back to my parents' home. I assumed there'd still be my bedroom—mine and Phee's—though when I arrived, there was already another me there—only she wasn't *all* there. As it turned out, *that* Peyton Herron suffered from cerebral hypoxia caused by a prolonged lack of oxygen to the brain that damages cells responsible for nearly everything relating to cognitive ability.

It was still light outside but she lay in bed in white underwear in fetal position mumbling to herself. This wasn't my universe. It was hers. X-ray projection allowed me to visualize the damaged sectors in her brain. Theresa Martinez had somehow mastered cellular regeneration but that was an ability I had yet to learn. I went over to the bed and sat down on the edge facing her. Her hair was oily and unkempt and fell over her face, clinging to her skin. I gently pulled it back only to reveal the scars from the rope that, like me, she had strangled herself with.

She half glanced up at me and then continued to mumble, "I don't want to go to school today, Mama. Theresaurus is there. Theresaurus won't ignore me. It won't stop. My head, my head, my head."

Poor thing, I thought to myself. "Come on," I said to her, "Let's get you a bath," then I pulled her up to a sitting position and held her against me. I could feel the bones from her spine. Her body stank and the sheets were wet from urine. "Up we go," I said, lifting her to her feet, struggling against her almost dead weight. I knew I could have drawn out a double of me to help or else have nullified her mass, but I thought that would have frightened her, so I steeled my muscles and walked her to the bathroom.

"Do you need to pee?" I asked.

She nodded. I pulled down the panties she was wearing and sat her down on the toilet seat. As I turned on the faucet for the tub I stared at her. She was emaciated beyond belief—the poster child for anorexia. Her ribs bulged through her skin. Her waist must have been eighteen inches and as much as I had struggled to move her, she must have weighed less than ninety pounds, which at five-foot-eight is life-threatening. *How could this have happened?* I wondered.

I could hear the trickle of urine splashing down into the water of the toilet bowl. And then it stopped and she just sat there, her eyes staring, vacant and unfocused, as though in her mind she wasn't even there. As tepid water filled the tub, I went over to her, tore off several sheets worth of toilet paper, and wiped her—once and then again. How strange it was I thought, unshaven as she was; never the case with me since puberty availed itself. But this was how women were, for the most part, since time immemorial. There were thin, blonde hairs on her legs and tufts under her arms. I gently raised her chin with my fingers and looked at her.

"When was the last time you've eaten?" I asked her.

"Who are you?" came her weak response. "Am I dead?"

"No, Sweetheart," I said, "but I'm here for you now. Everything's going to be all right. I promise." I undid the hooks of her bra and took it off of her. Her breasts were almost nonexistent, especially in that what's normal for me is a C-cup. I would have put her at an A. I shook my head to myself at the thought of what had happened to this version of me.

I got her to her feet and then walked her to the bathtub and helped her get in. The water having filled the tub halfway, I shut off the faucet, sat down on the edge, and with a washcloth and soap began to bathe her. I was amazed that she hadn't any bedsores. I just wondered how long she would have lasted if I hadn't come.

I gently daubed her face with the cloth and shampooed her hair. As I rubbed the washcloth over her back, she winced.

"Does that hurt?" I asked.

Her eyes still closed, she nodded.

I lathered my hand and rubbed her back gently. "How's this?" I asked.

"Good," she replied, though the words barely escaped her lips.

When all was done I said, "Let's both stand up."

It was hard for her. She slipped she was so weak but I caught her.

"I've got you," I told her. Then I helped her out of the tub, sat *her* down on its edge this time, and dried her with a towel. She stared at me and then reached up with her left hand and touched my face.

"Why do you look like me?" she asked in a weak voice. "Are you an angel?"

"I might be, for you," I said. It was the simplest explanation for her in her state of mind. There was a white terry robe on one of two hooks on the wall. I took it and put it on her and then wrapped the belt around her waist.

"There," I said as I looked at her, taking both of her hands in mine. "Good as new. Now let's get you downstairs and get some broth into you."

I led her barefoot down the stairs, ever vigilant that she not lose her balance and fall. There was a sickly sweet odor that I had smelled ever since we left her room that grew stronger with every downward step. Holding her but stopping time, I split off another of me, phased into the kitchen, and then gasped, my hand rising up to cover my mouth. There on the floor lay a corpse, her eyes open and white, the skin of her lips desiccated leaving her with an almost sardonic grin. I quickly phased us both to the county morgue, where I left a note as to who she was; who she was, was my mother, Katherine Elise Kimble Herron, or at least this timeline's version of her. This woman never knew me—never birthed me nor raised me—and yet I still felt hollow at the thought of her death. Would that I might have undone time to reverse her demise, but hers was a natural death from a weakened heart that no hospital could mend. I covered her body with a sheet and then phased back to the house where time once again had resumed.

The sickly version of me was at the kitchen table, sitting at an empty place. My other self was at the stove. I merged back into her, ladled out a bowl of chicken broth, brought it over, and then sat down beside her.

"You need to eat," I said.

"Mama said to me," she replied in the whisper of a voice, "that when I got older I would meet a man and fall in love and live happily ever after. That was when I was little." Her breathing became labored. "That was before the Theresaurus monster attacked me!" she screamed, slamming her fists down on the table again and again.

"Hey," I said softly, gently taking hold of her arms to quieten her, "that's all in the past. You have a guardian angel now."

She turned her head one way and then the other.

"Where's my mama?" she said and then called out, "Mama? Mama?"

"She's not here now," I told her.

"Where is she?" Peyton asked.

"She went out for a while," I replied.

"It's been so long," she said.

"I know," I said back. Then I brought a spoonful of broth up to her mouth for her to drink. "Right now, you need something in your stomach. We can talk later on."

She pursed her lips and then sucked the liquid in. "Promise?" she asked afterward.

"Of course," I replied as I brought another spoonful to her mouth.

129

CHAPTER XXI

Chloë
(The One Who was with Cleopatra)

Earth Year: 2033
Alternate Reality I

Despite that I had been in a coma for more than six years, and despite all the other time that I had spent in the past, Cleo and I phased into my bedroom the morning after I had left. Our arrival into those futuristic digs, from Cleo's perspective, was fascinating, not to mention the temperature-controlled environment. What piqued her curiosity first was when she went to the window and stared out into the yard.

"Where is this place?" she asked.

"It's called America," I replied, "sort of on the other side of the world from Egypt."

"In my time," she said, "it was known as Atlantis. Julius claimed to have met sailors from there who washed up on Hispania with features more like those from Serica.[21] But why hast thou brought us so far?"

"It is where I live," I told her. "This is my bedroom." When I looked around, however, I began noticing differences, like a typewriter where my laptop should have been. "Something's wrong," I said.

"What dost thou mean?" she asked.

"This is not the way I left it," I replied. "There are differences."

I walked over to the dresser and looked in the mirror over it. Behind me in the reflection was another one of me. I wheeled around but she wasn't there.

"Dost thou see her?" I asked.

---

[21] In Cleopatra's time, such was the Roman name for northern China.

"See whom?" came the reply. "I see no one other than thee."

Again, I turned to the mirror to look and there she was, seated at the desk, reading a book. But turning back, the chair was empty.

I walked over to the dresser and tried to pick up a brush that was lying on top of it but my hand went right through it.

"Why can I see *it* but not *her*?" I said aloud in English. "We must be out of phase in space and time."

"Is something wrong?" Cleopatra asked with great concern. "I do not understand thy words."

Just then another version of me walked into the room, sat down at the desk, and picked up a book to read. Though she said nothing, I could tell from her expression that this Chloë was one she could clearly see.

"I believe we are not truly in this reality," I said. I extended my arm toward her. "Here, grab hold of my hand. I need to take us into her plane of existence."

She did as I asked and I phased us into the other Chloë's world. It was as I did that the other version of me saw us appear out of nowhere, stood up, and turned toward us.

"Who *are* you?" she asked, her voice trembling, fear written over her face. "Why do you look like me?" Then she saw Cleopatra. "Peyton?" she said. "What's going on?" And then she fainted dead away.

CHAPTER XXII

Chloë
(The One Who Vanished Alone)

Earth Year: 2033
Alternate Reality III

I awoke to a soft purple glow that faintly illuminated the grave I had been phased into—a glow that was coming from just behind a remaining mass of decaying brain that resided in the carved-out skull that had once belonged to Peyton Herron. Her corpse was garbed in a silver Quantum Girl costume. The glow came from the god-stone that had been placed in her head by a being from a long-dead civilization. Dead is dead, though, whether for a trillion, trillion years or for barely a breath of time. And Peyton Herron was most discernably dead, under the soil, sharing her grave with me and some long-dead nameless corpse. Even though I also had a god-stone in my head, for whatever reason, it no longer worked. There had been four of me in ancient Egypt. Perhaps it has been pulled back into one of them or into the quantum fabric. All I knew was that I couldn't feel it in my head anymore. In truth, there was only one of each colored stone in the reconciled existence. There in her head was the purple one and it offered a way for me to escape.

It would have been disgusting enough to have reached in through the brains of a stranger, but this was Peyton Herron's that my fingers were pushing into, and Peyton had been my friend. At last, having wriggled through the decaying organ, my fingers gripped the glowing gem. I pulled back my hand and grimaced at the sight of bits of her brain coating my hands but I had no other choice if I wanted to live. Regardless, it became clear that the god-stone didn't care. As I placed it near my forehead it began to spin, shrink in size, and then phased into my head. I felt a sudden surge of power. I was a Quantum Girl again! I threw myself backward, taking a deep breath, and then lurched forward again as I felt the skeletal fingers of the other corpse entangled in my hair. Pulling myself free, I wound up face down, my face pressed up against yet another dead body—that of the Chloë Salinger from this reality, no doubt murdered by the imposter who had phased me into the grave. Seeing what appeared to be myself staring blankly at me with clouded white eyes caused me to gag and start to throw up. It was only after my stomach had emptied its contents that I was able to regain enough composure to phase myself out of the grave to the surface, cringing, only to realize that the fingers of the now-severed hand were still entwined in my hair. Reaching up, I grasped it with my *not* bony fingers and threw it to the ground shivering at the thought of whose hand it might have been. Death is something no one likes to think about because we know it awaits us all. Sooner or later, whether we wish for it or not, we are, each of us, destined for the grave. We can sugarcoat it with dreams of a merciful God, who will wrap our souls in the blanket of some eternal life, but the dream does not make death less real.

I found myself in an old cemetery—the kind with huge tombstones and monuments erected by those who years ago had followed their loved ones into the ground. It was a moonless night, quiet as the death beneath my feet but for the uncaring crickets that chirped out their mating calls. There was wet dirt in my eyes and mouth, but as I tried to wipe it away, I realized that the hand I was using was still covered in decaying brain. I quickly tore off my blouse and used it as a rag to wipe away as much of the loathsome soil and Peyton-remains as I could. *Thank goodness it's dark*, I thought to myself, *with me in just my bra*. I was so rattled, I did not even think to phase on more clothes.

I desperately wanted a shower but I couldn't go home. If my antimatter self's powers were anything like Peyton's I knew that I was no match for her. I sat down on the ground with my back against a tree, uncertain what to do.

133

A million thoughts raced through my head, all the while remembering how I had foolishly told everything I knew to the antimatter me. Yet when I was attacked, one would have thought that my powers would have automatically kicked in, but that didn't happen. *What if,* I thought to myself, *I had gone back in time from the here and now and taken it from me in order to save me from a battle I definitely would have lost?* I decided to test my theory out.

And so, I phased back before the antimatter me had entered, while Cameron and Erin were still in the bedroom and I had just stepped out of the shower—and then I froze time. Peyton had once said that it's impossible to get a god-stone out of someone's head without their consent, but the naked frozen me *was* me. So it was that I merged with her and then divided myself from her, taking the god-stone with me. That would prevent any resistance on her part and everything would repeat without what happened to Peyton happening to me. The odd thing was that having to strip myself in order to merge, when I did, none of the dirt came with, and wound up on the tile floor. Then, phasing into the closet, once separate again, I picked out a black silk dress with spaghetti straps and black heels. That outfit was necessary because I was on a mission and my attire needed to fit in. I wondered, though, what the counterfeit me had thought when she came across the mud on the now filthy bathroom floor. *Who knows?* I thought to myself and, more than that, *Who cares? Just as long as it isn't significant enough to change the course of events.*

There were no redlight districts in L.A.; strip clubs were located wherever permits allowed. Cameron had said that Peyton worked at the Pink Lady which according to my cellphone was located on Montana. The gentlemen's clubs as they were called before all gentlemen became extinct, without exception, were on the dark side—literally—so I was able to phase into the dim-lit club unnoticed for the most part. I say for the most part as the on-stage performer appeared to have gotten a glimpse of me. There was a doubletake, but then her attention was distracted back to the stage when one of the women seated up close placed a couple of bills down right in front of her. With the absence of men on the planet and the designer drug, Maxx which aroused, heightened, and prolonged the sexual experience, the girl-on-girl thing went viral. The room was filled with women of every age, color, and shape, each with a stash of dollar bills and the errant desire to take one of the girls home for fun, games, and party favors. Everyone entering at the ten-dollar admission price was obligated to buy two drinks which, of course, were laced with prodigious amounts of Maxx. Twenty dollars would buy a table dance. A hundred to a thousand would buy a private room for fifteen minutes to half an hour where *bargaining* took place—*bargaining* meaning sex.

Erin and I once snuck into one of the clubs before things changed. It was open audition night. We'd both recently turned seventeen and used fake IDs to get in. As pledges, it was part of initiation for Delta Beta Gamma, the sorority at our high school and we desperately wanted to be sisters. One of the girls' *actual* sister was the hostess at a club in Venice called The Flightless Beaver and so they designated her as the observer. Erin had been in queue to go first. She had stripped down to the bikini she had worn under her clothes, same as me. She'd just gone on stage and was holding the pole with one hand when she saw Brad with one girl getting a lap dance. There wasn't much to what the girl had on. She was nude other than a pair of gossamer-thin panties, grinding away at his lap as the music played for the dance that Erin was supposed to do—only her eyes fixed on Brad as he stared at the girl, so obvious to any observer that he was more than aroused by the act. Erin had been a virgin until Brad, who had sworn to her that he loved her and only her. Watching him, she gripped the pole with both of her hands, pulling herself into it. There were tears in her eyes as she watched the love of her life getting off with some strange girl. I saw it all from the door to the dressing room. I felt her trembling body brush against me as she rushed past me and grabbed her clothes, shedding tears, not even bothering to put them on as she raced from the back door of the club into the cold night air. She'd left her purse behind. I picked it up and followed her out.

"Erin!" I called after her, "Wait!" but in another moment she was lost to the darkness.

The next time I saw her was in school the following day. It was in English class. Both of us attended Braxton which is a prep school, Supposedly, preparing all of the students for college, though it would seem that public high schools do the same on a more economical scale. But Braxton is considered far more prestigious than Santa Monica High. Anyone with two nickels and a rich uncle goes there, so there I was sent—not that I have a rich uncle or anything. That's just an expression. Claire went before me as did Peyton and Ophelia and that awful Martinez girl.

Erin looked as though she'd been crying all night. Her eyes were red and swollen. As Miss Blake, our teacher, went on and on about the foreshadowing of the broken pickle jar in *Ethan Frome*, I slipped a note to Erin. It didn't say much; just, "I'm here for you. He's not worth it."

She passed back a note that read, "I can't help it. I love him."

I waited for her after the bell rang. It was the last class of the day. From there we were to go to cheerleading practice. I looked into her eyes as I faced her.

"I know it hurts," I said.

"He texted me last night," she sobbed, "after I got home."

"And?" I asked.

"He said he saw us as we were leaving," she wept, choking on her tears. "He accused me of following him there. He bragged about the stripper he was with. He said after the club closed they went back to her apartment and he fucked her all night. He said he didn't want to be with anyone who stalked him. Then he broke up with me!"

"Hey," I said, "There are a million guys so much better than him."

"You don't understand," she said, swallowing hard.

"Understand what?" I asked.

"I'm pregnant!" she replied and then unleashed a rain of tears.

I dropped the books I was holding and hugged her.

"Come with me to practice," I insisted, determined to keep an eye on her. "Once we're changed, we'll tell Coach that you just got your period and you can sit it out. We'll talk afterward."

We met on the bleachers when practice ended. She was there with me and then she was gone. And then she wasn't and she and Cameron and I wound up naked together in bed with never-in-my-life-would-I-have-ever-predicted results. There was no Brad or baby on the way, and the world had been turned upside down.

Peyton was on stage when I phased in. She was using the name—believe it or not—Quantum Girl. There were blacklights aimed down at her giving her an iridescent, violet look. She wore the same sort of cowl as the Quantum Girl costume I had come to know. Her iridescent tunic, though, was made of some thin and fragile material that fell off of her bit by bit as she danced, holding the pole, until she was totally nude. At the very last moment, she pulled off the cowl, shook out her hair, and then bowed to her onlookers. The second half of the set was all nude—spread legs, displayed masturbation, torrid moans.

But to say that she was gorgeous would have been an understatement. Her beauty was an indisputable fact recognized by nearly every woman in the room. This Quantum Girl, exuded sex with every move, with every breath, with every drop of pheromone that wafted from her flawless skin. What I couldn't figure out was why someone with quantum abilities would be working as a stripper. I needed to talk with her but after her set. The music she danced to was hypnotic, as was she. She would have been every man's dream but there were no men anymore. Still, there were women, whose hearts now throbbed at the sight of her—chemically enhanced perhaps but throbbed nonetheless. When her act was done, she went around the stage collecting all the bills that had been left for her as tips, offering eye contact and smiles for all those who had placed them there.

"Hey," I said to her when she happened to look in my direction. "Can we go somewhere private?"

"I have a session," she said glancing at a slender, well-dressed woman who had been eyeing her. "You can book me after that. A thousand for half an hour."

"I'm not here as a customer," I said with the realization that she had no idea who I was.

Peyton looked at me sideways. "Dancer, huh? I haven't seen you here before."

"First time," I said somewhat awkwardly. "Just hoping to get hired."

She gave me the once-over. "You look like you're in high school. A lot of the janes like that." She glanced over at her client, held up her index finger for her to wait, and then turned back toward me. "You got a name?" she asked.

"Chloë," I told her. "Chloë Salinger."

"No," she said, "a stage name."

"Isis," I replied.

"Have they tried you out?" she asked.

"Not yet," I replied.

"Hang on," she said and then walked to the DJ station where an older woman stood talking with one of the strippers. The woman turned to her, words were exchanged, and then both looked in my direction. A moment later, Peyton returned.

"Congrats," she said. "You're hired. You can change in the dressing room. You're on in three sets." She threw a glance at her customer who in turn gave her an *Are you ready?* look and then headed over to her, glancing back at me. "I should be done by the time you're on stage," she said. "I hope you're as good as you look. By the way, love your accent. Where're you from?"

"Perth," I replied as she walked away. "Australia. Lived there growing up!"

Rather than go to the dressing room where the other dancers were, I retreated to the loo and I phased into my Isis attire with modifications. My headdress and makeup were essentially the same as when I was back in time but barefoot and, instead of any costume, I was nude but for the illusion of a living, hissing boa constrictor with gold scales that clung to me and wrapped around me. The music I'd picked was the Prelude to the Cello Suite No. 2 in D minor by Johann Sebastian Bach. Making my body almost weightless, I was able to use the pole better than any trained gymnast and with sensual rather than athletic moves. No matter how I moved, though, the virtual snake covered what modesty dictated that it should. At the very end, as I leaned back against the pole, the snake slithered down to the stage floor revealing all of me. I lifted my arms over my head, and gripped the pole, thrusting out my chest as much as I could while seductively closing my eyes. Opening them again, letting go of the pole, I waved my arms as though magically and caused the snake to dissolve into a million flecks of gold. For the second half of the set, I was completely nude. Rather than trying to emulate all of the other dancers, I offered my rendition of a belly dance in the nude accompanied by rapid beats from a Doumbek.[22] When the music stopped, I went around the stage picking up all the bills that had been left for me, as well as several notes asking for private entertainment in one of the rooms including one from an older woman offering me a permanent place as a sex slave for her and her "love-starved" wife.

Peyton was at the edge of the stage floor as I picked up the last of the bills.

"That was incredible!" she said. "You said you wanted to talk. I have one more set then I'm done for the night. How about we go grab some cocoa after?"

Leaving the club through the back door, we walked to a nearby Ahab's and settled down in a booth. What Starbucks or, rather, Stubbs

---

[22] A Dombek is a large goblet-shaped drum, commonly used in traditional Egyptian music.

was to blended coffee, Ahab's was to chocolate brews, heavily caffeinated, and quite the thing it seemed.

"So," Peyton said with a smile, "where else have you danced before?"

"I haven't," I replied. "Other than one tryout that got cut short, this was my first time on the stage."

She brought her cup of Crème de Menthe cocoa to her lips and drank just a bit, never taking her eyes off of me which unnerved me just a bit. "You're a total contradiction," she said.

"What do you mean?" I asked.

"Well," she replied, setting down the cup, "up on stage, naked as a jaybird, you were calm as a cucumber, but now you seem as nervous as a mouse cornered by a cat. Just because you can tell that my intentions are less than honorable is no reason to suddenly turn shy."

She reached across the table and put her hand on mine.

"Don't you find me attractive?" she said with a look in her eyes that tried to pierce my soul.

"Yes, but," I replied, "you're almost like my sister."

"How so?" she asked.

"Well," I said, a bit unnerved as she interlaced her fingers with mine, "Claire's married to Ophelia."

"I don't know who either of them are, Kitten," she replied, "but I'm hoping you'll come home with me. That *is* why you approached me in the club, isn't it? Surely, you didn't just want my autograph?"

She didn't recognize me and I didn't know how to respond.

"You have no memory of all that went on?" I asked.

She looked at me strangely, as though wanting me to explain.

"Khattaaara?" I went on. "Rendenaaar?"

"If those are other strippers," she replied. "I don't know them— at least not by name."

She bit off a piece of one of the chocolate pretzel sticks she had ordered as she continued to stare at me.

"If they're part of the day shift," she said. "I definitely don't know them. I mostly work nights. That's where all the money is. Daycares—that's what we call the women who come for lunch—pun intended. The women don't tip worth shit." She offered me one of the sticks. "Want one?" she asked. I shook my head. "Your loss," she replied as she took another bite. "I've got to head back. Last bus. The invitation's still on." She stood up. "I've got a thing for pretty, young girls. Used to *be* one myself. Young I mean. Young*er*. I'm still fucking pretty, don't you think?"

"Definitely," I replied.

"You don't talk much, do you?" she said. "Come on. We can make out on the bus. No one uses it this late but me and the driver's eyes are on the road."

I stood up and went with her. It amazed me how some misstep in the past could change people's lives or erase them entirely. That made me deeply concerned about Claire's existence or lack thereof. And Ophelia's. And the kids. I had to know more but I didn't want to spook her, so I walked with her to the bus stop and waited on the bench next to her. Neither of us said a word, but she reached out her hand and took mine once more. After five minutes or so, the bus pulled up with its characteristic squishing sound from its brakes. As we stood up, the door opened with a whoosh.

"After you," she said.

Then followed a cringe-filled moment. As I mounted the first step, she reached under my dress and slid her fingers up my butt crack to my crotch. Thank God I had panties on!

I had hoped that all of this was just an act; that her being a stripper had some underlying purpose; but being up close to her I could tell there was no god-stone in her head. Beyond that, sexually this wasn't her. The Peyton Herron I knew didn't behave that way—at least she never behaved that way toward *me*. She was an entirely different person. And yet, I wondered, how could that be? I had pulled the god-stone from her decaying brain two years from then. Once on the bus in one of the back seats, as I leaned against the window, staring out into the night, wondering what to do next, I felt her hand under my dress again, threading its way up my thigh. I placed my hand on hers through the dress.

"Can we wait till we get to your place?" I asked. "I feel uncomfortable getting it on here."

"The driver's not watching," she replied.

"She has a rearview mirror," I insisted. "Besides, I want things to be special." I stared into her eyes. "Seriously," I said, "you're the most beautiful woman I've ever known and I was hoping…"

"What?" she asked as her eyes glistened with anticipation.

"That it could be for more than one night," I replied.

Her eyebrows raised ever so slightly at the suggestion.

"My mom kicked me out," I lied. "I don't have anywhere else to go."

"I don't see that as a problem," she said, again taking my hand in both of hers, this time bringing it to her lips and kissing it, never for a second taking her eyes off mine.

Her apartment was a couple of blocks from the end of the line, meaning the last stop. It had been a half-hour ride. The club was embedded in a rather seedy part of town. The building itself was embellished with pink *neon* lights—helium actually—running the width of the front, reading *The Pink Lady* and boasting *More Pink Than You Can Imagine*, as well as the outline of a naked woman, again in pink neon. Surrounding it all stood a shabby landscape of dilapidated structures with litter and graffiti and a hungry stray dog rummaging through the trash of an overturned garbage can. The end stop was a block away from Peyton's home—a loft in what was once a factory—a red brick dinosaur from an industrial era where men fought eight hours a day against metal machines long before 3D printers caused them to go extinct. A large freight elevator hoisted us up to the third floor where her apartment sat. The steel doors of the lift opened after the metal conveyance halted with a bump as it stopped. Peyton slid open the metal grate safety door that gave way directly into her flat. Turning a key in the mechanism after it had closed assured that no one could enter unexpectedly or uninvited. The lights she turned on illuminated what I would describe as steampunk décor—a ton of iron and obsolete artifacts coated in black enameled. It was all one large room with an enclosed toilet and clawfoot tub boxed off to one side. The bed like almost everything else was cast iron, accoutered with black and white striped sheets as though it had been placed there by the turnkey of some medieval gaol. Even the fridge was one of those antique types that stood on legs with a levered door and the condenser on top. Yet in sharp contrast to it and the rest of what was there stood a stainless steel microwave, a coffee maker, and a flat panel TV.

"How do you like my digs?" she said, turning to face me.

"Totally sick," I replied as I glanced around. "Hey, mind if I use the loo?" I asked. "I've been desperate to pee since we boarded the bus."

"Over there," she said, indicating the boxed-off section.

"*Merci mon amour*," I replied and then went there and closed myself in.

The inside was not typical for America. I'd seen conveniences like this when Claire and I were in Cairo. The sink was white porcelain, fixed on a pedestal with separate faucets for hot and cold. As for the toilet, in England it would have been considered Victorian; there was a water box mounted two meters up with a long pull chain that had a white porcelain pull handle at the end. I really did have to pee but that wasn't the only reason for my short retreat. After draining my bladder, I caused the violet god-stone to be drawn out from my head and held it respectfully with the fingers of my right hand. Emerging from the loo, there was Peyton, naked in the bed. She was sitting up with her back against the pillow that served as a buffer between her and the iron railing of the headboard. Her knees were straight up and bent, her legs just slightly spread, her hands toying with a purple latex dildo.

"Get naked," she said. "I hope you're as into this as I am."

I took a deep breath and then slid the straps of my dress over my shoulders, letting it drop to the floor. I stepped out of my shoes and climbed into bed with her. She reached out one arm and caressed my cheek.

"Hey," I said with a subtle smile. "You have a smudge just above your eyes."

She withdrew her hand and touched her forehead with it.

"No, here," I said. "Let *me*." I reached out my right hand with the god-stone and placed it against her skin. The gem at once began to spin, became almost microscopic, and then melted into her head. As it did, her body stiffened, her eyes glowed, her skin radiated violet. She looked at her hands, turning her palms toward herself. It was as though a shockwave had gone through her... or an epiphany. She stared at me, cocking her head just a bit.

"Chloë?" she uttered. "Why are you..." then, looking down on herself, said "Why are we in bed together naked? And where *is* this place?"

"Long story," I replied, getting out of bed. "If you don't mind, I'll tell you after I get dressed." I glanced in her direction. "And you might want to do the same."

CHAPTER XXIII

Chloë
*(The One Who Vanished Alone
then Met Herself)*

*Earth Year: 2033
Alternate Reality I*

Cleopatra stared, first at *me*, then at the other *version* of me who lay in a heap on the floor, and then back again at me. I wasn't quite sure what was going on but my eyes met with hers ever so briefly and then stared down at the collapsed figure on the floor. I could have asked for Cleo's help lifting her, but I thought it easier to just phase her onto the bed. Thus, after squatting down, I reached out and touched the unconscious form. As I did so, my other self vanished and then instantly reappeared on the bed on her back. I then stood over her and used the x-ray power I had learned from Jordan in order to look inside her. Cleopatra watched as the clothes, skin, and muscle of my double vanished layer by layer. Everything seemed fine. Her heart was beating, her lungs expanding then contracting, and, to my great relief, there was no god-stone in her head. Cleopatra took a step back.

"Great Isis," she proclaimed, "of all the scrolls I have read, there was no mention that thou possessed a *ka* in human form."

"She is not my *ka*," I replied as I retreated to the bathroom. I searched the cabinet beneath the sink, phased to the kitchen for a bottle of ammonia, dampened a cloth with it, and then phased back to wave it under the other Chloë's nose. When she stirred a bit I slapped her across the face a couple of times. She opened her eyes, coughed, and just stared at me in terror.

"Don't be afraid," I told her. "I know you're scared. I would be, too. I'm the same as you, just from another reality. In mine, I have

145

superpowers." I turned into Quantum Isis to show her but, apparently, that was too much for her in her emotional state. I glanced at Cleopatra. "She fainted again," I said.

More of the ammonia snapped her out of it for a second time.

"Hey," I said. "Please don't pass out on me again. Just let me explain."

She didn't move. She just laid there wide-eyed as I told her all the impossible things that I wondered if I would believe if I were in her situation.

"I didn't ask for any of this," I said. "And I most certainly didn't expect to find another version of me when I finally made it back, but here you are."

"Here you are, too," she replied.

"Kind of like identical twins," I said, "only the egg didn't have to split," I said.

That got half a laugh from her. I'd at least broken the ice and she was taking it better than I would have and so differently from the antimatter version of me who presumed to accept it without question. This Chloë seemed more like me, like how I was before all the shit hit the fan.

"And this isn't Peyton," I told her. "It's Cleopatra—the Cleopatra, who, by the way, doesn't understand a word of English."

She pulled herself up a bit in the bed and stared at Cleo. "You *are* joking, aren't you," she said.

I turned to Cleo. "Say something to her," I said in ancient Greek.

"Είναι τιμή μου να γνωρίσω αυτήν που δεν είναι η Θεά μου,"[23] she said to the other Chloë.

O.C. stared hard at her. "It's all Greek to me," she said, not realizing. "You' swear she's not Peyton and that this isn't all some sort of a joke? I mean, Peyton Herron's been damaged goods ever since she tried to kill herself."

---

[23] "I am honored to meet she who is not my Goddess."

146

"It is Greek," I said, "ancient, actually—not that there's much difference. And she looks like her because Peyton is Cleo's reincarnation."

"I know I'm dreaming," O.C. replied. "In a little while, I'll wake up and this will all make sense."

Meanwhile, Cleopatra just stood there staring at the girl.

"Please sit down," I said to Cleopatra. "Μας κάνεις και τους δύο να νιώθουμε άβολα να στεκόμαστε εκεί σαν να έχεις παγώσει στον χρόνο[24]."

The problem wasn't with her but with me. My bad. I only realized it because O.C. wasn't moving as well. I took a deep breath with the realization that, unlike Peyton, I didn't have the same control of my powers. I focused my will and restarted time again.

"Anyway," I said, "if you're cool with it, we need a place to stay for a while and I need to teach her English. —and help her learn how to use her powers."

"Just one thing, though," she replied. "How am I supposed to explain the two of you to my parents."

"We'll try and keep a low profile," I said. "I can become invisible. It's one of *my* powers."

"What about Erin, though?" she asked. "She spends an awful lot of time here."

"Girlfriend girlfriend?" I asked.

"God, no!" she replied. "Erin and I are best friends. But I *have* to tell her."

"How trustworthy is she?" I asked. "I don't want this getting out."

"It won't," she said. "But wait!. Were you two involved in your reality or whatever it was?"

"In the original reality, we were just best friends. In the rewrite, we had sex a couple of times," I told her. "Once with Cameron and

---

[24] "You're making us both uncomfortable, standing there like you're frozen in time."

once with Brad—more like a marathon. They gave me some drug. It totally messed with my inhibitions."

"Wait!" she replied. "Cameron Barkley? She's totally straight here. Wouldn't get naked in front of another girl if Coach ordered her into the girls' showers. I think her parents are Amish or Quaker or something. As for Brad Warren, he's a total douchebag who, unfortunately, Erin is head over heels for." O.C. looked at Cleopatra. "What about her?" O.C. asked.

"Just into men," I replied, "and powerful ones." I turned to Cleopatra. "Πρέπει να βρούμε τον Πέιτον," I told her, "αλλά υποθέτω ότι μπορεί να περιμένει. Πρέπει πρώτα να σας αμερικανοποιήσουμε και αυτό θα πάρει λίγο χρόνο." [25]

And it did—take time, I mean. When Peyton's mind was taken over by Khattaaara, Khattaaara was able to connect through the Internet and learn first English and then Russian almost instantly. The problem was, as I soon learned, the Internet didn't exist in this reality. Neither did cell phones or any electronics other than what could be made from vacuum tubes—the same as in the world where Payton had grown up. On the positive side, foreign languages didn't seem to be an obstacle for her, as she was already fluent in nine. As it turned out, she found English easy enough to speak, though difficult to read.

"Whoever invented its writing," she proclaimed after making her way through Huckleberry Finn, "must have been drunk at the time!" It took her only a month to become fluent, partly because of her natural aptitude and partly because of the god-stone in her head. Regardless, she had a bit of an accent that was in its own way charming.

I had kept her hidden in a pocket dimension most of the time— similar to the one the two of us had *landed* in. As the bedroom door was able to be locked, O.C. and I were able to share the one bed without fear of being walked in on though there was the issue of her

---

[25] "We need to find Peyton," I told her, "but I guess that can wait. We need to Americanize you first and that'll take some time."

spooning me at night. She had vehemently proclaimed she had no sapphic inclinations but that turned out to be—how shall I put it— prevarication. She feigned being asleep, though quite a number of times I felt her fingers entering my lady parts—not that I objected as it did produce the expected results—it just seemed a bit weird considering who it was who was fingering me. I never said anything, and whenever she placed mine on her, I reciprocated the act. We never spoke about any of it after the fact. It was just a weirdly erotic nighttime thing.

I did have fun posing as her, though. It made things a bit easier going around the house, just as long as we both weren't seen at the same time. We both looked identical, so her mom and dad were oblivious to my pretending to be her whenever I was around them. Sometimes, she'd be the one to attend school. Other times, I would. It did become complicated—this was before Erin got let in on what was going on—when Erin showed up unexpectedly through the bedroom window while O.C. and I were both asleep and climbed naked into bed with the both of us.

"What the fuck!" she exclaimed assuming that she was being cheated on. Another "What the fuck!" came out as she switched on the lamp on the nightstand. It took a bit of explaining and a demonstration of my quantum powers, but she eventually accepted things and was cool about keeping things secret afterward.

When emotions had settled down and Erin was convinced, I started to excuse myself, not wanting to be a third wheel, and said I would phase off to where Cleopatra was. Cameron grabbed my wrist to stop me.

"Like hell, you will," she said and then turned to O.C.. "You don't mind, do you?" she asked. "I mean, she's just another version of you."

"Just?" I exclaimed.

"*I'm* in," O.C. proclaimed.

I shrugged and then all of us got back into bed. Needless to say but not to be repeated in mixed company, it was a truly memorable night.

CHAPTER XXIV

Peyton

Earth Year: 2033
Alternate Reality I

It took two weeks of constant nurturing to bring the frail version of me somewhat back to health. From having been the richest woman on the planet, I became both caretaker and housemaid, but there was nothing less that I could do. This version of Peyton Herron was still a part of me and a sad reflection of what might have happened had Dhraaal not intervened.

It was just two days after I had phased Katherine Herron to the county morgue that the doorbell rang, followed by a heavy knocking. One of me, who had been making lunch, answered the door. A well-dressed man and woman stood on the other side.

"May I help you?" I asked.

"We're here for Peyton Herron," the woman said.

"*I'm* Peyton Herron," I replied.

"Peyton *Elise* Herron," the woman clarified.

"Yes," I said. "Who are *you*?"

"I'm Mrs. Martin," the woman said. "I'm with the Los Angeles Department of Public Social Services."

"And I'm Sgt. Det. Ryan," the man said, "Central Homicide Division."

The woman opened the manilla folder she was holding and then showed it to the cop. He stared at *it*, up at *me*, and then down at *it* again.

"Would it be all right if we came in," the detective sergeant asked.

"I suppose," I said with a bit of reluctance.

The two of them entered—Mrs. Martin first, the officer shutting the door behind him.

"Is your mother around?" Ryan asked, glancing around the room.

"No," I replied. "she went to visit a sick friend."

"You wouldn't by any chance happen to have a name or phone number, would you?" he asked, pen and notepad in hand.

"Martha Eldridge or Ellsbert—something like that," I replied, "and, sorry, no number."

"Our reports indicate," Mrs. Martin said, "that you're incapable of taking care of yourself."

"I was ill," I said, "but I've recovered."

"I'm afraid we have some bad news for you," Ryan said, looking at me again. "Two days ago, your mother's dead body mysteriously showed up on a table in the medical examiner's office."

"Oh, my God!" I said, feigning shock. I took a step back, forcing tears from my eyes. I caused myself to tremble. "No!" I said. "There must be some mistake!"

"Perhaps you'd like to sit down," Mrs. Martin said.

I glanced at the sofa that was just behind me and sank into it. Mrs. Martin took the overstuffed chair beside it and sat facing me. Ryan continued to stand. I glanced from one to the other through a veil of crocodile tears. Beyond all else, the body in question wasn't that of my mother who had been uncreated by events that had altered the reality she had been a part of.

"When was the last time you saw your mother?" Ryan asked.

"Two days ago," I said wiping away tears. "Early morning. That's when she left."

"Has she phoned you since then?" Ryan asked.

"No," I replied. "I don't know if there's a phone where she went. She said her friend lives up near Big Bear."

"Her car is still parked in the garage," Ryan went on. "And surveillance footage shows you inside the county morgue next to your mother's body the day after you claim your mother left to visit her friend. I'm afraid I'm going to have to ask you to come with us. If you'd please stand up and place your hands behind your back…"

It was on hearing those words that I froze time, went back two days, and phased the car with Peyton's mother's body in the driver's seat close to the emergency entrance of Cedars Sinai Hospital, positioned so that it blasted the horn. I then returned to when the bell rang, followed by the knocking at the door. A uniformed police officer and a woman stood on the other side.

"May I help you?" I asked.

"We're here for Peyton Herron," the woman said.

"*I'm* Peyton Herron," I replied.

"Peyton Elise Herron?" the woman clarified.

"Yes," I said. "Who are you?"

"I'm Mrs. Martin," the woman replied. "I'm with the Los Angeles Department of Public Social Services."

"And I'm Officer Sieczkowski," the man said, "Santa Monica P.D."

The woman opened the manilla folder she was holding, and then showed it to the cop. He stared at it, then up at me, then down at it again.

"I'm very sorry to tell you we have some bad news," the woman said as the cop looked back up at me again. "Two days ago, your mother's body was found in her car near the emergency entrance to Cedar's Sinai."

"Her body?" I replied, once more appearing shocked.

"I'm very sorry," the cop went on, "but it appears as though your mother was trying to get to the hospital when she passed away."

"Oh, my God!" I said, trembling, taking a step back, and streaming tears. "No!" I said. "There must be a mistake!"

"Perhaps you'd like to sit," Mrs. Martin said.

I went to the sofa and collapsed into it as the two of them stepped inside. Mrs. Martin sat down next to me and faced me. The cop took the overstuffed chair next to us and sat facing us.

"She told me," I wept, "that… she was going… to visit with her friend, Emma, for a couple of weeks. Emma has a cabin near Big

Bear, but there's no phone. I assumed that she made it there and that everything was all right. She was supposed to be back tonight." I paused and then asked, "How did she die?"

"The autopsy concluded it was from a heart attack," Mrs. Martin said. "Miss Herron," she went on, "I hate to have to bring this up at this time, but our records indicate that for the past eighteen years, you've been needing care as a result of asphyxia from a suicide attempt when you were fourteen." She stared hard at me. "You seem... recovered."

"Things change," I said. "People heal. Trust me, it was a long road to get to where I am."

"I'm glad to hear that," she replied. "One of the reasons we showed up was out of concern for your wellbeing."

"Thank you," I said, "but as you can see, I'm fine."

The two of them stood up. A moment later, I did as well and faced them. "When can I see my mother?" I asked.

"Anytime during business hours," the cop replied. He took a business card from his pocket, wrote on the back of it, and then handed it to me. "Here's the address. You can discuss any arrangements with them."

"Thank you," I said, my cheeks still wet from tears.

Mrs. Martin reached into her handbag, took out another card, and offered it to me. I took it, glanced down at it, and then looked up at her.

"It's for a grief center," she told me, "for those suffering the loss of a loved one. It's called Elysium. You can call them anytime. They offer phone support and meetings where you can talk among others who've lost those they've cared about, and share your grief."

"Thank you," I said, wiping away more tears.

I escorted them to the door and then closed it, watching them get into the car they had come in and drive away.

I met my other self in the hallway upstairs outside Peyton's bedroom where we merged back into one and then returned downstairs to the kitchen. The hot lunch I had prepared was cold. I phased back in time to just after I had left to answer the door. I could hear the first, and then the second version of events as time reset as the pottage I had been cooking still needed to be stirred as it warmed. Once done, I phased up to the bedroom door with the meal and some tea on a bed tray. This reality's Peyton looked so helpless and frail. She stared at me with vacant eyes as I entered. I placed the tray down on the dresser, went over and helped her up to a sitting position, brought the tray over, laid it over her lap, and sat down on the bed facing her.

"Come on, Sweetheart," I told her. "You need to get up your strength."

One by one, I brought spoonful after spoonful of the soup to her lips until it was all gone. I tried to get her to drink the tea but she shook her head.

"I don't want any," she said. "Tea rhymes with Phee and there is no Phee anymore, is there?"

"I don't know," I replied. Then I stopped time and scoured the house for evidence of Phee's existence. Peyton's room had only one bed and all of the photos, even of her as a child, were just of her. Then I had a thought. I remembered where my mother had always kept important papers—in her top dresser drawer. In it, under her lingerie was a manilla envelope, and among the various documents in it was Peyton's birth certificate, revealing that she was a twin but that her sibling, a girl, had died just shortly after birth. Another paper, a death certificate, revealed that the infant had been named Ophelia. How many dominos fell in the wrong direction, I wondered, when I had touched just one. Resuming my position on the bed, I caused time to restart.

"What do you remember about her?" I asked.

"I used to tell Mama all sorts of thing but she never believed me and she said that she was just my imaginary friend and I would get mad and pound my fists on the table and say, 'I am Khattaaara and I am the ruler of Rendenaaar!' but she would tell me there is no place called Rendenaaar and I would laugh and make fun of the way she pronounced it but I knew that there was and then I became Quantum Girl and then I died because of Theresaurus at school and I wanted to die and I tried I really did and put a rope around my neck and it hurt so bad but the pipe that I put the rope over broke and then I woke up in the hospital but things were different because I couldn't think clear anymore and my head hurt so much all the time and I want to die all over again but Mama said I mustn't and Papa he died in a car crash because after things happened to me he started to drink alcohol and he lost his job and he loved me but I disappointed him I think and so he died and now it's only Mama and me but I haven't seen Mama in a while and I was so hungry and I waited and waited but she never came maybe because she's disappointed in me too and then you came and you look so much like me but guardian angels are supposed to aren't they?"

"Peyton," I said and she looked at me. "I'm going to help you get better no matter how long it takes."

The fact of the matter was that I wasn't sure what to do. She had no one other than me to take care of her in this reality. Both parents dead, no sister, she'd wind up institutionalized for the rest of her life—the Quantum Girl who never was. I couldn't help feeling sorry for her, or perhaps I saw in her a reflection of what might have been me. I lay in bed with her at night. I held her when she trembled. I literally felt her bones through her skin. I dreamt that same night that I was her but trapped in a concentration camp with numbers and symbols indelibly inked onto my arm, wearing vertically striped clothes like pajamas symbolic of death. One of the guards came and got me and brought me to the commandant. I was ordered to undress, which I did, but it was now my skin that was striped. My body was as thin and frail as Peyton's. The music that played was *Nocturne 2* by Chopin, slow and laconic at first but then quickly turning into his dizzying *Fantaisie*. I danced faster and faster becoming more and more exhausted as the Nazis around me turned into skeletons in their uniforms and then everything became a blur. The music stopped and the skeletons fell into piles of bones that turned into sand with me in the middle of it all, first as Cleopatra, standing in the desert, and then as Quantum Girl in outer space as the universe around me blew up.

I woke in a cold sweat. Peyton lay beside me wide awake, staring at me. No lights were on but the room glowed with a violent iridescence that came from me, for in my sleep, from my nightmare, I had become my quantum self. This was her nightmare, too. Somehow, her death experience had connected her to whom she might have been, and from my unconscious transformation had come one of the many phantoms in her head so that she retreated into herself even more.

She became more of a ghost than a real human being after that. I had to move her like a puppet, phase food into her stomach, bathe, and dress her, unsure how to undo the damage I had unintentionally caused. Weeks passed. Her body became stronger but not her mind. Most of the time she was catatonic. It was on the forty-eighth night when a figure suddenly phased into the kitchen as I stood fixing dinner.

"Hello, sister," she said in a voice that resembled mine but with an accent I couldn't place. But it was not my sister—not Phee. It was another version of me.

"So, you're the famous Peyton Herron," she went on. She cocked her head a bit as she sized me up. "You don't appear to be mentally challenged."

"I'm not," I said.

"Then there must be three of us," she replied.

"And which one are you?" I demanded to know.

She smiled a subtle smile and said, "You may call me Cleopatra."

CHAPTER XXV

Peyton

The Next Universe
Planet Erebus: Year 1
Alternate Reality II

Life takes shape based on the conditions it finds itself in, each different from the next, unique unto itself, and beautiful in its reflection. Erebus had its own lifeforms thousands upon thousands of years before we arrived, upright on two legs but looking more like amphibians than human beings, and it was they who had built the cities that we sheltered in.

"But if that's the case," Phee asked me as we stood outside, breathing in the night sky, "why doesn't our new Chloë look like *them*?"

"I suppose they didn't anticipate our arrival," I said with a smile. "It might have, though, if they'd had four arms and four legs."

"I don't even want to imagine," she replied and then asked, "Have you heard anything from your other self?"

I just shook my head. "Nothing," I replied. "Not a word. Not a thought."

"Aren't you two still connected through the quantum fabric?" she asked.

"Yes and no," I replied. "I can sense her out there somewhere, but that's as far as it goes."

Phee stared at me. "What if she succeeds?" she asked.

"What do you mean?" I replied.

"Well," she said, "if she manages to prevent our universe from collapsing, then this one won't exist and what will happen to us? I don't have a quantum brain like you do, but I would think that if the universe we're in suddenly vanishes, then we'll go with it."

"I would never let that happen," I assured her. "Not the me here or there back in the past."

Phee stared up at the night sky. "They're all so different," she said. "The constellations are all gone—even the North Star. I miss the Earth. I miss the noise and the people." She looked at me again. "You always loved astronomy. Do you remember when we turned fifteen I gave you that meteorite?"

"Do you mean this one?" I asked, revealing it in my hand.

Phee smiled. "Of all the things you could have brought with you, you brought *that*."

"I told you when you gave it to me," I said, "it was the best present ever. How could I leave it behind?"

"But as Quantum Girl you could have your pick from millions everywhere."

"I suppose," I said, "but this one came from *you*."

CHAPTER XXVI

Peyton
(resurrected)

Earth Year: 2033
Alternate Reality III

The last thing I remembered clearly was realizing that the universe was about to end and that I needed to do something about it. The next instant I was naked in bed and there was Chloë, also naked— Chloë, who is six years younger than me and sort of like my sister-in-law once removed and, according to her, I had wanted to have sex with *her* of all people! I had no recollection of any of it or any other life. Whatever memories were in this body were lost to me or buried so deeply I couldn't find them. It seemed unfair to the one whose life I'd just usurped but I had no control of what had taken place. The last thing I remembered was taking Jordan to the park. A lump stuck in my throat. Where was Jordan in this new timeline? Or Phee? Or Claire? Chloë didn't know either.

"I'm sorry about before," I told her. We had both gotten dressed and sat on the sofa watching *Starport* and eating the Chinese food we'd ordered.

"Don't worry about it," she replied, cracking open her fortune cookie and reading what some Chinese cookie company randomly inferred was her future.

"What does it say?" I asked,

"The end of one journey marks the start of the next," she read aloud. "Someone must have a camera following me around." She looked at me. "What does yours say?" she asked.

I opened mine, pulled out the narrow paper strip, and read, "Let others see what is inside you."

"Well," Chloë said, "the god of fortune cookies appears, it would seem, to have our lives down pat. So," she went on, "what are we going to do?"

"About?" I asked.

"Putting things back the way they were," she replied. "You said you don't remember giving me the god-stone, so I'm assuming it was either future you or another version. Either way, I must have stepped on some pretty large butterflies in the past to mess things up this much."

"Let's get some sleep first," I suggested, "before we wrack our brains too hard." I stood up. "I hope you don't mind sharing, I promise to keep on my side."

"Oh, my God!" she said. "You mean we're *not* going to have sex?"

I stared at her aghast.

"I'm just messing with you," she went on with a smile. "I mean, you're like my older stepsister!"

"I've seen films about that," I said.

"Ewww!" she replied.

"Come on," I said. "Let's go raid the closet and see what my alter ego *has* in there."

It was embarrassing, actually—a lot of stripper clothes, bondage gear, handcuffs, and even a mechanical fucking machine. Chloë ran her fingers over the pink dildo that was meant to go back and forth when the device was turned on.

"Really?" she said smiling.

"I plead total ignorance to all of this," I said, "though *that* one does look as though it could be *interesting*."

We both laughed, found some nightwear, and, after our toiletries were attended to, went nodding off to slumberland.

CHAPTER XXVII

Peyton
(the stripper)

Earth Year: 2033
Alternate Reality III

When I awoke it was still dark in the room, but that was because of the blackout drapes. I guessed it was maybe ten or eleven, but my iPhone said 3:10 p.m. The little princess was still fast asleep. The problem was, I didn't remember *going* to sleep, though I did remember her getting in bed with me, and fuck if I could figure out how I wound up in a nightgown. But, *Whatever*, I thought to myself.

"Hey," I said to my dark-haired cumquat. "Wakey, wakey! We have to get down to the club. Our shift starts at four and we need to catch the bus."

She just moaned, probably half-remembering all the sex that we'd had, I thought to myself, though it was me who couldn't remember it.

"Coraline!" I said, trying to shake her from her sleep. "We need to get dressed and go! The bus comes in fourteen minutes!"

She squinted her eyes as I pulled back the drapes and let the sunlight glare in. Then she yawned and sat up in bed.

"What time is it?" she yawned. "And who's Coraline? I need to take a shower."

"No time!" I insisted. "Just sponge the pits and use some mouthwash from the medicine chest above the sink!"

"Okey-Dokey," she said, stretching as she rose from the bed, her tits crying out for attention there wasn't time for just them—sadly. "By the way," she called out from the bathroom, "do you have anything I can borrow to wear? My clothes are kind of *scented*. I left my entire wardrobe in the other reality. I'd phase on an outfit but my head is still reeling from the wine. I will never drink again!"

I went to the closet and got something for each of us to wear. My Quantum Girl costume was in my work locker. "Hey, Isis!" I shouted. "Do you have your stuff with you?"

"I left it at the club!" she shouted back.

"Sure hope you fed the snake," I said to myself as I laid out fresh clothes for her.

She exited the bathroom brushing her hair. "Why the rush to get back there?" she asked.

"Because we *work* there?" I answered.

She stopped in her tracks and just stared at me. "Peyton?" she said.

"Yes?" I replied.

"We're going back to strip again?" she went on.

"That *is* what strippers *do* in a strip club," I said.

"Shit!" she said. God knows why.

On the bus ride, she started asking me some fuck ass weird questions like, "Don't you remember anything about being Quantum Girl"

"Of course, I do," I told her. "It's my main act. The women like that shit and that's why you, Little Miss Isis, are going to be such a hit. By the way, how did you manage all that stuff with the snake?"

"The same way you get to Carnegie Hall," she replied.

"Huh?" I said back, but she just smiled.

CHAPTER XXVIII

Peyton
(resurrected)

Earth Year: 2033
Alternate Reality III

I was half-naked in the middle of some strip club. I wondered how it was that I'd gotten there, let alone center stage, upside-down hugging a stripper pole with my legs. I could feel a cowl over my face, but it wasn't the same as the one I was used to. This was actual cloth. The rest of my outfit was also similar to my Quantum Girl costume with the exception that it was cloth as well, and, instead of bikini bottoms, I was wearing a cutout-front thong. I stopped time, righted myself, and then divided into two of me—a, to look at myself, and b, to figure out what was going on. There were only women there, which I thought a bit odd. Chloë had told me about *the club*, so that was no shocker to me, as I'd been a stripper on Earth II, but where, I wondered, were all the men? She had failed, though, to mention anything about *that*. My initial thought at the time was that this might have just been a lesbian hangout. Pulling myself back together, I went in back to the dressing room, where I found Chloë dressed as an erotic ancient Egyptian, holding a golden boa constrictor just below its head, the two of them engaged in a staring contest.

"How exactly did I get here?" I asked after I unfroze her.

"You reverted when you woke up," she replied. "I wasn't sure how to handle things other than play along. I couldn't very well just blurt out how we both have quantum powers. The other version of you is definitely not altruistic and I did *not* want to risk her becoming another Dark God. Isn't there anything you can do to stop her from coming out again?"

I just shrugged and shook my head.

"Well," she went on, "just tell Maise you've come down with something or that your head is splitting, but you're going to need to finish your set."

"Maise?" I repeated.

"Over there," she replied with a motion of her head, "talking to the D.J. She does that a lot. I'm assuming you don't want to go into one of the back rooms."

"Meaning?" I asked.

"Meaning," she repeated, "it's not just stripping that goes on here. This place is a dive, literally. You—your other persona—told me. The women bid to have sex with us. High bid wins. Thank God, at least, this club is exclusive—you need to be a minimum 8 out of 10 for your age to make it through the door. Small consideration, but at least it keeps out the ones you wouldn't want to be with at all."

"What about you?" I asked her. "Getting hired, I mean."

"No probs," she answered, "I was won by Daisy McKenzie—bid five thousand on me and I get to keep half."

"You don't mind?" I asked with more than a hint of astonishment.

"I didn't used to be," she replied, "but it's a whole new world and I figure I may as well get used to it if we can't change it back."

"You've always had an open mind," I said.

"Legs now, too, I guess," she said. "Anyway, go climb back up your pole, restart the universe, and play to the salivating crowd."

"And you get back to where I unfroze you," I replied as I went back to the stage.

There are two dances to each set at a strip club. I know because as I mentioned, I had been a stripper in the rewritten timeline on Earth II. The first is in costume, the second, totally nude, or at least winds up that way. So, not only was I familiar with the pole but an expert at it and I knew how to work what Nature gave me. The ambiance of the club, though, was rather strange for me, never having played to an all-female, sex-starved crowd. For my second dance, I ditched the cloth outfit and phased on a quantum one. Little by little, I caused it to fade away, shooting off galaxies and stars until there was nothing left but the cowl which I didn't take off until the very end. I raked in nearly a hundred dollars in tips, took my bows, and then retreated to the dressing room.

"Seen Maise?" I asked the girl nearest where I chose to sit down. She shook her head and then went back to powdering her nose. "Anyone?" I asked, looking around.

"Anyone what?" said a voice from behind me, rough from years of smoke.

I turned around. The forty-something woman stared down at me, pulling the half-spent cigarette from her lips. "You were off your game tonight," she said. "They're not looking to watch Gypsy Rose Lee."

"Sorry," I replied. "I feel like my head's about to explode. Is it okay if I wrap up for the night?"

Maise shrugged. "Yeah, sure," she said. "Anyway, that girl you brought has everyone's attention with that snake act of hers. Where'd you find her?"

"She's my cousin," I replied.

"Well," she said, "I owe you one for that. And I don't want you getting sick. Go rest up. Take a couple of nights off."

"Thanks," I replied. "I'll wait till she's through. She's staying with me."

"I'd like to see the two of you work the stage together when you're back," she went on. "Quantum Girl and Isis. It'll play good in the ads."

It was nearly an hour before she was done, her hair tangled, her body scented with musk.

"I definitely need to shower," she said.

"How was it?" I asked.

"Pleasurable," she replied, "but still not sure if it's something I want to get used to. Can we get out of here?"

"I've just been waiting on *you*," I said.

We didn't take the bus back. We just phased straight into her flat.

"How do we straighten all this out?" she asked me.

"I don't know," I replied.

"How did you do it before?" came the next question out of her mouth.

"That was different," I replied. "I pulled all of the dimensions together, but I didn't undo any of the timelines."

"You're Quantum Girl," she said. "If anyone can do it, you can."

"Except one part of me is in another universe," I said, "and the other part of me here and now is slipping from one reality to another."

I found the décor of my apartment *interesting*—not my taste, but neither was it garish in any way. I did wonder why it was that I used a bus rather than a car to get to work until, rummaging through some papers in a desk drawer, I found court documents concerning a DUI that I'd gotten six months ago. I was also curious if there was a car that I owned in the garage or somewhere—not something I needed as Quantum Girl, but the other thread of me didn't have superpowers and, obviously, if she was pulled over for drunk driving, she must have had a car, at least at *that* time. The problem was that I couldn't very well question myself and my recollection of my existence as her was nonexistent.

After ordering a pizza—the fridge was barren— Chloë and I settled down to watch The Incredible Shrinking Man from the late 1950s on television. Chloë made a joke about male shrinkage which might have been funny, I pointed out, had not the entire male population been eradicated.

"It was just a joke," she said, looking at me like she had said something to offend me.

"I know," I said. "We'll get them all back."

"When we do," she said, sipping on her drink through a straw, "there might be a few we might want to leave out."

"Such as?" I asked.

"Elliot Page," she replied.

"Why…?" I asked.

"I don't know," she said. "I didn't like him in *Hard Candy*."

"Meaning him when he was a her?" I replied. "And *he's* probably still alive."

"Because…" I asked.

"Because he's a woman!" I snapped back.

"You don't have to be so snippy with me," she said.

"Well," I replied, "if her doctors were so snippy, she'd still *look* like a woman!"

We both laughed but she suddenly blurted out, "Ow!"

"What happened?" I asked.

"The drink went up my nose!" she replied, causing me to laugh so hard that tears came to my eyes.

"Don't laugh," she scolded me. "I could get brain damage."

I just looked at her and sighed.

"I *do* have a brain!" she said defensively.

"I didn't say a word," I replied innocently enough.

"You're not saying a word spoke volumes!" she said. "You're the one who's blonde!"

"Excuse me?" I replied. "I happened to have an IQ well over a thousand!"

"And I have one over a kagillion!" she said.

"There's no such thing!" I protested.

"They just haven't made up a word for how high it is!" she said.

"Or how high the drink went up your nose!" I shot back. "You okay?" I asked her.

"I'll survive," she said. "Don't know if my god-stone will, though."

We both laughed again.

"Let's get some sleep," I suggested. "It's been a long day."

"I *do* love you," she said after the lights were out and we were both in bed.

"I know," I replied. "Love you, too."

168

CHAPTER XXIX

Peyton
(the stripper)

Earth Year: 2033
Alternate Reality III

I woke up in the middle of the night wondering how I wound up in a nightgown. The last thing I remembered was being naked in bed with her. I looked at my cellphone, which said it was Wednesday. *What the hell* I thought to myself, *I've lost an entire day!*

"Hey!" I shouted, but it was like yelling at a corpse. "Hey!"

I shook her. It took that to wake her up and she came awake with a start.

"What?" she said opening her eyes.

"Where the fuck did yesterday go?" I shouted. Maybe shouting wasn't called for but anyone who loses a day of their life is bound to be upset.

"What do you mean?" she answered and then shook her head to shake out whatever sleep was left in her head. "You don't remember?" she asked.

"No!" I said. "Just getting in bed with you—then nothing!"

"Shit!" she said. "You're the other her."

"What the fuck's that supposed to mean?" I said back.

She sat up wearily in bed. "Can I have some coffee first?" she asked. "Then I'll try to explain."

"You didn't drug me or anything?" I said. The situation had caught me off-guard and I didn't know *what* to think.

"No, no…" she answered. "Coffee please. And maybe an aspirin. I'm not a night person. I think I have jet set lag."

She dragged herself out of bed and then went to take a leak while I put my Keurig to work.

"I can't find any aspirin!" she shouted through the wall.

"Bottom shelf in the medicine chest!" I shouted back. "There are some white pills!"

"Are you sure they're aspirin?" She shouted.

"Yes!" I shouted back.

"Why aren't they in the bottle?" she shouted.

"I needed the bottle for a urine specimen!" I shouted back. "Just take a couple then come back out! I want an explanation!"

As she emerged from the bathroom, looking at her, I felt I should have kicked myself for taking her in. I mean she was seriously fuckable but if I'd wound up having been drugged by her it wasn't worth it. *Fuck my sex drive,* I thought to myself. *Self-preservation comes first!*

After she sat down at the table and had a few sips of her caffeine-laced brew she stared at me and then spoke.

"I doubt you'll believe what I'm about to tell you," she said. That was followed by some superhero tale that even Stan Lee wouldn't have believed.

"I'm trusting you," she said. "You were always a good person. You always sacrificed yourself to help others. Please don't let me down. I know you wanted to sleep with me but I feel uncomfortable with that because you were more like an older sister to me and I never thought of you that way."

She told me everything and it was a lot to take in. "I've been through a lot in my life," I told her. "I once tried to hang myself but the damn pipe that I threw the rope over broke from my weight and I fell to the floor, soaked to the skin. I never had an Ophelia. It would have been nice to have had a sister—someone to share things with. Theresa Martinez—she had me jumped afterward and gang-raped while she watched. I wound up getting pregnant. My mother was a *Christian* woman. She wouldn't let me get an abortion. I carried to term, but neither would she let me keep him. I named him James— James Charles Herron after my father. I don't know what they renamed him. It was a closed adoption. 'You can't keep him,' my mother kept saying. 'You just turned fifteen. You have your whole life ahead of you.' Yeah, some life. I take my clothes off for a living and then fuck whatever woman's got the most cash." I looked up at her. "You said I have powers. Like what? And you don't have to worry about me misusing them. I figure I've got to make my life count for something if just for the sake of James. It's kind of strange, though."

"What is?" she asked.

"All that you said," I replied. "I had a dream just before I woke up. I was in my costume but it was different. It was the shit. Stars and galaxies moving all over it. But then there was this crazy thing. There were like ten of me."

"That's one of your powers," she said.

"Seriously?" I asked.

"Try ten to the power of ten," she replied.

"No fucking way!" I replied. "Hey," I went on. "I've got a favor to ask, since the other Peyton and I seem to be flipping back and forth. If and when you see her, would you ask her if we can meet? I mean, since she's got a grip on all this quantum stuff, maybe she can split apart so that only one of her turns back into me. I'd kind of like to get to know the me who had a different life than I did."

"Consider it done," she assured me. Beyond all the powers she said I had, it seemed like I also had a new real friend. My life having been so superficial for so long, that meant a lot to me.

CHAPTER XXX

Peyton

Earth Year: 2033
Alternate Reality I

How strange it was to find myself face-to-face with my former incarnation from ancient Egypt. I wondered how it could be that she, whose body I once cohabited, was able to phase through time to meet me. Her appearance was not quite identical to mine, but, still, she looked far more like me than my sister. A Quantum Cleopatra, dressed in her ancient regalia but with a purple quantum glow.

Her voice had the same accent I had heard when my mind had infiltrated her body—when I became an unintentional voyeur to her sexual encounter with the Dictator of Rome. "Isis told me, if anything went wrong, to try and find you," she said.

"Who is Isis?" I asked.

"She whom you knew as Chloë," came the reply. "She's gone."

Chloë! My God! I thought to myself. *Dead! Is that what she meant? After all that had gone on!* I suddenly felt sick. My legs gave out from under me and I started to collapse. Cleopatra caught me and helped me to a chair. Then she took one as well and told me all that she knew about everything that had gone on.

"I thought I was helping her," I wept, "by phasing a god-stone into her head. I thought I was saving her. Instead, I caused her so much pain."

"She lived two years she otherwise wouldn't have," Cleopatra said, trying to console me. "She kept me from ending my own life and brought me to your time. She taught me your language and your customs and how to use the stone. Yes, she's now gone in the flesh but she remains in my heart and in yours. No better friend could I have ever asked for. She became more to me than Caesar and Antony

172

combined—more to me than the throne of Egypt itself. Peyton Herron, hear this. If there is a God and a Heaven as your religion claims, He will find her soul and bring her there."

I wiped away my tears, smiled just a bit, and then stared up at the woman who was in ways the conscience of me. "Thank you for your words," I said. It was then, looking at her that a thought came into my head. "How is it," I said aloud, "that you can stand here so close with the god-stone in your head and there is no attraction between yours and mine? It's not the same as when I met Khattaaara."

"Because," she explained, "my goddess was wise and in her wisdom, she foretold this moment and so used her stone to place a quantum field around mine to prevent that from happening. Ours is the amethyst gem while hers was the ruby, more precious and powerful it seems."

Just then—just as she had spoken her words—there were sounds from upstairs. "Papa!" a voice that was like both of ours screamed. "Papa, cut me down!"

I quickly took Cleopatra's hand and phased us both to Peyton's room. Peyton was in bed having a nightmare. I sat down on the bed and shook her to rouse her from her sleep.

"What in the name of Ra is this?" Cleopatra asked. "Another one of us! How can this be?"

"Another reality," I said. I lifted Peyton up and held her in my arms. "It was just a bad dream," I told her. "Everything's all right now."

Peyton rested her head on my shoulder. "It hurt so bad," she said, crying. "I don't want it to hurt anymore."

"We'll get you some breakfast," I said, gently rubbing her back. "I made toast with raspberry jam and chocolate waffles with maple syrup. You like that, don't you?"

"Yes," she replied, "but I miss Mama— and Papa, too."

"I know," I said, "but we have each other now, don't we?"

"Yes," she said.

"And you know that I love you," I told her, "don't you?"

"Angels *only* love," she replied and then, staring at Cleopatra asked, "Is she an angel, too?"

I glanced back at Cleopatra. "Yes she is," I said.

"She's beautiful," Peyton said.

"That's because she looks like you, too," I replied in the gentlest of tones. I pulled back a bit to look into eyes that were still somewhat sunken in as were her cheeks.

"You *know* you're beautiful, don't you?" I said.

"Mama said I was the most beautiful girl in the whole world," she replied. "I almost had a sister," she went on. "but she died when she was born. I would have liked to have had a sister."

"Well," I said, "you have me."

"And her?" she asked.

"And her," I said.

"What's her name?" Peyton asked.

"Cleopatra," I told her.

"Like the pharaoh?" she asked.

"Uh-huh," I said. "Just like the pharaoh. Now, let's get you sponge-bathed and dressed and get some food in your stomach," and I tickled her there and she laughed.

After breakfast, I took her into the living room and left her to watch a Charlie Chaplin movie called *Modern Times*. There were no terrifying moments in it and, almost immediately, her eyes transfixed on the screen, she began to laugh. Cleopatra and I moved back to the kitchen to talk.

"She is what we would call in Egypt an *akh*, a ghost," she said.

"She suffered cerebral anoxia," I replied. "It's caused when all of the oxygen is cut off from the brain for too long."

"And what is her future?" she asked. "You told me she has no one. If it were me I would prefer death."

"I feel a kinship to her," I replied. "It's like she's the part of me that I've always had to suppress—the part who was terrified of the

174

girl who bullied me in school who filled me with so much fear and dread. I want to heal her mind."

"So, how will you do that?" Cleopatra asked. "Are you a physician?"

"No," I insisted, "but the god-stone in my head might be able to fix her brain."

"How?" she asked, staring at me with curiosity. "Isis did not tell me of such a power."

"There isn't one," I replied. "Only the mother stone has such ability but I never learned how to use it in that way."

"What are your plans, then?" she asked.

"To place my god-stone in her head to heal her," I replied.

"This is the difference between us," Cleopatra said. "I would never trust my power to another."

"And yet you gave *up* your power," I said.

"For the sake of the lives of the three children I had left," she replied. "They would have been killed had I remained."

"All because you loved them," I insisted. "And now I *love her*."

"When are you planning to do it?" she asked.

"Tonight," I said. "after she goes to sleep."

"I think you're a fool, Peyton Herron," she said, "but a romantic one. There's consolation at least in that."

The night fell without incident. I put Peyton to bed and pulled up a chair to sit beside her, holding a book from the library downstairs.

"I like when you read to me," Peyton said. "Mama always read to me at night before I went to sleep." She looked into my eyes. "When you go back to Heaven will you say hello to her?"

"Yes," I said. "Of course," and then I began to read.

They named him Loki after a story they had heard from Katherine's grandmother who had grown up in the land where the sun never sets or never rises depending upon the mood of the year.

"Mama's name is Katherine," Peyton said. "Is the story about her?"

"No, Sweetheart," I said. "It's about someone else with the same name. Would you like me to go on?"

"Yes, please," she replied.

They named him on the spur of a moment when, after a fortnight of tripping out names, Katherine exclaimed the four-letter word like it was a spell, and it was decided upon and accepted and stuck to the soft-furred pup like the scent of cut pine that clings to the Christmas air. Loki was the runt of the litter who had been thrust blindly into a human world—abandoned by she who sired it. But Katherine had taken to it as though it had been her own child, and she nursed it with milk and cradled it in her soft white hands whenever she had a moment to herself.

The pup grew into a strong dog child, a blaze of black fur that held like a mask to its face, and true to its namesake, it was filled with ancient mischief as it explored the world of the cabin in which they lived.

It was Katherine's dog, one could always tell—so protective and loyal, always there at her feet or asleep at her side—so much so that James would often shake his head and say that it was a lover from some past life, reborn into this shiftshape, to which Katherine would only laugh her wondrous laugh, then pat James's head, and say, "There, there," to him, "but I love you, too, for you were my loyal Sir Fourfoot in that same past life."

Her blue eyes glistened past the silk-like sheen of her straight blonde hair that intermixed itself with darker shades of brown. The delicate chin would draw taut, her soft lips would curl themselves into a pout, and then break into a smile. "Sure I did not come all this way to Klondike to pit the likes of two loves against themselves," she would say. Then, so gingerly, she would bring herself up to James, encircle his neck with her arms, and touch her lips to his face to soothe his maleness and kiss her gentleness upon him. James would feel the dog rub up against them both, and could almost hear its tail wagging the air. He loved Katherine. He knew, too, that even Loki must have been enchanted by her spirit, and so he simply locked his arms around her and returned her embrace with all the passion that his heart could hold.

Yet before those last words were even spoken, Peyton was fast asleep. I turned to Cleopatra, who had stood silently in the doorway, and whispered, "It's time."

CHAPTER XXXI

Cleopatra

Earth Year: 2033
Alternate Reality I

The room was immersed in darkness, broken only by the purple glow from Quantum Girl who stood beside the fragile Peyton Herron who lay asleep in her bed. As for myself, I stood nearby watching, wishing to observe but not wanting to interfere. As Quantum Girl, she removed the god-stone from her head and became mortal again, her radiance gone, only to have been replaced by an almost blinding light from the god-stone itself. Gingerly, she placed the now marble-sized crystal against the sleeping Peyton's forehead. As if by magic, it began to spin, faster and faster, until it became no larger than a pinprick and dissolved down through her skin. It was only seconds afterward that she began to change. Her sunken eyes filled out. Her cheeks filled in. Even her breasts swelled back to what they must have been before she had starved herself. In another minute, her skin began to give off the same violet glow as mine did whenever I drew forth the power of the gods. In one more instant, her eyelids burst open revealing glowing orbs of brightness that stared outward without any sign of consciousness. Suddenly, then, a ghostlike image of her rose from her body, half-human with pointed ears and a snakelike tail. The apparition hissed at me and then turned toward the Peyton who had just relinquished her power and, faster than thought, plunged its tail through her heart. Upon seeing this, I hurled a force beam at the one who lay in the bed. The projection dissolved but, as it did, the one who had been Quantum Girl collapsed to the floor in a pool of blood. So severe was the wound that there was no life left in her—no final words. She was just dead. To this day, I can still see the shock in her eyes as the razor-sharp appendage plunged into her chest. *This*, I thought to myself, *was the price of the love she had felt for her.*

It was a strange feeling to stare down at a corpse that looked like me. This was the second time, but back in Egypt that one was but a demon devoid of any soul. This was someone I had met and talked to, who had emotion and compassion and a spirit that defined her as unique. What was it that Isis had told me when we phased to her time and found that everything had changed? "The road to hell is paved with good intentions." My focus suddenly changed as the living Peyton moaned and awakened from whatever daze or trance she had been in. She looked around the room as she sat up, frightened and confused.

"What's going on?" she said. "Who are you? Why do you look like me only," and she paused, "older?"

"What do you mean, 'older?'" I asked. "How old do *you* think you are?"

"Fourteen," she replied. "And why is it so dark in here?"

She reached over to the nightstand to switch on the electric lamp.

"I wouldn't do that," I warned her.

Peyton grimaced. "Why not?" she asked, but before I could reply she had already turned it on. The room, now brightly lit, she looked around it and then saw the body on the floor, saw the carpet covered in blood, put her hands to her mouth, and screamed.

CHAPTER XXXII

Chloëbot

The Next Universe
Planet Erebus: Year 1
Alternate Reality II

I was passing by the rec room when I overheard the girls talking.

"She's not really Auntie Chloë," Jordan said. "She just thinks she is."

"Yes, she is!" said Zhana.

"Is not!" Jordan insisted.

"Is so!" resounded Samira.

"She's just a robot that looks like her," Jordan said.

"Well," Zhana said to Jordan, "I heard our Moms say that Auntie Peyton's not really your mom!"

"Then who is?" Jordan demanded.

"*My* mom!" Zhana shot back. "You were born in another dimension and growed up on Rendar and then when everything changed Auntie Peyton put you in her stomach and you got borned again!"

"Huh-uh!" Jordan said.

"Sami heard it, too!" Zhana said. "Didn't you, Sami?"

"They said you were all growed up," Samira replied, "and you helped save everyone!"

"Then why aren't I grown up now?" Jordan asked.

"I don't know," Zhana answered. "Maybe cause you died."

It was then that Jordan rushed from the room in tears. I caught her and squatted down to face her.

"Hey." I said, "What's wrong?"

"Zhan and Sami said my mom's not really my mom!" she wept.

"I don't know how that can be," I said to her. "I felt you when you were inside her and after she gave birth to you she held you in her arms."

"How can you know that?" Jordan said. "You're just a robot! You weren't even there!" And with that, she broke away from me and ran off sobbing.

I stood up and found Peyton. "You need to find Jordan," I said.

"Why?" she replied. "What's wrong?"

"The other girls told her that she's really Pheeli's daughter," I said, "and that she grew up on Rendenaaar."

I could see the anxiety as it built on Peyton's face.

"I was hoping to wait until she was older to tell her," she replied.

"She's just a little girl," I said, "who thinks she's lost her Mom."

"Do you know where she ran off to?" Peyton asked.

"I think her bedroom," I told her.

I followed Peyton there. All three girls shared the one room. Jordan was face down on her bed sobbing bitterly when we got there. Peyton sat down next to her and gently rubbed her back. "Hey, Lovebug," she said in a caring, quiet voice, "what's wrong?"

"Zhana and Samira said you weren't really my Mommy!" Jordan sobbed.

Peyton rolled her over to face her. Jordan's cheeks were stained with tears. Peyton gently wiped them away.

"Hey, hey, hey," she said softly. "Why do you think I'm not your Mom?"

"That's what they said," Jordan replied, crying.

"You know," Peyton told her, "I carried you for nine months inside me, just like Grandma carried Aunt Ophelia and me."

"You did?" Jordan asked, sniffing and then wiping her cheeks with the back of her hand.

"And I held you in my arms the moment you were born," Peyton said, "and I looked at you so, small and helpless, and I thought to myself that you were the most beautiful baby I'd ever seen. And I loved you so much I wouldn't let anyone touch you and so I took care of you all by myself." She smiled at her and then went on. "Of course, since I'm Quantum Girl I had a lot of help."

"'Cause you can make more of you, huh?" Jordan asked.

"Mmm, hmm," she replied, "though really it was all just me. And you know something else?"

Jordan shook her head.

"I knew," Peyton went on, "from before you were even born, that I was going to love you forever and ever and then some."

"So Zhana and Sami made it all up," she said.

"Well," Peyton answered, "there was another girl named Jordan and she grew up on a planet in a whole other universe—not this one or the one you and I were born in—and her mother was Aunt Ophelia. But because of all that happened, she couldn't be around anymore."

"You mean she died?" Jordan asked.

"In a way," Peyton said, "but not exactly. Do you know the story about Jesus that Grandma told you, and how when he was on the cross he cried out, 'My God, my God, why hath thou forsaken me?' The truth was that in the Old Testament God had done many bad things. Once he even flooded the Earth and killed many people."

"But why would He do that?" Jordan asked.

"Because even though he created men and women, He didn't understand them. And so He turned himself into an egg inside of a young girl named Mary, and the egg became a little boy, and nine months later she gave birth to Him and she named him Joshua, which means salvation."

"But I thought His name was Jesus?" Jordan said.

"That's just what the ancient Greeks called Him," Peyton said. "Anyway, Joshua didn't remember that he was God. He thought he was the Son of God, so there was no one to answer when he cried out in pain."

"But why did He want to be born again?" Jordan asked. "Didn't He like being God?"

"It wasn't that," Peyton said. "It was that He wanted to know what it was like to be human so that He could *understand* people and know their needs. The other Jordan had a hard *time* growing up. She was bullied by all the other children because she was different from them. And so, when I set things right, I thought it would be best for her if she could know what it was like to be born into a world where she would only know happiness and that's why you were born and why you can't remember anything from before."

"Did Joshua ever remember who He really was?" Jordan asked.

"Yes, He did," Peyton replied.

"What about me?" Jordan asked. "Will I ever remember about being the other Jordan?"

"Someday," Peyton replied, "when you're all grown up."

"I'm glad you're my Mommy," Jordan said.

Peyton smiled. "And I'm glad you're my little girl," she replied. "Now, you wipe off the rest of those tears and go back and play with Zhana and Sami."

Jordan rose from the bed. She stared up at me and then, without a second thought, raced from the room. Peyton, who had been standing at the foot of the bed, fell backward onto it with spread arms.

"Oh, my God!" she exclaimed. "The challenges of motherhood!"

"You did good," I told her.

"I can only imagine what started it all," she said, staring up at the ceiling.

"It was what Jordan said about me," I told her.

Peyton lifted her head and looked at me. "What do you mean?" she asked.

"Jordan," I said with a deep sigh, "told Zhana and Samira that I wasn't really me but that I was a robot. Then Zhana told her you weren't really her mom. *But where,* I wondered, *would Jordan have gotten that idea?* And then I began to think back. I don't remember crossing universes with you and the rest, and I really don't have any memories without Claire. I mean, everyone has their own memories

183

from when they're with other people or from when they're alone but I don't have *any* of them. It's as though everything about me came from Claire's head." I stared hard at her. "So, tell me, am I really Chloë or some machine who thinks she is?"

Peyton remained silent. In retrospect, I assume she had no idea what to say. As for me, my breathing became labored. I backed up into one wall.

"What *am* I?" I said. I could feel my face becoming flushed. I was sweating even though the air was tepid in the room.

Peyton sat up and looked at me with the seriousness of someone who doesn't want to hurt someone else.

"I don't know," she said. "But what I do know is that you care about each of us, especially the children. The *real* Chloë may be gone, her life ended with the universe, but however you came to be, you're real to me and I know that Claire is forever grateful that you saved Ophelia's life." She smiled at me and then said, "Come here."

I went over to her and she hugged me. Whatever I was or whatever I wasn't, whatever I knew or whatever I didn't know, at least at that moment in time, I knew that I was loved by *her*.

CHAPTER XXXIII

Peyton
(the one who just woke up)

Earth Year: 2033
Alternate Reality I

Mirrors don't lie. They just don't. I had lost nearly two decades of my life. That was longer than I had been alive before I had tried to end my existence. One thing was certain. I didn't look fourteen anymore. My skin was not as soft. There were crow's feet around my eyes that were just slightly sunken in. It wasn't that I looked old but, staring at my reflection, I just seemed aged. I had been in a virtual coma for all those years. I was retarded—mentally—from a damaged brain. How ironic that that was what Theresa the Terrible used to call me—*Retard!*—even though I got straight A's. But all of those years from then until I awakened were just a blank. The last thing I remember is trying to kill myself—on the night of my birthday no less. I had used a climbing rope to hang myself but it all went wrong. I remember being strangled. It had hurt so much and then I passed out only to be awakened as I was falling, though my thoughts were all muddy by then. It was strange as I thought back to that moment. It was as if it had happened in slow motion—falling, I mean—and then I hit the floor. I realized in retrospect that the water pipe I had thrown the rope over to hang myself had broken from all the struggling I must have done. Being strangled by a rope is not an easy thing. The rope hurts your neck but the worst of it all is that you can't breathe no matter how hard you try and you feel like your lungs are going to explode. The carpet was wet when I landed on it. The noose had loosened a little so I could finally exhale just a bit and take the smallest of breaths. The door to the closet was closed. The water soaked into the carpet and then got in my mouth and nose. I should have gotten up but my body wouldn't respond. I remember crying, and I wondered if all the water was from my tears. I couldn't think straight. In front of me floated the mouse from the desktop computer we'd thrown away after Mom and Dad bought me a laptop.[26] Then I closed my eyes. There were no thoughts after that, but a poem I'd heard somewhere kept repeating in my voice in my head.

I know that God exists because I saw him in a movie;
I know that I exist because I saw myself in a dream;
I know that need exists because I've heard my stomach rumble;
I know that fear exists because I've heard my larynx scream.

And then I passed out. That was the last thing I remembered until I woke up in my bed with a woman standing by the door. I saw her in the purple light that dimly lit the room. She looked so much like me only older. Then the lights came on and there was the body on the floor with blood all around it and I heard myself scream. Then suddenly the woman was sitting on the bed beside me. She didn't walk to the bed. She was just there. I squeezed my eyelids tightly together to try and make sense of it all. *I must have imagined that*, I thought to myself. *My head's unclear. The mind plays tricks sometimes.*

"Who *is* that?" I said trembling. "And why is there a dead woman in my room?"

---

[26] Whether there was a floating mouse or not remains questionable considering the condition of my mind at the time; perhaps it was just a hallucination, brought on by the lack of oxygen, triggering memories of a scene from one of my favorite books as a child—Alice in Wonderland:

'I wish I hadn't cried so much!' said Alice, as she swam about, trying to find her way out. 'I shall be punished for it now, I suppose, by being drowned in my own tears! That will be a queer thing, to be sure! However, everything is queer to–day.

Just then she heard something splashing about in the pool a little way off, and she swam nearer to make out what it was: at first she thought it must be a walrus or hippopotamus, but then she remembered how small she was now, and she soon made out that it was only a mouse that had slipped in like herself.

The other glanced back at the body on the floor and it disappeared.

"Where did it go?" I asked as my breath became labored.

"Is it not enough that she is gone?" she asked.

"I want my Mom and Dad!" I said.

"A lot has happened while you've been asleep," she replied.

"What do you mean?" I asked her.

It was when she said ten years had passed that I felt ill. She took hold of my shoulders and stared into my eyes.

"There are consequences for each action," she said, "like the crocodile that snatches an ibis with hungry jaws but then itself is taken as prey by the lion, its jaws filled, unable to defend itself. You chose to thread your suffering with a rope rather than defend yourself against the girl who attacked you. When she beat you, what did you do?"

"I turned away," I said.

"And what did that accomplish?" she asked. "She beat you again and again until you said, 'I want to die!' You turned the other cheek as your mother no doubt taught you from the god you call Jesus. And now you have lost nearly ten years of years of your life and your parents fill their graves!"

"No!" I wept, "That can't be!"

"Tears," she said in a stern voice, "drip into the earth and then are gone. They do not water the lily. They bring nothing back to life. If a cobra tries to strike you, you strike back and cut off its head. I once thought like you, wanting to end my own life, but my goddess showed me the path that we all must follow. You and I, our souls are intertwined. You are my future and you need to share my strength."

"Who *are* you?" I asked her.

She stood up and faced me, folding her arms. "I am Cleopatra," she told me. "I am Egypt. I am Queen of the Nile."

I started laughing through my tears but then she changed right in front of my eyes. She looked like Cleopatra but her skin turned violet and glowed even in the light. And then she changed back.

187

"The body you saw," she said, "she was my sister as are you."

"That wasn't my mind playing tricks?" I asked. "Where did she go?"

"I scattered her atoms throughout the fabric of time," she said. "Her heart beats no more. No air escapes her lungs. No blood rushes through her veins. She only lives in us."

"Cleopatra," I repeated trying to take it all in. "Didn't you die two thousand years ago?"

"It should be obvious that I did not," she replied.

She stood up and then offered her hand to help me out of bed. I walked to the bathroom, turned on the light switch, and stood before the mirror above the sink. I stared at my reflection. I looked so much older than I had been, my features more mature. This was to be expected, though, if I were no longer fourteen years old. I closed the door to the bedroom and then let my nightgown drop to the floor. Looking down I saw that my legs were more shapely, my breasts more full. My legs had been shaved, but I had more pubic hair than I remembered and there was hair under my arms. In that all of it was blonde it wasn't as obtrusive as it might have been but I needed to take care of what was there. Even at fourteen, I knew proper hygiene. I searched through the medicine chest but came up empty.

"Are there any razor blades?" I called out through the door.

In another instant, Cleopatra was standing there facing me. My heart jumped.

"Oh, my God!" I said. "Don't do that again!" I glanced down at myself, trying to cover myself with my arms. "And I'm naked!" I exclaimed.

She flashed off her clothes. "Now we both are," she said. "So, what? We are exactly the same. What do you need razor blades for? Do you wish to cut your wrists? If that is the case, I can help you."

"I just wanted to shave my body hair," I said.

Cleopatra shook her head to herself. "Hold up your arms," she said. Then her eyes glowed bright purple as she stared at me. When they dimmed, she said, "It is now gone."

I looked down at myself and then under my arms. There wasn't a trace of hair left.

"How did you do that?" I asked.

"I will teach you later," she said. "Now, take your bath or shower, and then get dressed. Trust me, despite the sponging off you were given," and she sniffed the air in my direction, "you still stink." That said, and with a turned-up nose, she vanished from the room.

I filled the tub with the grape-scented bath salts and the bubble bath that were in the cabinet below the sink and then stepped into the warm water. It felt soothing and made me feel almost weightless. The fruited aroma wafted its way into my nostrils and brought me back to the innocent times of my life when my parents and I used to go to the beach and Dad would buy a grape-flavored snow cone for me. I must have been five or six years old. I could still feel the grit of the sand as it scrunched between my toes as I walked alongside him. Mom would be back at the spot we had chosen, spreading out the blanket she had brought along and then taking out the lunch she had prepared and placed in the picnic basket along with one thermos of ice tea for her and Dad and another filled with lemonade for me. Mom always wore a one-piece bathing suit. She jokingly blamed me for ruining her figure and not being able to wear a two-piece, but when it seemed I had taken it to heart and began to cry, Dad told me that it wasn't my fault. It was Ophelia who had died in the womb because her umbilical cord had wrapped around her neck and strangled her (sadly foreshadowing her sister's act—my act—it seemed) and the doctors had to perform an emergency c-section, leaving her with a scar. As for Mom and Dad being dead, I had only the word of the *woman* who claimed to be Cleopatra, which at the time seemed a bit far-fetched, but I had seen it all with my own two eyes—and her. I considered the possibility that I had been given some hallucinogenic drug. That seemed to make more sense. There was no denying, though, that years had passed since I had hanged myself. I must have soaked for an hour.

When I emerged from the bathroom, dressed in a robe that I found hanging on a hook but didn't remember, I saw her standing there, waiting.

"Sorry it took so long," I said. "I just needed time to think."

"There is no need for you to apologize," she replied. "I phased through time, stopping when I saw the door begin to open."

I looked at her, curious. "If you're really Cleopatra," I asked, "how do you have all these powers?"

"From the god-stone in my head," she answered, "the same one as in yours."

"You're telling me," I said in disbelief, "that I can do all of that, too?"

"Once you learn," she replied.

"This is all ridiculous," I insisted. "Either I'm in a coma somewhere or I've been drugged or I'm dead and all of this is Hell."

"I told you," she replied. "We are very much alike. I am the Queen of the Nile and you are the Queen of Denial."

"This is not a joke!" I said back at her. "Okay, if I have some sort of rock in my head…"

"It is called a god-stone," she interrupted.

"Whatever!" I replied. "How did I get it?"

"You got it," she answered, "because the other Peyton—the one you saw dead on the floor—put it there before you killed her."

"What do you mean I killed her?" I said.

"You were unconscious," she replied. "I told her not to do it but she was insistent that it would heal you and it did."

"Why didn't she have one?" I asked.

"The one she gave you was hers," she answered. "She's been taking care of you. She felt it was her responsibility because you didn't have anyone else and you were an alternate reality version of her. She was a fool and I told her as much. But she was also a hero with powers far greater than mine."

"A superhero?" I asked. It all seemed so incredulous.

190

"She was Quantum Girl in her reality," she said. "Now, you're Quantum Girl in yours. Only you need to learn how to use the god-stone in your head."

CHAPTER XXXIV

Chloë

The Non-Superpowered One
Earth Year: 2033
Alternate Reality I

We were one and the same, sort of, and had become best friends. It was amazing. *She* was amazing. She took me back to ancient Egypt where we watched the Sphinx being carved into a lioness from an outcropping of rock, and then, hundreds of years later, to when the head had been re-sculpted—reshaped—to bear the face of Khafre, the Pharaoh of Egypt who later built the Great Pyramid of Giza. We bathed in the Nile. We ate dates and figs. We watched the Great Pyramid being built passing through time so fast that it was like time-lapse photography, until, at last, four Chloës, each dressed as the goddess, Isis, lifted the golden capstone and set it in place. The sky, dark with storm clouds, rain falling down in sheets, as the capstone had barely kissed the pyramid beneath it, a bolt of lightning struck the metal and reflected out, striking three of the four who looked like us. Two fell crashing down to the sand while one vanished entirely. As the fourth phased down to a black girl who stood watching, a second lightning bold struck the capstone and reflected down on her just as she was phasing with the girl. It was as though both her body and the girl's flashed negative, then positive, and then negative again, and then just vanished.

"That was me with Nefra," my Chloë said. "The two on the sand lost their ability to merge back or travel through time. I don't know what happened to the other one."

I grew up in a time when superheroes were a dime a dozen, at least in films. But this was real—kind of freaky at first but I got used to it, having someone who was exactly the same as me but who grew up with a different set of circumstances. My Claire and I never made it to Australia. Claire wound up hooking up with one of her classmates, a girl named Myra Kartinova, a scorchingly hot model who had immigrated from Russia when she was a child. Claire's a lesbian. We all kind of suspected it, even though she played it straight throughout high school. Then one day I caught her and Myra kissing in her bedroom.

"Get out!" Claire yelled at me, though later she came into my room after I'd gone to bed and apologized. I told her it didn't matter one way or another to me just as long as she was happy. It probably disappointed a lot of guys, though, after both of them came out. Mom and Dad still had me to be there to pop out grandkids for them one day. I was still a fucking virgin and if that isn't an oxymoron I don't know what is. It wasn't that I was saving myself or anything. I just hadn't met the right guy yet.

After Egypt and a few other historical places, I suggested traveling to the future. She agreed but when she tried, the furthest she was able to take me was March 12, 2036. After that, it was like there was nothing to go forward to.

"What's wrong?" I asked.

"I don't know," she replied. "But it's as though there's nothing there—like the universe doesn't exist after 10:46 p.m.."

"How can that be?" I asked.

My *doppelgänger* shook her head. "I'll try again," she said. "Be right back, I hope."

It was more than her not being able to go further ahead in time. The night itself was strange. We were at the 3rd Street Promenade mall. Hardly anyone was around. A crescent moon hung near some clouds, but there wasn't a single star even though the sky was clear. I watched as she began to phase forward in time, only there was something wrong, as a green mirror version appeared facing her. It was when the two of them touched that there was a blinding flash of light and then the air opened up and swallowed them both so quickly that, in the end, all that was left of them was the echo of their screams.

But there was more. As it happened, a fragment of something shot out of it and hit me in the head and I passed out. When I woke up. I was floating in total darkness. I couldn't see or hear or feel anything. Whatever it was, wherever I was terrified me. I wanted to be back where I'd been and then, suddenly, a red glow surrounded me and an instant later I was back, watching it happen all over again. The scene repeated and repeated—a hundred times, a thousand, a million—I don't know. I couldn't count. I couldn't change things. The words were the same each time that I spoke them. The end was the same and every time I would awaken in whatever kind of void or hell that it was. I wanted to go back farther in time but I didn't know how until at last, finally, I did.

An eternity later, I found myself in the same place where I'd been but it was day and there were now people all around. A thirty-something woman in a print dress did a second take as I appeared out of nowhere. When things like that happen, people tend to think it's just them, and so, after a second glance, she shook her head to herself and walked on to wherever it was she'd been headed.

There was no doubt as to where I was. The question was when? A newspaper from a magazine rack revealed the answer. I was now nearly a year from where I had been, though still two years ahead of my time. With that in mind, I took a bus home, wondering as it trudged along if I'd encounter another version of me when I got there.

The lawn was uncared for with wild grass and weeds, some that were more than three feet tall. The mailbox overflowed with envelopes and throwaways. There was an Amazon package in front of the door that looked as though it had been through torrents of rain. I used my key to get in.

"Mom?" I called out. "Dad?" but there was no answer.

The house looked as though it hadn't been lived in for years. Everything was still there but there were no signs of life. The kitchen sink was piled with dirty dishes. The fridge had disgusting, rotting food in it, no doubt because the power was off. Even the gas stove didn't work. Mom and Dad's room was a mess from the carpet to the bedsheets, but my room was just as I'd left it. *What had happened?* I wondered. *How did it get like this and where was everyone?*

There were a few sheets of paper on the floor in the hall. I picked one of them up. It was a missing poster with a photo of me on it. "Chloë Anne Salinger, If anyone has any information…" it read. *My God,* I thought to myself, *Mom and Dad and Claire must have been put through Hell!*

I sat down on my bed staring at the flier. From my perspective, I hadn't even been gone a day. I went to try and call Erin or Claire, but the phone line was dead. I shrugged to myself, gathered some clothes into an overnight bag, and set out to walk to a Stubbs about ten blocks away as I didn't want to waste what money I had on another ride. Once there, more than glad to drink something after my long trek, I ordered a frappé and then sat down, my mind a total blank. After a few minutes, I got up and went to the payphone toward the back and dialed up Claire.

"Chloë?" she answered. "Oh, my God! Where have you been? Are you okay?"

"I'm fine," I assured her. "Look, I'm at the Stubbs on Montana. Can you pick me up, please? I was over at the house but it's deserted."

"I'm on my way!" she said and then shouted, "Myra, it's Chloë!" and hung up.

Eighteen minutes later a red Ferrari convertible pulled up in front of the house and I got in. "My, aren't we slumming?" I said as I hoisted my suitcase into the back seat and then got in.

"Myra bought it for me for my birthday, if you must know," she said in a somewhat irritated tone. "Just where have you been all this time?"

"You're not going to believe it," I said as we got into the car. "What happened to the house?"

"You happened to the house," she repeated with more than a hint of anger. "Mom took a fatal overdose worrying about you. Meanwhile, Dad literally drove himself off a cliff. He's now paralyzed from the neck down, eating through a straw." She glanced at me. "We all thought you were dead. But look at you. You don't even show tread marks for all the time you've been gone!"

"That's because I traveled through time," I replied.

Claire slammed on the brakes and glared at me. "Do you think this is funny?" she exclaimed. "Our mother is feeding worms and our father is two steps away from the grave—not that he will ever walk again!"

The car behind us started honking, so Claire drove on. As for me, tears began to well up in my eyes.

"I'm sorry," I said, "but I didn't have any control. The other Chloë took me into the future and then she disappeared and I barely made it back this far!"

"I have no idea what you're talking about," she said in an exasperated tone and then threw a glance in my direction. "Have *you* been using drugs?"

It was as she said that, that I was no longer sitting in the car, but standing in the street ahead of her, flagging her down. Claire glanced at where I'd been and then stared ahead at where I now was and stopped the car, allowing me to get back in again.

"Kindly explain," she said, "how you did that?"

"I'm not sure," I replied, "but probably the same way that I got back in time to here. The other Chloë had powers. All I can think is that when she vanished or got killed or I don't know which, they passed onto me."

"Other Chloë?" Claire repeated. "What on earth are you talking about? What's going on?"

The fact was that I didn't know, although, thinking back at the time, it all seemed to have begun when I felt the whatever-it-was hit me in the head. I hadn't thought about it before but I pulled down the visor and stared in the mirror, lifting up my bangs. There was nothing there—not even the slightest mark.

"What are you looking at?" Claire asked.

"I got hit really hard in the head," I replied.

"When?" she asked.

"About a year from now," I said, pushing the visor back up.

It was at this moment that Claire pulled the car into the underground parking lot of the building where she and Myra owned a condo in a large modern complex.

"I don't know if this is all some practical joke," Claire said, "but I'm not laughing."

Tears came to my eyes. "Do you think I like the fact that Mom is dead or that Dad is permanently crippled? Do you? Well, if that's what you think then you really don't know me!" I got out and slammed the door. "Sorry," I said apologetically as Claire emerged. "I know it's an expensive car. It's just, everything was going along just fine, and then she popped in out of nowhere with Cleopatra of all people and the two of us got to be really good friends, and then suddenly she was gone and I'm two years in the future and everything's changed and not for anything good!"

We walked out of the lot and over to Claire and Myra's townhouse. Myra sprung up from the sofa as we entered. She looked at me holding my overnight bag.

"Hey, Chloë," she said.

"Myra," I replied. "I hope you don't mind the intrusion. There's no water or electricity in the house."

"Don't mention it," came the reply. "You're family."

After lugging my suitcase into the guest room that, fortunately, was on the ground floor, I shut the door, stripped down to my undies, climbed into bed, threw the top sheet over myself, and promptly fell asleep. Despite that the sun was still overhead, both my mind and body were spent.

It was after I'd fallen asleep that my mind seemed to go berserk. I began reliving the other Chloë's life at hyper speed. Image after image and thought after thought raced through my brain until I realized that it wasn't her. It wasn't the Chloë I'd been friends with. It wasn't *her* life that was crashing through my brain. It was the other one—the one I'd only caught a glimpse of before both of them disappeared—the reverse Chloë, the negative one. Those were *her* thoughts. I just had this gut feeling that they weren't the same as *my* Chloë (ridiculous as it was to say), as though there were two universes—one on top of the other—and she was from the other one. There were vast differences. The other Claire was married to a woman named Ophelia. In her universe, all of the males had been eradicated by some sort of manmade plague. I relived the other Chloë's encounters before and after the Great Dysanthropia or GD as it came to be called. I, who had been a virgin, had pummeled into my mind the orgasms of both guy-on-girl and girl-on-girl sex. Erin Masters was my best friend but I never thought of her in that way and yet, suddenly, there was the memory of my having had sex with her and Cameron Barkley and with Brad Warren, the guy Erin was so much in love with. And, suddenly, I who had always been a straight as they come (the word *sparrow* came to mind), understood what Claire saw in Myra and Ophelia and what Myra and Ophelia saw in Claire sexually. I didn't think I would ever be the same after that and I was right. And then there was the matter of the god-stone that had somehow made its way into my head. The name Quantum Girl kept reverberating inside my head, *but what did it mean*? I wondered. The question loomed oppressively in my unconscious mind and still remained when I finally awakened in a cold sweat—that is to say, when the three of me awakened.

It was both shocking and frightening for each of us or each of me… whatever. Communicating at first was impossible as we all spoke at the same time with the exact same words. When one of me gestured to let that one speak, the other two did the same. While this might have been great for synchronized swimming, it was getting on my/our nerves. It was like we were all wired together. Finally, we all screamed. "Stop!" which seemed to have awakened Myra and Claire, who came to the room and froze in their tracks as they saw the three of me.

"Sweet Mother of God!" Myra exclaimed.

"How is this possible?" said Claire.

"I don't know," we all replied in unison. "I told you I got hit in the forehead by something. I think it was what the other me—the one I told you took me time traveling—called a god-stone—some sort of alien crystal that gives you powers." We paused and then went on, "Look, this in-sync thing is driving me to the brink. Could each of you please take one of me into separate rooms to try and break the connection?"

Claire took one of me by the arm, Myra the other and each went off to separate rooms. I, the middle one, left to myself, flopped down on my back, threw my arms out to the sides, and breathed a sigh of relief. The other two felt slightly relieved as well. We all still knew each other's thoughts and could see what each of us saw and heard, but none of us could figure out how our body had been tripled. Claire and Myra both wanted to know what was going on but there was no real explanation other than, "I must have a god-stone in my head."

I had no explanation other than that somehow I now had the powers that the other me had had. It was difficult for me to accept. In *this* thread of existence, the only superheroes were in movies and comic books. There had never been a Quantum Girl or a Quantum Chloë. The word *quantum* was something just used by physicists and at that I didn't even know what it meant.

"Perhaps if you just willed yourself back together it might happen," Myra suggested, but however hard all of me tried, nothing worked. There were now three of me—of us—perhaps forever; we just didn't know.

Our wardrobe represented a bit of a problem that was solved somewhat by us traveling back to the house to retrieve the rest of our clothes. Sleeping arrangements were crowded at best. Myra and

Claire's place was only a one-bedroom with a guestroom that boasted only a full-sized bed. But at least the strings were cut and the three of me, while sharing consciousnesses, were able to act and speak independently. In order to differentiate one from the other, we referred to ourselves as Chlo, Chloë, and Chloë Anne and each did our hair differently. Chlo me took on a ponytail, Chloë me, a straight-haired look, and there were pigtails for the me who was Chloë Anne. All of us, though, still wore bangs.

As time passed, the three of me grew apart emotionally. Perhaps it was the environment or with whom each of me separately interacted, as we were no longer joined at the hip, so to speak. Sometimes one or the other would go out with Claire or Myra. Sometimes one would stub her toe or eat this or that, different from the other two. A lot of guys might fantasize about the three of me naked in bed together having sex with each other. The Chloë Anne me became insistent that we "try it at least once!" justifying it as *only* masturbation since in reality, we were "all the same person!" The other two of me found the idea embarrassing. "Who's going to know?" the Chloë Anne me kept saying. "Besides," she went on, "I keep having flashes of memories that weren't even ours about having sex with Erin and Cameron, and let's just say that my urges are *dampened* by them, literally." The other two of me reluctantly acceded to her incessant demands.

"It's the only way to get her to shut up," the Chlo one of me whispered to the Chloë. "We just need to think of ourselves as an extension of us and not as three separate people."

"Fine," the Chloë me whispered back, "but this is all strictly under protest."

To be honest, it was amazing, basically because we shared our thoughts and knew what we wanted, exactly where, and how to stimulate ourselves. But it was as we orgasmed simultaneously that it happened. We all began to glow red, brilliantly actually, at the precise moment we all came. The physical effect took us out of the moment like a crash of thunder waking someone abruptly from their sleep.

"What the fuck!" my Chloë self exclaimed, echoing the thoughts of my other two selves.

"What's going on?" said the Chloë me as we all sat up in the bed.

"Whatever it is," the me who was Chloë Anne said, "I feel charged. Let's all do it again."

The Chlo me gawked at her with a dropped jaw. "We're all glowing red and all you can think about is sex?" she exclaimed.

"And?" came the reply. "You have to admit it was incredible. We could never do that when we were just one."

"Ugh!" my Chlo self said back to the me who was Chloë Anne. "You and your vag! This is important! Maybe we can learn to control the god-stone that's in our heads and merge back into one."

"And what if I don't want to merge back?" my Chloë Anne self said. "What if I like being *me*? We're becoming different—evolving." She glared at the Chlo me. "You're now the intellectual, trying to figure out what we can do to recombine. And you," this directed at my Chloë self, "always wanting to prove yourself to Claire while turning your head from her lifestyle. Well, it's now *your* lifestyle, too, and don't tell me you didn't fucking enjoy what we just did! I'm out of here!" she exclaimed and then disappeared.

The two remaining ones of me stared at where she'd just been and then at each other. The glow had vanished, the room that was now only lit by the Lava Lamp on the nightstand with its everchanging red blobs rising and falling, separating and recombining, again and again.

"I can't hear her thoughts anymore," the Chlo one of me said.

"Neither can I," said the Chloë me, who stared at my other self. "What are we going to do?"

"I don't know," my Chlo self replied. "but apparently she's figured out how to use the god-stone."

CHAPTER XXXV

Peyton
(the one who just woke up)

Earth Year: 2033
Alternate Reality I

Cleopatra and I were sitting in a booth in a Little Caesar's Pizza restaurant (she thought the cartoon image of a diminutive Julius Caesar was hilarious) when the waitress came with our order—a large thick crust with pineapple, mushrooms, pepperoni, and sausage on one side and just pineapple and mushroom on the other. That last was mine.

"I take it there were no vegans in ancient Egypt," I said munching on a slice from my side.

"Vegans," Cleopatra mused. "Those who do not eat animals or anything that comes from them. But I notice that you eat cheese. Is that not derived from a goat?"

"A cow, actually," I replied. "Strictly speaking, I'm a vegetarian. Vegetarians don't eat animals, but milk and eggs are all right unless the egg has an embryo in it, which is gross."

"We ate many fruits and grains," Cleopatra said, "as well as pigs, sheep, and goats. I myself found lamb particularly tasty."

"I could never eat lamb," I said, "even if I weren't a vegetarian. I mean, it's basically a baby sheep."

"The Hebrew god," she replied, "had no problem killing the firstborn baby Egyptians according to your Bible."

"I'm sure He had a good reason for doing so," I said in no uncertain terms.

"And I," she remarked, "had a good reason for eating lamb. I enjoyed it. And what is this yellow fruit?"

It's called pineapple, I replied. "A lot of people think it's gross on

202

pizza but I like it." I took another bite, and then asked, "So, what about this power I supposedly have?"

"It is the power of the gods," she answered. "Unfortunately, the gods are all dead. But I will teach you just as Isis taught *me*."

"Cool," I replied and then resumed devouring what was left of my half.

We paid the bill with money that had been in the other Peyton's purse. I really felt bad about what had happened. I wished I could have met her. After all, she took care of me and then sacrificed her life so that I could be whole again. I figured that the only way to pay her back was to take up the reins, so to speak, and become the heroine she had been.

My education began the next morning. I had lost eleven years of my life but my Mama had taught me to believe in God and Jesus and maybe this was Their way of making it all up to me. Cleopatra believed in Isis and Osiris but the Third Commandment said, "Thou shalt have no other gods before me," so I guessed it was all right for her to worship them as well, just as long as she put God first. But in that Cleopatra had left her time twenty-five years before Jesus was born, I had taken it upon myself to teach her the Old Testament and the Gospel while she helped me learn how to use my powers—powers during the day, Bible studies at night. That was the deal.

I missed my parents desperately and felt guilty that my attempt at killing myself caused them so much heartache and grief. I was always Daddy's little girl and when I went full zombie, I guess it was just too much for him. The death certificate that I found said that he shot himself in the head. That left the burden on Mama to take care of me until she died—I'm not sure from what, but if it was a heart attack I'm sure that my having been nearly braindead for almost a decade was a big part of it.

The sky the next morning was filled with pouring rain, though Cleopatra inhaled it all—spiritually, I mean. She described it as "wondrous," having come from a land that abutted a desert that was filled with parched sand that had little to offer other than as a cemetery for long-dead pharaohs whose pilgrimage to the afterlife began with their being buried under millions of tons of stone.

As a teenager, the rain was inconvenient. It meant umbrellas and puddles that could soak your socks and ruin your shoes. As a child, though, it was different. It was fun. When I was little and it was hot outside Mama would dress me in my bathing suit and then turn on the sprinklers for me to run through with my imaginary playmate, Ophie whom I named from the book Papa gave me called Ophie the Ostrich; only my imaginary friend wasn't a giant flightless bird but a beautiful girl my same age with golden hair and bright blue eyes. As I got older, though, I would play with her less and less until I forgot about her altogether.

The first thing Cleopatra taught me—or, rather, tried to teach me—was how to phase. I was very bad at it at first. "You have to concentrate!" she would insist, followed by something like, "Great Mother Isis, what have you sent me to?" which I took as her version of an Oh, My God!

Maybe I was still a bit brain-dead because it was all very hard for me. I figured I seriously wondered if I might have been Quantum *Woman* by the time I got all my powers figured out. I said this aloud once. Cleopatra woefully agreed.

"You need to think where you want to be," she said. "The god-stone will do the rest. Look!" she said and then disappeared from where she was and reappeared just behind me. "See?"

I jumped. I thought I was going to have a heart attack. "Don't *do* that!" I said, holding my hand to my chest. "I'm *not* like *you*!"

"You're *exactly* like me," she said. "We are one and the same, just from different times." She looked hard at me and then went on. "I'm going to try and slap you in the face. All you have to do is wish that you were three feet over to your right and it won't happen."

Unfortunately, it did—three times. Each time I closed my eyes and wished that I were a yard to my right and each time I got slapped.

It really hurt and it seemed harder each time. When the fourth slap was about to strike I didn't phase as she put it but everything stopped, even the rain. At first, I was trapped. I tried to move but the falling water acted like a prison. Cleopatra stood frozen, her mouth open, ready to say something to me. I started to panic. Regardless that I was twenty-three, emotionally I was still only fifteen—just—and I was frightened out of my wits. My heart was racing. A flush came over me. The rain wasn't even wet. It was more like plastic. Plus, I was having trouble breathing. I closed my eyes and prayed to Jesus to let me move and, suddenly, I could. I found that I could push away the streaks of rain as though they were beads and I was able to inhale and exhale without the air feeling like sand. I breathed a sigh of relief but there still remained the problem of how to cause time to start again. Up in the sky, a jet airplane hung motionless thousands of feet in the air. A squirrel looked as though it had been taxidermied, posed as though it were about to jump onto a tree. There were no sounds. The air was unnervingly still. And it was cold. *Dear, Jesus,* I thought to myself, *please let me be warm again,* and suddenly I was.

Cleopatra hadn't moved in all this time—*not so much as a blink of her eye. No, wait!* I realized. *Her eyes had been wide open but now they were half closed.* I hadn't caused time to stop entirely, but rather caused it to move incredibly slow. Even so, everything around me was dimmer than it had been before, and the sun, as I looked at it poking through the clouds, was not as bright. *What if I was trapped like this forever?* I wondered. I needed to think. I needed to pray. Fortunately, the back door was open enough for me to squeeze past it. Pushing hard against the air, I went upstairs to my bedroom and lay down. The mattress and pillow felt as if they were carved from stone but I was so upset that, regardless, I quickly fell asleep.

Maybe the god-stone stored memories—I didn't know—but I had the strangest dream. I was poised high over the Earth wearing a dark costume that was patterned in galaxies and stars and shown with a violet hue. Behind me hung a cape of the same sort of material and to my left hung the moon. All around me in every direction stars shown with magnificent brilliance and when I focused really hard I could make out nebulas and galaxies that must have been billions of lightyears away. How wonderful Jupiter and Saturn appeared with their own moons and rings. And then it happened. The earth and moon began to shrink. The stars grew dimmer and dimmer and then everything around me vanished into itself until just seconds later when the explosions came, ripping *through* me and tearing me apart, causing me to awaken in a cold sweat.

I rose from the bed feeling *different*. I passed my closet door with its full-length mirror to view myself, not as Peyton Herron but as Quantum Girl. It wasn't as though I knew anything about her, but as if all of the experience from the other Peyton Herron had somehow projected itself into my brain—her abilities—her strengths. As for her memories, none of them came with. Such being the case, I phased back outside, leaned back against the tree, facing Cleopatra, and caused time to resume at its normal speed.

Cleopatra finished her blink, realized that I had disappeared from where I'd been, and found me, arms stretched down somewhat behind me, looking innocent enough in my Quantum Girl costume beneath the shade of the massive, agéd oak.

"How in the name of Isis did you do that?" she asked with her jaw dropped so low it might have brushed the ground—speaking in hyperbole, of course; Cleopatra in actuality would never have let her jaw drop more than half an inch despite any surprises— such being the mark of her ancient royalty.

"It was the god-stone," I replied, "or perhaps Jesus. I don't know."

"I've never seen such a costume," Cleopatra said, staring at it with fascination, "but Isis described it to me. She said it was worn by the Peyton who died." She thought a moment and then asked, "What else can you do?"

I reached out toward an overhanging branch. A purple flash shot from my hand, severing the limb, and causing it to crash down to the

206

ground. I then phased from one part of the yard to another and to another and on and on in a succession so fast that all she must have seen was a blur. After that, I split apart so that there were five of me, merged back into one, and then focused on her so that her clothes became invisible.

"Enough!" Cleopatra commanded, breaking my concentration, and allowing her clothes to be seen on her once again. "Do not forget that I am still of noble blood!" she said with some indignation.

"Sorry," I said with a smile. "It was just a joke." I phased back into my street clothes. "Hey," I said, "I'm kind of hungry. How about we order up some Chinese for lunch?"

"I am not a cannibal!" she replied. "I do not eat human beings!"

"Ugh!" I said back, rolling my eyes. " I meant Chinese food, not Chinese people!"

"Very well," the Queen of Egypt replied, "we shall savor their cuisine. Afterward, you may tell me about your god as we agreed."

Cleopatra liked the Chinese food that I ordered: mu shoo and cashew chicken, prefaced by egg drop soup with crispy fried wonton strips. She tried to drink the soup straight from the bowl, raising it to her lips but it spilled down the corners of her mouth. I began to laugh which made her angry.

"Hey," I said, "I'm sure I'd be just as much of a klutz back in your day!"

"What is the meaning of *klutz*?" she asked, wiping her mouth with her napkin.

"Awkward," I replied. "Here, Use the spoon. It works a whole lot better. And try the wonton."

The mu shoo, wrapped as it was, gave her a bit of struggle. At first, she tried to eat it with her fingers as was the practice in ancient times, but quickly caught onto our ways, watching me as I used a knife and fork. She explained to me that in her day, everyone ate using their hands with small bowls filled with water to dip their fingers in as they ate.

"I don't understand," she said. "Why do you not eat pizza the same way?"

She had me there. "Well," I said, "There are some things we eat with our hands, like hotdogs and hamburgers and sandwiches... and pizza, but with most other things we use knives and forks and spoons unless it's in a glass."

"It is a terrible thing to eat dogs," she replied.

"Oh, no," I assured her, "they're not really dogs. They're just called that. I'm not sure why. They're sort of like sausages made from ground-up meats." A thought occurred to me. "What did you and Isis eat all the time you were together?"

"Mainly fruits and nuts," she replied. "And a wonderful delicacy called chocolate. We had no such thing in Egypt. Truly, it is a food of the gods."

"Do you miss Isis and the other Peyton?" I asked.

"Isis very much," she replied. "The other Peyton, I did not know her well, though she seemed both intelligent and kind."

"I would have liked to have met her," I said.

"Look in the mirror," Cleopatra replied with a mouthful of cashew chicken, "and say hello."

"I may as well look at *you*," I replied, "but it's not the same. What makes us special is what's inside."

"Then," she replied, still chewing, "perhaps you should go back and become best friends. But there are consequences."

"What do you mean?" I asked.

"If you go back in time," she replied, "realizing she will be killed when she goes to heal you, she may decide against it. By doing so, you will never have been made well in order for you to be able to go back in time, thereby creating an unending loop in time that could destroy the entire universe. But it's your choice to make, not mine."

The subject then turned to religion. As I mentioned, Jesus had yet to be born during Cleopatra's lifetime, but she was familiar with the Jews with whom she had formed alliances.

"It was all political," she said. "I offered them protection and they became my ears in Macedonia and Rome. But they, like the Bedouins, were a filthy people who seldom bathed and whose men were unshaven. They reminded me of the camels they would ride. As for their god, I have read their Bible. It is filled with killing—the flooding of the Earth, the destruction of Sodom and Gomorrah, the murder of every first-born Egyptian, and on and on. It starts with all women having to suffer in childbirth for the one supposed sin of Eve because she took a bite from a piece of fruit that she was supposedly told not to eat. Why? So that it would rot on the tree? My ancestors in Macedonia had a similar story about a girl named Persephone who should not have eaten the six pomegranate seeds but in doing so created the six months of winter. I wonder what would have happened if she had eaten twelve. Then there was Job. God murdered his children, caused him to lose everything he owned, and then made boils erupt all over his body, simply because God made a bet with Satan to prove a point."

"But," I protested, "in the end, God rewarded Job by giving him long life, seven more sons, and three beautiful daughters."

"So what?" she replied. "Do you think that one child can replace another like some old coat? And what about all the others he murdered? He said they were wicked, but wicked by whose standards? I think the Romans were wicked with their slaves and orgies and games of death, but the god of the Hebrews did not destroy *them*."

"That's why God sent His Son to Earth," I said, "to walk among men and show them the meaning of forgiveness and love."

"And this son," she protested.

"Jesus," I clarified.

"If he was the son of God, why didn't he fix everything?"

"Because," I tried to explain, "God gave man free will."

Cleopatra looked at me and shook her head. "He gave man free will," she said, "until he decides when it is too much free will and then he kills or tortures him. And what made this Jesus so special?"

"He had powers," I said. "He could walk on water or heal the sick or turn water into wine."

"Just like your Moses," she replied, "who could turn his staff into a snake. Our magicians could do the same. Tricks," she went on. "Just tricks."

"But they weren't!" I insisted.

"Then perhaps," she insisted back, "your Jesus had another god-stone in his head."

"Jesus died for us," I said, "He was crucified by the Romans and then He rose from death and ascended to Heaven."

"And Osiris," she said, "was murdered by his brother, who then cut him up into pieces but my Isis put him back together and then brought him back to life. Only my Isis says this was not so. Osiris remains dead and so now does his wife."

"Jesus will save their souls," I replied. "He will bring all who believe in him to live forever in His glory."

"I wish that were so," she said back, "at least for Isis because she is someone I grew to love."

We left our religious discussions at that. We retired to separate bedrooms, exhausted both physically and in our minds. Three of me—for I had divided myself—talked for a while. One of me stood naked in the shower. A second was at the sink brushing my teeth, while the third sat on the toilet peeing.

When I was fourteen, I had a stubborn streak in me. Nine years had passed but it had passed *around* me, I hadn't passed *through* it or *with* it other than physically. As a result, I didn't want to listen to the warning Cleopatra had given me. I wanted to know about the other Peyton and so I decided that come morning I would go back in time.

"It doesn't make sense," said the me in the shower.

"That time can be changed," finished the second with her mouth full of toothpaste.

"How can you change what's already happened?" asked the one

210

of me on the toilet as a stream of urine gushed from my urethra. "It doesn't make any sense that one small event can cause the destruction of everything in existence."

The drenched me proclaimed, "She can't possibly be right."

The sinkuous me spat out toothpaste and said, "She's from ancient Egypt. Seriously, they believed that cats possessed magic."

The peeing one of me glanced to her side and frowned. "Could you find me some toilet paper?" she asked. "Totally out."

"I'm in the shower," said the wet me, "getting a back massage from the water. Besides, I'd make puddles all over the floor."

"No problem," said the pasted me as she spat out the last bit of toothpaste and then filled her mouth with a cupped handful of water, spat *that* out, and then looked in the cabinet under the sink, "I think we're out!" she said and then looked at the shower curtain and said, "Hey, keep it up. The water feels good on my back."

"Same here," the no-longer-peeing me said.

"I think there's a square box of Kleenex on the shelf in the closet," the naked me replied.

"Let me check," said the sinkopated me, who then phased into the closet. "Found it!" she shouted and then phased back with the box.

The toileted me pulled out a sheet to wipe my vag. "I think I'm going to wind up with a permanent ring around my butt!" I said, getting up and then flushing.

"Ow!" all three of us said in unison as the water in the shower suddenly turned hot.

"Sorry," the bare-butted, exposed vag me said as I pulled my jam bottoms back up.

The showered me turned the faucet off and then pulled back the curtain. "Should we merge back together again?" she said.

"I think you'd better dry off first said the me who had just gotten off the toilet."

"Good thought," said the tooth-brushed me as she threw her a dry towel.

"I'm starving!" exclaimed the me with the ring around her derriere.

"What do we want to eat?" asked the me who was drying herself.

"Waffles with sausages!" exclaimed the one with the now-bright smile.

"I doubt we have any of that," replied ex-pee.

"We can phase over to IHOP," the toweled-off me suggested.

And so we merged, though the box and the towel somehow fused together, leaving me not the slightest clue as to how to get them apart. *Oh, well!* I thought to myself. *Maybe they'll separate in the wash.*

Her Royal Majesty still asleep and not wanting to disturb her, I phased over to the restaurant and asked for a booth. The waitress handed me a menu. Twenty-five dollars for waffles? Inflation! Oh, my God! I only had twelve dollars and change in my purse. *No problem!* I thought to myself. I went outside, phased back to 1960, and then went back in and sat down again. $2.50 for the exact same thing! Cool! The waffles were delicious as was the hot cocoa. When I was done, I left a fifty-cent tip for the waitress and walked over to the register to pay. The woman there, whose nametag read Martha, eyed the five-dollar bill I handed her with suspicion.

"This don't look like no five-dollar bill I've ever seen," she said.

"It's one of the new ones," I said.

"Marv?" she called to the back.

A thin man in a dark suit with a white shirt and a narrow black tie walked up to her.

"What's wrong?" he asked.

"This here woman gave me this piece of paper she claims is a five-dollar bill." She handed it to him. "Does that look like any five-dollar bill you've ever seen? Part of it's pink!"

"No, ma'am," he replied. He looked up at me. "Where'd you get this, young lady?"

"From my Mama," I said.

"Well, then," he replied. "It would appear that your Mama is what

212

we refer to as a counterfeiter and, from the likes of this, not a very good one. Here at the International House of Pancakes, we offer real food in exchange for real currency. So, young lady, do you have any to pay for your meal?"

"No, Sir," I said.

"Should we telephone the police?" Martha asked.

The man picked up the bill, looked at it, and then shook his head. "No," he replied, "it's only a waffle and hot chocolate. I suppose I can make up the cost myself." He reached into his pocket, pulled out his wallet, placed three dollars down on the counter, and then looked at me. "Now, young lady," he said in no uncertain terms, "I could have called the cops on you but you seem like a nice person, so I'm going to overlook it this time. But if you ever come in here again, you'll need to show your money up front to the waitress."

"Yes, Sir," I said apologetically. "I appreciate it."

"And you tell your mama," he went on, " that she needs to find a better use for her artistic abilities."

"Yes, Sir," I said.

"I have a daughter around your age," he said, "or I might not have been so sympathetic to your predicament. Now, you go on and I hope you've learned from this experience."

"Yes, Sir," I repeated, "though I can't tell my Mama anything, as she died a few weeks ago, and what I gave you is all that she left me."

"Goll dang it!" the man said and he reached into his wallet again, this time taking out a ten-dollar bill that he handed to me. "Here," he said. "I don't want you to go hungry."

"Marv!" Martha exclaimed. "That's good money!"

"Well, then," Marv replied, "then I'm putting it to good use, so you hush up." He looked at me. "You make sure you feed yourself," he said to me, "and God bless you."

"Thank you," I said back to him, "and God bless you, too." I cast him a humble smile and then left.

Once outside and in a secluded spot, I phased back to my house, a week before I'd been awakened. I knew I shouldn't have done that but I did. I met her and I met myself. There, standing before me, living and breathing, was the corpse that I saw lying on the floor in that same room. My past self, the one who could barely think, was sitting up in bed staring, just staring.

"It's me," I said. "In the bed. It's me before you saved me."

"Saved you?" she replied.

"You put your god-stone in me," I told her, "and it worked, only you died. I killed you. I didn't mean to. I'm not worth it. You need to let me go."

The other Peyton nodded and then I disappeared. The other Peyton had listened. I hadn't been saved. But if I hadn't been saved I couldn't have gone back and warned her and so it was and on and on—a time loop, inescapable with millions, perhaps billions of repetitions until finally Cleopatra materialized just as I did and phased me away before the other Peyton noticed either of us.

"You are a foolish girl!" Cleopatra scolded once we returned to my time. "I warned you of the possible consequences and you ignored what I said."

"I know and I'm sorry," I said as tears began to flow, "but she was a good person and I killed her. I only wanted to make things right."

"By ending all existence?" she replied. "It was fortunate that I felt the ripple in time fast enough to place a quantum field around myself or there would have been no end to it." She just looked at me and shook her head. "You need to grow up."

It was at that moment that the doorbell rang. Cleopatra lagged behind as I went to see who was there. I opened the door to find twin girls in their late teens on the other side—who merged into one and then split apart again and again to a dizzying effect.

"Oh, my God!" I exclaimed and then yelled back toward the staircase, "Cleopatra!"

"I need help!" the girl begged, her voice varying from two girls speaking to one.

Cleopatra phased downstairs and stood by my side as she stared at the girl. "Isis!" she gasped. "How are you still alive?"

"Isis?" I repeated.

"Chloë Salinger, actually," the duo echoed.

"Let her in!" Cleopatra ordered.

"Her or them?" I asked.

Cleopatra gave me a sharp look, and so I stepped aside. The girl or girls entered. I shut the door behind her or them. It was very confusing at the time.

"I thought I'd lost you," Cleopatra said.

"I'm sorry," came the reverberated reply, "but I'm not her. I'm the other one." She looked at her with ingrained sadness. "The other Chloë died—at least I think she did. Then something went into my head. It's caused nothing but problems. There's a third one of me out there. She knows how to use whatever's inside us and I think she's…"

"What?" I interrupted.

She stared at me as though petrified by the very thought of what she was about to say. "Insane," she answered, her eyes fixed, her pupils dilated, her voice seeming to echo the words.

"Oh," I said, "Is *that* all? A version of you who is batshit crazy phasing around with a god-stone in her head."

"Wait!" she went on. "There's something else. When the stone went in my head I connected with another reality. Something happened there. All the men on the planet got wiped out by some biological disease."

"That means," I said, "there are other versions of us out there." I turned to Cleopatra. "Well, maybe not you, considering that you've supposedly been dead for two thousand years."

"A charming thought," she replied.

I turned Chloë—the Chloës—whatever—and said, "Maybe you can find a way to get us there."

Chloë shook her wavering head. "Not in my present condition," she replied. "I think I need the rest of me in order to pull myself back together, and God only knows where she is."

CHAPTER XXXVI

Chloë
(the batshit crazy one)

Earth Date: September 12, 1878
Deadwood, South Dakota
Alternate Reality I

The twenty-first century sucked as far as I was concerned. It was crowded, polluted, and filled with politics. I didn't need to watch superheroes in movies. I *was* one. After phasing off from my two duplicates, I decided to try my hand at the Old West. I'd seen the series, *Deadwood*, and so I thought, *Why not?*[27] I met Calamity Jane, who, without tryin' to be cruel, weren't nothin' to look at, and Bill Hickok, whose real Christian name was James, William having been his deceased father's name that he took on account of to honor him. Wild Bill as he got nicknamed, owned a mustache that could have been used to build a crow's nest and sported a hooked nose that was nothin' to sneeze at. But the two of them were quite amicable until Bill got shot in the back by some no-good named Jack McCall as he sat playing poker at the Nuttal & Mann's Saloon, holding two black aces and two black eights what later got to be called a dead man's hand because of that's what it got him, meaning dead, and Jane, she cried her eyes out after she heard about Bill. All this happened in Deadwood, which was in what was at the time the Dakota Territory. As I said, Jane, she took it right hard as the two of them had had amorous congress with each other on many needful occasions. But that was just on two years ago and as for Jack, he soon got caught and was eventually strung up. Hell, the folks mourned Bill so much they done buried Jack with the noose still 'round his neck.

---

[27] It is interesting how the mind—at least my mind—had adapted to the customs and language of the time.

I come back to Deadwood after a couple of stints in Cheyanne and Carson City. I'd phase from one to the next, sometimes as a gunfighter, sometimes as a saloon girl. A lot of men would come in just for me, but I'd only perform tiffs with the good-looking ones. One oily fat toad tried to force hisself on me, so I sent him to somewheres near the 'Dromeda galaxy where I 'spect he's orbiting one of the star systems waiting to be discovered by some extraterrestrial intelligencia. 'Dromeda's two and a half million light years from the Earth, so I reckon I was being right kind, as I could have as well dropped him into intergalactic space.

When I first arrived, damn did I look outta place. Al Swearengen who ran the Gem Theatre saloon in Deadwood—he took me in on acounta, he said, I had the purdiest white teeth he'd ever seen and none of them marks that those who'd been afflicted with the pox had. Plus, he said, I was young and filled with pulchritude. I didn't know what that meant at the time, but it turned out it were a compliment that I was beautiful at least in his eyes, and bein' that I was just nineteen, "ripe for pickin,'" he said, so he fitted me up with the same sorta dresses that the other saloon girls wore. None of 'em wore bloomers, though, as "they hindered the occupation" I was told and found that to be right correct information. I were given free room and board and got to keep half of what I took in 'ceptin' for the tips which were all mine. Sometimes, when a guy did it real right, I'd glow quantum red and the guy when he saw might get scared and all but I'd reassure him that was just how some girls were when men gave them ecstasy and on account of their egos, most took to believin' it. Got me pregnant a couple of times but then I'd just phase back to the future to get an abortion or in some cases, a pill as those weren't done or invented yet back then. When it were taken care of, I'd afterward phase back.

One girl, Lottie, who was a skinny little thing only fifteen, whose parents had died from the cholera, shared a room with me. She was there only a week before some brute started beating her up 'cause she refused to fuck him after she saw his dick was infected with pus and all. He gave her two black eyes and knocked out one of her teeth. Hearin' all the racket, I come into the room and he turned on me which was the last mistake he ever made as I blasted him and made a hole right through the middle of his chest. Lottie, who was beat up right bad just stared at me as I sent him into the Chinaman's pigsty for the hogs to have at him for their dinner. I figured it was his just desserts, him being their main course and that were a joke if you didn't get it. Well, as I said afore, Lottie, she just stared at me, kinda frightened I might add but I told her I was her guardian angel sent straight from Heaven to watch over her and protect her and excused myself for not attending to her needs sooner. She did forgive me, though, and we became the best of friends.

By August of '78, Lottie and I were in Abilene. We'd given up whorin' and decided to rob banks instead. We didn't *need* to do it but it was fun I s'pose. I named myself Clover Anne and there were wanted posters of me all 'cross the state. We'd go into the banks, guns ablazin'. Didn't take it upon ourselves to shoot no one but we did put the fear of death in a lot of s'poséd brave men. One of 'em, sure as shootin,' trickled a stream down his britches. Lottie laughed so hard she nearly busted a gut. That night after that happened, we drank our fill of whiskey, rolled around naked on the banknotes, and had us some long, sweet love.

"Know what?" Lottie asked after being all so breathless from the pleasure I concocted in her, "After all the men who abused me at the Gem, I rightful know that you're the only one fer me."

I looked over at her next to me. "Well," I said, "if I do say so myself, your cooch is a whole lot sweeter than most of them dirty old pricks Swearengen set us to accommodate on our knees." It was as I bent over and kissed her that she coughed somethin' fierce. I'd noticed her coughin' afore only I 'tributed it to all the trail dust. But it got so bad that night that I phased her back to 2033 to the emergency room at one hospital. I paced and paced till a woman doctor came out and told me that she had passed. 'Twas from consumption, what's now called tuberculosis. Let me tell you when I heard that I fell to my knees and pounded the floor and cried and screamed out, "No!" I can't 'member how many times, till a male doctor or orderly helped me up and tried to give me some sort of shot but the needle wouldn't go in and then I got mad, real mad, and I phased out right in front of them, not caring in the least whate'er in tarnation they might think.

To hell with it all! I thought to myself.

With nowhere I cared to be, I phased back to my bedroom, two years older than I should have been in that time. I'd lost the one great love of my life and didn't give a mule's ass if I lived or died. I just threw myself down on the sheet of my bed, curled up into a ball, and wept out all the tears I didn't even know I had in me.

It was my mother who found me lying there in a puddle of sorrow. She sat herself down on the edge of the bed and gently rubbed my back.

"What's wrong?" she asked in a gentle-like voice.

"I want to die," I said back.

"Why do you say that?" she asked. "What's wrong?"

I stared ahead into the nothing that was afore me. "The girl I loved, Mama," I said, "she done passed from consumption, and 'twere nothin' I could do about it. No matter how much powers I mighta had, I couldn't rightly save her."

"I'm sorry about that," she replied. "but why are you talking like that? Are you rehearsing for a play at school?"

I rolled over onto my back and looked at her. There was a gentleness in her countenance. "No, Mama," I said.

Her eyes teared up a bit as she looked down upon me. I could see how the years of bein' a wife and mother had taken their toll on her face. In the hallway there hung a photo of her and Papa when they first married. Theren't been a wrinkle on her face. But now her eyes looked worn by time, I thought to myself, and crow's feet stomped out from the corners of her eyes. I think she knew there was a sadness that fell hard upon my heart and a tear dripped from her eye and fell down upon my cheek and it was at that moment that something in me changed and I pulled myself up to a sitting position.

"I'm fine," I said. "It was a close friend of mine. I had to rush her to the hospital. They did everything they could but they couldn't save her. They said it was tuberculosis that had gone undiagnosed too long. There was too much damage to her lungs and her heart."

"I'm so sorry," she replied. Before Mom got married she was a registered nurse and knew the grieving process for when someone you care about or love passes away.

"Were the two of you close?" she asked.

I sat up straighter in the bed and looked her in the eye. "I was in love with her," I said. "I never in all my life thought I could love a girl that way, but I did. Is that wrong?"

Her hand reached beneath my hair and caressed my cheek. "Love is never wrong," she replied.

"I do still like guys," I said, "but there was something about her; something that just touched my heart and made it pound in my chest every time I even thought about her. There's just one thing."

"What's that?" she asked.

"Well," I said, "She doesn't have any family—not here or anywhere; and the hospital said that they would take care of all the arrangements and cremate her remains and I know I have the sixty thousand dollars that Grandma left me, but I was wondering if I could use some of it to have her buried. I mean, Granddad's body was lost at sea during the war and there's an empty plot that no one's ever going to use and I think she'd be comforted to lie there beside Grandma like Grandma's spirit would watch over her forever knowing how important she was to me and if the money left wasn't enough for my studies, I could work whatever jobs I needed to, to make up the difference."

I could see more tears about to come to my mother's eyes. "Of course, you can," she started to say and she choked on her words, "have her buried next to her. I know your Grandma would be pleased to have her company."

"Thank you, Mom," I said. "By the way, her name was Lottie; short for Charlotte. That was her baptized name—Charlotte Dorne. She was only seventeen."

"Just like you," she replied. "Why don't you draw yourself a bath and then change into some fresh clothes? Tomorrow, we can drive down to the coroner and make the arrangements." She got up, went to the door, and then turned back to face me. "I can fix you something to eat," she added. "You need some meat on your bones. What would you like?"

"If it's all right with you," I replied, "I'd like to go out for a hotdog. It's kind of been a while."

CHAPTER XXXVII

Ophelia

The Next Universe
Planet Erebus: Year V
Alternate Reality II

We'd been on Erebus for more than five years. I supposed that would have made it 2038 Earth time if there still had been an Earth. Zhana and Samira had just turned ten and Jordan was eleven, growing up in a world we had yet to fully explore. The Chloëbot hadn't aged a day. With some identity issues, she fast developed her own uniqueness from all of the new experiences and developed a propensity for revitalizing the ancient equipment that had filled the timeworn structures.

It was strange watching Jordan grow up—Jordan, who in our previous existence, had emerged from my womb and not Peyton's. This time, however, Jordan was maturing in a more normal way. On Erebus, despite that we were all that was left of humanity, she was not being ostracized. In fact, both Zhana and Samira looked up to her as a kind of older sister, which biologically she was, despite whose uterus had fed her during her gestation. That is not to say that the twins, as we often referred to them, didn't have personalities of their own, independent of her leadership. But trumping even Jordan was the Chloëbot whom the children referred to as Aunt Chloë. The Chloëbot served as both their nanny and friend. Their favorite pastime was acting out Peter Pan with the Chloëbot as Peter, Jordan as Wendy Darling and Samira and Zhana as Michael and John. Peter would fight the imaginary Captain Hook, often rescuing Wendy and her *brothers* from Hook and his pirates. Occasionally, when there was time, either Claire or Peyton or I or all of us would participate. Claire would pretend to be Tiger Lilly while I would be Mrs. Darling back in

Kensington Gardens, grieving for the loss of her children. Peyton would be Mr. Darling or Captain Hook or all of the pirates because she could turn herself into so many. It made me think about how people must have entertained themselves before the advent of movies or television, and although we had no books to read, I was reminded of a sonnet I once read.

In Kensington, there is a spot where stands
A statue of a boy born long ago
In a forgotten realm, that many know
By Barrie's tale of Never Never lands.
The one he told of had ambitious hands
Upon short sword that clashed with Hook, his foe.
But Tinkerbell used magic dust to show
Him how to fly and led him to far sands;
And there he met young Wendy Darling, oh—
Blonde hair and gentle smile and pale blue eyes—
Who being just a child to his long years,
Took needle, thread and did his shadow sew
On back, and made him whole and glad and wise;
And with her love, she ended all his fears.

It was the Chloëbot who had fixed the ancient fabricator when it had broken down and made a stovepipe hat and glasses and an umbrella for Zhana and a teddy bear for Samira to carry around. It was wonderful fun for them all and for us when we chose or were begged to participate. It was five years of family and peace, of love and contentment, until that one dark day when the invasion began.

When I say invasion I don't mean hoards of spaceships descending from the sky or legions of aliens armed with weapons. It was actually worse than that. The children were playing as usual. Wendy, aka Jordan, was fleeing from Captain Hook aka Peyton, when the ground gave way under her. Peyton froze time and caught her but what became apparent was that there was an underground cavern beneath our feet.

"What is it?" Jordan asked after Peyton had set her down.

"A cave of some sort," Peyton replied.

"Why don't we have a look?" Claire said.

"I want to go, too!" Jordan insisted.

"Me, too! Me, too!" cried out the twins.

"Later," Peyton said. "After we know what's down there."

"But I was the one who found it!" Jordan insisted.

Peyton shook her head. "It wasn't *you* who found *it*," she said. "It was *it* that found *you*."

A moment later, she turned into Quantum Girl and phased us down—*us* meaning her, Claire, and me. The Chloëbot stayed behind with the kids. We didn't call her Chloëbot to her face or to each other though. Not anymore. She was just Chloë now. It was an honor that she had earned.

The cavern was immense, stretching as far as the eye could see in every direction with row upon row of pods stacked one upon another, each containing something similar to how the Chloëbot had appeared before she changed. There must have been thousands, if not millions, of them. It was eerie being entombed with them. The floor of the cavern lay covered in perhaps half an inch of water, our footsteps echoing as Claire and I followed Peyton over to one of the endless banks of pods. It was as we reached it that Claire lost her footing only to catch herself by grabbing hold of one of them. We all breathed a sigh of relief that nothing happened. But a moment later, the pod nearest us began to emit a violet glow followed by a domino effect. One by one, in rapid succession, each of the other pods followed suit, lighting up the cavern. What was worse was that not only were the pods awakening but also what was inside.

I turned to Peyton. "It must be the god-stone," I said. "It's activating them the way it must have done with Chloë!"

Peyton changed back to herself as she heard me. I shook my head.

"It's too late!" I said.

Claire looked panicked. We all did. "We need to get out of here!" she exclaimed, as one bot and then another began to emerge from the pods—looking like us and others we'd known!

There were duplicates of Peyton and Claire and Liam and me and Chloë and Theresa Martinez and Daisy McKenzie and Myra Kartinova and our parents— even our teachers including Mr. Chatterjee. Human or alien, it didn't appear to matter. Khattaaara, Dhraaal, and Thara-Klo were among them, as well as both myself and Claire in Rend form. There was even a Quantum Girl. It seemed that everyone we ever had contact with who was prevalent in our minds was brought to life from the robotic forms—even the adult version of Jordan, but there were no children. Peyton phased us out of the cavern and then sealed the opening but it was to no avail. The bots came from a technology centuries if not millennia in advance of our own. They came, one after another, materializing out of thin air, apparently similar to how Peyton phases, and then they phased out *en masse*. It was Zhana who first screamed. Peyton responded, becoming six Quantum Girls. Each grabbed a hold of one of us and phased us back home.

"I've placed a quantum barrier around the building," she said as she merged back into one. "but there are millions of them."

"What do you think they want?" I asked.

"And why do they all look like us or someone we knew?" Claire chimed in.

"Maybe Chloë can tell us," Jordan suggested.

"How would I know?" Chloë answered.

"Because you're a robot…" Jordan started to say.

"Expert!" Peyton interrupted, giving Jordan a sharp look. "A robot expert."

"No idea," Chloë answered.

"What if they all go back into the cavern?" Claire asked.

"Doubtful," Peyton replied causing the outer wall to become

transparent.

The duplicates filled the window she had created but the figures weren't just mulling. They were staring—at us!

"What do they want?" I asked.

Peyton glanced at me as she ended her X-ray projection. "Only one way to find out," she said. Another Quantum Girl split out of her and then phased from the room.

CHAPTER XXXVIII

Peyton

The Next Universe
Planet Erebus: Year V
Alternate Reality II

I phased out into the hoard of replicas. The experience was oppressive. I was amazed that I was able to phase there at all with so little room, the bots all so crowded together. My sudden presence pushed several of them out of the way, but I felt like a sardine in a tin. How ironic that I came face to face with a duplicate of the Peyton form of myself, with one of Phee and a Claire on either side. They were all talking at once, mostly mindlessly repeating conversations from the past, but their jabbering *en masse* created an incoherent din. Meanwhile, those nearest me were all pushing against each other *and* me to try and get inside the building we had claimed as our home.

"Why do you look like me?" The Peyton bot said only inches from my face. "Are you my quantum split?" It thought for a moment and then concluded, "No. You can't be. I can't hear your thoughts. Oh, my God!" it then exclaimed. "You're Payton from Earth II, aren't you? I've missed you so much! I know you wanted us to have sex together. We couldn't before but we can do it now," and she began to undress in front of me—tried to—but her movements were being hindered by the oppressive crowd.

"What's going on?" said the Pheebot into my ear. "Why are there so many of us? We're not like *you*. We can't divide ourselves. Or can we? Are we all Quantum Girls and Guys now? Am I a blue one? That's my favorite color, you know."

This was all too much for me. I phased into the air five hundred and then a thousand feet above it all. The crowd of replicas stretched for miles in every direction. Worse, similar throngs had emerged all across the planet. There were bots of Jasmine, the deaf-mute Chinese slave I'd had an affair with as Liam, and the Russian human traffickers who'd enslaved me when Khattaaara had taken over my mind. Phasing ten years into the future, things had gotten worse. The replicas were at each other's throats. Their world was in utter chaos and much of it was on fire. Arms and legs and heads and torsos lay strewn everywhere. It was as though the bots all had been infected with a virus that had driven them even more insane. I phased into our home. It was now littered with broken bots—Peytons and Ophelias and Claires and all the rest. A Quantum Girl bot with an almost completely severed head stared vacantly outward repeating "Pey-Pey-Peyton" in mechanical tones. *But where was my family?* I wondered. *Had I gone back to when I'd left and rescued them?* As I was considering the possibilities I heard an explosion not far off in the distance and phased over to it. There was rubble and *dead* bots all around. I walked over to one of the bodies—one of the Ophelias. I stared at it and then used my X-ray projection to make certain it wasn't Phee. Suddenly, a young woman's voice yelled out at me. "Hold it right there! Don't move!"

I turned to see a pretty, young woman with chin-length light brown hair in her early twenties aiming what appeared to be a rod at me. Assuming it to be a weapon, I immediately phased out of the line of fire and reappeared beside her. She turned sharply to face me as I snatched the weapon from her hand at quantum speed.

"Who *are* you?" she exclaimed. "*What* are you?"

"Jonni?" I heard another young female voice call out from the shadows. "Are you all right?"

In another moment, two young women emerged into the sunlight. One had short blonde hair and the other was… Jordan! All grown up! Both had tube weapons aimed at me.

"Don't move!" the blonde girl cried out as the two of them approached. As they did I phased back into myself.

Jordan froze in her tracks. "Mama?" she cried out. Then she

229

glanced to her left. "Mira!" she said. "Lower your pulser! It's my Mom!"

"That's impossible!" Mira replied. "She died years ago! The Frags killed her!"

Jordan walked up to me, looked me over, and then hugged me. "Thank God!" she exclaimed, tears streaming from her eyes. She pulled back and stared at me. "How did you survive?"

"It's only been a few minutes for me," I replied. "I split off and went to see what was happening outside." I looked around and past her. "Where're Phee and Claire?"

Jordan pulled back a couple of feet. "Dead," she answered. "The Frags murdered them."

"And Chloë?" I asked.

"Here," came the reply from off to one side.

Straggling over was what remained of the Chloëbot. Half of her left arm was gone as was part of her left foot and a portion of the right side of her head and face. I stared at her in disbelief.

"She saved us," Mira said, the beautiful blonde girl who tearfully looked even more like Phee than did Jor.

"They came in at night," Mira explained. "We were human. They weren't. They used pulsers to burn holes right through our Moms' hearts. Chloë killed them—all of them—but not before they nearly destroyed *her*."

"I've tried to raise them as you and Claire and Pheeli would have," Chloë said. Her voice was mechanical and broken. "I did the best I could but there's not much left of me."

"What's been going on?" I asked.

"The Frags are what's left of the civilization that built all of this," Jordan explained. "They built millions of them to replenish their people. Their world—this planet—was about to be hit by an extinction-level asteroid. They were going to implant their consciousness into each of the Frags. But then something went wrong. The event took place too soon for them to act. Everyone was killed but the Frags remained dormant in the network of caves underground."

"Until my god-stone triggered them," I said. "I'm responsible for all of this." I turned to the other two. "And for the deaths of both of your mothers." A question occurred to me. "How exactly did I die?" I asked looking from one to the next.

"We're not certain," Jonni—Zhana—replied, "but you're buried just outside the compound."

As we walked to the gravesite, Zhana said in a low voice and a motion of her head toward Jordan, "It was hardest on *her*. She tried not to show it but it was as though her heart went into the grave with you—or her. It's all so confusing now."

The grave itself was unmarked. All that could be made of it was a slight mound that had been kept free of any weeds or grass.

"We didn't want any of the Frags digging you up," Zhana explained.

I used my X-ray projection to reveal the body that lay beneath the soil. Jordan turned away as I did. Astonishingly, there was no decay. What lay six feet under was a Quantum Girl that radiated a yellow hue. Focusing on the ground, I caused the soil to erupt and the corpse to rise from the grave. The dirt having filled in the abscess beneath it, I laid it on top and examined it from its pores to its organs, from its fingerprints to its quantum signature.

"It's not me," I said.

"What do you mean?" Samira asked as Jordan turned to face it and us.

"She was from another universe," I replied.

"Another dimension?" Jordan asked looking from it to me.

"No," I said. "She's made of antimatter. If it weren't for her god-stone, this entire planet would have been destroyed. It contained her within a quantum field."

"She *is* dead," asked Zhana, "isn't she? I mean we buried her nearly a decade ago."

"Unfortunately," I replied.

"And the other you?" Jordan asked.

"Dead as well, no doubt," I said, "exhumed from *her* grave by the antimatter version of me." I paused as I stared at my opposite's remains. "I need to extract the god-stone from her without blowing up the planet."

I focused on the corpse and then watched as it disappeared with the yellow god-stone appearing in my hand.

"Where did she go?" Samira asked.

Staring at the god-stone, I glanced up at her. "I phased her," I said, "to the middle of the black hole at the center of the galaxy we're in. I assume my counterpart in the antimatter universe did the same with my remains as well."

"How can her god-stone help?" Zhana asked.

Jordan and Samira looked at me for an answer.

"I don't know," I said. "All I do know is that, even if we go back in time, we can't stay on this planet."

"So where are we *supposed* to go?" Samira said, "Another planet? The universe after this one? Maybe back to Rendenaaar where we can all be considered freaks like Jordan was?"

"I need to go back in time and undo all of this," I replied.

"Wait!" Jordan exclaimed as I was about to phase back to the past. "If you do that, everything we've done since we were children, our thoughts, our lives, will be undone. It will be like killing us. You need to take us back in time with you."

"But if she takes us back," said Zhana, "and prevents any of this from ever happening, won't our existence as we are now be erased anyway?"

"Not if she puts a quantum field around us," Jordan replied, "like she did around Aunt Ophelia when she was on Earth II." She turned to me. "That would still work," she asked me, "wouldn't it?"

"It would," I replied.

"See," Samira said aside to Zhana, looking at Jordan, "she thinks of everything."

Hearing that made me smile. My little girl, all grown up. It saddened me, though, that she had to be on her own for so long. But at least I was comforted by the thought that she had her cousins… and the droid.

I turned to Samira and gave her a questioning look.

"I'm game," she said.

Zhana nodded her head in agreement and then added with insistence, "Chloë, too."

The robot who believed she was Chloë had remained in the background. It was Jordan who looked at her intensely and insisted with a motion of her head that she come to where the rest of us stood.

Limping over to us, she said in a shallow voice, "I don't want to hold you back. Besides, I'm one of *them*."

"Don't be ridiculous," Jordan insisted. "You're as much a part of our family as *any* of us!"

"You've been like a mother to us all these years," Samira told her.

"If it wasn't for you," Zhana went on, "we'd probably be dead!"

"Beyond all else," Jordan added, "We all love you. I think I speak for all of us in saying that if you won't go neither will we!"

The android who wanted—no, needed—to be human wiped a tear from her eye, nodding consent.

So, it was decided. I would phase us all into the past. The problem was that I didn't act fast enough. My quantum presence had triggered the Quantum Girl Frags that were in the vicinity, and in the middle of the night, eight of them appeared inside the building we had sheltered in. The alien droids did not break in, though. They did not smash through doors or break windows. They phased inside. Somehow the Frag's mimetic ability allowed the Quantum Girl variety to create a synthetic god-stone that was able to draw power from mine. Unlike our Chloë, however, the others, for whatever reason—were hellbent on destroying organic non-plant lifeforms and, according to the girls, had decimated nearly all of the land creatures on the planet.

233

The first shriek of terror came from Samira, quickly followed by a "Go away!" from Zhana. It was Jordan who stayed calm while remaining vigilant.

"Mom!" she called out to me while staring at half a dozen Quantum Girl Frags, each with glowing violet eyes.

I immediately phased to the room where she and the other two girls were and divided myself into the same number as the invaders. I used force fields to fend them off but they used them as well, drawing their power from the god-stone I possessed. The remaining two Frags phased behind us, each of them doubling themselves and grabbing all six of me by the arms. There was no doubt that they were winning.

"Girls!" I shouted. "Get out of here while they're distracted!" Zhana and Samina rushed from the room but Jordan hesitated. "Go!" I insisted. She hesitated but then, reluctantly did as I asked. I felt myself growing weak, my power waning. I thought, *This is the end*, but then, suddenly, I heard Chloë's voice.

"Merge back into one!" she shouted at me, "and place a barrier around yourself!"

Using every ounce of strength that was left in me I did as she said. Wearily, I looked up to see her as her body began to glow with brightness as fierce as any star. And then she exploded, taking the Frags with her. As for me, I felt myself collapse, and then everything went black.

I woke up on my back on a bed in what ten years ago had been my room. The first thing I saw when I opened my eyes was Jordan, sitting on the edge of the bed, patting my forehead with a cold compress. Then she glanced back toward the door.

"She's awake!" she called out.

Zhana and Samira rushed into the room.

"I must have passed out," I said groggily.

"You've been in a coma for nearly two weeks," Jordan replied. "It's fortunate there were no more Quantum Girl Frags, or maybe

234

there weren't any because you were unconscious. But we're going to need to get out of here."

I started to get up but then sank down again. "Some protector," I said. "I'm here less than a day and I bring all this down on your heads."

"Here," said Samira, "give her some of this."

Jordan took the cup she was holding from her and brought it to my lips. It smelled awful.

"What is it?" I asked.

"An herbal tea," Samira replied, "made from indigenous plants. It helps with healing."

"It's one of the many things we've learned," Zhana added, "being forced to survive on our own."

I began to drink it, making a face.

"It may taste awful," she went on, "but it works. A lot of the plants here have medicinal value. You just have to know which ones."

I handed the cup back to Samira when I had drunk as much as I could bear. "What happened to Chloë?" I asked. "There was a brilliant burst of light before I passed out."

"She sacrificed herself to save you," Jordan replied. "To save us all. But we need to leave here ASAP if we're going to survive. Your waking up may trigger more Frags."

I dragged myself out of bed with Jordan's and Zhana's help and then shook my head to try and spark more consciousness into my brain. "Where's the antimatter god-stone," I asked.

Jordan handed me the yellow marble-sized gem which I clenched in my fist. How it could help was a mystery, but one that needed to be solved later on. Clenching my fist around it, I phased the four of us back in time to just before all hell had broken loose—out of the frying pan and into the fire as they say.

CHAPTER XXXIX

Cleopatra

Earth Year: 2033
Alternate Reality I

I have sat on the throne of Egypt. I have had lovers who commanded legions of soldiers and who ruled half of the civilized world. I have seen wars where men were struck down like wheat at harvest. I have witnessed births and deaths and even met a god but never could I have imagined the world I entered when I traveled forward two millennia in time! The pyramids and the Sphinx were in ruins. The gods of old were gone, replaced by one mortal woman known as Quantum Girl who, too, had perished. All that remained of her was the pale reflection of herself who was left to fill her shoes—a superheroine with little world experience, but who, like myself, had powers that derived from the untread parts of the heavens. I, too, was mortal, but my days of valor were over. The walls of existence, it seemed, depended on *her*.

Oh, but listen still. I was told by the now-dead Quantum Girl that all of existence was about to end, though she offered no means by which to change that. I myself have had a long life, most of which was spent as Pharaoh. Here in this future time, I stand unrecognized—not as Royal Egypt, not as the Queen of Kings. Those who would pass me on the street would give me no second glance other than for my obvious beauty. Admittedly, it has been a long two years since I left my home to come here to the land of plastic and machines. My body, however, still hungers for the carnal pleasures it once knew.

As I continued to wonder about the loss of the third of the two Chloës who had appeared at the door, I decided to explore the nightlife in the city. After phasing around the main streets several thousand times in an instant, I caught sight of a building with a line of younger attractive people in interesting attires, especially the girls. I caused my clothing to appear similar to one of them, a dress of metallic cloth and glitter that left little of my body to the imagination. To that, I added my royal headdress. As the stilted shoes proved difficult to walk in, I phased them off of my feet and created the illusion of sandals instead. I then phased inside the building onto a crowded dance floor with blaring, beating music, to find myself pressed against a girl in her late teens with pale skin, blue eyes, and pink and blue straight hair that fell over her forehead like the Chloës but, everywhere else, fell down to her chin. She might as well have been a boy for all the bosom she possessed. Upon her dress, which was very short, were strands of small beads that shook as she moved.

"Hey!" she said as our bodies collided. Then she looked up and down my figure. "Cool threads!" she went on, having to shout above the noise, "and I love the tiara or whatever it is!." She extended her hand toward me. "My name's Kayla, by the way!"

"Cleopatra!" I shouted back as I briefly took her hand in mine.

"It fits!" she shouted back. "You'd probably have given her a run for the money—back then, I mean!"

"No doubt!" I replied.

"You want to get out of here?" she yelled. "A friend of mine's an artist and he's having an exhibition! I promised I'd make it there before it wound down!"

I glanced around the room. The music was deafening. The people, other than their costumes, seemed insipid. "I would be pleased to accompany you!" I replied.

We left the club through a back door and then walked to her conveyance which she called "her bike" which I later learned was a motorcycle.

"You ever ridden one?" she asked.

"No," I replied.

She put on a pink helmet, straddled the machine, and then told me to do the same with the other one she had. "Just wrap your arms around my waist," she said, "and lean with me when I turn." She used her right foot to start the engine and then it began to move.

It was both frightening and exhilarating—the rush of movement, the wind in our faces, blowing our hair. The red and green traffic lights reminded me of the carnelian and turquoise stones that often comprised the jewelry of my people. How sad it was to think that even their bones had been ground to dust by the ravages of time.

We traveled for about ten minute to a house in a somewhat poor area. Kayla stopped the motorcycle and we both got off and went to the door upon which she knocked two times, then three times, and then once again. A man—a tall, slim Nubian in his late twenties—answered the door wearing trousers and what I later learned was called a wife beater—a sleeveless undershirt with a low-cut neckline. His hair was in what Kayla called dreadlocks and his face was unshaven although he did not have a beard—and his breath smelled of spice.

"K.K.," he said in a deep raspy voice. "What brings you to my crib?" He looked me up and down. "And who is your fuckably exotic friend?"

"Her name's Cleopatra," Kayla said.

"Hello, Cleopatra," the yet-to-be-named man said. "Mmm, mmm, mmm," he went on, staring at me, and then licking his lips.

Had this been Egypt, with those words directed at me, I would have had him beheaded.

"Down, Tiger," Kayla said. "Are you going to let us in or do we need a written invitation?"

The man, whose name turned out to be Leroy, took a step back, extended one arm, and bowed. "Enter the kingdom," he replied, and so we went in.

How little this infidel knows of kingdoms or kings, I thought to myself.

The doorway opened into a large room furnished with padded chairs and sofas of varying colors and designs. There was nothing attractive about the décor. In one chair sat a bearded man in his mid-thirties with dark hair, wearing a red plaid shirt and jeans, holding a can of what I later learned was beer in his left hand. Straddling him sat a pretty girl around twenty years old with red hair and blue eyes, wearing only an open blouse. Apparently, the man was penetrating her, as she was rocking back and forth on his lap making furtive cries that soon became louder as she began to bounce up and down, holding onto his shoulders for support.

"That's Duke and Princess," Leroy pointed out. "Duke is addicted to Viagra and Princess is addicted to the results plus the money he gives her." He turned to Kayla and then to me. "Set your fine asses down on the loveseat," he went on, and then asked, "Can I get either of you anything? Beer? Whiskey? A Leroy lollypop?"

"Don't be bourgeois," Kayla replied as she sat down, encouraging me to do the same.

"Bourgeois!" Leroy called out, first to the mating two, and then to Kayla, and said, "What else are we learning in college? Hopefully, they are teaching you skills in oral presentation."

"Got any mollies?" Kayla asked.

"For which I get?" Leroy asked.

"Whatever you want," Kayla replied. "though I know what that is."

"To penetrate that fine pink pussy of yours," Leroy said back. He looked at me. "And what can I get the exquisite Cleopatra?"

"Get her a roofie," Kayla said. "She should enjoy that."

"A roofie for the newbie," Leroy chuckled as he went to the kitchen and momentarily disappeared.

I turned to Kayla. "What are such things?" I asked.

"They're pills that make you feel good," she replied.

"How does this happen?" I pressed on.

"I don't know," she said. "They just do."

A moment later, Leroy returned with two pills and handed each of us one of them. Kayla swallowed hers and then looked at me with an expression that insisted I do the same. With the stoic belief that nothing could harm me with my quantum abilities, I swallowed the pill I had been given. That was the last thing I remembered until I awakened naked on a bed in a disheveled room. I was dizzy and disoriented and my vision was blurred. There was light coming through the windows—light which hurt my eyes. Kayla was in the bed beside me, passed out but naked as well. Leroy stood near a dresser, also naked. I tried to sit up but my head was spinning and I collapsed into unconsciousness again. It must have been night again when I came to, only to find a fat mixed-race man on top of me, naked and inside me. This time, though, my head was clear. I glared at him as he continued to thrust his phallus into my vagina again and again. Rage filled my every pore. *How dare a stranger defile the Queen of Egypt!* I thought to myself. Projecting a forcefield, I threw him across the room, obliterated him with a burst of energy, and then rose from the bed, and stopped time. Leroy, dressed as before, was taking money from one man while others in the room stood or sat. On a low table was a sheet of paper with a list of names on it, some of which had been crossed off. One man, frozen like the rest, was exiting out the door to the outside. Phasing backward in time, I observed what had gone on. Men had arrived to pay money to have sex with me while I was drugged. Returning to the present, I started time back up again. Everyone stared at me, including Leroy, but that was the last thing they would ever do. Death was too good for them. I phased them all to the middle of the Sahara desert. *Let them die of heat and thirst!* I thought, and then I followed the quantum trail of Kayla and her motorbike to her apartment, to She Who Had Gotten Me Drugged and caused all of this. Mercy had left me long ago when as a small child a handmaid had dared to strike me. Kayla turned and looked at me, startled.

"How did you get *in* here?" she asked.

"That is not the question," I replied. "The question is, how will *you* get out?" and, with that said, I phased her to one of the sealed

240

chambers in the Great Pyramid, there to scream with no one to hear her, there to beg for mercy from the long-dead gods, and there to die from fear or suffocation, I cared not which. Once that was done, I went outside, filled my lungs with the cool night air, and then phased back to Peyton's home.

CHAPTER XL

Peyton

Earth Year: 2033
Alternate Reality III

It was all over the news—a yellow-costumed Quantum Girl had appeared in the sky above Manhattan. Chloë said that she'd encountered her before and that she called herself Quantum Queen, an antimatter version of herself. But, I wanted to know, why was she was bent on destruction, and how did she manage to get to our universe in the first place? I became Quantum Girl, stopped time, and then phased to where she was. She was frozen, hanging midair, focused on the ground a thousand feet away. I reached out and touched her but as I did it was as though quantum energy had wrapped itself around me. Not only that but from where I had touched her, the color of her costume changed to gold. I stared at her. Chloë was right. In the antimatter universe, it wasn't me who had taken on the quantum costume, but the reflection of Chloë. And how, I wondered, even with existence paused she sensed my presence. Her eyes moved just a bit in my direction as though she was fighting to break free of time itself in order to challenge me. Seeing that, I phased back to my apartment.

"Oh, my God!" Chloë exclaimed as she stared at me.

"What's wrong?" I asked.

"Look in the mirror," she replied.

I turned to catch my reflection in the freestanding mirror that stood in one corner. My violet costume was now silver. It had changed just as hers had.

"It must have happened," I said, "when I touched her."

"Dear God," Chloë replied, her lungs two vessels of trepidation.

"I don't understand," I said. "It's just a different color."

"No, you *don't* understand," she went on. "That was the color of your costume when I woke up next to you in the grave!"

"What do you mean?" I asked. "What grave?"

"Where do you think I found the god-stone that I put in your head?" I asked.

"I didn't know *you* put it in me," I replied. "Wasn't it there since Dhraaal gave it to me?"

She shook her head. "Not in this reality," I said. "Honestly, I don't know what's going on. This is some sort of chicken and the egg reality that God or the quantum fabric seems to be playing with us." She took a deep breath as though to give herself a second or two in order to compose her thoughts.

"You were dead!" she exclaimed. "All right? Another Quantum Girl, one in a gold costume, phased me into a grave with you. Half of your head was blown away but I reached into it and got your god-stone all covered in gooey, rotting brain stuff! And now it's all repeating and I don't want you to die again!"

"Hey!" I said back. "I've lived a long life and if that's the way things are meant to be, that's just the way it is."

Chloë glared at me. "Then how are you going to save us?" she yelled. "You're a hero! That's who you are, from saving everyone in the Twin Towers and from the planes to the girl in the car crash to the cat in the tree!"

"That last one was Theresa," I calmly said.

"Grrrr!" she replied. "You know what I mean! You're caring and selfless and kind and you've always used your powers to help others!"

"You have a god-stone, too," I replied.

"I'm not *like* you!" she said. "Oh, I could tell Claire what dress to wear or demand she be on time, but when I got my powers as an adult what was the first thing I did? I fucked Brad and Erin and Cameron and I probably would have fucked my other self if she hadn't turned out to be the dark version of me! I don't have what it takes to be a superhero! I'm sorry but that's the just way it is and I don't want you to die! Every time I look at you I keep seeing you beside me in the grave!"

"Perhaps it's just meant to be," I replied.

"There must be some other way!" she insisted.

"There isn't," I replied.

I guess I must have zoned out for a moment because her next comment was, "You *still* want us to work at the club?"

"What are you talking about?" I asked.

She shook her head and stared at me, "I was talking to *her*, er, you, the other you," she said. "You do realize that you have two personalities in that quantum brain of yours, don't you?"

"I most certainly do not, did not," I replied.

"Well, you do!" she said, "And it can be a bit off-putting, seeing as the stripper you is trying to get my clothes off in order to fuck me half of the time!"

"Sorry," I replied. "Maybe you should take it as a compliment."

"Not funny!" she said. "I mean, I love you and all but not in that way!" She stared at me, her eyes going down and then up my form. "It would be like having sex with my sister!"

"Which you haven't, I hope," I said, "meaning Claire."

"Shut up!" she replied. "Seriously, what are we going to do about keeping you from dying?"

"I think," I remarked, "we should first try and figure out where the god-stone that's now in my head came from. You can't have gotten it from me in the future to give it to me in the past."

"I don't understand," she replied.

"A boy owns a pocket watch that he got from his father," I began to explain. "He goes back in time, meets his father, and gives him the watch that his father later passes on to him. The watch had to have come from somewhere in the first place, the same as the god-stone in question."

"So, from where then?" she asked.

"I know that I eliminated all parallel dimensions," I said, "but not the possibility of coexisting realities."

"Explain," she replied.

"Parallel dimensions," I said, "existed as though they were universes unto themselves. Alternate realities, theoretically, would exist or coexist where the quantum fabric becomes fractured."

"That just sounds like a lot of gobbledygook," she replied.

"It's not, though," I insisted. "Quantum reality doesn't depend on causality but neither is it impervious to change. Religious devotees maintain that God created the universe. But, then, who created God? How could God have existed forever? There would have had to have been some starting point where God came into being. By that same reasoning, the quantum fabric would have to have had a beginning somewhere. That would be the argument of common sense, but not in terms of quantum reasoning."

"Your point being?" she asked, followed by, "No, I don't want to have sex with you. It would be totally gross!"

"What are you talking about?" I asked.

"Sorry," she replied. "Other you briefly came out, literally. We've been talking for more than an hour. You'll need to excuse me. I have to go pee. Go on. I can still hear you from the loo."

She got up from the bed where we were both sitting—*Strange, though*, I thought to myself. *We were on the sofa when the conversation began.*

"My guess," I told her, raising my voice a bit, "is that the quantum fabric somehow became fractured."

"You don't need to shout," she said. "I have quantum hearing, same as you, you know."

"Sorry," I replied in a normal voice and then went on. "There may even be an antimatter equivalent to the godlike woman I met in the fabric. Regardless, there needs to be a reconciliation to it all. What part my death plays in this I don't know, but if in fact I wind up in that grave again, you need to be prepared to take on the role of Quantum Girl and prevent the universe from imploding."

"There isn't any replacing you," she said. "We need to figure this out."

"Hang on," I said. I phased into the quantum fabric and then back again. "According to my calculations, you and I have lived through this same moment more than four billion times."

"And what?" she raved on. "I'm supposed to let you die again so that we can relive it four billion more?"

"No," a voice said from behind us with a heavy Gaaalthaaaran, lizard-like accent, "There is another solution."

We both turned and saw Khattaaara.

"Which one are you?" I asked, filled with trepidation.

"The one with you," came the reply, "or, rather, the other one of you."

"Payton?" I exclaimed, tilting my head as I stared at her.

"None other than," she said with a smile—an alien smile, but a smile nevertheless.

CHAPTER XLI

Peyton

The Next Universe
Planet Erebus: Year V
Alternate Reality II

We phased into a paradox just hours before eleven-year-old Jordan was about to step onto a piece of ground that would give way beneath her feet and cause a world of hurt to all of us. It was the crack of dawn and none of the past versions of us were awake.

"Do you remember where it was?" I asked Jordan.

"Like it was yesterday," she replied. "Over near that rock, just to the left."

I used my X-ray projection to reveal the cause. "There's a trapdoor under the dirt with a rusted latch." I focused on it, rearranging the molecules to their original structure. "It won't collapse again."

"What do we tell them when they wake up?" Samira asked.

"The truth," I replied.

"So, none of our mothers have to die," Zhana said.

"And you, as children," I went on, "won't have to fend for yourselves, especially with the three of you as their big sisters."

"From now on," Jordan added, "like Clairey and Claire."

"Unless and until any of you decide you want to merge," I replied.

"I think it'll be cool," Zhana remarked, "but let's say we trade off."

Samira's eyebrows raised at that. "What do you mean?" she asked.

"Well," Zhana answered, "I can mentor young Jordan, Jor can mentor young Samira, and Mira, you can mentor the younger version of me."

"Sounds like a plan," Jordan replied, "though it might be a bit confusing with names. Mira, your Mom used to call you Sami, so that's no problem. How about Anna[28] for you and Danna for me?"

"I guess," Zhana said with a bit of reluctance in her voice. "But would it be all right if we used our own names in private? I've sort of gotten used to mine."

"Of course, sister, dear!" Jordan agreed. "Just try and remember what we were like back then. As I recall I had a bit of a superiority complex in that I was a full year older than the two of you. Zhana, you could be overly inquisitive, and Mira, you could be a bit of a brat."

"Hey!" Mira objected.

"But a cherished one," Jordan added. "You do know that Zhana and I would never have hesitated to sacrifice our own lives to protect yours?"

Mira's bit of anger broke down hearing that.

"See?" Jordan went on. "There's a smile erupting. *She* knows she's *loved*."

It was at that moment that three young girls raced from the compound but then suddenly stopped upon seeing us. It was young Jordan who stared at me in particular.

"Mom?" she said. "I just left you inside talking to Aunt Claire."

"Why do they look like us?" young Samira asked and then slowly walked up to the older version of herself. "What's your *name*?" she asked.

"Mira," came the reply.

"And who are the other two?" Sami pressed on, staring at the older versions of her sisters.

"That's Anna," Mira said, "and the other one's Danna."

"And where did they all come from?" Zhana, now emboldened, asked as she stared at me. "There wasn't supposed to be anyone else here but us."

---

[28] Pronounced Ahna.

"We're from the future," now Anna explained.

Zhana turned on her sharply. "No one asked *you*!" she declared. "I asked Aunt Peyton!"

"We *have* come from the future," I confirmed. "Ten years to be precise."

"So, that would mean you're us!" young Jordan deduced. "Holy fucking crap!"

"Jordan!" came the sound of my voice emerging from the complex. "Haven't I told you not to swear?" her voice tapering off as she saw the four of us. She stared at me. "You're back!" she said, "and you brought three others with you." Suddenly, she stopped as she caught sight of she who was now to be known as Danna. "Jordan?" she said, questioning. "How? How is this possible? Wait! Are you *my* daughter grown up or Phee's?"

"Yours, Mama," she replied. The other one of me rushed over to her, looked her up and down, and then embraced her. "I've missed you so much!" she went on.

When the hugging ended, the other one of me turned to me and asked, "How is this possible? I mean there was Clairey and young Liam and Li, but they were from different dimensions."

I shook my head, glanced toward Heaven, and then merged back into her. "I hate long explanations," I said to Danna with a smile. "Now, if you'll kindly excuse me, I need to get out of one of these sets of clothes," that, due to the fact that I was now attired in all of what we both had been dressed in—and, by the way, I totally ruined both pairs of shoes! I shook my head to myself as I stared down at them. Phee was in the kitchen, cleaning up from breakfast as I entered.

"What was all the commotion outside?" Phee asked. "And what on earth are you wearing?" Then came the sudden realization. "Oh, my God! You're back!" She rushed over and hugged me. "Five years!" she went on, gushing tears. "We all thought you were dead!"

She pulled away just a bit to stare into my eyes and then hugged me again. As she did I noticed Claire's profile, appearing seven or eight months pregnant.

"How is that possible?" I asked. "This isn't Jurassic Park."

"Apparently," Phee explained, "something about your having merged me with Liam allowed me to change *into* him at night while I'm asleep. Kind of freaky, huh?"

"Lucky Claire," I replied. Just then I noticed Chloë standing off to one side, motioning her head toward the other side of the room. I looked over and saw Claire in the doorway. "Congratulations," I said. "Thought up a name yet?" Then, I realized, "Oh, yes, you already told me. Wyatt. My bad." I paused and then added, "If you two lovebirds will excuse me, I need to go change into something a bit less confining."

"Good to have you back," Claire replied. "I mean the other half of you. Sami told me."

I smiled and then left the room where I was met by Chloë who put her finger to her lips and then led me to my room.

"What's up?" I asked in a low voice.

"What happened to me in the future?" she asked. "I mean, you and Jordan and Samir and Zhana came back, but not me."

"You sacrificed yourself for all of us," I said. "Not to worry, though. *That* future isn't part of *yours*. Not anymore." I paused for a moment and then added, "Back on Earth, we were pretty good friends. I hope we can be friends here, too."

She didn't utter a single word in return. She just looked up at me, looked into my eyes, and then hugged me. She was like Pinocchio at the end of his story, like the puppet that became real—at least she became real to me.

CHAPTER XLII

Peyton
(the one who just woke up)

Earth Year: 2033
Alternate Reality I

I didn't ask for this. I didn't know if I even wanted it. Having superpowers was awesome, but the responsibilities that came with them were not. "Learn to do right," said Isaiah. "Seek justice. Defend the oppressed." It was my mother who espoused this and it was she who taught me the Bible. She brought me up to have faith, to believe in righteousness, and to be grateful that Jesus died for us on the cross. There was no mention of Quantum Girl in either the Old Testament or in the Gospel.

I was twenty-three years old but emotionally and in terms of experience still just fourteen. I'd never had a boyfriend. I'd lost so much of my life. That girl, Theresa, I didn't know why she hated me so much. *Maybe it was me*, I thought. *Maybe I did something wrong to deserve all of this.* Suddenly, I was supposed to be someone I was not. I was supposed to be *her*, the other Peyton, and fill her shoes but I didn't know how. I didn't know if I could. I had no friends. My mother was dead. Papa was dead. I thought, *maybe because of me!* There was no one to love me and no one for me to love. I just felt so alone!

Two girls sat on the sofa in my living room, then one, and then two again. I had no idea what I was supposed to do. I hadn't the slightest clue how to fix them. It was like a bad horror film. It was like there was a woodpecker pounding on my head. Together, then apart, then together again, their voices doubled as they spoke—or was it as she spoke? I couldn't take it anymore. I needed to get out of there. Regardless, I tried to be the polite hostess that my mother had taught

251

me to be.

"Do you mind if I go out for some fresh air?" I asked them (or her).

"Not at all," she (or they) said in unison. My God! It was like being in a room with Tweedle Dum and Tweedle Dee!

"Would you like some tea before I go?" I asked.

"No thank you," came the reply (or was it replies)? "We'll just wait for Cleopatra to return. Maybe she has some ideas."

"There's food in the fridge if you're hungry," I said, "and there's a guest bedroom down the hall if you get worn out from sitting too long."

"Thank you so much," they both said at once and then briefly merged together again.

I put on my sweater—the blue one that was lying on the striped upholstered chair where Mama had always left it. Then I exited the house and quietly shut the door behind me, all too glad to inhale the cool night air.

I began to walk—blindly. I didn't look at buildings or signs or cars coming when I crossed the street. I looked down at the ground, one foot in front of the other, guided only by the need to get away from the craziness of it all. I could return anytime. But that thought was at the back of my mind and didn't challenge my impetus or direction. My heart was hurting from having no one and nothing. I must have walked for miles until I stopped. The neighborhood was not like mine. The houses looked shabby. A Mexican-looking man sat on his front porch in an open shirt with a bottle of beer in his hand.

"Come here, *Chiqueta*," he said in a graveled Mexican voice. "Come show me your *pinocha*."

I turned away, backing into the mailbox of the house next door, causing some of the letters that were overflowing to spill from it. I bent down to pick them up and put them back. As I did, my eye caught sight of whom they were addressed to—Occupant, Occupant, Theresa Martinez! *Could it be?* I wondered. On one of them were written the words, "Class Reunion Braxton High!" It *was* her, I realized. This was her house! I looked down at the ground. There was a large round gray stone on the grass near the mailbox pole. I picked it up, took aim, and hurled it at one of the front windows. The stone hit its mark accompanied by a loud crash. The man on the porch next door turned to look.

"Angry *Chiqueta*," he laughed in a loud drunken voice. "Don't bite off my dick! I've got two balls, but my dick, I've only got one!"

The lights in the house went on in the front room. A dark-haired girl around my age pulled back the curtains and looked through the broken window. The front door opened a moment later and she stood there, glaring in my direction, wearing only a short silk nightgown.

She shouted something angrily in Spanish and then came charging at me. When she got to me, she suddenly stopped dead in her tracks.

"Oh, my God!" she exclaimed. "You're her! You're Peyton! You're the one who tried to kill yourself! I thought you were in an institution!"

"And you're the one who put me there," I replied.

"Why are you here?" she asked. She glanced back at the window. "Just to throw a rock?"

"I don't know," I said. "Coincidence. Just walking. Then I saw the name on your mail. You were the one who made me want to die."

Her anger calmed. "I'm so sorry," she said. "I was angry all the time back then."

"We barely knew each other," I replied.

"I know. I know," she said. "You can't imagine how I felt when I heard that you tried to hang yourself and I knew it was because of me. I used to cut myself because of it. Please," she insisted. "Come inside and we can talk."

She ushered me in, offered me the sofa, and then sat down beside me, facing me on my left, her right arm resting on the back of the sofa, her right leg bent immodestly on it as her left leg hung down toward the floor.

"Would you like anything to drink?" she asked. "Coffee, tea, soda?"

"No, thank you," I answered, trying desperately not to glance at her perhaps inadvertently exposed vag. "But I have a question?" I said.

"Of course," she replied, catching the motion of my eyes, glancing down at herself but doing nothing to cover what was obviously exposed.

"Why me?" I asked. "I mean, as far as I can remember I never did anything to you. Why did you put a target on my back?"

"It's kind of hard to explain," she replied, "embarrassing, I suppose." She hesitated but then went on. "When I was a young girl my uncle lived with us—with me and my mom. He was in his middle twenties, I guess. I was nine. My mom, she used to work the graveyard shift doing cleaning at an office building. When she was gone, my uncle used to come into my bedroom and do things to me. He told me that if I told anyone that he'd hurt me and then he'd hurt my mom. This went on for years. Just before I got into Braxton, he got me pregnant and took me to an abortion clinic and made me go through with the procedure. I was brought up Catholic. We don't believe in such things. We think of it as murder. I cried for weeks after that. My mom kept asking me what was wrong and I kept telling her, 'Nothing. Nothing, Mama. Nothing's wrong.' Then I just exploded. When my mom was at work I screamed at my uncle, telling him that if he didn't get out I would go to the police and tell them all that he'd done to me. He left that night. When my mom came home I told her all that had gone on but she didn't believe me. She said I made it all up. I guess if she accepted what had happened it would have meant that she hadn't protected me. Anyway, it made me angry. And what I'd been through with my uncle made me hate the thought of being touched by men. Then, when I got enrolled at Braxton, I saw *you*. You didn't see me, but looking at you made my heart pound in my chest. You were the most beautiful girl I'd ever seen. I tried to go up to you so many times but it was like I was invisible to you. I wanted to be friends. I wanted to be able to stand at your locker and laugh with you. I wanted to walk down the hallway holding your hand. But you never noticed me back and all the anger I had in me from my uncle got directed toward you. I know that was wrong now but I was fourteen years old and hella immature. Then I heard what you'd done to yourself and I realized it was because of me and I wanted to kill myself and I tried so many times but I never had the nerve to ever go through with it."

She held out her left wrist and showed me all the scars from her cutting herself. I showed her mine.

"I guess we have something in common, then," she said with a slightly sardonic laugh.

"I guess we do," I replied.

"My mother died a few years ago," she went on. "I couldn't afford to go to college on my own. It's all just been hard work in clothing stores and restaurants. Hell, I even tried working in a strip club once but I couldn't deal with all the men looking at me. It brought back too many memories. Anyway, if it's any consolidation for what I did to you I've been alone ever since—all my life, actually."

"Same here," I replied, "though I can't remember the last nine years."

"I'm not asking you to forgive me," she said. "I just wanted you to understand the reasons for me doing what I did."

I stared into her eyes, damp with tears that had yet to fall. "The Bible says," I told her, "For if ye forgive men their trespasses, your heavenly Father will also forgive you."

"Matthew 6:14," she replied.

"I have sins of my own," I said. "Someone died because of me. It wasn't intentional but it happened nevertheless. My mother's dead, too. *And* my dad. I don't have anyone. Not really. Not to talk to. Not to cry to. Not even to hug. I've never had a boyfriend. I've never had anyone."

Theresa held out her arms. "Come here," she said. I leaned into her and she hugged me and I hugged her back. There wasn't any thought to it. There were no memories of the torment I'd been put through. It was as though both of us had somehow been reborn just then and that God, watching over me, said it was okay. When the hug ended I said to her, "I guess I'd better be going."

Theresa glanced at her wristwatch. "It's really late," she said. "Why don't you spend the night and then go home in the morning?"

I didn't tell her that I could have just phased back to the house. The truth was that I'd enjoyed her company, hearing the reasons for all that had gone on, and realizing that beyond all the powers I now possessed I had one even greater and that was the power of forgiveness—one that I shared with our Lord and Savior, Jesus Christ—so I agreed.

She led me to her bedroom. "I hope you don't mind sharing," she said. "I've used the other bedroom for storage."

I glanced back toward the living room. "I can sleep on the couch," I said. "I don't mind," but I really wanted to be able to sleep next to her, to feel another human breath, to hear another heartbeat.

"Your back would wind up a mess if you did," she replied. "You just take the right side and I'll take the left. It's a full-size bed. There's plenty of room. I'll grab a nightgown for you to change into."

I changed in the room with her. She turned her back but I caught her glancing toward me from the corner of my eye when I was undressed. Strange to say, it did not make me feel uncomfortable. After I'd changed, I got into the bed. She flicked off the light switch on the wall by the door and then climbed into the bed on her side.

As I lay on my back and she lay facing me, she reached over and took hold of my left hand. "When I was a little girl," she said, "I would pretend that I was a beautiful princess, trapped in an ivory tower and that some handsome brave knight would come and rescue me. He'd gather me up in his arms and kiss me passionately, steal me away to his castle and we'd live happily ever after. That never

256

happened and I don't feel like the beautiful princess anymore."

"Well, you *are* beautiful," I told her.

"But not the princess. I'm the scullery maid, trapped in a meaningless existence."

"Please!" I said. "I've felt trapped all my life, waiting to be rescued by someone—anyone."

"Even me?" she asked.

"Even you," I replied. "Even you."

She moved in closer to me. Then she raised herself up over me and kissed me on the lips. I wrapped my arms around her and kissed her back. Her breasts pressed against mine, I felt her arousal and I became aroused as well. I could hear her heart pounding the way that mine was and my quantum sense could smell the result of her lap pressing hard against mine. I felt a pleasurable sensation in my groin and such a want as I had never known.

"I love you," she said and I knew at that moment that I loved her, too, yet fear took hold of me. But then a thought crossed my mind. A verse from the Bible I had read: "God gave them up unto vile affections: for even their women did change the natural use into that which is against nature." *Dear Jesus, forgive me,* I thought to myself and so I phased from the room, back to my house, and back to my own bed, not even considering what could have gone through her mind when she held me in her arms and I just disappeared.

CHAPTER XLIII

Chloë
(the one from Ancient Egypt)

Earth Year: 2033
Alternate Reality I

I had been marooned more than four thousand years in the past. Foolishly, in retrospect, I had divided into four in the middle of a lightning storm. Two of me had vanished when bolts had struck us all. Of the two that remained, either the god-stone had been damaged or something in my head or heads had been, so that I or we couldn't merge back into one or return to our time. It took another two millennia for us to be merged back together. Meanwhile, mosquitos were dosing out malaria, while fleas spread bubonic plague, otherwise known as the Black Death, and where dead bodies were piled everywhere, even in the streets, until those who weren't sick *yet* got around to burning them. During the Middle Ages, the stench of death was everywhere. There was no heat during the winter other than from burning logs and summers were sweltering with neither electric fans nor air conditioners. Antiperspirants had yet to be invented, and as bathing was often a yearly ritual, many good townsfolk just stank. God help you if you got sick or had a toothache. Butchers and barbers back then often doubled as doctors and thought fit to either bleed you with leeches or drill holes in your head. Needless to say, most people had bad teeth from poor dental hygiene and pock marks from smallpox for which there was yet no vaccine. Women having seven or eight children during their lifetimes was not uncommon as there was no birth control but infant mortality was high and the act of giving birth sometimes took the mother's life along with the child. They were trying times for humanity but it was what the two of me had to live through. The worst part of it was that we had to move

258

every twenty or so years before people realized that we weren't aging at the same rate as they were. People saw us as twins. We did not want to be branded witches.

The two of me would take lovers on occasion. Between us, we gave birth to and raised forty-seven children over the centuries. What effect that would have on the timeline, we couldn't even begin to guess.

Being from the future wasn't all bad, though—as a single person once more after the other Chloë had fused us back together. I managed to witness the death of Julius Caesar and the birth of Jesus Christ (who oddly both had the same initials) and the signing of the Magna Carta.[29] I watched as Michelangelo painted the Sistine Chapel, and the Wright brothers as they made their first flight. I heard the gunshots from the grassy knoll in Dallas as JFK was assassinated, and watched the takeoff of every manned space mission up to and including Challenger. I gave up after that—watching it blow up took the thrill out of it all. I invested in every major stock from its onset, amassed a collection of rare books, antiques, and real estate, slept with Douglas Fairbanks, Charles Chaplin, Clark Gable, Errol Flynn, Gary Cooper, William Holden, and Marlene Dietrich when she was just eighteen. Immortality can make for monotony but I tried my best not to be bored, considering that I'd suffered through more than four thousand years. But after all of that, there I was on the painted side of the front door to Peyton Herron's parents' home, about to touch my finger to the doorbell.

Strangely enough, the door was answered by me or, as it later turned out, an alternate version of me, who apparently was caught in a quantum discontinuity—two of her quantum selves phasing in and out of each other, reminding me of my psychedelic experiences with LSD in the 1960s.

---

[29] King John had really bad breath and a very small dick, but he did enjoy my company in his bed so much that he presented me with a diamond and ruby necklace, which I still own.

"We were wondering when you'd return?" they said.

"How would you know I was even coming?" I asked.

"We need to figure out how to get us all back together," they said. "It was not cool of you to just phase off like that. I see you got rid of the pigtails. You're just going to confuse things. I mean, look at us. We're... unstable."

"I think," I said, "You're confusing me with another one of you."

"You're not Chloë Anne?" they asked.

It was becoming annoying. "Chloë Anne Salinger," I replied, "but if there's another one of you, it isn't me."

"We've been trying to get back together," they said in rather discordant tones, "but we're not sure how. We're not even sure how we split apart."

"Where's the other one of you?" I asked.

"We're not sure," they said. "After *we* split, *she* split."

"Just stand still," I told them. "I don't know about C3, but I think I can fix the two of you."

It was actually ironic because the god-stone in their head for some unknown reason appeared to be repairing the damage to the part of my brain that controlled the god-stone in *my* head. Whether it was due to the proximity or to quantum entanglement. I had not the slightest clue. But after more than two thousand years my powers were back and I was able to stabilize their physical existence in this reality.

The twins—and I use the term loosely as they were in reality both the same person—expressed relief.

"Thank you so much!" said one.

"You can't imagine what it's been like," said the other.

"I'm exhausted," said the first.

"Likewise," said the second.

"Let's go to bed," said the first.

"It's still light outside," I replied.

"You can come *with* us," said the second. "It'll be fun like before," then, remembering, added, "Oh, I forgot, that wasn't you.

But anyway you can still come. It'll be mostly the same."

"The same what?" I asked, half knowing.

"Having sex!" they both said at once.

That's all I needed, I thought to myself, having sex with the Bobbsey Twins who were both alternate versions of me! "I'll pass for now," I replied.

"We'll leave the door unlocked, just in case you decide," said number one or number two, it didn't matter.

"I'll keep that in mind," I answered as the two of them scrambled off to the guest room, one tickling the other's waist. I just shook my head to myself. *Children!* I thought to myself. I hoped I was never like that but the truth was I couldn't remember, it had been so long ago.

I sank down on the couch, but the moans from the guestroom became annoying. *Was that how I sounded when I had sex*, I wondered? Wearily, I rose from the comfort of the cushions, trudged up the stairs, and looked around. It has been a long time since I'd lived here with Peyton and her parents and Claire and Ophelia—and Liam, who was really Ophelia in a man suit... sort of.

Whichever reality I was in at that time, though, neither Ophelia nor Liam was in it. It was the strangest of feelings because no one had told me. I just knew—probably from the god-stone. And then I heard sobbing crying coming from what used to be Peyton and Ophelia's room but there and then it was just Peyton's—Peyton, who was an only child. Her room was to the right of the hall. I knocked gently and then entered without invitation.

She was lying on the bed clutching her pillow, her back to the door, immersed in tears. I walked over to her and sat down next to her.

"What's wrong?" I asked.

"Whoever you are," she wept, "just go away!"

"I can't do that," I said in a gentle voice. "You've done too much for me and Claire."

"I haven't done anything to help anyone," she went on. "I've only hurt people all my life. I don't deserve to live!"

"You can't mean that," I replied. "I wouldn't even be here if it weren't for you."

"Not me!" she sobbed. "I'm not *her*! And she's *dead* because of me! My parents are dead because of me! And the first time I think I've fallen in love with someone, it's someone God would send me to Hell for being in love with!"

"What are you talking about?" I asked.

She rolled over and stared at me with tear-drenched eyes. "I'm not your Peyton!" she wept. "I'm not a superheroine! I'm just another version who took the easy way out and wound up literally brain-dead for nearly ten years! *Your* Peyton cared for me! *Your* Peyton loved me! *Your* Peyton died because when she put the god-stone in my head to heal me I wound up killing her with it! And then… And then… And then… when fate sends me to the one person I could find love with, that I'm attracted to, it's someone the Bible says is sinful to love!"

"Why would the Bible say it's sinful to love *anyone*?" I asked.

"Because it's another woman!" she sobbed. "I'm just a sinner and I'm destined for hell!"

I gently brushed her hair off her face. "Hey," I said, "It's not a sin to love someone no matter who they are."

"But it's wicked," she sobbed, "one woman lying with another."

"Then I should hate my sister, I suppose," I said.

Peyton stared at me through tear-drenched eyes. "Your sister," she said, "is she… does she…?"

"Yes," I said, "and she's with the sister of the Peyton who cared for you."

"It's too late," Peyton wept. "I left her. I phased out from under her. She'll be freaked out and won't ever want to even touch me again!"

"One advantage to being Quantum Girl," I said, "is that you can go back in time."

She wiped her eyes with one hand. "I didn't think of that," she replied.

"So, you go back to the exact moment that you left," I told her. "You do what your heart tells you. You make love like there were no yesterdays and like there are no tomorrows."

"I will," she said.

Time rewritten, I would have to deal with the twins all over again. Such was my regret as I watched her disappear, her innocence soon to be a thing of the past, but with a future, hopefully, suffused with love.

CHAPTER XLIV

Peyton

(the one who just woke up)

Earth Year: 2033
Alternate Reality I

She never realized that I'd been gone. She never wondered why my cheeks were wet with tears. I felt her kisses against my lips. I felt her breasts pressed down against mine. I felt wanted and needed, and for once in my life I no longer felt alone.

Theresa Martinez was beautiful. She was tall and slender with hazel eyes and long dark straight hair. Her figure was perfect. Her skin was soft, her fingers gentle and skilled when they reached down to cause an ecstasy in me unrivaled by any other experience. I had never had a partner before—never kissed a boy, let alone a girl—but this was so much more than that.

Beyond how her uncle had defiled her, she said that she had never been with anyone she cared about and that, from the moment she first saw me, her only thoughts of sex or love were fantasies of me. I could feel her heart pound as our breasts seemed to melt into each other. I could smell the scent of her desire as it wafted up into my nostrils. She guided me gently through unimaginable acts, invoking pleasures I had never dreamt possible. And I reciprocated whatever she did to me on her. If she kissed my ear, I kissed hers. Where her tongue went, so did mine. There were no words. There was only the sound of our breath and our desire. If what we did to each other was a sin in God's eyes, then perhaps God is blind to love. At the end of it all, exhausted, our bodies laced with sweat and the pungent scent of our need, we both lay on our backs naked, the fingers of my right hand interlaced with those of her left. Ever so gently, she urged my hand up to her lips and kissed it.

"How could I ever have hurt you?" she said. "I stole so much of your life."

She rose from the bed, went to her dresser, and took something out of the top drawer. She returned with a gold necklace wrapped around the fingers of her right hand but all I could see was her—from her slender legs, to the line of her sex, to her breasts that swayed just a bit as she moved, to her beautiful face. She sat down on the bed and then reached out toward me.

"Raise up just a bit," she said.

I lifted myself enough for her to fasten the chain around my neck. Hanging from the end of it was an antique diamond ring.

"This belonged to my mother," she said, "and my grandmother before her. It's very special to me but now so are you."

"I couldn't take it from you," I protested.

"I want you to have it," she replied. "I was actually hoping…"

"What?" I asked.

"That it could be like a promise ring."

I sat up in bed, and then reached back behind my neck and undid the clasp from the chain. As I did, her face appeared riddled with anxiety.

"What are you doing?" she asked.

"A promise ring," I said pulling it off the chain, "shouldn't be hanging from my neck. It needs to be on my ring finger," and so I placed it on mine. I stared into her eyes. "You know, the ancient Romans believed that the vein for the left ring finger went straight to the heart."

"My God!" she said staring back. "I love you so much." She moved in toward me, wrapped her arms around me, and kissed me so passionately that my heart was like a hammer in my chest. I could feel the peaks of her breasts harden with her fervor as did mine. My arms reached around her. My fingers gently clawed at her naked back. Hers reciprocated that, and then my head fell into the cradle of her neck as hers did into mine.

"I love you back," I whispered to her.

"You can't imagine how much I've longed to hear you say those words," she whispered back.

But there were things I needed to tell her and I was filled with foreboding as to how she would react, but for that moment in time, all I could think, and not even clearly, was that I needed her to make love to me again.

There is only so much sex one can inhale in a single breath, though. I remember a joke that was being bantered around Braxton when I was fourteen that, at the time, I didn't fully understand. In the beginning, after God was nearly done with his creations, there were only two things left that he decided he should divide between Adam and Eve. The first He told them, was the ability to pee standing up. Adam immediately begged for that one. He claimed it would help him when he tended the Garden or named the animals, one by one. He was so adamant (no pun intended) that Eve told God to just give it to him and so He did. Adam celebrated by peeing on the nearest tree without a problem. All that remained was Eve's gift. "What is it?" asked Eve, fearing that it might have been the worse of the two. "Thou must suffer the curse of multiple orgasms," God told her. "What is an orgasm?" Eve asked. God explained and, without touching her, gave her several of them. Adam stared at his new wife, who lay writhing on the grass with a strange expression on her face. "Oh, Merciful God," he cried out. "Hast Thou tried to kill her?" But it was Eve who replied. "No, dear Husband," she said. "But do go on with your peeing, for no doubt it was the best of these two gifts."

Thus, it came about for apparently, sexually, women can go on forever. Truly, I think that Theresa would have been willing to give up breakfast, lunch, and dinner for a couple of days if given the opportunity to go on and on nonstop. I supposed I would have as well other than I had the subject of my being Quantum Girl to broach with her and it filled me with dread.

"Mind if I run a bath?" I asked as her fingers once again ran down the line of my sex.

"Mind if I share?" she asked.

"Not at all," I replied.

There are two ways two people can share a tub: with both facing each other—but then, with most bathtubs, one or the other winds up with the faucet in her back—or to sit spooned which is the option we both chose. Theresa sat behind me, rubbing my back with her hands, rubbing my breasts, and rubbing herself up against me. When for the third or fourth time her hands came forward again I took them in mine.

"There's something I need to tell you," I said.

"You're a sex-crazed nymphomaniac," she replied.

"That's not it," I said back, "though I think that's redundant."

"Aren't you the as*tucia lingüística*?" she said.

"What does *astucia* mean?" I asked.

"Cunning," she replied.

I half glanced back at her. "Is that all you ever think about?" I said.

"With you," came the answer.

"No," I said. "Seriously."

"Okay," she replied. "Tell me."

"I have superpowers," I said with great hesitancy in my voice.

"So," she said back. "You're like Captain Marvel."

"Kind of," I replied, "only Captain Marvel isn't real."

"And what kind of powers do you have," she said, "if I may be so bold as to ask?"

"Well," I said, "I can do this," and I phased out of the tub to suddenly appear standing, dripping, next to it facing her.

Theresa would have fallen backward in the tub if there was room. As it was, her arms, which had been gently rubbing my breasts, splashed down suddenly in the water, throwing her off-balance.

"*¡Mierda! ¡Qué carajo!*" she exclaimed. Translation: "*Holy shit! What the fuck!*" She stared at me with her jaw hanging. "You're not,

267

like, some ET who's going to impregnate me with an alien creature or anything, are you?"

I curled my lip at her. "Not that I know of," I replied.

"Then how?" she asked.

"I'm not entirely sure," I told her, "other than that I got something called a god-stone put in my head. That's what healed me and gave me…" and I hesitated, searching for the right word, "abilities."

Theresa stood up in the bathtub, water running down her naked form. Quantum me could see it all in slow motion. *Oh, Jesus, she was hot!* was the one thought that crossed my mind, followed with, *Thou shalt not use the Lord's name in vain!* But, *Sweet Jesus!*

"What else can you do?" she asked, grabbing a towel off a hook to dry herself.

"Time travel," I replied, "make more of me, phase anywhere, hurl out force fields, and I'm not sure what else. Cleopatra hasn't taught me everything."

"Cleopatra?" she repeated. "You actually know Gal Gadot?"

"No, no," I replied. "The original Cleopatra. Chloë Salinger brought her here from ancient times." I paused for a moment, perplexed by my own words. "One of the Chloë Salingers, at any rate."

"And you can make duplicates of yourself," she said and I nodded. "Then show me," she insisted.

I created three more of me, all dripping and naked. Theresa stared at me. Gawked is probably a better word.

"Hold on," she said spreading out her hands. "Don't do anything else except all of you just get into bed now. Please!"

And so I did, all of me. And so she did. And we had sex again— and again and again and again and again! Well, there *were* four of me! Anyway, I was glad she took it well—my having become a superheroine, I mean.

CHAPTER XLV

Danna
(formerly Jordan)

The Next Universe
Planet Erebus: Year V
Alternate Reality II

Being a big sister wasn't a new experience for me, but neither was it easy. So, there I was with young Jordan as my protegee. We sat in the girls' bedroom, Jordan sitting at a makeshift desk, her back to me, with her elbows on the surface, propping up her chin with her fists.

"I don't understand," Jordan said, "if my mom changed things so that I never broke through to the Frag cavern, how is it that the three of you didn't get erased with the new timeline?"

"Because your mom put a quantum field around us," I replied.

"Good thing for you she thought of that," Jordan said. "Otherwise it would have been poof and you'd all have been gone."

"Yep," I said. "Good thing."

There was an awkward silence that Jordan finally broke. She glanced back at me.

"I thought Mira was supposed to be my big sister," she said.

"We decided to each go with our younger versions," I replied, "because we each know ourselves better."

"Makes sense," she said. "So what was it like?"

"What do you mean?" I asked.

"It's kind of obvious something really bad happened," she said. Otherwise, where are the other versions of Aunt Ophelia and Aunt Claire and Chloë?

"Well," I replied, "there were all the Frags—like Chloë but violent and there were millions of them. Aunt Claire and Aunt Ophelia were both murdered and Mom was killed or zapped into the antimatter universe, so we all had to survive on our own, and when all that happened, we were your age."

"But you managed," Jordan concluded. By this time, I had seated myself on the desk to face her.

"It wasn't easy," I replied. "Zhana was very impulsive and Sami was... stubborn."

"*Tell* me about it," Jordan said, rolling her eyes.

"Anyway..." I went on, "After Mom died right in front of us—or at least that's what we thought—everyone's mood changed. It was hardest on me, I suppose. I refused to cry and I refused to let anyone help me dig the grave. The Frags attacked the next night. Aunt Ophelia and Aunt Claire tried to protect us but they wound up getting killed. It was strange and terrifying because they were murdered by Frags who looked just like them."

"Why are they called Frags?" Jordan asked.

"Because," I answered, "They came out of the cavern naked and then garbed themselves in whatever clothing or rags they could find. 'All of them like zombies,' I said, 'dressed in fucking rags.' Frags."

Jordan looked at me. "So, what did you do?" she asked.

"We hid," I replied. "We tried to make the best of things. Chloë became like a surrogate mother to us."

"But isn't she a Frag, too?" Jordan said.

"Yes and no," I replied. "For whatever reason, Chloë's different. I suspect she was manufactured in a way that didn't fit in with whatever purpose the civilization that built them all had in mind. Remember, we found her outside the cavern."

"What happened to Chloë?" Jordan asked.

"She died protecting us," I replied.

"She," Jordan repeated. "But isn't *she* just a machine?"

"Was Pinocchio *just* a marionette?" I asked. "Whatever it is that we call a soul found its way into her. So, here we are back in time and there she is, alive again."

"What happened afterward," Jordan asked, "when you were

growing up?"

"We each took on different roles," I replied. "When the Frags destroyed the power source for our food synthesizer, finding food became a challenge. Sami was our huntress, having become skilled with the bow she made. Zhana found she had a knack for figuring out the ancient electronics that Chloë couldn't tap into, and managed to construct a force field around our compound."

"What about you?" she pressed on.

"I took it upon myself," I told her, "to search for the other five god-stones that my mother—our mother—had hidden away."

"I thought they were all in her head," Jordan replied.

"They were," I explained, "but she feared too much power, even in herself. She remembered what had happened when her mind was taken over by Khattaaara and she knew that if that ever happened again with all of the god-stones in her it could mean the end of all existence."

"You said five, and one in her made six. But weren't there seven?" she asked.

"She tried to put one in the real Chloë's head before the universe imploded," I explained. "That one could be anywhere."

"So, did you find the other stones?" she asked.

"I did," I replied.

"Where are they?" she pressed on.

"Gone," I said. "Vanished in front of my eyes."

"Gone where?" she asked, looking at me with curious eyes—eyes that I knew from long ago.

"I'm not sure," I replied, "but tomorrow morning I'm going to dig them up all over again."

"Timeline stuff, huh?" she said.

"Timeline stuff," I repeated. "Want to come with?"

"Sure!" she replied and then hesitated. "We're not going to tell the others, are we?"

"Just you and me," I said.

271

She smiled the widest smile. Then she had a sudden thought. "But what about the Frags?"

"We don't need to worry about them," I assured her.

"Why not?" came the reply.

"Because, Buttercup," I told her, "they're still buried underground."

I flicked the tip of her nose with my finger, and she smiled at me again. The thought crossed my mind that everyone should have the chance to interact with themselves as a child. It gives one a sense of meaning as to how you became an adult.

CHAPTER XLVI

Chloë

Earth Year: 2033
Alternate Reality III

This was the first time I had ever seen a being from Rendenaaar. Peyton had described them to me—to all of us—the beings from the planet she'd lived on in a former incarnation.

"I'm Khattaaara," she said in an alien-sounding voice. Peyton stared at her and then took a step back, undoubtedly shocked at the sight of her.

"What's going on?" she said.

"What do you mean?" I asked.

"Who or, rather, *what* the *fuck* is *she*?" she replied.

"You don't know?" I asked, amazed that she didn't.

Khattaaara, who had been staring at her, suddenly turned her attention toward *me*. "What is going on?" she asked. "Why doesn't she know me?"

"This isn't your Peyton," I answered. "She's from an alternate timeline. They just both share the same body."

That certainly was news to the Peyton who stood with us. "You didn't answer my question," she said to me. "What the fuck's going on?"

"Do you know what quantum reality is?" I asked her.

"Isn't that where the FBI has its headquarters?" she replied, staring at Khattaaara. "What? Are you telling me she's some sort of federal agent?"

"No," I replied, "that's Quantico. Quantum reality is the basis for everything that exists, and you—the other you—is Quantum Girl, a bonified superhero."

"And I'm supposed to believe that?" she replied. "What? Is this

273

supposed other me, able to leap tall buildings in a single bound?"

I looked at her and shook my head. I was about to try and explain when Khattaaara interrupted.

"Wait!" she exclaimed. "I think I can help."

She moved toward Peyton, who backed up into a wall. Khattaaara became almost transparent and, in another instant, disappeared into Peyton who seemed to become electric. Her clothes disintegrated off of her. Her eyes glowed purple and then white and, as she screamed, the same blinding light filled the cavern of her mouth. And then it stopped as though a switch had been flicked. She stood a moment more and then collapsed. I caught her in my arms and helped her into a chair.

"Are you all right," I asked.

She nodded as another one of her briefly rose from the naked form in a Quantum Girl costume.

"Khattaaara?" I asked.

There came another nod with the faintest of smiles.

"So," I went on, "you were the one in the grave."

"Not yet," she said, "but soon."

"Why give up your life?" I asked. "Why can't Peyton just duplicate herself," I asked, "let just that one be killed?"

"The other Quantum Girl would sense the connection," she replied, "and destroy her as well."

"How did you know to come here?" I asked.

"There are filaments in the quantum fabric," she said, "that reach through time and space—even through universes."

She sank back toward Peyton and disappeared into her.

Peyton just stared up at me.

"Is Khattaaara inside of you?" I asked.

"Khattaaara and the Payton who was part of her," she replied. "But I'm exhausted. Would you just help me into bed?"

I did and then covered her with the bedsheet. She stared upward at the ceiling with little expression on her face.

"I not only remember *this* timeline," she said in a detached voice. "but two others. How did all of this fall on me?"

"You're not alone," I said as I sat down on the edge of the bed next to her. "You have Isis to help you for what that's worth."

"Thank you," she said and smiled. Then she rolled over onto her side, clutched her pillow, and closed her eyes to sleep.

As for myself, I phased up to the rooftop and stared at the stars in the cold night sky, contemplating existence, and feeling as insignificant as one tiny grain of sand in the desert. What would happen in the end? Who would live and who would die? *God only knows*, I thought to myself, *but if there is no God, then there is only unknowing.*

CHAPTER XLVII

Peyton
(the one who just woke up)

Earth Year: 2033
Alternate Reality I

I was back home alone when there was a knock on the door. The one Chloë had gone shopping and the other two were up to no good in the bedroom, so, for the most part, I had the house to myself. I had been engrossed in a movie called, *Death Breathes Deep*. It was a screwball comedy about a man being haunted by his ex. I hated to miss the rest of it but *Oh, well!* I thought to myself, heading down the stairs at a rabbit's pace as the knocking began again. "Coming, I'm coming!" I called out toward the door.

I supposed I could have just phased down, I thought, but what if whoever was knocking decided to look through the window? Opening the door I saw a good-looking man in his mid-thirties with light brown hair, blue eyes, and wire-framed glasses. He was dressed in a brown plaid sports jacket, white shirt, and slacks.

"May I help you?" I asked.

"I would hope so," he replied. "Do you have any idea what it took for me to track you down?"

"Why would you want to?" I asked.

"Why would I want...?" he started to say and then broke off. "Do you have any idea how many Peyton Herrons there are in the country? I tried using your sister's name but drew a blank. Finally, I remembered you'd mentioned a Claire Wrenley Salinger. I managed to get her parents' address and it was her mother who gave me this one. Except she was under the impression that you were in some sort of perpetual catatonic state since—she said —you'd attempted suicide at age fourteen."

"Are we supposed to know each other?" I asked.

The man scratched his head. "You were in my office three weeks ago, revealing yourself as Quantum Girl. You get hit on the head or something?"

"That wasn't me," I said. "That was her."

"Her?" he replied. "Who her?" He looked hard at me. "Your name wouldn't happen to be Ophelia, would it?"

"Sorry," I said. "I don't have a sister You can come in if you want and I'll try and explain."

The man entered, looked around the room, and then went over to the sofa. "Here okay?" he asked.

"It's fine," I replied. "Would you like me to get you something to drink?"

"Scotch or bourbon," he said. "It doesn't much matter to me."

"I was thinking more along the lines of orange juice or ice tea," I replied.

"Ice tea, then," came his answer as I went into the kitchen. "I'm still unclear what's going on."

"You said she told you about Quantum Girl," I said in a loud voice.

"Nearly gave me a heart attack!" he replied, shouting back. "There were two of you that merged into one right in front of me!"

"They were both her!" I said. "I'm from a different timeline!"

"A different what?" he asked.

"Timeline," I said, returning with two glasses of ice tea.

I placed his drink down on the coffee table in front of the sofa and then sat down in the overstuffed chair off to the side, facing him.

"Presumably," I said, "something happened in the past that caused the timeline to change. I'm another version of her."

"And where is she now?" he asked.

"Dead," I replied as I swallowed a mouthful of ice tea.

"How?" came the shocked response.

And so I told him all that I knew about what had gone on. "Were you two close?" I asked afterward.

"Not really," he replied. "We had actually just met."

"But she trusted you enough to reveal herself," I said with half a question.

"Apparently so," he replied, standing up and extending his hand to me. "By the way, I don't think I introduced myself. I'm Mark Marsden, former reporter for the Manhattan Mirror."

I took his hand and shook it. "Former?" I repeated.

"My editor and those in charge," he replied, "thought it best to can someone who was to them obviously losing their mind."

"Because you told them about Quantum Girl," I said.

Marsden shrugged. "Without naming names," he replied. "I'm curious though," he went on, "why the other Peyton Herron even approached me. It must have been for more than just tracking down her sister."

"Don't know," I replied. "But there is the other raging question. Why did you spend all that time and expense trying to track her down? I mean, there's the obvious curiosity about her being *unique* and all, but I suspect there's more to it than that."

He paused for a moment, considering how to word what he was going to say, and then answered, "Did you ever meet someone that you found overwhelmingly attractive, that you felt this was the one person you've wanted to be with for the rest of your life, just from one casual encounter?"

I wanted to say yes. I wanted to tell the whole world about Theresa but I held my tongue.

"That's the way I felt about her," he said. "I realize that sounds about as insane as trying to convince the paper I used to work for about some superheroine."

"No," I said, "not at all. But here you are, face to face with her again, only it's not her."

"Maybe not," he replied, "but maybe so."

"What do you mean?" I asked.

"The same person," he replied, "just a different version." He paused and then apologized. "I'm sorry," he went on. "As you said, you're not actually her."

It was at that moment that the unthinkable happened. A yellow-costumed Quantum Girl suddenly appeared in the room behind him—a Quantum Girl that looked a whole lot like Chloë. We both stood up and faced her as her eyes began to glow. She held her arms out in front of her. In another instant, a yellow ball of energy appeared in her hands. As she was about to hurl it at me, Marsden jumped in its path, grabbing hold of me—protecting me from it. His face turned pale and he collapsed to the ground. I stared at my quantum enemy and then phased both Marsden and myself back in time to the street just outside the same restaurant in 1960 only moments after I had left. It was all that I could think of what with everything happening the way it did.

"Help!" I screamed out at the top of my lungs. "Help!"

People gathered. There wasn't the indifference that existed in my day and age. One man ran to a phone booth and called for an ambulance. I suppose I could have phased us to a hospital, but I had no idea where one was.

"What happened?" asked one woman.

"Maybe it was a heart attack," said one man.

"He looks too young for that," another replied. "Maybe a stroke."

An ambulance arrived within minutes with a wailing siren—not the kind I was familiar with. It looked more like an old-fashioned hearse painted white. After it pulled up near us, two men emerged and rushed up to us. One of them squatted down next to him, checked for a pulse, and then his breathing. He put a stethoscope to his chest and listened to his heart. I was trembling. I didn't know if he was unconscious or dead.

"We were walking and he just collapsed," I lied, though there were genuine tears on my cheeks. I felt that somehow this was all my fault. It was like I was a bad penny. Everyone I touched wound up getting hurt… or worse!

The team rushed to the back of their vehicle, took out a stretcher, and brought it over to us. Then they lifted him onto it, strapped him down, lifted it and him, and placed him in the ambulance. One of the men got in with him and then the other shut the door. I turned to that one and touched his shoulder as he turned and was about to walk toward the driver's door.

"Would it be all right if I rode along?" I asked.

"Is he your husband?" the man replied.

"Yes," I answered.

"Get in, then," the man said.

I got in next to him in the front seat and we drove off to the hospital to the emergency entrance. I paced in the waiting room for more than two hours before a doctor came out and approached me.

"How is he?" I asked.

The doctor was solemn. "He suffered serious burns to his back," he said, "We did what we could. The rest is up to him."

"When can I see him?" I asked.

"He'll be in recovery for the next twelve hours," he replied.

"Why don't you go home," he said, "get some rest, and come back in the morning."

I nodded. Then he walked away. I wasn't quite sure what to do. There was no home for me to go to and I didn't dare go back to my time—at least not yet. I walked from Beverly Boulevard where the hospital was, to Wilshire, blindly staring into store windows in more or less of a stupor. Sooner or later, Mark (I'd gotten to thinking of him as Mark) was going to be released from the hospital, assuming he survived, and he would need to go somewhere and there would be all the doctors' bills to be paid. My experience was that of a fourteen-year-old. I didn't know what to do.

I stopped in front of the Bullocks Department Store at one of the window displays. In it was a man struggling to dress a female mannequin, trying to attach one of its arms under a blouse and jacket.

Exasperated, he pulled the arm out of the sleeve, threw it down, and then began yelling at the fiberglass woman like it was her fault. There were others who passed by on the sidewalk, most merely glancing at what was going on. It seemed that I was the only one engrossed in the theatre of the scene. My quantum hearing allowed me to listen in on the rantings of the man as he screamed at the helpless statue in Italian which I couldn't understand. Finally, he threw up his arms and stormed out of the display. *Poor, poor, mannequin,* I thought to myself, *being screamed at by that miserable man and yet smiling through it all. I could never be that strong!*

I considered the situation for a moment and then entered through the large brass-framed glass doors. Once inside, I asked one of the clerks where they did the hiring and then rode the elevator up to the fifth floor. As soon as the doors opened, I heard the same man's voice yelling in English and cursing in Italian, all ending with, "I quit!" followed by more Italian ramblings as he marched out from one office to the elevator where he began to beat up the button for him to go down. The doors finally opened, and he went in. And then they closed and that was the last I ever saw of him, although I could hear his Italian ramblings and curses as he descended to the first floor. My attention turned away suddenly from all that when a woman's voice addressed me from behind with, "May I help you?"

I walked up to the desk where the woman whose voice it was sat and asked, "Could you tell me who does the hiring?"

The woman, who was well-dressed, nice-looking, and about thirty years old, eyed me with curiosity. I obviously was not dressed the part for a job interview—at least for back then.

"We're full up on sales positions," she said.

"Oh," I replied, "I'm not looking to sell anyone anything. I was wondering if there might be an opening to work window displays."

The woman considered for a moment and then pressed a button on her intercom.

"Yes, Miss Larrabee?" a male voice asked.

"There's a woman inquiring if there are any openings for a window display position."

"Window display?" the man's voice repeated. "Yes, send her in."

The woman looked up at me. "Down the hallway to the right. Second door on the left. Mr. Randolph."

At the door in question, I took a deep breath and then entered a paneled room with a large picture window that viewed the Santa Monica Mountains in the near distance. A balding man in his late fifties sat behind a somewhat massive wooden desk. A cigar lay in a geometric metal ashtray to his right, wafting off thin wisps of white smoke from its lit end.

The man eyed me with curiosity. "Miss Larrabee said that you want to apply as a window designer," he announced in an accent that had a hint of Texas in it. "So far all of our window designers have been ill-tempered, middle-aged men. You don't look middle-aged and you are most certainly not a man. How is your temperament?"

"Sweet as cherry pie on a hot summer's day," I said in my best Southern drawl.

"And you can dress windows *and* mannequins?" he went on.

"Yes, Sir," I told him.

"Where was your last place of employment?" he asked.

"Abilene," I replied.

"And which establishment?" he asked.

As I had no idea what stores were in Abilene, I froze time and phased there, jumping from place to place until I found a small department store that looked like a good place to reference. Then I phased back and restarted time.

"Grissom's, Sir," I said. "They only have two picture windows, so I wound up working on most of the clothing displays as well."

That was enough proof for him as to my qualifications—*Lord, Jesus, forgive me my sins for having lied to the man*, I prayed—and so I was hired, Southern accent and all. My salary was set at twenty-five dollars per week which was about a quarter of what men made but it was a job and I sorely needed one. I managed to rent a room for Twelve dollars per week from a gentle old woman named Mrs. Langford, over in Hollywood, on the promise of payment after my first check, playing on her kindheartedness, with the story that my husband had been injured and was in the hospital on the road to recovery and I hoped those last words were true.

Once I was settled in and had a moment to take in my new abode, I phased over to the hospital and went up to the room to which Mark had been assigned. His eyes were closed but he opened them when I took his hand in mine.

"You're here," he said and tried to smile, though I could tell he was in pain.

"You risked your life to save mine," I told him. "Why would you do that? We barely met."

"You said the Peyton I met died," he replied. "I wasn't about to let that happen again."

I stared hard at him. "You fell in love with her," I said, "didn't you?"

He didn't say anything. He just shrugged.

"I'm not her, you know," I told him.

"I know," he replied.

"So, don't go getting any ideas about me because I'm not available."

He just smiled at me and squeezed my hand.

CHAPTER XLVIII

Young Jordan

The Next Universe
Planet Erebus: Year V
Alternate Reality II

It was kind of cool being able to see what I'd look like when I grew up, especially the boobs—not that there were any guys around to appreciate them. All three of us—Zhana and Sami and me—we all pretended that we didn't care about boys. "Who needs them!" we would all say, but the truth was we knew they were our other half and without them, we wouldn't be whole. At least that's what I believed. I mean, I didn't want to criticize Auntie Ophelia and Auntie Claire. They were who they were and that was their choice. People are all different. But I was not attracted to girls and I didn't think Sami or Zhan were either. Personally, I found the whole idea of two women, kissing and all, kind of disgusting, but that was just me. The problem was that it was getting harder and harder to even remember what boys looked like. My mom said that when she was my age she had a crush on Chris Hemsworth, who she said was "older but still hot." I kind of remembered him in one of the Avengers movies—sort of. But moving on...

It wasn't like a treasure hunt or anything, finding the god-stones. Danna had done all the searching before in the future. It turned out they were buried six feet under my bed which didn't make them easy to get out in that the floor was made of some kind of material that was as hard as steel even though it wasn't metal. We figured that our mom must have phased them to where they were.

"How did you know where to look?" I asked Future Me.

"I didn't," she replied. "Not at first. It wasn't until Zhana figured out how to work an ancient energy detector that I was able to find them."

The problem, though, was how to get the god-stones out from where they were without attracting attention. The answer came in the form of Chloë who possessed extraordinary strength, even though at that point in time she didn't realize it.

"How am I supposed to break through the floor?" she asked. "From what I remember I was barely able to make it through junior girls wrestling."

"Just try," Danna insisted after we moved the bed aside.

"All right," Chloë sighed. Then she banged the side of her fist down on the floor as hard as she could to find, to her amazement, it made a huge dent. She looked at her fist and then at the floor. A few more hammers and she had actually punched through it and, within minutes, she had created a hole five feet across. That much accomplished, she rose to her feet and stared at us.

"Anyone mind telling me how I was able to do that?" she asked, still believing that she was actually the Chloë who was human.

"The god-stones we all used to cross into this universe," I replied. "Do you remember giving yours back?"

Chloë thought for a moment and then replied, "I don't."

"There's your answer," I said and then went on to lie with, "It must still be in you."

It took two days to dig down to where the god-stones had been buried. *Thank goodness!* we both thought, Danna and I, that Mom hadn't buried them deeper. I suppose she thought it a safe enough distance, not expecting me to spend the next ten years looking for them, only to find them the day she turned up and announced that we were all to go back in time. It's kind of a strange thing how time works.

Because the god-stones vanished from the future, we had to dig them up in the past. But what if they hadn't vanished? Then there would be two sets of them which Mom said couldn't happen because they'd absorb into each other. But if they *hadn't* vanished in the future and Danna *had* brought them back, would the ones Danna brought back have merged into the buried ones or would the buried ones have merged into the ones in her hand? And why did they vanish at all; just because they got unburied didn't make any sense. It was kind of like they had a mind of their own. Anyway, it made my head hurt trying to figure it all out.

"What are we going to do with them?" I asked, staring at the five god-stones in her hand.

"Put them in a safe place," she replied.

"They *were* in a safe place," I said. "We just unsafe-placed them."

"Not the safe place I was referring to," she answered, her eyes pointing upward, meaning in her head.

"Not fair!" I complained. "I should at least get one!"

"You will," she said. "Just not yet. I need to do something first."

"Like what?" I asked with a frown.

"Like find out who we were before," she replied.

"Before what?" I asked.

"Before we were born," she said. "Do you remember the time you overheard Mom talking with Aunt Ophelia about Rendenaaar and about how she lived out her life as one of them?"

I nodded.

"And how Aunt Ophelia's human daughter came forward through time," she went on, "in order to help save everyone from Khattaaara? She mentioned our name, only at the time I thought she was referring to me, but she wasn't. She was referring to Aunt Ophelia's daughter. But why would Mom give us the same name as her? And when she merged all the dimensions together, she was the only one missing. Unless…"

"We're her!" I exclaimed.

"I want to find out if the god-stones can restore the memory of any past life."

"You still don't need *all* of them!" I complained.

"You never know," she replied. "Besides, I can always eject

them."

One by one, she placed the god-stones to her head and, one by one, they began spinning, becoming smaller, and melted through her skin. When the last one had disappeared, she stared out into space.

"Do you remember anything?" I asked her.

"No," she said. "Nothing."

"Oh, well," I replied.

"We have a bigger problem than remembering who we were," she said. Her eyes fixed hard on mine.

"What do you mean?" I asked.

"When we removed the god-stones, it interfered with the quantum field around them."

"And?" I asked.

"The mother stone just reactivated the Frags," she replied.

"But they're still in the cavern," I said, "and the cavern is sealed. Isn't it?"

"Yes," she replied, "but they'll eventually get out. Trust me."

"Not good," I said. "Definitely not good. So, what do we do?"

"We need to leave," she replied.

"And go where?" I asked.

"I don't know," she replied, "but this planet is, as they say, a fuse waiting for a match."

CHAPTER XLIX

Peyton
(the one who just woke up)

Earth Year: 1960
Alternate Reality I

With absolutely no experience in window dressing, I managed to pull it off. I found I even had a flare for it. For Mother's Day, I made a mannequin appear pregnant, pushing a baby carriage with a baby mannequin in it which I convinced Mr. Randolph to let me buy from the Wolf & Vine Mannequin Company that was located just ten miles away. Back then, mannequins weren't as lifelike as they would later become, but the display I created wound up getting a lot of attention and got me a ten-dollar-a-week raise, all of which went toward Mark's hospital bills.

Every day after work I would go visit him. For the first few weeks, he was pretty much under from the pain medication he was given, but gradually, as he began to heal he became more...lucid. I remember looking that word up in the thesaurus I checked out from the library. I had been trying to increase my vocabulary and knowledge in general, having missed so much school for so many years. The history and the science books only covered up to 1960 but that was okay. I mean, I couldn't get books from my time.

It was an interesting era, though. Eisenhower was President with Richard Nixon as his VP. All cars had tailfins and a lot of them were two-tone, meaning some color plus white. Hardly any of them had air conditioners or seatbelts. All of the refrigerators had heavy levers to open them which locked them shut, making them dangerous for children who might get trapped inside and suffocate when they broke and were left outside. I managed to save one little boy, hearing him and then seeing him inside with my quantum vision. I got so mad that after I got him out, I phased the refrigerator to the moon. I wondered what future astronauts would think when they found it there. I brought him home to his mother who burst into tears upon hearing what had happened and what had almost caused him to die. She knelt down and hugged him with tears flowing, and then pulled back and began to scold him. As the boy began to cry, she hugged him again and so there they were, both in tears.

"I am so grateful," she said and then extended her hand. "My name's Sharon. Sharon Costner."

"Peyton Herron," I replied.

"Sometimes I just don't know what to do with this child," she went on.

A boy about ten appeared in the living room where we stood. "I can't find my baseball mitt," he said.

"Where did you put it?" Mrs. Costner asked.

"If I knew that," the boy replied, "I wouldn't be asking."

"I have no idea where it is," she told him. "Why don't you take your brother back to your room and he can help you look for it."

"Aw, gee, Ma!" the boy groaned. "He just gets in the way!"

Sharon Costner's face turned stern. "Your brother nearly died today and this kind lady saved him. She gave him a chance to grow up to do great things!"

"Yeah, right," the boy said.

"Just go to your room!" his mother said and then turned to me as the boy marched to his room. "Honestly," she went on, "raising two boys is a twenty-four-hour job, but I already lost one in childbirth, so thank you for saving my Kevin."

I left feeling good about myself. I worried about altering the timeline by saving him. I just couldn't bear to let him die. The odds were that he'd probably just grow up and blend in with the rest of the population and not make any difference in the world. Anyway, that was my justification for doing what I did.

I spent a lot of time with Mark while he was recovering in the hospital. We really got to know each other and found that we had a lot in common. It wasn't as if it were about things like sports or art or even books we had read, and I knew absolutely nothing about the movies he had seen, mostly in black and white and with movie stars I had never heard of. It was about the way we felt about things like nature and the stars and love and God. Mark was raised a Catholic, which my Mama, being a devout Presbyterian, thought was the Devil's religion, but we got past all that because we both believed in Jesus and Him having died for our sins. We would talk for hours about little things and make stupid jokes that we both laughed at. Then one day, as I was sitting in a chair next to his bed, he said he wanted to whisper something to me and asked me to bend down so that he could.

"Why do you need to whisper anything?" I asked, glancing around the room. "There's no one else here." He had a roommate, but the man, unfortunately, had passed away the night before, so Mark for the moment had the room to himself.

"Because I want to tell you something," he insisted.

So, wanting to oblige him, I bend down, placing my ear near his lips to hear him say, "I love you," for the very first time.

I turned my head to look at him, only inches away. "I love you, too," I said. Then we kissed and he put his arms around me and pulled me close to him. I had my cheek laid against his chest, hearing his heart—with no quantum help I might add.

"I want to ask you something," he said in a quiet voice. "I know that we started out as strangers, but we've become… friends. I said that I love you but that was a half-truth. The fact of the matter is that I'm *in* love with you, Peyton Herron. I've lived most of my life never knowing you but now I can't imagine living a day of my life without you." He paused for a moment, gathering up courage. He reached out and took hold of my hand with his. His heart was beating wildly but then it slowed, almost to a stop. I didn't move. I couldn't, as my heart synchronized with his. I didn't think about Theresa. This was a different kind of love and, beyond that, I didn't know if I'd ever return to my time.

CHAPTER L

Cleopatra

Earth Year: 2033
Alternate Reality I

Despite the constant threat of war, things were a lot simpler when I was Queen of Egypt. This future was more complicated, especially around those I had encountered. I returned to the House of Herron to find one Chloë sleeping on the couch in the living room. There were noises, however, down the hallway—moaning sounds. Phasing into the room whence the sounds came, I found two more of her naked in bed in opposite directions, stimulating each other sexually. I needed to clear my throat loudly several times before they realized they were not alone in the room.

"Is this how you spend your time?" I asked. "I see you found your third."

"That's not her," one of them said. "She's from another timeline."

"By the Great Sphinx," I replied, "how many of you are there?"

"Four that we know of," said the other.

"Five, if you count the one who died," said the first.

"That was my Isis," I replied. "Kindly do not disgrace her memory in your depravéd state."

It was then that I heard voices from the living room. I went there to see the Chloë on the couch, now risen, speaking to another. Both turned in my direction as they saw me enter but then appeared to glance past me. I turned to see the other pair standing naked, apparently as surprised as myself to see that their other third had returned.

"Where have you been?" the naked ones asked in unison.

"What does it matter?" the other answered. "I'm back."

One of the naked ones looked at me. "Can you help us get back

292

together?" she asked.

I turned to the third and asked, "Is that all right with you?"

"Fine," she said grudgingly, "though I was kind of getting used to being my own self."

"You'd better undress," I said. "I don't want your clothing getting in the way."

Number three glanced up at me as she was taking off her clothes. "You *have* done this before," she asked, "haven't you?"

"Did you have practice when you split apart?" I replied.

"No, but…" she began, as she removed the last vestige of her apparel.

"In Egypt," I interrupted, "we had a word we used for such questions. *Ekhras!*"

"And that means…?" she asked.

"It means, 'Shut up!'" I said. "Now go stand with your other selves."

Once they had gathered together, I focused my thoughts on combining them into one. The figures all wavered and then began to merge together. Unfortunately, something unexpected happened. The fourth mixed in with them as well, clothes and all.

"That wasn't supposed to happen," said the now-combined one. "I don't suppose you know how to separate the ancient part of me?"

"No idea," I confessed. "I think it had to do with your all having the same god-stone, unprotected by a quantum field."

The newly formed Chloë took a deep breath. "Well," she said. "What's done is done. It's just strange having all these extra memories. I think I need to get some sleep to let them sort out." She glanced around the room and then looked back at me. "By the way," she asked, "have you seen Peyton?"

"She's not upstairs in her room?" I replied.

"I don't think so," she answered. "I called out to her when I got back in. I thought she might have gone out with *you.*"

I shook my head, phased from room to room, and then back to

293

Chloë. "She isn't here," I said. "It isn't like her to disappear without at least leaving a note. I'm concerned. Emotionally, she's still a child."

"Yes," Chloë replied, "a child alone with a god-stone in her head."

CHAPTER LI

Peyton
(the one who just woke up)

Earth Year: 1960
Alternate Reality I

After three weeks, the hospital allowed Mark to go home, meaning home to me. Mrs. Langford was very understanding, especially in that I had told her that Mark and I had been married only days before his accident. I said that we had been walking down the street at night when a robber threatened us with a gun and that Mark had fought back and had gotten shot. I couldn't very well tell her the truth, that some yellow-costumed Quantum Girl tried to murder me nearly three-quarters of a century in the future with an energy beam, but that Mark had jumped in its path in order to save me. I could only imagine her reaction.

Mark needed to use a cane to walk at first. The ordeal had made him very weak. They didn't have walkers back then. Plus, I asked Mrs. Langford if it would be all right if we rented a cot for me to sleep on since Mark was still quite frail. Her words were, "Nonsense! There's one in the attic you can use. I'll have a couple of the men bring it down when they return from work." The cot made the room a bit crowded but I was more concerned about Mark's health.

It's a strange thing about living in close quarters with someone. Having been an only child and never having gone to college to experience dorm life, this was a new experience for me. The thing about it was that Mark never got on my nerves. I found him endearing and we only grew closer together. It turned out that he grew up in Des Moines and then left for New York after graduating from the University of Iowa with a major in journalism. How touching it was that he left it all to find me—or, rather, search out the other me. I often wondered what her reaction would have been to his unannounced appearance. And I wonder even now how our relationship would have progressed if he hadn't risked his life to save mine so that we wound up together in the past.

Mostly, Mark and I ate in our room, but on Sundays, Mrs. Langford made supper for all of her guests—I think that's the right word, even though everyone paid rent. It was about a week or so after Mark came to stay there that I was at the dinner table with her and her other three tenants: Mr. Baird, a college professor in his sixties with glasses and a goatee, Mr. Lindstrom, a Swede in his mid-forties, who worked as a cabinetmaker, and Miss Braven, in her late twenties, who worked behind the lunch counter at Schwab's Pharmacy on Sunset Boulevard where supposedly actress, Lana Turner at age sixteen was discovered by director, Mervyn LeRoy.[30] Mark wasn't feeling well enough to come down.

"I hear that Richard Nixon is running for President," Mr. Baird said. "Fine candidate if you ask me."

"Running against that senator," Mr. Lindstrom added. "I forget his name."

"John F. Kennedy," Mr. Baird exclaimed. "Catholic I think. Doesn't stand a chance!"

"Gentlemen," Mrs. Langford interrupted. "No politics at the table, please."

"I'm just glad that Elvis Presley's back from being in the service," Miss Braven quietly said.

I barely heard them, though. My mind was focused on the empty chair next to me.

"What do you think about Elvis?" Miss Braven asked me. "Mrs. Marsden?"

---

[30] The story, which became legend, was entirely false. According to Lana Turner, she was actually discovered at the Top Hat Café, a block away from Hollywood High where she was a student, by Billy Wilkerson, then publisher of the Hollywood Reporter.

I woke from my reverie as she addressed me. "I asked you what you thought about Elvis Presley?"

"He's all right," I replied. "I've only seen him a couple of times on YouTube."

"What's YouTube?" she asked.

"Oh," I said. "I meant on the boob tube." That was what Pops, my granddad, used to call television sets.

"Well, I think he's just dreamy," Miss Braven said.

It was as I was cutting the roast beef on my plate that Mrs. Langford commented. "Peyton," she said to me, "what happened to your wedding ring?"

My heart jumped a beat at the realization that I was supposedly married but wasn't wearing one. I had taken off the one Theresa had given me because I didn't want Mark to think that I was married. "Oh," I said, embarrassed, "I had to sell it to help pay the hospital bill." To my discredit, it seemed that I was getting all too good at lying. Jesus forgive me.

"Well, we'll need to do something about that," she said. "Come see me after the table's cleared and everything's put away."

"Yes, Ma'am," I replied.

An hour or so later, when all was done, I knocked on the door to her room.

"Come in," she said.

I entered and she stared at me for a moment and then said, "Sit down, Dear." She paused for a moment, which was her way, and then went on. "You remind me of my son. You have the same kind eyes. We got into an argument and never spoke again. He had wanted to join the military to go fight in Korea and I didn't want him to go. The truth was that I was afraid something would happen to him. We exchanged words in the heat of the moment and I said things that I wished I hadn't. I don't know if we had words because of the military or because, after his father had died, I remarried and he was angry with me for that, but we never spoke again. As it turned out, he not only survived the war but was honored as a hero."

She got up from where she was sitting, went to her dresser, took out a newspaper clipping, and brought it back to show me. The headline for the article read, "Soldier Saves Platoon." I glanced at her and then read on. "Corporal Joseph Charles Herron of Culver City was awarded the Medal of Honor for saving the lives of seven men in his company when an enemy sniper had shot them. According to Sgt. Edward Blackstone, Cpl. Herron risked his life going out into enemy fire and dragging those wounded to safety." Within the article was a photo, beneath which read, "Cpl. Joseph C. Herron receives Medal of Honor beside wife, Janice, and son, James."

I stared at the clipping and then looked back up at her. *The universe*, I thought, *must play tricks. This woman, Mrs. Langford, was my great-grandmother! But how, of all the places I might have gone to, to rent a room did I wind up here?* She looked at me again and then opened her closed fist, revealing a diamond ring.

"This had belonged to my first husband," she said, "Joseph's father. I want you to have it. No woman should be married without a wedding ring."

"Oh," I said, "I couldn't."

"Edwin would want you to have it," she said, taking my left hand and placing the ring on my finger. "And I think that Joseph would have wanted you to have it, too."

My eyes began to tear up. "Thank you," I said. "I'll never take it off. I never knew any grandparents on my father's side, but I wish you could have been one of them."[31]

"You go on now, Dear," she said. "All these memories dredged up, I'm afraid I need to lie down for a while."

Back in our room, I changed into my nightgown in the dark and then climbed into my cot. I tried to be as quiet as I could but I guess I wasn't quiet enough.

---

[31] As I came to learn, the other Peyton did know her paternal grandfather, Pops, but in my timeline, he died before I was born.

"The moonlight through the window," Mark said in a soft voice, "makes you look like an angel." He paused and then went on with, "How was dinner?"

"Roast beef and mashed potatoes," I said. "Cecilia Braven, it seems, is an Elvis fan. Mrs. Randolph called me to her room afterward and gave me this." I held out my hand. "She doesn't know it but it turns out she's my great-grandmother on my father's side. She said a married woman should have a wedding ring."

"And I think," he replied, "that a woman with a wedding ring should have a husband. Proper decorum would dictate that I get down on one knee, but my doctor would disagree." He took a deep breath and then exhaled. "Peyton Elise Herron," he said, "will you marry me?"

"I never thought you'd ask," I said.

"Well, I did," he replied.

"Of course, I will," I said.

I got up, walked around the bed, and stood staring at him. I know the moonlight through the window behind me had shown through my nightgown because he stared up and down my form. Then I gently climbed into bed, snuggled beside him, and we kissed again and again.

CHAPTER LII

Peyton

Earth Year: 2033
Alternate Reality III

I opened my eyes in bed on my back to find the yellow-costumed Quantum Girl hovering just inches above me, facing me, shadowing me. I didn't know how it came about—whether it was caused by my subconscious mind phasing her there or from the god-stone going in—but there she was. And regardless that I had gone to sleep in my nightgown, I awoke in my Quantum Girl outfit. My right hand reached up to touch hers. Sparks of electricity danced between our fingers. As my head went from side to side, hers mimicked my every move. "Who are you?" I asked as she said the same. It was as though she were a mirror image of me. But then the appearance of any reflection vanished as she broke into what I can only describe as evil laughter. Her fingers laced into mine. What had at first been a mild tingling from the energy between us amplified into excruciating pain. I tried to pull free but she refused to let go. I tried to scream but no sound came from my mouth. As hard as I struggled, I could not escape her grip. Her breasts merged into mine, then her legs, and then her feet. The ends of her hair attached to the ends of mine, causing both to become shorter, pulling our faces together. Then came a blinding light between us—a light so hot it seared my flesh. The pain was unrelenting. My mouth fused into hers so that I couldn't even breathe. Soon, the brilliance was everywhere, as though both of us had exploded like a supernova. And then I woke up.

I was in my nightgown in bed, covered in sweat—my hair, matted to my face—the bedsheet and pillow, soaked in perspiration. It must have been early morning, just at the edge of dawn. I could hear birds chirping outside. Miles in the distance, there was the wail of a fire engine racing somewhere. And there was the sound of my heart, beating like there was no tomorrow—perhaps it was a foreshadowing of days to come. I didn't know. I couldn't tell. I was in a world that was unlike the one I had left. It was one of two divergent universes that had somehow been created by the red god-stone I had phased into Chloë's head as our universe was about to implode. It was back then that I had divided, with one of me going back to Rendenaaar and the other into the new universe with Phee and Claire and the kids. What had happened to either of them afterward I didn't know. It was as though I were me before that had happened. And who or what was that other Quantum Girl that I had dreamt about, the yellow one that Chloë said would kill me? I rose from the bed to find Chloë asleep in the overstuffed chair near the window. Throwing on a robe, I fetched a spare blanket from the footlocker where I kept all my bedding and covered her with it. Then I fixed myself some cocoa and phased out to the fire escape where I had a folding chair set up. I sipped my brew, stared outward at the growing light in the sky, and drowned myself in thought.

The universe was barreling toward its end, although it seemed that there might be two of them now. I had combined all the parallel dimensions but then I'd caused reality to diverge. I had to go to that other reality and find out what was happening there. Would that Earth be identical to this one, also bereft of men, and doomed to extinction as a result?

It was then, however, that I noticed a figure in the distance high overhead. It was her—real this time—the yellow Quantum Girl! Something strange happened then. A violet Quantum Girl emerged from me without me willing her to.

"How?" I asked.

She stared at me. "You don't remember," she said with a strange accent. "Your mind is still trying to sort out the two timelines you were in." She paused and then smiled. "You merged with me last night. I can't let you be killed and create a time loop from which there may be no escape. I'm the one who needs to fight that one."

"I can help," I said.

"You must not risk yourself," she replied. "Your universe depends on you."

"My universe?" I repeated, perplexed.

"I am Khattaaara," she replied. "And a part of you."

"But you'll be killed," I said. "Chloë told me."

"No," she replied. "My consciousness is still connected to my other self on Rendenaaar." She stared up at the yellow Quantum Girl in the sky and then looked back at me. "One more thing," she said. "I'll be leaving a friend behind," and, as she spoke those words, Payton emerged from her. Then Khattaaara phased off to meet the one who would complete the cycle and phase her soulless body into the grave.

Payton looked at me and smiled, and then stretched. "It's good to be human again," she said. "Hello, Peyton, dear," she went on. "In another moment the god-stone in my head will draw me into you but for the moment it's good to see you."

"The universe is done for," I told her. "It's up to me to save it."

"No," she replied, shaking her head. "It's up to us," her words fading into nothing as she was pulled into me—she becoming a part of me and I becoming a part of her. Suddenly, another reality slammed into my head—the one where Khattaaara and I combined—the one that overwrote reality before and created the other Ophelia and Sarabeth. It caused my head to ache. I took a deep breath, steeled myself, went back inside, and roused Chloë from her sleep.

"What's wrong?" she asked sleepily. "What time is it?"

"I need to leave," I said.

"To where?" she replied.

"To the timeline that overlays this one," I told her. "I need answers. I have to find out if there's another one of me there."

"I'll come with you," she said. "There's nothing for me here."

"Don't you like being a stripper?" I asked.

302

"No more than I'd want to ride a roller coaster forever," came her response. "It *can* get old after a while."

"I don't know," I replied. "I found it somewhat empowering."

"Wait!" she exclaimed. "You remember all of it? How you lusted after me? You still don't feel that way, do you?"

"Does someone who's drunk," I replied, "feel the same way once they're sober?"

"I get your point," she said. "Only please don't ever get drunk again."

I smiled at her. "You have my word," I assured her. "As for coming with me, I want you to wait one day just in case I phase into a trap."

She smiled and then hugged me, and then she disappeared.

CHAPTER LIII

Chloë

Earth Year: 2033
Alternate Reality III

I wasn't quite sure what to do after Peyton left for parts or realities unknown. Both she and Khattaaara were gone. After all that time it was still difficult to get my head wrapped around it all. *Shit*, I thought, *life could be complicated sometimes!* The thing was I had to leave soon. My former self would arrive in the early afternoon the next day. I supposed to myself that I could stay and watch her do battle with the yellow Quantum Girl, but then, I thought, what if she saw me, or what if our god-stones pulled us into each other? What then? Tempting as it was, there was just too much at stake to risk it.

I went back to the strip club one more time. It had become addicting. Sex is addicting. Being wanted is addicting. Orgasms and need are as necessary to humanity as are water and air. My goal—my fucking goal—was to perform and then have sex with at least three women—pretty ones, needful ones. I would give each of them a memory they would never forget, and I would get three or four (or five if there was time) in return—to take *with* me—to hold *in* me—steadfast in my brain to shiver down my loins on whatever nights I would spend alone.

There I was with one of the most powerful elements in the universe in my head, using it to facilitate my sexual gratification. How selfish was that? Nevertheless, I had my last fling as Isis—two brunettes, one blonde, and one dyed henna—twenty-four, twenty-six, twenty-two, and forty-four respectively. The forty-four-year-old had deeply ingrained stepdaughter issues, insisting on roleplay and willing to pay for the privilege with talk like: "But what if your father walks in?" "What are you doing?" "Why are you touching me there?"

304

"Yes, it feels good." "Oh, my God, don't stop!" "Yes, oh yes, I want to do it all to you!" It was an hour of nonstop sex from touching to tribbing. In the end (no pun intended) she tipped me four hundred dollars. That was on top of the thousand-dollar session fee. The fact of the matter, though, was that I didn't care about the money. But with Quantum Queen on my tail, facing imminent danger and possible death, I figured I was entitled to at least one full night of debauchery.

I phased back to Peyton's apartment for a good night's rest, to find Khattaaara outside on the fire escape staring up at the stars.

"They're all different," she said, hearing me come in. "And there are so few of them."

"That's just the lights from the city," I replied. "Out in the country, they're like glitter thrown up into the sky."

"You forget," she replied, glancing back at me as I walked up to her, "I can see past what the lights of the city hide. I meant that on Rendenaaar the nearby stars were like a rainbow of colors and there were nebulae in almost every direction. Now it's all gone and I'm the only one who remembers. And when I'm gone, what then?" She paused for a moment and then went on. "It's a strange feeling to know the exact hour of one's death."

"I thought you said your consciousness would go on?" I replied.

"I lied to her," she said. "My mind will continue in the one of me I left behind, but I'm no longer part of her. When I'm killed tomorrow, my thoughts will die *with* me."

"You don't have to do this, you know," I told her. "You can come with me to the other reality and live."

"You forget that would create a paradox," she replied. "I can't let that happen. I still remember how Peyton, who was a part of me for so long, loved her world."

"I need to leave," I said. "I promised Peyton I would follow her."

"I know," she replied. "There was an expression on Rendenaaar. It went something like, 'Don't walk over steps you haven't taken,' meaning don't try to predict the future. The problem is that the future

305

already knows the steps you're going to take." She looked me straight in the eye. "Good luck," she said.

"You, too," I replied. Then I phased from the room, following Peyton's path to the other reality.

CHAPTER LIV

Khattaaara

Earth Year: 2033
Alternate Reality III

The morning sun poked through the billowing white clouds as it rose in the eastern sky, but its nuclear fire could not compare in the slightest to the power of a single god-stone, despite the unfathomable difference in size. The Judeo-Christian Bible makes no reference to god-stones, but, then, neither does it mention galaxies or nebulae or other planets and their moons. Meanwhile, the ancients of this world, who had their separate gods, similarly believed that the Earth was the center of all existence and that everything in the heavens hung majestically over it. And whilst visions of limitless realms for an afterlife danced within their mortal heads, none, until most recent times, could bring themselves to believe that there was more to their tiny universe—as they perceived it—other than them.

It was that arrogance of mankind that amazed me, for of the trillions of intelligent lifeforms in this universe alone, humans have drawn their gods to look exactly like them—not like unto the trilobites that existed for more than two hundred, seventy million years, nor like any of the dinosaurs that ruled their planet for nearly one hundred sixty-five million years. Neither has any of their gods been drawn to resemble the more than thirty million insects that tread upon their planet. And, not so surprisingly, they have no explanation as to why their god or gods waited four and a half billion years after He or they created the Earth to create them, although some will naïvely insist that the planet just popped into existence only six thousand or so of their years ago. It is their contention that their species—mankind—was the most perfect creation imaginable with arms and legs and opposable thumbs and, with some, Original Sin to explain the pain that comes with their childbirth; such pain as did not exist among Gaaalthaaarans, who were indeed the image of perfection, and who procreated, not through vaginas that were forever hid, but, more sensibly, through *yaaarghig* that we proudly displayed.

I have been to thousands of planets with civilizations, none of which were human, so it begs the question, especially to all of their minister and priests, *Who created them and in whose image, and why do intelligent lifeforms all not look the same, and, more to the point, not look like them?* Life shares uniqueness with snowflakes, and its complexity ensures that no two are exactly alike. I found it odd even that humans bore so much in common with Gaaalthaaarans until I learned that Dhraaal had used his god-stone to coax the shape of human life on Earth. But enough of this philosophizing!

As I hung in the sky, a flock of geese flew in its V-shaped formation below me. A jet airliner, high above, sailed across the ocean of sky, filled with anxious humans, each so blissfully ignorant that their entire universe was about to end. I looked all around me, the cool air billowing out my cape. Everything seemed calm and peaceful, but then the clouds grew dark, fierce winds raged through the sky, and she appeared—the other Quantum Girl—poised in the near distance, having phased only twenty yards from me.

She was dressed like me but there was a yellow aura around her. She said nothing, but instead just stared at me and then hurled out a blast of quantum force or so I thought at first. I looked down at myself as my violet costume wavered, flickering on and off with a strobe-like effect. I felt a burning sensation everywhere unlike anything I had ever known. The thought then came to me. She wasn't from this universe or from an alternate or parallel one. She was made of antimatter and I had little protection against that.

"What do you want?" I called out to her.

"Your having collapsed all dimensions into one caused my universe to end!" she shouted back. "I'm all that's left and I want all of you dead!"

"All of humanity?" I asked.

"No!" she replied. "Just you, Peyton Herron—every one of you—and anyone else who gets in my way!"

She hurled another blast of anti-quantum energy at me. I threw up a barrier. The air sizzled as the two force fields met. Then followed an explosion, pushing both of us backward. My fall was downward, though, and into a tree, breaking branch after branch, until I hit the ground. The fall stunned me and threw me off balance. One of the branches had pierced me through and through. Azure blood melted into my costume as the pain from the injury pulsed into my brain like an unrelenting knife. She phased down in front of me, not a shred of remorse on her face. I lay there helpless, bleeding to death, waiting for the final onslaught that I knew would come. I thought about Thara-Klo and about Ophelia. I thought about my sister before she died. I wondered whether she would find me in whatever afterlife there was if there was one.

Another blast came only seconds later. It felt as though every cell in me became electrified all at the same moment. I stared upward at the impassive sky. I tried to split off a part of me but as I did there came the final blow as the anti-quantum energy tore through my chest. With my last bit of life, I stared down at myself. There was a hole in my chest that I could have put my fist through had I been able to lift my arm. I wanted to look up at her. I wanted to see the expression on her face, knowing that she had defeated me, but there was no heart left to pump blood to my brain, and so I died.

Inexplicably, however it happened, as death took hold, my mind was hurled back to Rendenaaar, back into my body back there, the same as when Theresa had done as much. I had expected that my life would end. I had told Chloë as much, but my lie to Peyton had come true. I had not died. Perhaps the Silver God had intervened. Perhaps it was the god-stone that was responsible. I only knew that I was grateful to have been counted among the living.

CHAPTER LV

Peyton
(the one who just woke up)

Earth Year: 1960
Alternate Reality I

Mark and I were married three weeks after Great Grams, who didn't know she was, gave me her wedding ring. Mark had fully recovered by that time. It was only a justice of the peace ceremony, though, with all the standard "to have and to hold, in sickness and in health," and all of that, though I hesitated at the "obey" part of it at which Mark just silently smiled. Afterward, with a couple of bags packed, I phased us both to Tahiti where we spent our days on the beach and our nights making love.

Our vacation lasted two weeks, which was as long as our money held out. I returned us to our room only minutes after we had left. I could not afford to take two weeks off from my job. Money was an issue. Besides the hospital bills, there were two of us now, and Mark wasn't ready to go look for work just yet. Rather than struggle, I chose to do something about it. So, while Mark was taking a bath, I quietly phased back to ancient Rome to Adrianople, August 10, 378, making adjustments for the Julian calendar. Adrianople later became Edirne, Turkey—at least that's what the history book I borrowed from the library said. The Roman army took heavy losses. It was nauseating to see all the blood and dead bodies—soldiers on each side, run through with swords or dismembered. Arms and legs and even decapitated heads lay all around. Some were still alive, crying out in pain or moaning in their private agony. A few lay crushed under fallen horses. It was all more than I could bear to look at. I just took what I had come for—a Roman sword belonging to the emperor who was also killed in the battle. And then I left.

Back in 1960, I took the sword to an antique dealer in Beverly Hills. It was really wonderful. The handle was made of carved ivory with the head of a lion cast in solid gold at the end. The shop was run by a thin, elderly, balding man who wore a white shirt and black silk vest. He examined the artifact carefully and then looked up at me.

"Where did you get this?" he asked.

"It was handed down to me," I replied.

"Such wonderful condition," he went on. "Do you know anything of its history?"

"I was told that it is late Fourth Century," I said, "and that it belonged to the Roman Emperor, Valens."

"This should be in a museum," he replied. "I'm afraid I cannot give you anything near what it's worth."

"What *can* you give me?" I asked.

"Thirty thousand dollars," came the reply.

"Done," I said.

The man stared at the sword one more time and then looked up at me again. "I just need to see some identification."

I reached into my handbag and took out my ID card. When a person can stop time it is easy enough to go down to the DMV and enter whatever records you will need.

"If you like," he went on, "you can meet me at the California Federal just down the street," indicating the direction with a motion of his head. "I don't keep that much money in the shop. Say in half an hour?"

"That would be fine," I replied and then began to leave.

"You might want to wrap that up in something," he went on. "Wouldn't want anyone to think you were planning on robbing the place."

We met thirty minutes later at the savings and loan. There were no computers—not back then—at least not in banks. There were no credit cards other than Diners' Club and the Bank Americard, which later became Visa. As neither I nor Mark had bank accounts, I received the thirty thousand dollars in American Express Traveler's Checks. I used much of it to purchase a three-bedroom house on the beach in Malibu. Not a bad deal, I thought, considering that it would be worth around thirty million in 2033. Then we packed up what little we had and bid goodbye to great grandma who didn't know she was even related to me. Still, I invited her to visit sometime and "dig her feet into the sand."

The house has a wooden exterior that was painted sea breeze blue, trimmed with white. We furnished it simply and even bought a Zenith black and white television. Mark became a devotee of *The Untouchables* and *Gunsmoke*; I preferred *The Roaring '20s* and *Route 66*, as I'm not so much into guns. We both liked *Thriller*, though.

Six months passed and everything was going along swimmingly as they say—as someone once said—as I did back in the days when wars were cold and when Communist dictators pounded their shoes on desks to make a point. Halloween was cool, though. When kids would come, I'd answer the door as Quantum Girl, who might just as well have been a monster as far as they were concerned. The new reign of superheroes had just barely begun. There was no Spider, Iron, or Ant-Man, no Fantastic Four, no Incredible Hunk, and no Avengers. Superman was dead or, at least, the actor who portrayed him—a gunshot wound to the head, ruled to be self-inflicted. So, it appeared that superheroes could in fact be killed, and not just by kryptonite. Mark was a comic book nut it seemed. They were ten cents back then—mainly Superman and Batman and Mad Magazine—that cost twenty-five cents. He didn't bother with Supergirl or Wonder Woman. He had me.

It was the night before Christmas that we had an unexpected visitor phase into our living room. It was somewhat cold outside and raining. It does that around the holidays in L.A. It makes up for the dry times most of the rest of the year. I remember hearing the raindrops splashing into puddles that had already been made. I remember hearing the sand on our beach take a beating from the relentless pounding of waves. And then there was her.

"How did you find us?" I asked.

She glanced at Mark and then glared at me. "I wasn't looking for *him*," she said.

"She's not one of your split-offs?" Mark asked, glancing back and forth between me and our *guest*.

"No," I said. "It's Cleopatra."

"You were not easy to find," she replied. "You erased your quantum trail."

"Then how?" I asked.

"From his death certificate," she said, staring at him. "He died March 23, 1996."

"But how would you even know about him?" I asked.

"Because she's not Cleopatra," Mark replied. "She's the one we ran from—the one who nearly killed me."

From that instant, everything appeared to slow down. The one posing as Cleopatra hurled an energy blast at Mark to finish the job. I screamed out, "No!" I tried to freeze time but I wasn't fast enough. I watched in slow motion as every atom in his body grew bright and then disappeared. Tears from what had just happened turned into rage as I faced her in hysterical anger. I hurled a quantum blast at her as she countered with one of her own. But there was something else— something more. The energy she was projecting ate into mine, went past it, and touched my skin. I felt it burn. I phased outside the house but she followed me. I tried to get away, phasing this way and that but each time she was there. Finally, I split into a thousand of me and then phased off in different directions. The last one of me saw her looking around, perplexed. For whatever reason, she couldn't duplicate herself to follow, though she did attack that one. The others saw and felt the death of the me who couldn't escape in time. A narrow beam of radiation, if that was what it was, leaked from her, and struck the one me that remained like a bomb. It turned that one of me into a mass of light that exploded outward in every direction,

313

destroying the house, cratering the beach, and creating a tsunami that must have been felt in China.

Regardless, that it was just one part of me that had died, the rest of me felt the pain. I needed to escape. I merged back into one and then phased a hundred years into the future to face an explosion of a different kind as I did. All matter appeared to have collapsed wherever it was and then exploded outward in every direction.

CHAPTER LVI

Peyton
(the one who just woke up)

The New Universe
Five Minutes after the Big Bang
Alternate Reality I

In space, perhaps it is true that no one can hear you scream, but you still can cry. Your tears just float away. I loved Mark. It wasn't about sex. It was far deeper than that. We shared interests; liked the same things; laughed at the same time. Now, he was gone but then so was the Earth. So was the universe, it seemed. It had just blown up and become something else—a new existence. "Let there be light," God said, "and there was light. And God saw the light, that it was good." Only this wasn't good and there was no light—not yet—no stars, no galaxies, nothing but subatomic particles shooting in every direction, creating hydrogen and helium, shaping space this way and that. There were quarks, grouping into threes, held together by gluons. And then there were the rest—individuals and pairs that scientists from some future world would call dark matter. How did I know that? I wondered. Perhaps, I thought, it had something to do with the god-stone in my head.

This existence was born from the soul of our universe, stealing everything in it to turn it all into something else. The thought of it fomented anger in my brain. And then sadness came from the loss—and then fear. I was totally alone in this new universe and the only air I had to breathe was what had come with me, trapped within the quantum bubble that shielded me from the otherwise insurmountable and deadly radiation.

I couldn't stay there. I didn't know if I could go back but I had to try. I phased into the quantum fabric and it was there that I saw

315

something strange. There were multiple colored threads. This was a part of the quantum fabric that I hadn't been to before—not this part of it—not in this time—so I followed them *through* time to a point where they became entangled. Eventually, they led me to a star system in the far distant future with twelve planets, and then to one that seemed similar to Earth with what appeared to be a breathable atmosphere. There were cities and buildings that lay in ruins, engulfed by the native vegetation, though at the same time impervious to it. The thread brought me to the night side of the planet to a building in a metropolis that was not deserted like the rest. There were lights coming from within one of the structures. I phased down invisible— a power that Chloë had taught me to use.

Once inside, I went from room to room, though it was in the sleeping quarters that I came across signs of life, and human life at that! Three girls lay asleep in one room, two women in another. Remarkably, Chloë was in a third. Another room held three younger women—in their twenties I guessed—who sat on beds talking to each other, while in yet another bedroom there appeared to be a sleeping version of me!

Then, suddenly, she was behind me, wide awake, holding onto my arms.

"I don't know who you are," she said, "but if you try and phase away from here, I'll phase with you and I'll still be holding on."

She held my arms even tighter and it hurt. Whether she was stronger than me or not, she had the advantage.

"I'm Peyton Herron," I said.

"Wrong answer!" she replied, pulling my arms closer together behind my back.

I phased out of my Quantum Girl costume and turned my head toward her. "I'm Peyton Herron," I insisted. "I'm just not the one you are."

Her grip relaxed. I guess the fact that she saw my face meant something. A moment later, she let go. I rubbed my arms.

"I followed your trail here," I told her. "I had to escape from the yellow Quantum Girl. I phased into the future but everything was gone and then there was an explosion. I didn't think that I'd survive."

"Our universe ended," she said, "and this one was born from the ashes. In 1949, an English astronomer named Fred Hoyle called it the Big Bang. He named it but didn't believe it. It theorized that our universe was created from a single point that exploded in all directions. He criticized its proponents, insisting that the universe always existed and always would exist. Both arguments were wrong. The matter in each universe explodes fifth-dimensionally. It becomes immense and then gradually loses energy becoming smaller and smaller until the cycle repeats again. That's why we're here, my family and I. We escaped using the god-stones. We thought we were alone until the girls found the body of a Quantum Girl from an antimatter universe. I thought you might have been another one of her."

"Not guilty," I replied. "But she murdered Mark," "At least one of her did. Mark was my husband. Look," I said, "I'm fairly new to all of this quantum power stuff. If not for me, he would still be alive."

"You can't blame yourself for things that are out of your control," she replied.

"So, what's going to happen?" I asked. "Eleven females on a planet on the edge of nowhere. We all live out our lives and then what? The last one standing buries herself in the futility of it all?"

"We go back," came a voice from behind us both. "We go back and fix it all."

We both turned to see another one of us—another one of me—standing in the doorway.

"How?" I said to her.

"I thought you were dead," said the Peyton nearest me.

The other looked at her in a knowing way.

"Oh," the one near me said.

"What?" I asked turning from one to the other.

"We're the same person," the newly arrived Peyton said. "We share our thoughts."

"Then why don't you just merge back together?"

"I need to take a shower first," the newly one arrived commented. "I'm covered in space dust. I did some exploring before I came here."

"And?" I asked.

"I found these," she said as she opened her clenched fist. In it were two gems—one black, the other blue.

"God-stones?" I asked.

"Yes," she replied, "only they're..."

"Antimatter," said the Peyton next to me.

"I'm going to clean up," the other said and then stared at me. "Afterward, I want to find out more *about* you, Sarabeth."

"That's not my name," I said. "It's Peyton, just like yours."

She smiled and shook her head to herself as she left.

"Who's Sarabeth?" I called after her.

The other took my hand. "Come on," she said. "I'll clue you in on everything you need to know."

They say a girl becomes a woman once she shares intimacy for the first time. Until then, she's just a child who plays with dolls and calls out rhymes as she skips rope or plays hopscotch. Sex is part of becoming an adult. It shocks the mind more than any spark of electricity can, but love shapes who the child will become, especially when it's reciprocated. That's what Mark and I had. It was more than simply intercourse. It was universes and dimensions away from what I had shared with Theresa. It was the sort of emotion that separates human beings from AI. Love wasn't created in some explosion of primordial matter. It didn't suddenly appear like the Phoenix out of what used to be. It comes into being out of want and need but it is more than that. It is unselfish and it is what defines the essence of our souls. For me, though, it was a shadow of the past—something inescapable and unconquerable but lost in everything but a memory that would grow fainter with every moment that went by.

After she was done telling me all that had gone on for them, I described to her in painful detail the life I never had. I never got to really grow up. No alien ever intervened on my behalf to give me time to do so. I never had a sister to share my life with nor was I given the opportunity to save the world. And while we are who we are, we are also what fate allows us to be. My story was interrupted, however, as her other self came back into the room and merged into her. Watching it was like having double vision that suddenly came into focus. It seemed strange. Being able to do something oneself is one thing, but seeing it from the outside is another. The two of us were physically identical with similar upbringings but that was as far as it went. Once she reunited with her other self, I went on with my story. Hours went by until, as morning awakened, so did the children—so animated and adorable that the thought stuck in me that Mark and I were never allowed such joy as they must have brought to this other self of mine and to her sister and her sister's wife.

It was a strange feeling when Jordan entered the room at half a gallop, outpacing the other two, and raced up to me out of breath.

"Mama," she gasped, "Sami and Zhan and I want to go swimming after breakfast! Is that okay?"

"She not the one to ask," the other Peyton said. She had gone into what they had made into their kitchen and was returning with two cups of herbal tea that she had brewed from the leaves of some indigenous plant.

Jordan turned to see her and then looked back at me.

"She's from an alternate timeline," Peyton explained. "She arrived in the middle of the night from her Earth." She handed me one of the cups. "She may be a stranger," she went on, "but you girls treat her like she's family. She's one of us now."

"You must be Jordan," I said, addressing the platinum-blonde girl who had mistaken me.

"Uh-huh," she replied. "But what do I call you?"

"Peyton," I replied. "It's my name. Hers, too, only you came from

319

her belly, not mine. You're a very pretty girl. I'm sure your mama's proud."

"Who wants pancakes?" the other Peyton said to the girls.

"I do!" "I do!" "I do!" they each shouted, almost in unison.

Pancakes it was. The three others came to breakfast shortly afterward bearing a striking resemblance to their younger selves. I knew. Peyton had explained. I wondered what would have happened if I had gone back in time and warned myself about the bullying or had taken the rope from the closet before I had a chance to hang myself. Would I have changed what was meant to be? And if I had, what then? Would I have altered the timeline so that *this* me would have ceased to exist and the one in my place would never have gone back to change what never happened so that it *would* happen again and on and on—an endless loop in time like the last one but with no one to rescue me from it? That meant that I couldn't go back and save myself. Not ever. Whatever horrible things I'd been put through or put myself through I was stuck with forever.

None of the three time-lost versions of the girls said anything. They just silently ate, occasionally staring up at me and exchanging looks. They could tell there was a difference between me and the other Peyton. It was the older Jordan who finally broke the uncomfortable silence.

"What was your reality like?" she asked.

"You're Jordan," I replied with half a question.

"It's Danna now," she said and then sipped from the cup she held. "Less confusing."

"In mine," I said, "there was no alien to save me when I tried to kill myself. I was rescued but there was brain damage. I lost nearly a decade until one of her," I said, motioning toward my other self, "put her god-stone in my head to heal me. Unfortunately, things didn't work out as planned. As I was being healed, a quantum spirit emerged from me and projected an energy blast that killed her. It killed her because she didn't have the god-stone in her anymore to protect her.

Then I woke up, things happened, and here I am."

"*What* happened?" That was Mira.

"I fell in love with an incredible guy," I said, "who was nearly killed trying to save me from the yellow Quantum Girl. I phased us both into the past. It was touch and go for a while but then finally he got better. We fell in love and got married but then she found us and finished the job. He didn't survive. I didn't want to stay in the past without him, so I phased into the future to get away. Only once I got back, the universe was gone. Your trails through the quantum fabric led me here."

"I'm so sorry," the one now calling herself Anna said.

I looked up to see three more women in the room, listening as they stood. Two of them, blonde and brunette were holding hands. They were both my age. The blonde one let go of her companion and went over to me. "I'm Ophelia," she said. "Where *we* came from, I was your sister. Where you came from, was there another one of me?" I shook my head. "I don't exist in all realities," she went on; "not like you. My sister and I, we were joined at the hip, but that doesn't mean I can't be your sister, too." She paused and then added, "If you want me to be."

"Thanks," I replied. "Ophelia, right?"

"Like in Hamlet," she said with a smile.

"How far back in time will we be going," Anna asked. "Earth time, I mean?"

"Whatever happened in the past," she said, appears to have delayed the Armageddon by a couple of years. We can go back just after we had left.

"But wouldn't that have created a paradox?" Danna asked. "I mean, if the universe wasn't going to detonate for another two years, that would have meant that we wouldn't have escaped when we did."

"It's kind of worse than that," I said. "In my reality, no one of the children existed."

"Or me," added Ophelia.

"The only one there is Chloë," I replied.

"Wait!" Claire exclaimed. "Chloë's alive? An alternate version…"

I shook my head. "I don't think so," I said. "She has a god-stone in her head."

Claire backed up into the wall that w as just behind her, overwhelmed with emotion, and began to cry. Both Zhana and Samira went over to her to hug her. Claire wiped her tears with one hand and then put her arms around them both.

"Don't cry, Mama," Zhana said.

"Hey!" Jordan called at her. "She's crying because she's happy."

"I am," Claire said.

"Aunt Chloë's a Quantum Girl," Jordan said. Then she turned to her mother. "Isn't she?" she asked.

"I would seem she is," came the reply, "which could explain the critical mass delay. Hopefully, it will give me enough time to prevent the end entirely."

"But how do we all go back?" Anna asked. "There are eleven of us now and there are only six god-stones."

"Peyton has one in her head," she replied, "and I found three others. Plus, there are the ones I hid."

"You mean these?" Danna asked, revealing them in her hand. "Next time, pick a better hiding place from your daughters."

She went over and handed them to her.

"We're still one short," Mira said. "Or did you forget Chloë?"

Chloë's figure emerged from the shadows. "I'm not going," she replied.

"What are you talking about?" Jordan said with great concern.

"The Frags on this planet are too dangerous," she replied. "They have to be destroyed."

"How will your staying here help?" Anna asked.

"I'm not human," she replied. "Remember? In my chest is a neutronium-cased sphere containing quarks and antiquarks that

322

power my systems."

Ophelia raised her eyes in concern. ' And?" she said. "Just what are you getting at?"

"I know that I look like Chloë," she replied, "but I'm not her. I'm the Frag that sealed the rest in the caverns, a guardian of them all, only I became damaged and the kindness in Claire's heart turned me into one of you. But I'm *not* one of you—not really—and I have a responsibility to end the Frag threat."

"End it how?" Claire asked.

"I can mix the quarks and antiquarks together all at once," she said, "to cause a reaction strong enough to destroy this planet and with it the Frag threat."

"No!" Jordan wept. She turned to Peyton. "Mama, don't let her! Please!"

Peyton looked at Jordan and then at Chloë.

"There's no other choice," the Chloëbot said. "Besides, there aren't enough god-stones to take me with you."

By this time, both Samira and Zhana were sobbing as well. "But we love you," Sami said, her eyes bleeding out tears.

"I love you, too," the Chloëbot said, "but this has to be done. If the Frags awaken, they could find their way back to your universe. I can't let that happen. Your lives, all of them, mean too much to me."

There were tears in Peyton's eyes as well as she sadly nodded in agreement. The girls rushed the machine that had become human and hugged it and the Chloëbot hugged them back and then kissed each one on the top of their head. An hour later, we all watched from outer space as the planet we had called Erebus burst into more fragments than Krypton.

CHAPTER LVII

Peyton
(the original)

Earth Year: 2033
Alternate Reality I

The lot of us who had returned from Erebus were gathered in the living room of my parents' home, only to find Chloë—the human one—standing over the dead body of whom we were told was Cleopatra, my former incarnation. Chloë looked up at us mournfully.

"She killed her," she said. "For no reason. She just killed her. I don't know why, but she left me alone. She just stared at me and then phased off somewhere. To Hell, I hope, but that's just wishful thinking."

Beyond her words, I could see that the death was affecting the Peyton from this timeline as well. Almost at once, she dropped to her knees in front of the now corpse and began to shake her.

"No, no, no!" she wailed as tears rained down from her eyes. "You can't be dead! You can't." Then she looked up at me and sobbed, "Isn't there anything you can do?"

I shook my head. "The only one who was able to resurrect the dead was Theresa Martinez," I replied, "and the antimatter blast would prevent me from reversing time past when she was hit."

Peyton perked. She wiped the veil of tears from her cheeks. "I know her," she said. "Maybe she could…"

"That was a different Theresa," I interrupted. "A different timeline. *That* Theresa no longer exists."

Suddenly, Mira's voice broke through the somber moment.

"Look!" she exclaimed, staring at the dead body.

Cleopatra's body began to glow violet and then stopped. The aura that had surrounded her faded, but that wasn't all. Her body began to age before our eyes. She became an old woman and then her skin withered and turned brown like a mummy without its wrappings. It was hideous to look at and each of the elder girls took hold of their younger selves and buried their faces against themselves to protect them from seeing the decay that made mockery of the beauty that had once brought emperors and kings to their knees.

"I'll bury her out back," Mira said.

"There's a shovel in the toolshed," I told her.

"No need," she replied. "I still have a god-stone." She then bent down, put her hand on the remains, and then phased both it and herself out behind the house. Danna started to go to Peyton when Phee intervened. "I've got this," she said as she helped Peyton to her feet and then led her upstairs to the bedroom that in another lifetime used to be both mine and Phee's.

The question remained as to why the yellow Quantum Girl killed Cleopatra but not Chloë. It was as I was having that thought that Mira returned from the interment.

"We'll need a headstone or marker or something," she said. "It's only proper, no matter which gods she bowed down to."

"I'll have something made," I replied. "A monument. I know a sculptor."

There was a long pause as I went over to the sofa and sat down. Anna sat down beside me. "What are we going to do?" she asked.

"Try and figure out a way to save the universe," I replied.

"I mean about the yellow Quantum Girl," she said.

"Stand our ground," I replied. "By the way," I went on, "you didn't think I forgot, did you? Your birthday. I made a promise before I gave birth to you. I never go back on my word."

"What was it?" she asked.

I looked at her and caused her eyes to glow. Her face grew blank, her head tilted back, and then she looked at me again. "Thank you," she said.

"Phee!" I called out. "Would you come in here again?"

As Phee entered the room, Danna stood and faced her. There were tears in her eyes as she looked at her. Phee tilted her head as though to ask, *What's going on?*

"I remember," Danna said.

"Remember what?" Phee asked.

"That you were my mother," she said, "before all of this."

Phee looked at me and I nodded. Then she turned to Danna. There was an awkward moment but then the two of them embraced, both now in tears.

"Oh, Mama!" Danna wept. "I didn't remember till just now!" She pulled back to look at her. "Why didn't you say anything?"

"You have another mother," she replied. "One who gave birth to you in the new reality so that you could still exist—my sister and my best friend."

Danna looked back at me and smiled. "I love you both," she said. Then she hugged her tightly again.

"Hey, Lovebug," I said, interrupting the moment. "I need to phase to Chicago for some answers. Want to come with?"

Danna looked in my direction and then at Phee who motioned at her with her chin and quietly said, "Go."

Danna smiled at her and then came over to me. "We're going to need to change," I said.

"What's wrong with how we're dressed?" she asked.

"We don't want people to stare at us?" I replied.

"Why would they stare?" she said.

"Because," I replied, "these aren't the sort of clothes women wore in 1929."

CHAPTER LVIII

Ophelia

Earth Year: 2033
Alternate Reality I

I have met several Peytons but never one as fragile as the one upstairs and in her room—*her* room, not ours. I never existed in this reality. This Peyton never had a sister. This Peyton succeeded, at least partially, in taking her own life. Fortunately for her, she just lost part of it. Animals live their lives never once thinking about the inevitability of death. The fear they hold within them is what confronts them in the present; not what awaits them in the future. This Peyton, like mine, once saw her future as bleak and filled with unbearable pain. She saw death as a way out—death by suicide—the word derived from the Middle English *seoifcwale*—literally, self-slaughter. In *my* Peyton's life, a being from a long-dead civilization revived her. In *this* one, she was nearly brain-dead after the pipe she had used to hang herself had finally given way under her weight. And yet, it seems, with every Peyton Herron, Fate steps in and saves her, only this one lost nearly ten years of her life. Other than what she had come to experience over the last couple of years, she was emotionally still a child—still just a teenage girl—trapped in the body of a woman whose reflection she barely knew. Regardless that we grew up in disparate realities, I still felt a connection to her. She was the sister who might have been had things been different.

"I think you should lie down," I told her.

She quietly, wearily nodded, and then began to strip off her outer clothes. "Is there a nightgown in the closet?" I asked. Another nod as she mechanically folded her blouse and then set it down neatly on one chair. As I went into the closet—that same one where, like her, my Peyton and Sarabeth both hanged themselves, she spoke for the first time.

"She shouldn't have died," she said in a barely audible tone. "She was my friend. She shouldn't have died."

I handed her the nightgown I'd found. "Thanks," she said. Then she threw it on over her head and then doffed the panties and bra, stepping out of them after they'd fallen to the floor. I bent down, picked them up, and looked at them.

"Odd," I said.

"What is?" came the reply.

"Peyton," I said, "my Peyton, wore the exact same brand."

"I didn't buy them," she said, as she climbed into bed. "My mother did. She bought them for me when I was still…"

"Injured?" I interrupted.

"I was going to say retarded," she replied, "but euphemisms are always good. They tend to insulate bad words. That's what my freshman English teacher once said. I was insulated for a long time. Then I woke up. Now, I'm in a world without insulation—except for what's in the walls." She paused and then stared up at me. "That was meant to be a joke," she said, "though perhaps it's not the right time. It's never the right time anymore it seems. People keep dying. First Mark. Now Cleopatra."

"Who's Mark?" I asked.

"He was my husband," she replied and then looked hard at me. "You and Claire," she went on. "You two…?"

"We're a couple," I said. "Married actually. Growing up, I never dreamt that I'd fall in love with another woman."

"Why not?" she asked. "Women are people like anyone else. We're all human beings. You should be able to share your heart with whomever you want."

"Cleopatra was your friend," I said with half a question on my lips.

"She was there," she replied, "from the moment I woke up, and despite that she had been the queen of Egypt, she treated me with

328

understanding and kindness when I was no one to her. So odd, though."

"How so?" I asked.

"She told me," came the reply, "that I was her reincarnation." She looked at me then, a dumbfounded expression on her face. "How could that be? How could two versions of the same person meet each other?"

"Time travel allows for a lot of strange things," I replied.

"I supposed," she said, "only then I wonder if it's somehow narcissistic of me to miss her. But the fact is that I do."

"You know," I replied, "History records that Cleopatra died in ancient Egypt, so whatever time she had here was a gift. Now, you get some rest. You've been through a lot."

As I went to the door to leave, she quietly said, "Thank you, Ophelia. I wish you could have been *my* sister, too."

I smiled as I quietly closed the door. I thought to myself that no version of Peyton Herron could ever be anything but gentle and kind. Such was her mark on the world.

CHAPTER LIX

Danna

Earth Year: 1929
Chicago, Illinois
Pre-Divergent Reality

When I was small, I had a mother but no father and two aunts—Claire and Ophelia. My mother always baked a cake for me on my birthday for as long as I could remember. Each was piled with fruit on top—blueberries, strawberries, Mandarin oranges, and kiwi. Sliced almonds covered the sides. There were no candles. There were flames that hovered above the cake that I would always do my best to blow out. It was a trick on Nature that my mother played. She could do things like that, that were normally impossible because she was Quantum Girl. At the time, I had thought that all mothers were like her. When I was five years old, I went to the birthday of my cousins, Zhana and Samira. Their cake had candles. When they blew them out, I picked up one with its black-tipped wick. I smelled it and then bit off half and began to chew it. My Auntie Ophelia, as I called her back then, was the only one to notice and rushed up to me, put her fingers in my mouth, and pulled it out. As everyone turned to look, I began to cry. My mother came over and hugged me and I hugged her back.

"Everything's going to be all right," she assured me.

When my crying stopped and everyone but me and Auntie Ophelia were in the dining room, I scowled at her with anger. "I hate you!" I said. Then I raced into the living room where everyone else was. The ire in children soon gives way to forgiveness, but after being given back my memories from Rendenaaar, I could hardly begin to imagine the pain my words had caused that day to the one, who for twenty-four years had been the mother I had forgotten, who had weaned me from the milk in her breasts. How it must have pierced

330

her very heart to have watched the little girl who had once emerged from her womb call another, Mother, even though that other was her sister and best friend. I often wondered why my Quantum Girl mother chose to do things the way she did, giving rebirth to me rather than allowing me to be born again to her twin. But perhaps she knew that children are only children for their parents once, and that, in just one more year, Zhana would be born and need a mother who would give her every ounce of her affection and attention, regardless of the bounty that my aunt, now remembered mother, had such an abundance to give.

Mama and I phased to Chicago, March 16, 1929. We checked into the Blackstone Hotel to a room on the twelfth floor with a view of Lake Michigan. I'd never traveled back this far in time—Earth time anyway. It amazed me how White everyone was—not just at the hotel but almost everywhere around it. Mama said that neighborhoods were segregated back then. Blacks—they were called negroes or coloreds at the time—lived on the southside. Asians—mainly Chinese—culminated in scattered sections of the city. If there were any Hispanics, none of them reared their heads. No one appeared to give it much thought, though, other than in terms of keeping separate—separate bathrooms, separate entrances, separate drinking fountains—separatism.

We both were outfitted for the time. Mama wore a long navy dress that came just above her ankles with a jacket trimmed in white fox fur along with a matching navy cloche on her head. My dress was a bit more daring, falling to just below the knees, forest green, with a matching jacket with bold stripes, also with a matching cloche, both of us hiding our long hair which was definitely not in vogue for that day and age.

A bellhop led us to our room and carried our just recently acquired luggage up to our room. Everything was posh and comfortable. Little did any of the wealthy guests suspect that in just six months' time, their world would come tumbling down with the Wall Street Crash,

331

Black Thursday, October 24th, ushering in what would be called The Great Depression. But, for the moment, everyone there lived in ignorant bliss.

Our target in going back in time was the 27-year-old Werner Heisenberg, who would be lecturing at the University of Chicago. Heisenberg was a German theoretical physicist who, just two years before, had created a branch of science that he called quantum physics.

As Heisenberg wasn't due to lecture until Monday and our arrival was on Saturday afternoon, we decided to spend the next day at the Field Museum. The museum, according to the brochures we were handed, boasted that its size was upwards of four hundred, eighty thousand square feet. Its exhibits consisted in part of a huge collection of taxidermized wild animals from all over the world, a nearly complete T.rex skeleton, and a vast array of Egyptian mummies in the basement, with air, I must say, that was filled with the musty odor of desiccated death. Seeing that, after having buried Cleopatra, was more than I could bear.

"Can we go back to the hotel now?" I asked.

"I didn't realize this was here," Mama replied. "Of course."

Entering the nearest ladies' room, we waited until no one else was there and then phased back to our room.

"There's no escape," I said, "is there? I mean, sooner or later, we're all going to wind up like them."

"Life is like everything else," she said. "No matter how bright it appears at the start, it gets worn out after time. 'Gather ye rosebuds while ye may, old Time is still a-flying. And this same flower that smiles today, tomorrow will be dying.' We all live our lives as best we can and try not to wonder when they'll end."

"Grandma believed in God and Jesus," I said. "What do you believe?"

"*Some*thing created all of this," she replied. "I don't know if it was God or a fluke or a science experiment. All I know is that while we have breath in our lungs and love in our hearts, we should use our time as best we can."

At ten a.m. the next morning, we phased over to the physics department at the university and were directed to one of the lecture halls. Heisenberg was in the midst of his talk on relativistic quantum mechanics. He was not a tall man at five foot seven but he had an erudite look about him. He was single at the time and would neither meet nor marry his future wife for another eight years. The lecture went on for an hour as more than one hundred students, all male, listened attentively as he spoke with his German accent and drew numerous mathematical equations on the chalkboard behind him. When he had finished and most of those in attendance had exited the room, we approached him.

"Professor Heisenberg?" my mother said. "I was wondering if you could spare a moment to talk?"

He looked at both of us. "I wasn't aware there were any women attending my lectures," he said, "but my notes will be available at the library by tomorrow."

Mama shook her head. "This doesn't have anything to do with the lecture," she replied. "It has to do with the contraction of matter—the illusion that spacetime is expanding when in fact it is quite the reverse."

"And from where have you garnered such a speculation?" he asked.

"It's not a speculation," she replied defensively.

"You should listen to her," I told him. "She knows what she's talking about."

"Can we go somewhere private," she asked, "so I can show you proof?"

"The university put me up in a room on the other side of the campus," he replied. "I supposed we could go there."

"This hall is locked up at night, isn't it?" Mama asked him.

"I suppose," he replied. "But I don't have authorization to get in."

"No need," she said, "then she phased the three of us twelve hours forward in time."

Heisenberg rushed to one of the windows to look out at the then night sky, turned back, and stared at her. "How did you do that?" he exclaimed. "This is some sort of a trick. Like, like, your magician, Houdini!"

"Houdini died five years ago," Mama told him, calm written on her face.

The man kept glancing out the window, dumbfounded at what had just occurred. "Then how is this possible?" he demanded to know.

"I took us twelve hours forward from where we were," she said.

"Time travel!" Heisenberg scoffed. "Einstein would have everyone convinced that you get into a rocket ship, travel at nearly the speed of light, and wind up in the future! A*ch der Lieber!* The arguments we have had about that! 'Albert,' I said, 'time can no more be stretched than my desk or the *Bleistift* in my hand!'"[32]

"We're from the future," I told him. "The year 2033 to be exact. Back there," and I glanced at Mama, "she's known as Quantum Girl."

Heisenberg appeared as though he felt that he was losing his mind and sank down onto one of the desks.

I glanced at Mama. "Show him," I said.

Instantly, Mama became Quantum Girl. "*Mein Gott!*" Heisenberg exclaimed as his hand went up to cover his mouth. Then, slowly, he stood up again, walked over *to* her, and then *around* her like she was Michelangelo's *Pietà* that had suddenly and miraculously appeared out of nowhere.

"How is this possible?" he said, glancing at me, as though Mama were not even real.

"It's called a god-stone," I replied. "There's one in *her* head and in mine as well." In another instant, a hundred of me appeared around the room, each of them taking a seat in the gallery.

---

[32] *Bleistift* is the German word for pencil.

"Nein, nein!" he exclaimed. "You, you, you have hypnotized me!"

Each one of me sighed deeply and then merged back into the one who was standing next to him.

Mama turned back into herself and then said, "You know Munich, don't you?"

"Of course," he replied. "I received my doctorate there five years ago."

"You know the buildings," she said, "the motorcars, the way people dress, don't you?"

"Of course," he replied, suddenly curious.

"Then let us show you how it looks in our time," she said, throwing a knowing glance at me.

In another instant, we were in the heart of Munich in the middle of the day in 2033. Cars honked their horns. Noise filled the air. People stared at our odd, out-of-place clothing. Overhead, a 747 cut a path through the sky.

Heisenberg looked this way and that in astonished wonder. "This is the *Marienplatz!*" he exclaimed. "And there is St. Peters! And, and there the Theatine Church! But everything else is different! And the people! The woman! How they are dressed! And what sort of motorcars are these?"

"Why don't we sit down somewhere?" I said. I took my iPhone from my handbag and said, "Hey, Siri, where is a McDonald's near me?"

"There is a McDonald's on Tal," Siri replied, "approximately a quarter mile to your west. I can call it or get directions."

"Get directions," I said.

"Getting walking directions to McDonald's," Siri went on. "Head southeast on *Marienplatz* for a quarter mile, then turn left on *Viktualienmarkt.*"

Heisenberg stared at the phone. "What sort of magic is this?" he demanded to know.

"It's called an iPhone," I replied.

"It's a telephone and a computer," Mama explained.

The man shook his head to himself.

"Come on," I said to him, taking his hand. "Let's go get something to eat."

"This reminds me of the moving picture by Fritz Lang that I watched last year called Metropolis. So this is what the world is meant to become!"

At the McDonald's, Mama, who speaks fluent German, did the ordering. "*Wir werden drei Hamburger Royal mit Tomaten und Salat, drei große Pommes und drei Schoko-Milchshakes haben.*"[33] She then used the Apple Pay on her phone, followed with a "*Danke.*" from the man who took her order, though he stared at us curiously. Mama looked down at her dress and then back up at him. "Cosplay," she said.

"Ah!" the man replied with a smile.

Dr. Heisenberg ate his food with the enthusiasm of a starving man who had at last been given a meal.

"This is *wunderbar!*" he said with a mouthful of food. "I must get the recipe!"

"If you wait another twenty-five years or so, "Mama replied, "you'll be able to order as much as you want."

"So," he said, wiping the corner of his mouth with a paper napkin. "What is it you want to talk with me about?"

"Where we are now in time," she began, "the universe is about to end. Two days ago, in your time, an American astronomer named Edwin Hubble published a paper in the *Proceedings of the National Academy of Sciences* describing, from his observations of the red shift of light from distant stars, how the universe was expanding. He concluded this because the farther away stars are, the more they

---

[33] "We'll have three Big Macs with tomatoes and lettuce, three large fries, and three chocolate milkshakes."

exhibit a uniformly greater change toward the red end of the spectrum."

"That would appear logical," Heisenberg said.

"The problem," Mama went on, "is that he was wrong. In just two years, a Belgian cosmologist and priest by the name of Georges Lemaître will propose a revolutionary theory that the universe began from what will later be named the Big Bang. In 1963, two scientists at Bell Labs, Arno Penzias and Robert Wilson, will discover what they will call *cosmic background radiation* from that initial explosion. But while the premise of the universe having begun thirteen point eight billion years ago is correct, the idea that it came into being from a single point or that it is expanding are both wrong, presumably due to the fact that when you stick an idea in someone's head and then amplify it, it's hard to think of anything else."

"Go on," he replied.

"The unfortunate truth," she continued, "is that it isn't spacetime that is expanding, being pulled apart by some mysterious, yet-to-be-discovered dark energy, but that matter is uniformly shrinking. Our universe is one of trillions upon trillions that had existed before it, each built from the stardust, so to speak, of the previous one. When the matter from a universe contracts to a critical mass, it explodes from wherever it is. Those points become the building blocks of stars and galaxies in the next universe, like the Phoenix rising from the ashes of the one before it. Within no more than a few years from now, all the matter in this universe will reach its critical mass and explode into the next. Nothing will be left."

"But is there any way for this to be stopped?" the physicist asked.

"That's why we came to you," she replied.

"You're one of the greatest scientific minds in modern history," I added.

Heisenberg smiled and then looked at Mama. "Your daughter," he said, "appears to think more of me than most. This is a lot to—how do you Americans say it?—take in. If you would provide me with as

337

much information as you can and also about your quantum abilities, perhaps I can figure something out."

"I'll do more than that," Mama said to him. "If you don't mind being a guest in our home for a few days, I can provide you with a state-of-the-art laptop and access to the Internet. Afterward, we can return you to the exact moment you left, so you won't miss any of your lectures."

Heisenberg agreed, but he appeared confused as to what the Internet was and amusingly thought a laptop involved something sexual. After several days of calculations and considerations, he seemed to have had a eureka moment.

"I believe I have an answer," he proclaimed, "but it is not an easy one. Your god-stones need to be positioned all around the circumference of the universe and then used to inflate matter again."

"But the universe is more than 28 billion lightyears in diameter," Mama told him. "That would take trillions upon trillions of Quantum Girls to put in place!"

"That is not all," he said. "It would require an equivalent amount of antimatter to accomplish it."

"Oh, great!" I said. "And most of the antimatter god-stones are in the hands of the Quantum Girl who's been on a murderous streak!"

"'scuse me!" said my younger self, who'd been listening in. "If all the god-stones get blown up and Mama's so far away, what happens to *her*?"

Mama shrugged knowingly. Younger me saw her and yelled out sobbing, "No! No! No! No!" and rushed up to her and hugged her around the waist.

Mama put her hands around her to try and comfort her.

"Hey, Jor," I said. "It hasn't happened yet, and since we need the yellow Quantum Girl to help, it probably never will."

Later that night, Mama came into my room. "You *know* this is a serious situation," she said. "Countless lives are at stake—not just on Earth but everywhere."

"We can't even find the yellow Quantum Girl," I said, "let alone get her cooperation."

"Beyond that," Mama added, "there's the matter of me having to split into trillions of selves and then phase each of us to the edge of the universe." She looked at me. "I've never done anything even close to that before."

"If it comes to that," I said, "let me be the one, Mama. I've had god-stones in me since I was a child on Rendenaaar. The world needs Quantum Girl."

"And I need *you* to be safe," she replied.

"There's still that younger version of me," I insisted.

My mother shook her head. "I love both of you," she proclaimed, "and so does your other mother. I've lived through billions of years—more than anyone else. There comes a time in life when even gods breathe no more." She paused and then said, "Come here." I went to her and she hugged me so tight. "My little Lovebug, all grown up," she said as a whisper in my ear.

"I love you, Mama," I said.

"Love you more," she replied.

Feeling her hold me, with me holding her, I never wanted to let go. I never wanted that moment to end.

CHAPTER LX

Peyton
(the original)

Earth Year: 2033
Alternate Reality I

I returned Dr. Heisenberg to the lecture hall a moment before we had met, erasing the memory of his encounter with us. In the quantum fabric, I met up with another one of me—or version of me.

"Which one *are* you?" she asked.

"The one who went back to Rendenaaar," I replied.

"As did I," she said, " but it seems that reality diverged at some point in time and it divided us and caused us to go in separate directions."

"We should merge back," I suggested.

"No shit," came the reply. "No sense talking to ourselves."

Thus it was that we *integrated* into each other so that both our memories converged. Part of me became saddened by the loss of the one who had helped the damaged Peyton. The other part of me was embarrassed and aroused by the nakedness and lurid sex that had happened on a nightly basis at the strip club.

Thus, it was that I was alone once more with nary a clue as to how to find the yellow Quantum Girl who had thus far murdered two versions of me—Cleopatra and Khattaaara. Where, I wondered, was the universe she was from, and why was she so determined to end my existence?

The answer to my question came from behind.

All that you desire to know, it said, *lies within you.*

I phased through myself to face the other direction. There before me stood the being I had seen twice before, glowing with silver radiance.

Gaia! I thought back at her. *You told me that was your name.*

The godlike creature stared back at me and smiled. *I told you I had many names,* she said in my mind. *Gaia is just one of them. And Khii. And one other that might interest you—Peyton Herron.*

Wait! I replied. *You're telling me that I'm you—that you're me?*

I'm telling you, she said, *that I am all of you. All the Peyton Herrons. All the Khattaaaras. All the Cleopatras and all the rest. Even the antimatter one.*

Why me? I asked. *Why am I so special?*

Because you are the one, she replied. *In the beginning, you were a thought. Then the thought became self-aware. There was only darkness. You were frightened and alone. But out of that fright came electrons and quarks and from them came light. 'Let there be light,' you thought to yourself, and there was light and you felt it and could see it and for you it was good. You shaped the first stars, built the first galaxies, created gravity and time, sparked the first life, and put your consciousness into some of your creations so that you would no longer feel alone. Unfortunately, the first time you became Khattaaara, you went insane. Come phase into me so that you will remember. There is a universe you want to save.*

As I merged into her I could feel incredible power. It was more than the god-stones had ever given me. I remembered everything from the very beginning. In the beginning, I created the Heavens and the Earth. *No,* I thought to myself. *That isn't right. I'm not God! Not even close! I'm Peyton Elise Herron. I'm a human being and imperfect. I never asked to be special. I never asked for superpowers. I just wanted to be ordinary—to be able to live my life like everyone else.*

But you are not like everyone else, the voice inside me said. *We are not like everyone else. Here in this time, we are the reason that everything exists. Mankind are our children and we are their mother. And now that you know all, you know what we must do.* And I did.

I followed the quantum trail that Yellow had left. It led me to the other reality a moment after Chloë had arrived and saw her other selves and merged with them with Cleopatra's help. Yellow had just materialized as well and was about to murder the other Peyton, the innocent one. I phased her to safety, where Yellow would never think to look. I froze time but Yellow pulled out of it and faced me. But she did not see Peyton Herron or Quantum Girl. Instead, she saw the Silver Goddess who I now was.

"Who the fuck are you?" she screamed.

"Why are you so angry?" I asked in a calm voice.

"She destroyed my entire universe!" she shouted. "Everyone I ever cared about! Everyone I ever loved!" Then she broke down in tears.

"It wasn't her," I replied. "It just was meant to be. Universes burgeon into existence, but they also eventually die. If you want to save yours—restore yours—you will have to work with me."

"How?" she wept, desperately wanting to know.

"First, I need to protect them," I said, referring to everyone in the room, and so, one by one, I sent each of them one hour ahead, the god-stones in them dropping like marbles to the floor, and then shooting up into my hand.

"What do you want me to do," she asked.

"I'll need your god-stones," I replied. "I'll do the rest."

"If I give it to you," she replied, "I'll be killed. I'm made of what you call antimatter."

"No," I said, shaking my head. "I've placed a quantum field around you to protect you. But I need the five you still have in order to do what needs to be done. At the proper moment, I'll send you home. You won't be Quantum Girl anymore, but you'll be alive and well and so will everyone you love."

"Go ahead and take them," Yellow said, and so I did and watched as she changed, not into another version of me, but into one of Chloë.

"Take care of yourself, Chloë Salinger," I said. "Perhaps you will think kindly of me someday."

Those were my last words. I phased off to intergalactic space, far beyond the local cluster, and then duplicated myself a trillion, trillion times, more than I had thought possible, and positioned each one of me at every edge of the universe, all but one of me, who remained behind, hovering in empty space. As for the rest, the explosion of twelve god-stones—matter and antimatter—reshaped spacetime and gave this existence and its counterpart another hundred billion years of life. None of those who had triggered the blast had survived. Afterward, I did as I promised and returned the antimatter Chloë to her universe where she would live out her youth, grow old, and die as most of humanity does. Phee and Claire and our Chloë and the children would all find their places on the Earth in good time. As for the other Peyton, I gave her the gift that I once had—a second chance at life and the power to do good. And if you're still feeling sad about the artificial Chloë, you needn't be. I resurrected her and she's safe now by my side.

CHAPTER LXI

Peyton
(the one who woke up)

Earth Year: 2025

It was strange that I remembered everything, even though things had changed. I was fourteen years old again. Tomorrow was my birthday, mine and Phee's. So odd that I now had a sister with memories that may or may not have been mine of how close we always were. I was at school and there was a flood of students going this way and that as the lunch bell rang only seconds before. The din of the throng was not uncomfortable, though. It was a sign of life, teeming all around me. And then there was Phee just ten feet away, who tripped and crashed into another girl with both of them spilling their books. Well, to be perfectly honest, I was the one who, with the slightest of force fields aimed at her feet caused her to trip. As the two of them bent down and began to sort through the pile to figure out whose was whose, they exchanged looks and smiles at each other, and when they both rose to their feet, they shared words.

"Sorry about that," Phee said as she picked up the pieces of her bagged lunch. "I've been known to have two left feet sometimes."

"Don't worry about it," the other replied.

"My name's Ophelia," Phee told her, "Ophelia Herron."

"Claire Salinger," said the other and then looked at Phee with curiosity. "You're the one with the sister."

"Guilty as charged," Phee replied.

"She's in my chem class," Claire went on. "Peyton. Smart."

"Genius on the Hawking scale, I think," she replied.

"Hey!" Claire said, "I'm headed over to the cafeteria. How about I buy you lunch to replace what my history book did to yours?"

"I don't know," Phee said with hesitation, glancing back at me. "I generally eat with Peyton."

"Well, I don't want to intrude," Claire replied at which point I mouthed to Phee, "Go!"

Phee threw me an *Is it really okay?* look, to which I emphatically nodded.

"Sure," Phee said to Claire. "It's all right. I have lunch with her all the time. I think she'll survive."

The two of them walked off together.

"I haven't seen you around," Phee said.

"Oh," Claire replied, "I just transferred in. We were supposed to have relocated to Australia, but then my dad broke his leg and so here I am, doomed to remain in America. I think our dog's the happiest about it, though. If we were to have moved, we'd have had to leave her here with friends."

"What kind of dog?" Phee asked.

"A blue merle collie," Claire replied. "Her name's Niska. Maybe I can introduce you to her someday."

"I think I'd like that," Phee said. "I'm definitely a dog person. We used to have what my dad referred to as a curbstone setter otherwise known as a mutt, but it ran off one day, never to return."

And thus a soon-to-be-romance began. As for myself, I ducked into the girls' bathroom, went into an empty stall, and then phased to the hall of a high school on Long Island. One girl seemed to have caught a glimpse of me coming from out of nowhere, but then just shook her head to herself and dismissed it as her just seeing things. Most of the attention, though, was focused on a ruckus in the other direction. With others watching, one boy was being bullied by another. I walked over at a brisk pace.

"Hey!" I shouted at the brute. "Leave him alone!"

"Whoa! Whoa! Whoa!" the brute said. "What have we here? Hot stuff!" Then he reached down and lifted up my skirt.

"Touch me again," I said, "and you'll regret it!"

345

"Yeah?" he said. "What're ya gonna do? Pussy whip me to death?"

It was at that point that the other boy, who was on the floor lunged at him, toppled him to the ground, and began beating him till he bled. Then he stood up and scowled at the bully who wasn't a bully anymore.

"Apologize to her!" he demanded.

The other, seeing blood on his hand from his cut lip, looked up and me and said, "I'm sorry."

The victor said back, "She didn't hear you!"

"I'm sorry," he repeated louder. "I'm sorry!"

"Come on," the boy who had defended me said. "Let's get out of here."

And that was how I first met Mark—in this reality, that is.

CHAPTER LXII

Peyton
(the one who woke up)

Earth Year: 2028

Phee and Claire were married in a small ceremony at the rose garden in the Los Angeles County Arboretum, the cost split by both sets of parents. Chloë and I were bridesmaids. Dad gave Phee away and Mr. Salinger gave away Claire. Vows and rings were exchanged. The marriage was pronounced and then Claire and Phee kissed. It was all more beautiful than I could ever have imagined. When the bouquets were thrown, I caught one and Chloë caught the other, though she looked at me with an odd expression on her face which was understandable considering that she was only fifteen years old.

"Just wait," I said aside to her.

She shrugged and then ran up to the newly married pair to congratulate them and give them hugs. Within the next year, Phee would become mysteriously pregnant and give birth to a beautiful blonde-haired girl she would name Jordan. She and Claire would tell everyone that the birth was the result of artificial insemination, but we all knew better. More than two thousand years had passed since the last immaculate conception presumably had occurred and we wouldn't have wanted anyone to get the wrong idea. As for me, standing alone, holding my bouquet as all attention was turned to the newly-married brides, I heard a voice from behind me.

"Hey," it said.

"Yes, Mark?" I replied as I turned to see him handsomely dressed in his tux.

"I've been thinking," he said.

"Thinking is good," I replied.

"The book I've been working on," he said. "I think it will sell."

"Of course, it will," I replied.

"Well," he went on, "I figured if that happened, I could afford a down payment on a house in Massapequa."

"Why Massapequa?" I asked.

He shrugged and said, "I thought it might be a good place to raise kids."

"Mark Marsden," I replied, "are you asking me to marry you?"

"Yes," he said with great affirmation. "Yes, I am."

"You know," I told him, "you're going to have to ask my father's permission."

"I already did," he said.

"And what did he say?" I asked.

"He said," Mark replied, "What the hell took you so long?" He looked me in the eye and tilted his head. "So, are you going to marry me or not?"

I looked back at him. "Well," I said, "when you put it *that* way… Yes! Of course, yes, you ding-a-ling!"

He lifted me in his arms and spun me around. When my feet finally hit the ground, we kissed.

"Let's wait to tell everyone," I said. "We don't want to overshadow their moment."

Six weeks later we were married in the exact same place. Poor Chloë caught the bridal bouquet again and just shook her head to herself. Mark didn't know I was Quantum Girl. I didn't want him to fall in love with a superhero—just me. A couple of years later I became pregnant and, nine months after that, welcomed two non-identical twins whom we named Zhana and Samira. They and Jordan would eventually become best friends with Jordan always in the lead and Samira defiant as was her way. Oh, and I brought out Liam again briefly, which explained how Claire also became pregnant. It was only fair, her having miscarried on Earth II. It would be a boy who would grow up to have his mother's eyes and his father's chiseled face. Many years from then, Claire and Phee would still be together and there would be many grandchildren to fill their declining years. So, perhaps I should say that everyone lived happily ever after, but the fact is that with a superhero in your family, you just never know.

CHAPTER LXIII

Payton

Earth Year: 2033

The two of them were asleep in bed when I rose out of her. She moaned just a bit and then rolled over onto her side. I put on some clothes and then phased to a rather shady part of town in front of a familiar house.

I looked down at the ground. There was a large round gray stone on the grass near the mailbox pole. I picked it up, took aim, and hurled it at one of the front windows. The stone hit its mark accompanied by a loud crash. The man on the porch next door turned to look.

"Angry *Chiqueta*," he laughed in a loud drunken voice. "Don't bite off my dick! I've got two balls, but my dick, I've only got one!"

The lights in the house went on in the front room. A dark-haired girl around my age pulled back the curtains and looked through the broken window. The front door opened a moment later and she stood there, glaring in my direction, wearing only a short silk nightgown.

She shouted something angrily in Spanish and then came charging at me. When she got to me, she suddenly stopped dead in her tracks.

"Oh, my God!" she exclaimed. "You're her! You're Peyton! You're the one who tried to kill yourself! I thought you were in an institution!"

"And you're the one who put me there," I replied.

"Why are you here?" she asked. She glanced back at the window. "Just to throw a rock?"

"I don't know," I said. "Coincidence. Just walking. Then I saw the name on your mail. You were the one who made me want to die."

Her anger calmed. "I'm so sorry," she said. "I was angry all the time back then."

"We barely knew each other," I replied.

350

"I know. I know," she said. "You can't imagine how I felt when I heard that you tried to hang yourself and I knew it was because of me. I used to cut myself because of it. Please," she insisted. "Come inside and we can talk."

She ushered me in, offered me the sofa, and then sat down beside me, facing me on my left, her right arm resting on the back of the sofa, her right leg bent immodestly on it as her left leg hung down toward the floor.

"Would you like anything to drink?" she asked. "Coffee, tea, soda?"

"No, thank you," I answered, trying desperately not to glance at her perhaps inadvertently exposed vag. "But I have a question?" I said.

"Of course," she replied, catching the motion of my eyes, glancing down at herself but doing nothing to cover what was obviously exposed.

"Why me?" I asked. "I mean, as far as I can remember I never did anything to you. Why did you put a target on my back?"

"It's kind of hard to explain," she replied, "embarrassing, I suppose." She hesitated but then went on. "When I was a young girl my uncle lived with us—with me and my mom. He was in his middle twenties, I guess. I was nine. My mom, she used to work the graveyard shift doing cleaning at an office building. When she was gone, my uncle used to come into my bedroom and do things to me. He told me that if I told anyone that he'd hurt me and then he'd hurt my mom. This went on for years. Just before I got into Braxton, he got me pregnant and took me to an abortion clinic and made me go through with the procedure. I was brought up Catholic. We don't believe in such things. We think of it as murder. I cried for weeks after that. My mom kept asking me what was wrong and I kept telling her, 'Nothing. Nothing, Mama. Nothing's wrong.' Then I just exploded. When my mom was at work I screamed at my uncle, telling him that if he didn't get out I would go to the police and tell them all

351

that he'd done to me. He left that night. When my mom came home I told her all that had gone on but she didn't believe me. She said I made it all up. I guess if she accepted what had happened it would have meant that she hadn't protected me. Anyway, it made me angry. And what I'd been through with my uncle made me hate the thought of being touched by men. Then, when I got enrolled at Braxton, I saw *you*. You didn't see me, but looking at you made my heart pound in my chest. You were the most beautiful girl I'd ever seen. I tried to go up to you so many times but it was like I was invisible to you. I wanted to be friends. I wanted to be able to stand at your locker and laugh with you. I wanted to walk down the hallway holding your hand. But you never noticed me back and all the anger I had in me from my uncle got directed toward you. I know that was wrong now but I was fourteen years old and hella immature. Then I heard what you'd done to yourself and I realized it was because of me and I wanted to kill myself and I tried so many times but I never had the nerve to ever go through with it."

She held out her left wrist and showed me all the scars from her cutting herself. I showed her mine.

"I guess we have something in common, then," she said with a slightly sardonic laugh.

"I guess we do," I replied.

"My mother died a few years ago," she went on. "I couldn't afford to go to college on my own. It's all just been hard work in clothing stores and restaurants. Hell, I even tried working in a strip club once but I couldn't deal with all the men looking at me. It brought back too many memories. Anyway, if it's any consolidation for what I did to you I've been alone ever since—all my life, actually."

"Same here," I replied, "though I can't remember the last nine years."

"I'm not asking you to forgive me," she said. "I just wanted you to understand the reasons for me doing what I did."

I stared into her eyes, damp with tears that had yet to fall. "The

Bible says," I told her, "For if ye forgive men their trespasses, your heavenly Father will also forgive you."

"Matthew 6:14," she replied.

"I have sins of my own," I said. "Someone died because of me. It wasn't intentional but it happened nevertheless. My mother's dead, too. *And* my dad. I don't have anyone. Not really. Not to talk to. Not to cry to. Not even to hug. I've never had a boyfriend. I've never had anyone."

Theresa held out her arms. "Come here," she said. I leaned into her and she hugged me and I hugged her back. There wasn't any thought to it. There were no memories of the torment I'd been put through. It was as though both of us had somehow been reborn just then and that God, watching over me, said it was okay. When the hug ended I said to her, "I guess I'd better be going."

Theresa glanced at her wristwatch. "It's really late," she said. "Why don't you spend the night and then go home in the morning?"

I didn't tell her that I could have just phased back to the house. The truth was that I'd enjoyed her company, hearing the reasons for all that had gone on, and realizing that beyond all the powers I now possessed I had one even greater and that was the power of forgiveness—one that I shared with our Lord and Savior, Jesus Christ—so I agreed.

She led me to her bedroom. "I hope you don't mind sharing," she said. "I've used the other bedroom for storage."

I glanced back toward the living room. "I can sleep on the couch," I said. "I don't mind," but I really wanted to be able to sleep next to her, to feel another human breath, to hear another heartbeat.

"Your back would wind up a mess if you did," she replied. "You just take the right side and I'll take the left. It's a full-size bed. There's plenty of room. I'll grab a nightgown for you to change into."

I changed in the room with her. She turned her back but I caught her glancing toward me from the corner of my eye when I was undressed. Strange to say, it did not make me feel uncomfortable.

After I'd changed, I got into the bed. She flicked off the light switch on the wall by the door and then climbed into the bed on her side.

As I lay on my back and she lay facing me, she reached over and took hold of my left hand. "When I was a little girl," she said, "I would pretend that I was a beautiful princess, trapped in an ivory tower and that some handsome brave knight would come and rescue me. He'd gather me up in his arms and kiss me passionately, steal me away to his castle and we'd live happily ever after. That never happened and I don't feel like the beautiful princess anymore."

"Well, you *are* beautiful," I told her.

"But not the princess. I'm the scullery maid, trapped in a meaningless existence."

"Please!" I said. "I've felt trapped all my life, waiting to be rescued by someone—anyone."

"Even me?" she asked.

"Even you," I replied. "Even you."

She moved in closer to me. Then she raised herself up over me and kissed me on the lips. I wrapped my arms around her and kissed her back. Her breasts pressed against mine, I felt her arousal and I became aroused as well. I could hear her heart pounding the way that mine was and my quantum sense could smell the result of her lap pressing hard against mine. I felt a pleasurable sensation in my groin and such a want as I had never known.

"I love you," she said.

"I love you, too," I replied.

No one knows what the future brings—not for any of us—not even for a Quantum Girl. And that, as they say, is that.

AFTERWORD

The Quantum Girl Saga deals with a lot more than aliens and superpowers. They touch upon bullying, self-harm, and suicide. These are issues faced by young people today. As a teenager myself, I strongly encourage anyone twenty-five or younger, who is facing those issues or others such as sexual assault or date rape, substance abuse, child abuse, sexual trafficking, anxiety or depression, or if things are bad at home and you are considering running away, please call the Thursday's Child hotline at 1 (800) USA KIDS from a landline, or (818) 831-1234 internationally or from a cellphone. Phone lines are open 24/7 and are confidential and free. They care. I care. I'm Peyton Herron, Quantum Girl, and spokesperson for Thursday's Child. Their website is www.thursdayschild.org, where you can also get help.